MAX-CATT

The Beginning

By

Bill Diamond

ShieldCrest

ISBN: 978-1-913839-46-8

MMXXII

A CIP catalogue record for this is available from the
British Library

Published by
ShieldCrest Publishing,
Bicker, Lincs, PE20 3BT England
Tel: +44 (0) 333 8000 890
www.shieldcrest.co.uk

To my wife, Julia, whose support and love
has taught me so much

FORESHADOWING OF MAX-CATT

'Let's walk back to camp Terry; it'll be a doddle compared to our speed marching.'

'Of course sir, it's a good clear night to walk as well.'

Maximus put two hundred pounds over the bar for the boys; then the two early leavers left the now rowdy pub. They had walked for about ten minutes along Beachley Road towards Tutshill when Max stopped. He heard an unexpected sound that he couldn't associate with being in the middle of the countryside. A strange sound for the still of the night with no traffic, although it could, Max supposed, be a wild animal scurrying away. At that particular moment Max was explaining his ideas to Terry about three-platoon's duties when they are in Afghanistan. Well, the lieutenant thought he was talking to Terry! His corporal had gone.

Max looked behind and was stunned rigid to see Terry struggling with a dark shadow moving behind his corporal. The lieutenant could make out the glint of the moonlight's reflection bouncing off a knife blade that was held close to the corporal's neck.

'Stay there.' Screamed the attacker. Max could now make out the assailant was wearing a dark balaclava.

Max inched closer to Terry but stopped again as the masked man gestured a threatening upward movement closer to Terry's throat.

'Stop and don't move or I'll fucking slice him!'

Max sensed he wasn't messing.

'Here's my money, take it all.' Max threw his wallet towards the assailant's feet. But it wasn't money the attacker wanted this night.

Max's concentration on his corporal's situation was broken; from the lieutenant's left side another masked attacker approached at speed. Simultaneously a third man entered the affray, this time from behind Max. He attempted to drag the lieutenant down to the ground with his arm around the young officer's neck, almost choking him. Max moved quickly to his right and spun round to face the third assailant. As this man turned his head to follow Max's defensive manoeuvre, Max lunged with his middle and index fingers spread, finding their targets in both of the attacker's eyes. The counter-assault by Max was so violent that he felt one of his fingers entering deep into the attacker's eye socket, coming to rest against warm soft tissue. The assailant dropped his knife, screaming and holding his face in great pain. The second attacker threw himself at Max, wielding a knife out in front of him. While this was happening, Terry's assailant, who was still pressing a knife to Terry's neck, was again threatening that he would slit the corporal's throat. The young lieutenant had no choice but to defend himself, being forced to ignore the threat to his corporal. Max's self-defence skills had already kicked in. Max grabbed the rushing attacker's wrist and pulled him in close, kneeing him viciously in his groin, followed by a head butt planted on the flat of his nose. The semi-conscious man dropped like a stone. Before the one with damaged eyes could recover, Max pounded him with several heavy, well-directed punches to his already swollen face before the attacker collapsed. The now one-eyed assailant held his head, writhing in pain and fell to his knees. Max finished him off with a flurry of well-directed kicks. The young officer now had a moment to see what the first man was doing with Terry. The attacker still had the knife menacingly close to his corporal's throat, and looking over Terry's shoulder, he stared menacingly at Max. The young lieutenant gasped in horror with what happened next: the crazed man in a balaclava slit the hapless corporal's throat with one violent movement. Max couldn't believe what he had just witnessed; it quickly became a surreal blur at this crazy, mad moment.

The vision of Terry dropping to his knees with blood squirting from his neck like a fountain was captured in the moonlight, like some horror movie. Max had only one course of action; assist Corporal Terry Dixon. Terry was on his knees, still spraying and pumping his red, life-giving fluid into the air. Terry stared wide-eyed at his lieutenant from his kneeling posture as if thinking aloud: Why?

The two thugs struggled to their feet, one helping the other, then joined their brutal accomplice, the throat butcher. All three disappeared as quickly as they arrived, through the hedgerow. These vicious men were, at this moment, the least of Max's concern. Terry was dying in front of his lieutenant. The young officer phoned 999, calling for an ambulance and police. Max explained a man was dying.

'A man has had his throat cut'. Max shouted this with urgency. He gave the operator the exact location but didn't stop to answer her many obvious questions, ending the call abruptly! Maximus then phoned his sergeant, who was still in full song at the pub. He told Tim straight, Terry is dying. Max demanded, over the din, that Forbes must get the bar staff to cut a metre of plastic pump-line and bring it to him. Screaming at Forbes to come as quickly as he could. Terry Dixon was running out of time! The young officer ordered the sergeant to borrow or hijack a car and come to the location Max gave him.

'I'll be right there, sir!' The quick-thinking lieutenant removed his underpants and socks to use them as a pad and strapping. He pressed his finger into the open cut and found the windpipe, attempting to stop Terry's blood from being sucked into his lungs. Max was no doctor, but he knew his first aid. He could see by his phone torch that his corporal's jugular small vein had been severed, but thankfully not the larger one of the two. The officer could hear air gurgling from Terry's neck, which meant the windpipe was penetrated. Tim Forbes arrived; Max didn't speak to his sergeant but grabbed the plastic drink-line from the sergeant's hand. Max, with Tim now holding the phone torch, inserted the beer pump-line into Terry's severed windpipe very carefully, ensuring no further blood was sucked in. Max hoped his first attempt at a tracheostomy was successful.

Finally, placing his underpants over the open wound as a pad he then banded this by his socks tied together, holding the makeshift padding in place.

Both Max and Tim tried to comfort their comrade, but he had slipped into unconsciousness. Despite the first-aider's efforts, Terry still lost a great deal of blood. The sound of the ambulance, police or both was getting nearer; it happened that both the emergency services arrived at the same time. Blue lights were flashing from both vehicles manufacturing a shadowy blue intermittent outline along the hedgerows. Paramedics were out with all the gear they could carry and immediately took over from Max. The medics asked the army officer what had happened and had the victim ingested any drugs. Max explained about the pipe that they could see clearly for themselves sticking out from Terry's throat. To Max's surprise, they left the beer pipe in place, lifted Terry onto a rolling gurney and into the ambulance. They removed Max's pants and socks to replace them with a clean dressing. Terry was injected and a saline drip attached; the ambulance sped away with the blue lights flashing and a screaming siren.....

1

Twenty-Two Years Earlier

Maximus Churchill Hainsworth-Catt was born to Mr Christopher and Mrs Virginia Hainsworth-Catt at the family's ancestral home, Brandscombe Manor, set upon a thousand-acre estate. Mrs Cooper, the family nanny, cook, housekeeper and trained midwife, delivered Maximus with no fuss. The newborn's middle name was in honour of the war leader who took Britain through its darkest hour. Winston. Christopher's father, Granville Hainsworth-Catt, told many tales of the great statesman. Granville, himself a WW2 hero who joined the newly formed SBS (Special Boat Section) had inherited Brandscombe from his father. Granville saw action in the North Africa campaign and in 1943 received a Victoria Cross, the highest military medal for bravery. He won the prestigious decoration at the Salerno-landings, where he was severely injured and honourably discharged. Granville then returned to Brandscombe Manor. The estate occupies a thousand acres within the rolling Surrey countryside. The manor was a fine example of early Elizabethan architecture that has been in the Hainsworth-Catt family since the early 17th century apart from two years during the first English civil war when the family fled from the Parliamentarian army under orders from Mr Oliver Cromwell to help feed his Roundheads in the region.

Archie, the eldest son, took to the estate naturally and Christopher was confident he will one day take over the running of the thousand acres. Pippa had a penchant for the family's press and publishing interests. It was planned that she would go straight into the publishing enterprise after university.

As for little Maximus, he hadn't shown much interest in the estate or media, but he did long to hear his father's stories about his grandfather's war adventures. Unfortunately, they were second-hand. The brave Granville had died prematurely, probably brought on by former war wounds.

Max's siblings went to the best private schools. Pippa attended one of the highest-rated schools for girls in England. Archie went to Tadley Grange and boarded. Max was expected to follow Archie into Tadley, but the younger brother's determination ensured he followed in the footsteps of his father and grandfather who had both attended Carrow Abbey.

So on September 6th, Maximus Churchill Hainsworth-Catt joined Sark House, Carrow Abbey School. Just ten days before is 11th birthday. Max was introduced to his room-mate Rory Slater who would turn out to be Max's best pal for life. The two friends were inseparable through their early years at Carrow. Max excelled at rugby and athletics, becoming the Surrey hundred metres county champion.

2

Three Years Later

Dinner at Brandscombe was often formal and this evening was no exception. It was attended this Friday night by Christopher, Virginia, Archie and his girlfriend Charlotte, Pippa, Thomas and his mutually ruinous wife, Samantha. They sat down at 19:30hr, after traditional aperitifs in the drawing-room. Max could see his uncle and auntie were both quite drunk. A usual occurrence and embarrassment for the whole family.

It didn't take long for Uncle Tom to start his rude performance. He began with a tirade at Christopher in his drunken state and egged on by his wife. Unfounded but typical of brother Tom.

'You only invited Sam and me tonight to gloat and show off; half this place should be mine! It's not fucking fair; nothing is!' Samantha joined in the attack.

'Yeah, and where's the fairness, you got all the estate and a generous income from those glossy magazines and papers you print. It's Tom's birthright; he should have at least half of the fortune? We could easily run a simple paper business. You are nothing but a tight bastar.....!' Samantha couldn't finish what she was saying. She slumped back into her chair as if too tired to continue her attack, her head bowed. Although not an adult, Carrow school has shown Max many things, how to behave within reason, recognise bullies and stand up for what one thinks is right. So Maximus wasn't going to let his uncle get away with his rude outburst! 'Don't ever talk to my father like that again.

You are drunk Uncle Tom and should go to bed now and take Auntie Sam with you; she is incoherent now anyway. Please leave now!' The whole dining room went into silence before Tom shot to his feet, tipping his chair backwards crashing it onto the floor, stirring Samantha for a few seconds who then slipped back into her stupor. How dare you speak to me like that! You little shit, never talk to me in that tone again!' Thomas screamed at his young nephew, but Max stood his ground only inches away from his uncle. He didn't say any more, just stared at his Uncle Thomas.

'How bloody dare you, now apologise you brat. Christopher, are you going to let your son get away with such rudeness?' Thomas was now losing control.

'If you acted as an adult should Uncle Thomas, I wouldn't have spoken to you like that and no, I certainly am not going to apologise to you, and as I said, don't talk to my father like that again or I'll thump you here and now.' Max, at fourteen, was as tall as his uncle and more muscular that defied his years.

Christopher rarely loses his temper; he did now! He grabbed his younger brother by the lapels of his dinner suit and laid into him assertively but in a controlled manner.

'Thomas, you inherited one million pounds from our father and all the shares in the family's diamond mines worth a minimum of twenty-five million pounds. Where's the income from your shareholder dividends? You ought to be getting at least two hundred thousand a year from them. What have you done with it all? Where's it gone?' Christopher instructed Jarvis to ask Marshall to bring the car round and take his brother and Samantha home. 'They can collect their car tomorrow when they have sobered up.' Jarvis, the family butler, scurried away to find Marshall.

After breakfast the next day, Max went back to his room to dress for a quad ride with his dad; when he heard a car pulling up. He saw his Uncle Thomas getting out of a taxi from his window. He thought it best to stay in his room, not wanting another confrontation with Uncle Tom.

A loud conversation started between Christopher and his brother, who had both gone into Christopher's study. Max heard them, but it was now muffled from where he was on the landing. Nevertheless, the young son was intrigued and wanted to listen to their conversation, so Maximus crept downstairs to listen outside the study door.

'I invited you to dinner to have you included as part of our family. I felt sorry for you as you only have us as kin; just look how you repaid me! You and Samantha are a disgrace and it took my fourteen-year-old son to bring your outburst to an end. Are you not ashamed, Tom?

'I need ten thousand pounds by the end of next week; otherwise I will be beaten up or even worse.' There was a smack of desperation in Thomas's appeal.

'You had better tell me what the hell this is all about and from the beginning.' Christopher just about kept his control.

'I have been so stupid. I was not getting enough returns from my two mines, so I borrowed against them. The payments got less and less each month from South Africa, until hardly anything went into my bank account. I was so worried that I even went to the mines myself to find out what was happening. I met with the mine's manager, who declared major problems with strikes, flooding and even gang attacks from the townships. He said a government agency might be interested in taking over the two mines. I arranged a meeting with a government official and he offered two hundred thousand pounds sterling. I owed about half of that in gambling debts that were then getting serious; the cash was too much temptation knowing my predicament. It was all done so quickly. A government official turned up at the mine's office, we both signed the contracts, and he gave me twenty thousand pounds sterling in cash. He then showed me the transfer into my U.K. account for the balance. I paid a hundred thousand to the loan shark who had dangerous thugs as collectors. The balance all but twenty thousand went to pay my account at Le Croupiers. That was six months ago, now I've mortgaged my house and need ten grand, or God knows what they will do to me. So you have got to help me Chris.'

The older brother was astounded, even by Tom's standards. Finally, and in disgust, Chris laid into his irresponsible sibling.

'You have made big mistakes throughout your life, and our father was kind enough to bail you out each time. Do you know those mines you sold are worth twenty-five million? Well, at least twenty fucking million! You have given them away; you have blown your inheritance through an obvious scam and your signature. The South African government wouldn't have bought mines; they can't afford to anyway. I'm not helping you this time because you never learn. If I give you this money you'd be back time and time again for more,' Christopher was raging while Thomas was snivelling, 'damn it; I'll give you the ten thousand, but that is definitely the very last handout. Now get out of my house and don't ever come back; you are nothing but a weak, good-for-nothing, bloody fool!'

Max scurried back upstairs as he heard the brothers coming out of the study. He watched his Uncle Thomas leave holding his father's money.

3

The Inter-House tournament came, Sark was in the quarter-final.

There was a bully in the Sark House. His name was Josh Fordham, a big lad who looked more like sixteen than his almost fifteen years. He threw his weight around, particularly in the face of Maximus Hainsworth-Catt. Probably because Max wouldn't kowtow to him as most other boys did. After a training match, Josh Fordham waited outside the changing rooms for Max. As the unsuspecting Max came through the door he was punched straight between the eyes, making his nose bleed profusely. Before Max could defend himself, Fordham kicked him in the groin so hard it doubled Max over. Then, Fordham's shadow, Dominic, attacked Max from the back by hitting the defenceless boy with a baseball bat across the kidneys. Dominic swung the bat again, this time to the back of Max's legs behind the knees. Max crumpled to the ground. He was momentarily too dazed even to defend himself.

Josh Fordham leaned over Max, whispering, 'Play another game of rugby for Sark, and I'll make sure you don't walk properly ever again.' Dominic twirled his bat in a triumphant gesture as the two inseparable thugs left with a swagger. Max stayed motionless for about twenty minutes. He eventually staggered to his feet and stumbled back to his room. Rory was there to greet him. 'My God Max what have you done? That wasn't done on the rugby pitch.' Max just nodded with his swollen face, went to the bathroom and gingerly cleaned himself up as best he could. Thankfully he didn't need stitches. The Sark house master quizzed Max suggesting it was Fordham who beat him. Max didn't reveal who his attacker was. The master knew differently as Fordham was under watch for similar attacks on pupils but they all were too frightened to report him.

Max returned to his room; he had decided what he would do about his beating. Max made a vow to himself: *"Mr bloody Fordham isn't going to get away with what he did to me, nor his buddy Dominic. I am the grandson of a VC hero; I must defend the honour of the Hainsworth-Catt family, especially against cowardly bullies."*

After dinner Max and Rory strolled back to Sark house with a few other pals. Maximus said to the others, 'I have to go somewhere now; I'll see you guys later.'

Max jogged to the other side of the lake and exited the school onto Pond Lane, leading to the town centre. He called a cab and asked to be taken to Pat's gym in Windsor, a few miles away from his school. The taxi dropped Max outside a converted warehouse. Pushing a pair of swing doors open, he entered a new world that would help change his young life for good. Walking towards Max was a muscular man in his fifties; he was well built and had the flattest, bent nose imaginable. The disfigurement restricted his speech and accentuated his nasal voice. 'What do you want son? It looks like you've had a few rounds already.' He scoffed at his own joke. Not surprisingly, Max didn't share his humour. 'Can I learn to box here?' Max asked expectantly.

'We can teach you, but I can't say you'll learn, mind you. Most lads give up after a couple of weeks anyway.

'I'll give it my best shot sir, that I promise.'

'What's your name son?' Flat nose asked.

'Maximus.' The coach ushered Max into his gym; the young student was amazed that so much was going on.

'What is that?' Max enquired, pointing at two men fighting inside a cage. He was intrigued and wanted to see more. Old broken nose who greeted Max was the gym owner, Mr Patrick McCoubrey, originally from Northern Ireland. He took Max across the gym to the cage.

'This is called the Hexagon Ring; the rules are pretty simple, you have to overpower your opponent, but that is easier said than done. It comes under MMA rules (Mixed Martial Arts). There are three five-minute rounds, and it can be dangerous; we do have a junior section, but I wouldn't recommend it to youngsters, especially those new to it.

'What are the rules that apply in the cage fight?' Max asked.

'You can't gouge eyes, head butt, strike to the groin, bending or breaking fingers, attacking the eyes, kicks to the back of the head and a few more I can't recall.'

'Wow that's incredible; what can you do?'

'It's gloved boxing, part Muay Thai, Karate, Taekwondo, a bit of Thai boxing and wrestling. Some Jiu-Jitsu thrown in, excuse the pun on that one.' Again Pat sniggered quite nasally at his own joke.

'Well what do you suggest I should do, Mr McCoubrey.'

'I think we'll start you on basics in the junior section with weight training and core muscle work; I'll give you some basics in the art of boxing to show you how to hit a punch bag.

How does that sound? The fees are a hundred pounds a month or fifty for just the use of the equipment. I must have your parents permission in writing as well, but I will give you a free workout now if you like.'

Max nodded a grateful approval.

'Okay son, when do you want to start?'

'Tomorrow evening, if that's okay.'

'Right you are then son, don't forget to get your parents permission and bring the signed authorisation to me.'

Max returned to Carrow and jotted down the first street name he passed in Windsor to use as a fictitious home address. He used his own phone number as his fathers. He signed the fake parental authority as Christopher H-C.

Two weeks later and Max had clocked up fourteen hours at the gym. Rory played his part, lowering the rope ladder for Max's covert entry into their room.

Christopher Hainsworth-Catt was still fuming, still in disbelief that his brother had sold the family diamond mines that Granville, his father, worked so hard to acquire and develop from virtually nothing into a highly viable, worker-friendly mining business. Their worth at today's value was around twenty to thirty million. Chris discussed the situation over lunch with his wife, Virginia. He spoke softly.

'Christopher, you have helped your brother out so many times, giving him lots of your time, advice and now more money. Sadly, it will not help him because he will gamble or drink the money away again and host lavish parties to impress friends of that tramp Samantha. I'm sorry, I'm losing my temper now; I really shouldn't do that. God knows we have tried Chris.'

'I know Ginny, I know, but he is still my little brother. I'm just so thankful dad isn't here to witness how Tom has turned out. I'm not bailing him out again; it's a total waste of time.'

The following day, Pippa, who was at university, phoned home and asked if her boyfriend could spend Christmas at Brandscombe. Virginia replied in her motherly voice, 'Of course darling, is it still Toby?'

'No mother his name is Benjamin Collins, and he's gorgeous; you will love him.'

'When will you arrive dear?'

'On the 24th December, we'll visit his parents for a few days before coming home to Brandscombe. Mummy, I can't wait to see you and daddy. Will Archie bring Charlotte?'

'That's quite spooky Pippa, we were only just discussing that yesterday and yes, Charlotte is invited.'

'Mummy, it will be a great family Christmas; I can't wait. Love you lots. Bye.'

4

Max got his first ABA fight. The bout started; Max let the Uxbridge boy come on to him, his opponent did, like a bull charging, Max sidestepped, weaved left and right, danced from trouble to work him as Pat instructed. A barrage of jabs from Max pushed him back onto the ropes; using his natural speed, he hit him with a left hook that caught Max's opponent's jaw that put him on the canvas. The second round was going Max's way as well, finishing like the first, with a flurry of punches to the opponent's body and keeping to Pat's plan.

It was very much the same in the third, but with more of Max's punches landing on his opponent's body. The Uxbridge lad was visibly tiring. Round four and Max sensed his opponent's demise as the Uxbridge lad continually backed away. It was time to go in to finish the fight; Max did within the first minute of the fifth. With a rapid flurry of left and right jabs and a continued pummelling of his opponent's body, the ref stepped between the young fighters to stop the contest. Max was delighted but nowhere near as Pat was. He was bouncing up and down with utter pleasure seeing his protege win; Pat McCoubrey was elated.

Sark had reached the inter-house rugby final, winning their semi 26-22, Sark now have a chance to win the coveted trophy that has eluded the famous house for more than seventy years. Max played his part as captain and his father, who also played for Sark, was elated.

The relationship didn't get better between Max and Fordham. He had slipped a note inside Max's locker. It read. *"I'll get you Hainsworth-Catt. You're dead. JF"*

Max knew he had to be ready for the bully next time, with or without the bat-wielding Dominic to help him.

Back at Pat's gym, Mr David Chinn who had some Chinese, Nigerian and Liverpudlian thrown into his ancestral mix, was one of the best coaches of MMA in the South of England, specialising in cage fighting and Thai boxing. Pat introduced Max to him. They shook hands. 'I want to learn all aspects of the Hexagon cage, please, Mr Chinn.'

'Call me David and yes, I can train you, I watched your fight the other night, and I was mightily impressed; you have incredible speed. We shall start your training tonight.

The next day Max was at rugby training, the last one before the inter-house final. Max asked to leave the field ten minutes early as he had agreed to phone his father.

'Hi dad.'

. 'Good gracious Max, you are spot on time. 17:25hrs, that makes a change.'

Max ignored the sarcastic remark and gave Christopher the details of the rugby final.

'Max, I am sure you will be in the team, judging from your last two performances. I can't wait. Have you found out who you are playing in the final yet?'

'Yes, dad it's Witherdrew, we are confident but not blasé; it could go either way, we'll see.'

'What date are you finishing for Christmas Max, and what time do you want Marshall to pick you up?'

'We finish on 20th December, we pack up early at noon that day, so I think 13.00hrs would be great, thanks dad.'

Upon his return from Pat's gym, he went around the back, climbed over the fence and gave Rory the usual signal, a handful of gravel at the window; it opened as expected; Max looked up and went into temporary shock. The look on his face must have been a picture. It wasn't Rory at the window! The house and headmaster had replaced his friend. 'Oh fuck, I've had it now!' Max realised he was in deep doo-doo.

'Go around to the front door and I will let you in Hainsworth-Catt.'

Max faced both the headmaster and Mr Dobbs in his housemaster's study. Max awaited severe chastisement for being out after lock-up. But it was much worse than he imagined. The school headmaster opened the questioning.

'Maximus, you are in serious trouble! I want nothing from you but the truth, so consider your answers carefully as I expect you to answer all our questions truthfully! After the rugby practice this afternoon, a Rolex watch was stolen from Martin Timms's locker. Somebody broke into it, and a valuable watch was stolen. You left the rugby field early, evidently in a hurry and in front of all the other players. Fortunately, Mario Bartelli, who was in the shower at the time had heard a loud noise; he went to investigate and saw you opening Timms's locker at 17:35hrs. He is certain of that precise time because he had just checked his watch and thought he would be late for chess club. It looks, without a doubt, that the theft you committed is proven; we hold a master key to all lockers so we opened yours. Under a towel, we found the stolen Rolex. The timepiece was identified as it had Timms's name engraved on it. So please, Mr Hainsworth-Catt, do not deny the charge we are bringing against you. Stealing property upon Carrow Abbey school premises is very serious; if found guilty, which it very much looks like you are, you will be instantly expelled. What is your reply to our charge sir?'

'Sir, I have stolen nothing in my life, I did not steal the watch.' Max defended himself earnestly.

'I would like to believe you Maximus, you are from an honourable family; however, the facts before us leave no alternative but to proceed with our investigation. Until proven and this matter is decided upon, you will continue with your studies and activities in school. We will be informing your parents of course. You will appreciate this is an expulsion offence. As soon as we have completed our investigations and internal enquiries, we will let you know our decision. Mr Timms senior wants the culprit expelled as quickly as possible; he is furious. The school will compensate Timms as we would not like this torrid incident to go public. Although we try to deal with such matters internally, we have the proud name of the school to consider.

Your house master will deal with your absconding after lock-up separately. We do not tolerate thieving at Carrow Abbey school.

I will ask you again, did you steal that watch?'

'No sir, I didn't.'

'Understand Maximus; it doesn't look good for you. Consider the facts: an eyewitness makes an identification of you unlocking Timms's locker at the specific time of 17:35hrs; the stolen watch was found in your locker by your housemaster and me, and you asked to leave the field five minutes before the end of rugby practice. All these facts add up to one thing, you being the thief. I'm sorry to say these facts will be put to the governors at an emergency meeting on the 19th December, the day before the school breaks for Christmas. I will be speaking with your parents tomorrow morning.' Max knew he had to speak with his father before the headmaster!

'What is it son? Are you okay?' Christopher was concerned at such an early call from his son.

'Dad, I have been accused of stealing a Rolex watch from another student's locker that turned up in mine. But worse still, someone said they saw me open that locker. I didn't, dad, I swear!'

'Good God Max, what in heavens is going on? Are you winding me up?'

'I only wish I was dad, unless I can get evidence to prove my innocence by Christmas they will expel me as it will be decided at the next board of governors meeting. They have called an EGM on 19th December with one topic on the agenda. Me.'

'I believe you Max.'

'I have to go dad; I mustn't be late for breakfast. I'm in enough trouble; oh, and the headmaster is phoning you later. So please keep your cool.'

Maximus had to see Mario Bartelli quickly; a rugby teammate fortunately had Bartelli's number.

'Mario, I need to speak with you urgently, it's Hainsworth-Catt here. I need just five minutes please!'

'No, I can't, I really can't.' Bartelli was clearly scared.

'I know about the blackmail, and it's that I want to speak about.' Max bluffed.

'Who told you eh......., I mean, listen, I'll meet you for five minutes only. Where?'

'In the fifth year's common room at 18.00hrs this evening.'

'Okay I'll be there, but only five minutes and come alone.' Max agreed.

Max met up with Rory as arranged earlier. 'Now you know what to do, Rory; it's important.'

'Leave it to me Max,'

'Thanks for coming, Mario; I do appreciate it.'

'What do you know about the blackmail? Who told you about that?' Bartelli asked nervously.

'Mario, it's obvious, I've done nothing to you; what else would make you lie and get me expelled for something I didn't do?'

'Look, I can't say anything that....... Max, show me your phone.' Max put his phone on the table and exclaimed.

'Mario, why are you so nervous.'

'You don't know the half of it; I'm only telling you this, so as you understand, it's not what I wanted to do. I have been stupid myself and did something I shouldn't have. The student who made me say I saw you break into the locker knew what I had done, and he threatened to expose me. He said it was only a prank and that you wouldn't get into trouble, well, not serious anyway. He didn't mention the Rolex being stolen though.'

'What on earth did this someone have over you Mario. To get you so scared you couldn't refuse this person's demand?'

'I lost my key to my locker, the duty prefect lent me the master key. My blackmailer took the key from me and took a BluTac impression and got a master key cut. You can work out the rest.'

'Okay, I get that, but what's he got on you to make you do such a thing to me.'

'My father is into heavy porn from Italy, he distributes DVD's all over Europe; his base is in Turin. So I started nicking from his stock that he keeps at our home in London. I began making copies on my DVD recorder and selling them here at school. That is until that bastard, well, the one who made me lie as a witness, found out about my porno racket and said he would bubble me if I didn't do what he asked me to do.'

'Mario, you must help me and do the right thing!'

'I said no, and that's final. This meeting never happened; it's over. Have you got that?'

5

It was the day of the rugby final. Sark versus Witherdrew. It was a well contested match, but Sark came out the winners. Max lifted the trophy that was presented by the headmaster. It was an awkward moment for both at the handover of the cup. The first time Sark had won the trophy in over seven decades. Only the shadow of the Rolex eclipsed what would have been a sensational day.

Christopher and Max met up in the cafe after the final as arranged. Max told his father about Mario, then pointed to his dad's phone.

'Give me your mobile a moment, dad!' Christopher threw his son a quizzical look and slid his phone over the table. Max flicked through his father's messages and previous calls locating the day they spoke about Christmas and the forthcoming rugby final. There it was! 17:23hrs! Length of call time 27 minutes. Max stood up and shouted excitedly!

'Dad, do you know what this means? You have recorded my innocence! My call on the afternoon of the theft is not erased on your phone, so let me check my corresponding call as well. Yes dad, it corresponds, which confirms the date and time are identical. This proves you and I were speaking when Bartelli said he saw me opening Timms's locker..

'Hello Rory, were you able to do what I asked?'
'Yes, of course, and it's as clear as a bell!'
'Brilliant, thanks so much, can you come at once with your phone to the cafeteria.'

Max had set up an urgent meeting with Dobbs and the headmaster.

The Head greeted Mr Hainsworth-Catt. 'It's a pleasure to see you again but sadly not under such circumstances Christopher,' the Head shook his hand, 'please take a seat everybody, and Maximus, please explain what this is all about. Are you doing the decent thing and confessing to stealing the Rolex?'

'On the contrary sir! At the exact time of the alleged witnessed theft of the Rolex, my father and I were having a phone conversation. With the exact date and time recorded precisely between me leaving the rugby practice field and the rest of the players getting back into the locker rooms at 17:40hrs. In Bartelli's words and his signed statement, he saw me at precisely 17:35hrs, opening Timms's locker. Impossible sir! I can't be in two places simultaneously. Now sir, please listen to the recording of the conversation between Mario Bartelli, the locker witness, and me in the 5th year's common room this afternoon,'

The phone played back the entire conversation. 'That proves my innocence beyond reasonable doubt!'

Dobbs's face was beaming; he couldn't hold back any longer. 'I just knew you were innocent, Max, I knew it! I even told you so, didn't I.'

The Head cleared his throat and told Mr Dobbs to calm himself.

'I must apologise to you, Maximus, but you must understand all the evidence I received was heavily stacked against you. You should consider becoming a barrister Maximus; you could be Queen's Counsel, I'll wager. I did notice in the recording, Bartelli stopped short of disclosing the real culprit. Who is it, Maximus?'

'I have my suspicions, sir, but I really would not like to say; Bartelli is the one who should tell you, as mine would have no foundation, only motive.' The Head replied.

'You even sound like a barrister,' the Head chuckled.

Max went to see Mr Dobbs and got dispensation to go to Pat's via the front door this time. Max heard from his housemaster that Bartelli would not divulge the blackmailer's name. However, he did admit to selling heavy porn films to school colleagues and telling lies about Maximus Hainsworth-Catt. Mario was expelled in disgrace!

Josh Fordham sent one of his lackeys to Max, telling him he wanted to sort Max out once and for all so put down a challenge in "*The Ring*." It is how serious disputes are settled at Carrow Abbey; of course, it's unofficial and banned from taking place, but even most teachers turn a blind eye to this gladiatorial type contest. The fight occurs in a human ring of boys four or five deep. It was arranged for 18:00hrs the following evening. Anyone failing to meet the challenge is deemed a coward. The loser must grovel forgiveness. Of course wagers are made, but the book had closed as no one apart from a few pals and his rugby teammates bet on Max. The fourth former against a fifth-year boy with a bad reputation. The next evening the ring formed. Ominous chatter amongst the swollen crowd added excitement; there hadn't been a ring fight like this for ten years at Carrow Abbey. A large group of two hundred boys gathered and jostled for a viewpoint. Finally, Josh Fordham arrived with his overweight shadow, Dominic; the ring parted to let them in. There was no Max; most of the group were disappointed but thought he had sensibly backed out.

Then coming from the north side lawn with a backpack, Max arrived to a great roar from the crowd; someone started the chant! Max, Max, Max, Max! Finally, the ring parted, and Max looking very relaxed, spoke to Fordham and his sidekick Dom.

'Okay, you two listen good, put on these gloves and I'll take you both on at the same time.' The large crowd fell silent. The two thugs looked at each other and laughed.

'Okay no problem,' Fordham sneered into Max's face. 'You are going to get the hiding of your life. The last time we hammered you was only a warm-up, eh Dom?' The overweight friend nodded approvingly, while tapping a beat with his baseball bat into his gloved hand, menacingly.

He stripped down to his singlet, accentuating his young but muscular physique, a powerful body that surprised the growing ring of boys.

The two combatants laughed again when Max approached, stopped and bowed to them both. Finally the whistle blew to start the contest.

It was amazing to watch the speed of Max's opening fight gambit, a flying dropkick that caught Fordham under the chin and sent him at least three metres backwards, landing at the many feet of the human ring.

Max went to the overweight Dom, who raised his baseball bat to strike Max, who dodged the incoming blow. Then, simultaneously moving in close to large Dom, Max threw a flurry of punches so quickly that the boy just covered his head without response. Another barrage to his fat body finished him off; he broke out of the ring and ran. Fordham got up and screamed insults and threats about what he was about to do to Max.

The young Hainsworth-Catt circled his opponent very slowly, moving ever closer; Fordham swung a full punch, but Max dipped away, and his opponent hit mid-air twice. Before Fordham could recover his lost balance, Max attacked at close quarters with a right punch to Fordham's stomach. It made him lurch forward; however, before he could regain composure, Max, with lightning-fast hands, demolished Fordham, who was flat out on his back; he finally got up, only to be dropped kicked backwards to finish flat on his back again. Fordham turned and crawled away from Max. 'I haven't finished with you,' Max yanked him up by his hair and shouted. 'tell these boys that it was you who took the watch and blackmailed Mario, who is now sadly expelled because of you.' Fordham retorted. 'No, go and fuck yourself.'

Max pulled his opponent up off the ground, took five paces back and, with speed, performed perfect flying neck scissors to Fordham, bringing him down to the ground again. This time he had Max's bulging muscular legs around his neck with squeezing increments to an unbearable level. Finally, the school thug managed a choking scream, 'Okay, no more, I admit I blackmailed Bartelli into lying and taking the watch from Timms's locker. Now for fucks sake, let me go, please!'

With that confession, Max struck him once more in the midriff that bent Fordham forward and then Maximus gave him the most brutal kick up the arse Max could muster, propelling him into the wall of boys, only to be pushed back in. But Max left the bully whimpering on his knees and clasping his battered body. The ring of boys went wild, so much so that teachers were arriving from everywhere to see what was going on, but they couldn't control this raucous crowd. In the space of two days, Maximus became a hero at Carrow Abbey for a second time. The personal score had been settled for the Hainsworth-Catt family, especially grandad Granville, Max's hero. Max found Dominic who willingly signed a statement condemning Fordham.

Rory's parents were skiing in the Alps and Rory didn't fancy that so Max invited him to Brandscombe for Christmas.

Marshall collected the two pals from Carrow Abbey as arranged on 20th December. When they arrived at the entrance of the great manor house, Rory just stared in disbelief, he had no idea Max lived in a home so grand.

The talk at dinner was about Uncle Thomas and Auntie Samantha. Max's mother warned.

'If they come and live in Rose Cottage, they may cause us more problems; you can't keep bailing him out, Christopher, he'll be up here all the time for money, and you know how that upsets you.'

'I know Ginny, you are right, he will always be a spoilt, ungrateful, and useless person, but he is my brother, and it is Christmas. So from tomorrow, he will be homeless.' Max sat upright and addressed his parents.

'Do I hear correct? Uncle Thomas is coming to live in Rose Cottage. Is that our Rose Cottage on the estate?'

'Yes, he has lost everything to bad investments, gambling and drinking, not necessarily in that order. He lost the mines in South Africa, ran up tens of thousands of pounds in gambling debt and tomorrow, Queensclere House, his home, is being repossessed by bailiffs, at

Christmas as well; he moves into Rose Cottage tomorrow, and that's that.'

'Will he have Christmas lunch with us?' Max asked.

'Yes. Tom and Sam are having Christmas lunch with us; we couldn't leave them without a Christmas or family. So I hope it works out, but I do have reservations with them coming to live on the estate.' Virginia said with a tremor in her voice.

'How much has Uncle Tom lost altogether.' Max enquired.

'About twenty-five million pounds give or take a million or two.' Max, quite stunned, asked almost rhetorically.

'How can anyone lose that amount of money?' Max happened to look at Rory, whose perplexed facial expression confirmed his shocked reaction to the previously discussed colossal figure. Then finally, Christopher answered Max's possible rhetorical question.

'Your Uncle Tom lost that kind of money by being weak of character and downright bloody foolish and now can we please change the subject and eat our dinner.'

Pippa arrived later in the evening with another new boyfriend. By the time they arrived there was a thick snow blanket covering the estate and it was still falling; the taxi did well to get grip from his tyres as he eventually skidded away back down the drive, leaving tracks in the snow likened to a drunk driver attempting a slalom exit.

Christopher went to see Tom at Rose Cottage, although a picture-postcard appearance on the outside, it was cold and a little damp inside. Instead of lighting a fire and unpacking, Thomas and Samantha had a whiskey bottle opened and were sat at the kitchen table. The only heat was from a liquid gas heater situated about a metre away from the drinkers. Christopher said in a quiet but exasperated voice. 'So Tom, it has come to this! You had a chance to improve the mines and invest in a property venture I offered you; now look at you. Why, Tom, why?'

Tom replied. 'If you've come here to gloat, just fuck off back to your mansion.' Thomas snarled at his older brother.

'I have actually come to ask you to join my family for Christmas lunch tomorrow. But I'm warning you both, any nonsense, and I'll kick you both out myself. So please control yourselves and lay off heavy drinking. Do you both understand me?'

Samantha replied. 'Yes Chris, we understand, and yes we will behave. Otherwise, we don't eat. What time?'

'Come over about 12.00 noon. Merry Christmas both.' Chris let himself out.

'Fancy a night spin on my quad; it will be a lark in the snow,' said Max.

'Yeah, great.' replied Max's reliable pal, Rory. Max knew he had to be back for the traditional special Christmas Eve dinner.

The boys took the back road from the rear of the house; they had the headlights on full beam as it was pitch dark; it was super fun skidding the bike on the fresh snow, the way Max's father had taught him. They skirted the woods that would take them up past Rose Cottage around the estate's ring road towards the main highway then turning back to the gated entrance of Brandscombe. As they came into view of Rose Cottage, they could see the house dimly lit, but what caught Max's attention was a car with three lights. Apart from the usual twin ones to the front, a larger halogen in the centre made it look different from other vehicles at night. It was parked outside the cottage. Max thought it strange that Thomas would entertain guests or visitors so late when he had only just moved in and not even unpacked especially on Christmas Eve.

So being curious and not trusting his uncle, Max turned off the quad lights.

'I'm just being inquisitive; wait here with the quad, Rory; if Thomas is up to something, I'd like to know about it as I don't trust him.'

Max slowly walked the snow-covered path to the rear of the cottage, away from the light of the front porch. Max climbed over the stone boundary wall to the rear garden and passed a garden shed and a large greenhouse to his right, edging to the back wall of the house. The snow had drifted here and was up to Max's knees. He picked his way to the rear window from which the light formed outside shadows. He could hear shouting from inside; stealthily he moved closer to the window. What he saw stunned Max ridged! Two burly guys were beating Thomas! Samantha was sat on a chair, tied up and crying. One of the men had a knife, evidently threatening Thomas with it. Max distinctly heard one guy say. 'You have until 27th to get the fifty grand. Fail, and you are both dead!

The bigger one of the two hit Thomas twice more full-on, in the face. Tom groaned as his head dropped onto his chest; he was either dead or unconscious from the beating. Max doubted that they would see him at the Christmas table tomorrow.

6

'I forgot to get the After Eights on my way back from work today; your mum will shoot me. It's too late to ask poor Marshall to go shopping; he wants to leave to see his family, so I'll go to Tesco Express, they are open until 22.00hrs tonight. Do you want to keep me company, Max?'

Max answered his father with a nod. They picked up the chocolate mints and returned. Before they reached the main gates of Brandscombe, an impatient driver behind got very close. Max turned to see how close it was. Max couldn't believe what he saw. It was three eyes, about twenty feet behind. In an instant the strange looking car overtook Christopher's Land-Rover. It was heading towards Brandscombe. Max wondered if the car with the three lights was going back to Rose Cottage. He decided to find out as he had an intense feeling of something not being quite right. So he decided to go over to Rose Cottage later this evening, covertly. Later that evening when the lads were in their bedroom. Max went down the fire escape at the rear.

Max crept out the back to his quad, dressed in the bike gear, and ever so slowly drove down the estate ring road to the woods and the cottage. This time he parked the bike on the edge of the thicket and walked to the house. Again, the black frog looking car with three eyes was parked outside. This time with its eyes closed.

Max used the same track he had taken earlier in the evening, moving slowly around the house, remembering the snow drift. Max's last footprints were lost from a further snowfall. As Max drew level with the cottage, he froze but not with the biting cold night air! To his left, about fifty metres away, there was a human cough and the stamping of feet. *"He's bound to see me."* Max thought. It was very dark with just a hint of light struggling to get through the curtains. Max dropped deep into the snow to hide. Max's eyes were adjusting to the dark that helped him see the person burst into illumination for a second or two; his face glowed from the striking of a match, the man was lighting up a cigarette and now leaning on the front door inside the open porch. He hadn't seen Max, who waited for the guard to turn away then slowly moved past the cottage's side and rear, climbing over the same stone wall he had done on his earlier visit. He crept slowly to the house's rear elevation. Max looked through the kitchen window and couldn't believe his eyes. Thomas, Samantha and the two thugs, who assaulted his uncle earlier were now sitting at the table, all pals with a bottle of whiskey in the middle of them. The conversation was surprisingly cordial this time. It confused Max, and he thought rhetorically. *"How can these scenes change from beating the crap out of Thomas literally a few hours ago to drinking together in what appeared to be quite a civil but earnest conversation."*

Unlike earlier, when they were shouting, it was now harder to hear what they were saying through the glass. There was a lot of gesturing with arms aloft. Max definitely heard Pippa's name mentioned at least twice, so he knew he wasn't mistaken. How in heavens name is Pippa involved with these low life scum! Max pondered.

The teenager heard footsteps getting louder. Max moved behind the protruding chimney breast just enough to hide him from the approaching person providing he didn't come any closer. Should he attack him, run for it or try and talk his way out. Max was thinking quickly about what to do. Thankfully a decision was not required; the man turned and walked several paces towards the garden, stopped and pissed all over the white topped cabbages. "*Dirty bastard*" Max thought; the guy turned back, briefly looked around then went back, presumably to the front porch. Scare over. He missed a few minutes of the meeting but thought it best to get a bit nearer to the window. Max was straining to hear, daring to get as close as he could, pressing his ear to the ice-cold glass hidden from the occupants by a thin curtain. He heard "*tomorrow night*" but couldn't make out in what context.

There were raised voices with one thug swallowing his drink, and from their movements, Max realised the gang were about to leave. It was time for Max to go! Back at Brandscombe, Max entered via the fire escape through the door he left unlocked for his return entry. Max decided not to tell his father about his brother, well not until Christmas Day was over!

'Time to turn in Rory; it's hard to believe it's Christmas Eve with all that's going on. Good night my friend, and Merry Christmas.'

'Good night Max.'

Max woke first and threw a present at Rory's bed that startled the young guest.

'Merry Christmas, I hope you like your present.
Open it.'

They were the latest Nike trainers, the blue ones with white soles, the ones Rory had kept on about in school.

Rory was delighted.

With breakfast over, Christopher ushered everybody into the hall to gather around the massive spruce Christmas tree that spiralled all the way up through the gallery stairs. Then, behind the gathering and through the wide Gothic door walked Thomas and Samantha; they were carrying gifts stacked so high one couldn't see their faces. What's more, they were both sober!!!

They put the presents under the tree and took off their coats. 'Merry Christmas, everyone.' Samantha seemed sincere with her greetings. Max thought: *"Have my uncle and aunt become good people overnight? Something is not quite right about these two!"*

It was time for the family's highlight of the day and Christopher's favourite time as head of the family. He started Christmas lunch proceedings by saying grace, the welcoming speech, and finally, a toast to the family's good health and fortune. Everybody tucked into a marvellous cooking performance by Mrs Cooper. It was always so good.

The family retired to the drawing room for Christmas games and a good chat. Everybody circulated with drink in hand.

Thomas waited until Pippa had gone to the loo, intercepting her in the hall by the Christmas tree. 'Pippa, did you like your present?'

'I...I don't remember seeing one from you, Uncle Tom.'

'Oh dear, yours must still be in my car, we had so many presents in the back. Be an angel, please go and get it; my car is around the side of the house towards the stables; here are the keys. The doors will automatically unlock as you approach. You know my car.'

'Sure, Uncle Thomas, that's very sweet of you.'

Thomas went back to the lounge to mingle with his family. Samantha mainly wanted to engage with Benjamin and was chatting when Thomas arrived and joined in the family conversations.

Pippa's search for her present was brutally interrupted, a hand around her neck and another was stopping her breathing. A large man held a cloth over her face, covering her nose and mouth. She let out a muffled scream for about three seconds and collapsed into the arms of her assailant. She was carried between two men who bundled her into the boot of the car with three headlights! It drove to the entrance gates and turned left towards the town. After fifteen minutes of idle chat, Ben looked around for his new love, Pippa.

'Have you seen Pippa about?'

'I saw her at the opening of presents; obviously, she was at Christmas lunch, which probably was the last time I saw her. So she must be about somewhere.' Thomas remarked while looking around the room.

'She may have popped up to her room to freshen up.' Samantha suggested. Ben replied.

'Of course, I'll go up to check on her.'

Thomas and Samantha looked sheepishly at each other then went across to Virginia.

'Lovely Christmas, Virginia.' Samantha declared insincerely.

'So glad you could make it. Have you unpacked and settled into the cottage?'

'We are in, but the boiler isn't working. We are relying on a liquid gas heater.'

'Well, it's good to see you both; I hope you will be happy in Rose Cottage. It's nice having you back on the estate. We'll chat after Christmas about possible work for you on the paper or our magazines if you like.'

'Yes, of course, we'll chat about that later.' Thomas replied as if he wasn't really interested in any sort of work.

Ben came back into the family lounge, looking flustered; he found Christopher. 'Mr Hainsworth-Catt, have you seen Pippa in the last half hour?'

'No, I haven't. Pippa is around somewhere; perhaps she has gone to her room to do what girls do, most probably.'

'I have checked her room; she's not in it.'

Chris replied. 'I can't help you then, Ben. You could try the stables; she may be feeding the horses some leftovers of veg from dinner; she was always with the horses as a girl.'

Ben left the room again and went outside in search of his girlfriend. Max went over to speak with Archie and Charlotte, who were getting stuck into Champagne. 'Fancy a glass, Maximus?'

'Don't mind if I do, bruv. How are you, Charlie?'

'Very well, thanks Maximus; how is Carrow Abbey treating you? Your father was raving over you playing in some rugby final or something, telling us you played brilliantly for his old house and that Sark hadn't won the final for seventy years. So well done for that.' Max explained to Archie all about his Rose Cottage excursions, what he'd seen and heard on his two trips yesterday. Max was looking for some advice.

'Do you think I should tell mum and dad? I didn't want to worry them or spoil their Christmas. What should I do, Archie?'

'Bloody hell Max, this could be serious, we should go to dad, you and me both, let's ask to see him in his study. Charlie, will you be okay for five minutes?'

'Yes of course, Archie, you two go; I will say nothing.'

Archie and Max went to their father and asked if they could see him in his study. Now! The two brothers followed Christopher into his locked office. Immediately they were in, and the door had closed, Max repeated what he had witnessed at Rose Cottage on both occasions. Christopher had a worried look.

'Max, why didn't you tell me sooner?' Christopher barked at his son. A typical human response from an anxious parent.

Max explained his reasons. 'Dad, I can see now that I should have told you last night. It was Christmas Eve, and considering mum's special dinner, I waited until now, once Christmas lunch was over. I was wrong in my judgement. I am so sorry dad.'

7

'We have your daughter; listen well.' There was a pause, and the recognisable sobbing voice of Pippa was put on the phone.

'Please help me dad, but don't go to the police. They said they would rape and then kill me please d....'

The phone clicked off. Christopher and Virginia hurried down to the lounge where the family and guests were grouped, awaiting news. For the Hainsworth-Catt family, Christmas was truly over. Do they bring in the police? Christopher warned, 'The most crucial thing is Pippa's safety. We must negotiate and hope to God they will return her unharmed.' The family just looked on, not knowing what to say or suggest.

After an hour, the phone rang again. 'Tomorrow at noon, you will take one million pounds in a holdall, in fifty pound used notes to Dontin lake near Godalming. You will hire a boat and go to the middle of the lake—an xFold Dragon x12 drone will find you; it will hover above you low enough for you to reach the hook on its undercarriage. Place the holdall on the hook but don't hold or pull at the drone. Give me your mobile number and keep your phone with you tomorrow. There is a little present for you at your entrance gate, to show you why you don't go to the police'.......

There was no time to reply or ask further questions to the kidnappers.

Christopher said to Archie. 'Go to the gate quick and see what's there.'

'I'll go with you, Archie,' Max left with his brother. 'Come on, I'll take you on the quad.'

They returned and gave Christopher a sealed cardboard parcel. Christopher opened it; inside was the smallest, blooded digit of a left foot.

'No, no, no, please don't let it be what I think it is, oh my God, no!' Sadly it was the severed small toe from Pippa's left foot.

Also inside the small package was a ruby ring. Pippa's grandmother had given it to her; she always wore it. Christopher and Virginia were beside themselves with fear and anxiety for their daughter. Virginia was clearly in shock and collapsed into a chair sobbing. Christopher now had his mind made up for him. He would not call the police; he would get the high-value ransom together. Chris had a special relationship with his private merchant bankers, Steinhart and Cohen, which made it possible to get the ransom money together over the Christmas bank holiday. High street banks would not even be open at this time.

'There will be no police; we must not tell anyone else about this, only our immediate family that are here present. So please don't mention it to Thomas or Samantha or our guests. I know you believe that Thomas and Samantha are implicated, Max, but I want Pippa back before investigating my brother and Sam.'

Although Max was itching to drag the information out of Thomas, he could understand his father's careful approach.

The phone rang; Christopher took the call in his study. Archie and Max were in attendance. It was Steinhart and Cohen. They said the money was ready and they would deliver it to Brandscombe in thirty minutes by an armoured security van with a guard and accompanied by a director to obtain a signature. The whole Hainsworth-Catt family were getting very twitchy.

The armoured vehicle arrived. Thomas was directed away, as he was showing too much interest. Christopher signed for the cash in his study and transferred it to a leather holdall.

Christopher, Archie and Max travelled to Dontin lake; surprisingly, the recreational lake was open on Boxing day, which was obviously why the kidnappers had chosen this location. They arrived at 11.30hrs, hired a boat, and then rowed out to where they considered to be the middle of the lake. At three minutes to twelve, Christopher had a call on his mobile.

'Good so far. We are watching you. Do you have the cash?

'Yes, do you have my daughter because if anything happens to her, I will have you hunted down and killed?' Chris was showing anger that the sons had never witnessed.

'Your daughter is, apart from a sore toe, okay; as soon as we receive the money, we will tell you where she is. Do you understand?'

Christopher told the voice. 'We can find you if Pippa is not returned to us safely now! We will interrogate my brother Thomas; we are sure he knows something about you scum.'

The man on the other end of the call went very quiet. This was obviously not in his plan. Max wondered to himself if his dad had done the right thing by saying that, but on the other hand, it may protect Pippa if they think they could be caught. Chris's remark had thrown the kidnappers, but events were still moving fast. The voice advised. 'I'll call you when I've checked the money'.........

The family heard a burring noise getting closer; out from the trees from the far bank came a large heavy-duty drone that came in high above the boat and lowered vertically to a metre above the boat. Chris stood up and hooked the money bag onto the hook, and away it flew out of sight.

They rowed back to the boathouse and waited in the Land-Rover anxiously for the call—all of them praying for Pippa's safe return. Then finally, Christopher's phone went; the three jumped. The voice barked instructions.

'It is all there. You will find a note we have left for you under the largest stone by the metal litter bin, in the flower bed next to the boathouse cafeteria. The message will tell you where the girl is......'

'I'll go.' Max sprinted back to the boathouse, about one hundred metres from the car park.

Max found the bin and the sizeable adjacent stone. It had to be the one. There was an envelope that Max retrieved for his father. It was an address and reasonably close. 'Come on, put this place into the Sat Nav.' Demanded Chris. When they got to the address, it appeared to be an empty house. The front door was locked, so they broke in through a window at the back, allowing Max to climb in.

Maximus let his dad and Archie in through the back door. A muffled noise came from upstairs. Max was away, climbing two steps at a time to the first floor. Christopher was shouting for him to wait. There was no chance of that!

'Thank God, Pippa, are you okay?' As Max removed her gag, Christopher and Archie came crashing into the room. Chris hugged his daughter while she was still tied to a chair. Max cut the ropes with a knife and released his sister. Apart from her apparent stressful state, she appeared all right. She broke into tears and, with heavy sobbing, tried to speak. Christopher, in a fatherly, comforting way, said. 'Come on, let's get you to hospital for a checkup.'

Thomas and Samantha went back to Rose Cottage; they were unpacking boxes when a knock on the door startled them. Samantha opened it.

'We have the money. It went according to plan, dead easy.' The kidnapper spokesman grinned.

'Come in, and give us our cut. Two hundred thousand was agreed, but Thomas and I have been thinking we demand three hundred thousand less the fifty thousand we owe your boss. The extra is on account that we planned it all and set up the girl to be taken. The extra is not negotiable. We demand it!' As Samantha turned to go back to the unpacking room, a muffled thud sounded as a silenced bullet split Sam's occiput. A neat hole in the back of her head ensured she was dead by the time she hit the floor.

Thomas came to the front hallway to see what the noise was. His mouth wide open, it was Thomas's last expression ever! Two shots into his face, one in his left eye, the other in his chin, had put him down in under a second, it left a protruding trail of his brain across the hall wall as far as the stairs.

Maximus will not get revenge for his sister after all, Thomas and Samantha are no more. So the bad side of Hainsworth-Catt family were both eliminated. Not a bad thing, many might say.

The male members of the Hainsworth-Catt family all arrived back at Brandscombe with Pippa. Apart from a Tetanus injection and antibiotics for her amputated toe, Pippa was now in good spirits and was enjoying her family's attention; the relief in the room was almost tangible.

'We need to see Thomas now.' Max urged his father. So Christopher agreed that the three Hainsworth-Catt men could take out two quads to ride to Rose Cottage, which had become a frequent journey for Maximus.

The door was surprisingly locked; it appeared nobody was in. They knocked several times; Max went around the back but could see nothing through the same window where he witnessed the kidnapping plan being hatched previously.

Christopher looked through the front door letterbox and yelled.

'Oh, God, no, no, no!! They are both dead.' After his initial shock, he phoned the police. They waited until three police cars arrived. The sight was surreal; the bodies were in top and tail position like neat sardines in a tin.

They were lying in a pool of their joint blood that was already clotting on the floor, attracting rats, who were evidently feasting on the freshly butchered carcasses of Tom and Samantha Hainsworth-Catt. Max felt no loss, just some pity for their souls. He thought of the massive inheritance Thomas received. So many life opportunities, but the weakness of character and lack of self-discipline led swiftly to his premature demise.

Life settled down into normality again over the next few days, but Max wasn't going to leave it. The callous kidnappers severed his sister's toe and got a million out of his dad. He asked Archie to help him, and the fact he could draw himself away from Charlotte and perpetual bonking impressed Max when Archie agreed to help. The older brother also had a car. Most essential in the search for the gang.

They didn't say anything to their father; he had enough on his plate with Virginia worrying so and looking after Pippa, who was lapping up all the attention from everybody. 'Our only lead is their car with its strange centre front light. I'm sure it has been fitted by a local garage somewhere close, so we will start locally in town as that was the direction they came from the night I heard them at Rose Cottage.' So, after ticking off several garages, they phoned Uphill garage on the town's outskirts; a mechanic answered the question they wanted to hear.

'Yes, I do recall the job, a strange one, although it must have been six weeks or more ago. I remember it clearly because the man was aggressively obnoxious, but he was unequivocal in his requirements. Nasty bloke mind, he never smiled once, insisting he paid for the job that included many other alterations for £3,000 in cash. He got the hump because I wouldn't knock the VAT off his bill for cash. Our garage had just undergone a VAT inspection; the boss got a hefty fine, so he hasn't messed with the VAT from then on. He said we are not to do cash jobs anymore apart from his family members.'

'Can you give us his address?' Max asked.

'Afraid not, owing to data protection, but I didn't like the guy, so I'll tell you where he drinks; I've seen him in there a few times. It's the Lamb and Compass at Blindley Heath, just outside Croydon. I don't know you, but be careful; he looks a right handful.'

After five nights of going to the Lamb and Compass without success, Archibald decided he couldn't carry on with the surveillance; he was committed to Charlotte's parents New Year's Eve party that was pre-arranged. Max will continue but realised transport would be a problem without Archie's car.

Both brothers felt disappointed with no breakthrough, but it was always going to be a long shot anyway.

Max has known Marshall since he was a small boy; and always enjoyed his humour and wit. He, on many occasions, could have dropped Maximus into trouble but didn't. He was an excellent person to have around. But Max needed his help now.

'Mr Marshall, can you please take me, um.... unofficially to the Lamb and Compass at Blindley. It's near Croydon.'

'I know where it is. Do you fancy a pint, Max?' Marshall chuckled to himself.

'Does your father know? When do you want to go?'

'Now, and no and no. I'm not drinking or meeting a girl. I'm looking for a three-eyed car. If you see one on the road, try and take its number, Mr Marshall.'

'Okay, I'll take you, wait here. I'll bring the car around. By the way, either call me Marshall or Mick; I'm not too fond of the Mr bit if it's all the same to you.'

'Of course, Mick, I'll walk to the garage with you, then we can go straight out.'

They turned left towards the town to pick up the A22 to Blindley Heath and the Lamb and Compass pub, arriving at 20.00hrs. They stayed until 21.30hrs but with no luck. "*Another nil return*.." Max thought.

'I'm so sorry, Mr...er Mick, waiting for nothing. We can go home now. Thanks for taking me.'

'Are you going to tell me what is so interesting about this car we are looking for? What is your connection Max?'

'I'd rather not say at the moment, Mick, as I don't want to implicate you.'

'Now you are intriguing me, Maximus. Just be careful, okay.'

The next day, Max chatted with his sister Pippa, asking her if she could remember anything about her kidnappers. Appearance, mannerism, anything. Pippa was rather uncomfortable talking about it, which was understandable.

'Why does my fifteen-year-old brother want to know about my horrible experience? I don't particularly like talking about it. I told the police everything I knew. Sorry Maximus, I didn't mean to be irritable.'

'That's okay Pippa, quite understandable; I just wondered, that's all.'

'I do remember one had a distinctive, broad Northern accent, Yorkshire, I think.'

Mick Marshall gave Max his mobile number, which helped considerably. He took him up on his kind offer to help. Max called him to set up another visit to the pub. Marshall said he was going into town for Christopher to collect some bits for him; he suggested he could drop Max off at lunchtime at the Lamb and Compass then pick him up later, on his way back.

'When Mr Marshall?'

'I'll meet you at the garage in ten minutes if that suits, and it's Mick, remember.'

'Sorry Mick, too much Carrow Abbey training, I think. I'll be at the garage in ten minutes, thanks.'

Mick dropped Max off; he said he would ring when he left town, suggesting picking him up at the pub's entrance.

Max went into the pub, buying a can of coke and a meat pie. There was a big guy to his right just being served by another barmaid. In a broad Yorkshire accent he asked. 'Ee lass, ah cud eat oven door if it wor buthard'

Max took his refreshments and returned to the car park, thinking back to what Pippa had said about one of her kidnappers with a strong Yorkshire accent. The guy at the bar couldn't have had a stronger one if he tried. Maximus thought this lead was worth a try. He went straight back into the lounge, looking through to the main public bar area where Yorkie was still ordering. Max photographed him on burst mode, taking random shots around the pub. He put the phone on record and went back into the main bar, casually strolling over to where Yorkie was sitting. Max stuck his nose into a menu, recording the best he could from a three-way conversation. Nothing he could pick up apart from *"something being too risky"*. Because Max was standing close, Yorkie put his finger to his mouth and said something that obviously got a reaction as they all went quiet. Max thought it time to leave. The Carrovian detective looked in both the Lamb and Compass car parks, but no three-eyed car was there. So Max phoned Mick, asking him to collect him ASAP, telling him he'd explain upon his arrival.

Max went back to the picnic bench where he'd left his coke and pie, sitting down to watch the exit door for Yorkie and Co. to come out.

Thankfully, forty minutes later, the Land Rover pulled in, and Max flagged Marshall down, getting in, and directing Marshall to an empty parking spot under a large Oak tree that gave them a full view of the entrance door. Max explained the people he required information about but left out the details for a reason. He promised Mick the full story on their way home, but first, he wanted him to follow a car unless the gang left by taxi. After fifteen minutes, Marshall was getting twitchy and said. 'Maximus, we can't stay much longer; I have to deliver some packages to your dad.'

'Okay, Mick, I'm sure it won't be long; please bear with me; I'll sort it with dad, I promise.'

Another twenty minutes went past. Then, at last, out came Yorkie with two other guys; Max pointed them out to Mick; they turned right, vanishing behind the front of the pub.

'Sod's law Mick, they are parked in the other car park. No matter, drive forward so we can watch the other exit onto the road.' They didn't have to wait long. A white Qashqai with Yorkie and his two easily recognisable companions, one having a mop of ginger hair, drove away. Max snapped away in burst mode again with magnification to the maximum on his phone camera. He got the number plate as they turned right onto the A22, passing them as they went by. Marshall pulled out behind them, staying a steady hundred metres back. Luckily, they were heading in the Land-Rover's direction, which pleased the chauffeur.

After about ten miles, the Qashqai turned left onto a B road to Thrupp. Marshall followed, keeping his distance; The gang had no indication that they were aware they were being followed.

'I wish I knew what you are up to; this is all a bit cloak and dagger for my liking.' A slight trepidation was creeping into Mick's voice.

Five more minutes later, the white SUV turned off the road, down a farm track; Max told Mick to drive straight on for half a mile then turn into a farm gate that accessed a field. After the intentional delay, they pulled out of the field and turned back to where the SUV turned off; Mick parked up. Max left their vehicle, saying he would only be five minutes.

Maximus walked down the single-track lane for about two hundred metres, then left the tarmac road and continued into the paddock close to the hedge running parallel to the lane. After another one hundred and fifty metres on, Max came to some trees; he could see a large house, probably a farm, he stayed close to the hedgerow that formed the property's entrance and boundary. To Max's surprise, at the front of the property was the white Qashqai and old three eyes. Max's heart was racing with excitement; he had found the bastards that kidnapped Pippa, also the ones that no doubt murdered Thomas and Samantha. He ran back to Mick. 'Let's go home and thank you so much for waiting.'

Mick replied sarcastically. 'Yes, master.'

Max laid on his bed, staring at the ceiling, watching a spider making its web using the ceiling rose as an anchor point. What to do, what to do? He thought of his options. He could go to the police, let them sort it out, or find out more himself to exact revenge for his sister and dad.

Max still pondered; he had done all the work himself from that night he eavesdropped on the thugs beating up Thomas. It was his case. Maximus decided to carry on alone, for the time being anyway. He would need the help of Archie to drive him to the farmhouse for a closer look.

First, he had to make sure it was the thugs he followed. So he decided to show Pippa the Yorkie photos and video. Next, Max phoned his sister to ask her if she could manage to come to his room, with her amputation still relatively fresh.

'Yes, I need to exercise my legs and foot for the circulation; I'll be up directly.'

'What's this all about, Max? We haven't had secret meetings for many years; it used to be after we raided Mrs Cooper pantry, do you remember?'

'Yes, like yesterday. Before I tell you something sensitive, you must promise not to tell anyone, is that clear?'

'Yes, of course, but what is it?'

Max showed Pippa the photo clip of Yorkie.

'Oh my God! It's that big man who threatened to kill me; I'd recognise that Yorkshire accent anywhere. It's definitely him. Where the hell did you get this video and photos? I really can't believe it; seeing that horrible bastard again makes me shudder with the thought. Are you going to the police with these pictures of him? I can vouch it's him from the photos, for sure.' Pippa baulked at what she saw. Almost an instinctive, defensive reaction.

'No, Pippa, I have some more investigative work first.'

'What is that, Max? Please do nothing stupid. Let the police deal with it. But Max, these men are dangerous. I promise you; I've met them. Oh my god, Max!'

'Please don't worry, Pippa, I will not take risks.'

Pippa went to her room, somewhat shaken from what she had seen. Max required Archie's help with using his car, so he phoned him, hoping he would respond.

'Archie, I need your help tonight. Please trust me on this and don't mention anything to mum or dad. It'll not require you to stay over at Brandscombe unless you want to. I suppose you'll want to return to Charlotte's tonight. Can you help me, please Archie?'

'I don't know what you are up to Max, but yes, let me ask Charlie out of courtesy. Can you wait a minute?'........

'Max, yes I'll be over in about two hours. We are just about to eat.' 'Thanks, Archie; phone me before you get to our gates, and I'll meet you there.'

'This had better be good, Max.......!'

8

It was 19:30hrs when Max's phone rang. Archie was still a couple of miles away. Max rode his quad down to the gates and hid his transport in the bushes.

'Thanks, Archie' Max climbed into his brother's car. 'We are heading towards town, after about ten miles we turn right onto a B road to Thrupp. Come on, let's go.' They nearly missed the turning to Thrupp. The darkness and speed they were travelling didn't help despite the satnav guidance. They drove up past the lane leading to the kidnappers' hideout, a farmhouse well hidden off the beaten track. Archie parked up in a small passing point a hundred metres further on. They walked back to the farmhouse lane, now in total darkness, with only a pencil torch to navigate the way.

'Stay here, Archie. I have to check on a couple of things nearer the house, and I need to know if the kidnappers are inside. I'll be back within five minutes.' Max moved towards the light emanating from the house; all was quiet. His senses easily determined the distinct smell of a coal fire; he now had a clear view of the room. Max was able to confirm people were inside. Working his way back around the front yard, keeping the two cars between him and the house, from this closer angle, the Carrovian detective could see movement in the front room; he edged towards three-eyes and photographed its number plate low down to hide the flash from his phone camera. Max only chanced one shot; it was the same car at Rose Cottage. Max gambled on a closer look and recognised three of the four men. He contacted the police inspector who is investigating Tom and Samantha's murders.

'Come on, Archie, it was the correct place, and the bastards are inside. Now for the fireworks.'

They walked back to Archie's car and waited for the expected armed police. Max had suggested to the police chief that his cars did not put blue lights and sirens on.

Two squad cars blocked off the road on either side of the farm lane. The inspector got out of his car.

'Are you Maximus Hainsworth-Catt?

'That's me, sir.'

'This had better not be a prank; we have a squad of six armed response officers here with automatic weapons; according to your story, this could get dangerous.'

'Sir, before I take you to the best observation spot, let me give you some information that will help: firstly, keep your blue lights off. They may see them from the house. There are four men, and they are in the house now. I checked before calling you. They're armed, I am sure. I would suggest you call in another armed squad as there is access at the rear; they could make a run for it at the back across a paddock and onto the other B road connecting to Thrupp. You will have the advantage of surprise, but I do think you may need more armed police to cover the rear.'

Although shocked, the inspector was impressed with the intel he received from young Max; he agreed that another armed unit was necessary so he called up reinforcements. The inspector ordered them to keep their blue lights and sirens off. Once the backup arrived, Max led what seemed like an army, stealthily moving up the lane.

Max took the inspector alone to the spot behind the cars; he pointed to the lit room, telling the officer they were all in there.

'Okay, son, now I want you to go back to your brother's car and drive home, no ifs or buts.

That's a police instruction. Now go. Hopefully, we shall be in touch tonight; thanks for what you have done, excellent detective work by the way, now go.'

Max got back to Archie, who thought he was in some film set.

'We have to go home, Archie, police orders.'

Maximus explained the whole story on their way home. How he'd spoken to the police inspector earlier that afternoon to tell him what he knew but emphasised he wasn't a hundred per cent sure they were the suspects. He thought Max was playing a prank until he told him who he was the son of; then thankfully he took Max seriously. The inspector respected Christopher and had been to the manor for charity events. Max explained also to the inspector that the men in the farmhouse were definitely the ones at Rose Cottage. The same men who were involved in the abduction of Pippa and the murder of his uncle and auntie.

The inspector with two detectives arrived at Brandscombe in one car. The staff were curious to know why the coppers were visiting their employer's home so late at night. The police party were taken to Christopher's study—the inspector, with justification to be proud, gave a detailed account of his team's success at the farmhouse. The lawman was confident in bringing charges against the four held in custody and explained. 'They gave up without a fight. Of course, the gang pleaded their innocence, saying they had nothing to do with the kidnapping or murder of Mr Thomas and Mrs Samantha Hainsworth-Catt. We are holding them in custody and require Pippa and Maximus to identify them. We will use other evidence to back-up our prosecution, such as the vehicle at the scene and their hide-out. These will give us their DNA. The weapon taken at the farmhouse matches the one used to shoot Mr and Mrs Hainsworth-Catt.'

Max and his two siblings travelled to the central police station in Croydon where the Farmhouse Four were being detained. The quartet faced a one-way viewing window individually then collectively. They were ordered to turn about, and finally asked to recite a couple of sentences. In both Pippa's and Max's judgment, there was no doubt that these were the kidnappers and, evidently, the murderers. Conclusively, Pippa remembered the striking tattoo of a mermaid and anchor on one of the gang's left hand.

With Max and Pippa's emphatic identifications, the tyre prints left in the snow outside Rose Cottage matching the treads of old three eyes, Max's photo of the car at the cottage and the farmhouse, this will seal the gang's fate. However, the gang would not say where the million pounds ransom was.

Max had a pretty busy and unusual Christmas, no doubt about that, but he thought he'd try and find the gangs retirement fund. He had nothing better to do.

Max thought it couldn't be far away because of the short time since the money exchange. He thought it was either at the farmhouse or nearby en-route from Rose Cottage. Max decided to start tomorrow. He couldn't get into the farmhouse as the police forensic team were still working meticulously there. It'll be a couple of days before they will be finished. It turned out that the gang had rented the farmhouse. There work was specialising in debt collection with menaces. Kidnapping was a new opportunity with a much larger revenue, set up and devised by Thomas to save his neck and make twenty per cent of the million. This information came from Christopher, who knew the detective inspector quite well.

New Year's Eve came and went. Max poured himself a flute of Champagne, and just after midnight, when all the hugging and Auld Lang Syneing was over, he slipped away with his glass of bubbly in hand; stood at the entrance door staring out at the chilly white landscape. Max pondered what the new year had in store for him. He also wondered if the police forensics had finished at the farmhouse. He will check tomorrow, as he knew Mick was off until the second of January.

Max will require him to drive to the farm as Archie was at Charlotte's parents for the new year.

Max had four days before he returned to Carrow, and as Mick had agreed to take him to the farm this lunchtime, he wanted to get on with the treasure-hunt.

Marshall pulled up outside the farmhouse, finding it deserted. That was good news as Max can get stuck into the hunt for the gang's loot, that's if the police hadn't already discovered it, which Max doubted as Christopher would have been notified. Max asked Mick to stay in the car. Marshall wasn't comfortable with that but was persuaded; he soon got stuck into his newspaper and sandwiches that Mrs Cooper always made for his lunch. Max didn't bother with the house as the forensic team would have stripped the place looking for evidence and the stolen ransom money. Instead, he went to the sheds and outhouses; after forty minutes, Max had found nothing. Next, he targeted the outside toilet; the smell was disgusting, the flush was broken, with dark shit caked all up the pan's sides. It made Max retch violently with the stink and the thought. He couldn't cope with the sickening smell so retreated from the appalling loo. He thought for a moment about the flush and wondered what had caused the malfunction of the cistern. Could it be some object that impeded it. *"Something like a bag of money perhaps?"* Max wondered. The police, he was sure, would have given it a miss, owing to the sheer stench; with one look in the pan, they would have cut their search and retreated. It was disgusting!

Max put a scarf around his face to re-enter the repulsive loo. It was an old cast-iron cistern. He used a stick to flick the toilet lid down to stand on. He lifted the lid off the cistern and felt pretty optimistic as there was something inside. Maximus pulled a large plastic bag out, dripping wet. He had found the money! He excitedly tipped out the bag's contents outside the loo and far enough away from the stench—only porn magazines fell out. Although disappointed, it made Max laugh that some bloke, probably married, had a stash of these dirty books in the loo. He probably went there once or twice a week to *"spank the monkey"*. He must have forgotten his mags when he sold up; it was funny, although disappointing.

Max moved to the rear garden, it had been neglected for years by the looks, judging by the overgrowth. He walked around the large kitchen garden; it still had some pockets of snow lingering in the shaded north-facing areas. Nothing showed any recent disturbance of the ground. Max carried on further beyond the garden and made his way to a small orchard that was monochrome in the wintery light, just a misty colourless scene with patches of white snow still lingering after the partial thaw. Maximus entered the orchard, coming across some small pet gravestones, about five, all overgrown. However, what did get his interest was the grass with dying foliage spread next to the memorial stone of Rex, obviously a family dog in years past.

He moved the foliage with his foot to expose loose brown, recently disturbed earth. Just what Max was looking out for. He went back to the car to tell Mick that he would be another half hour. Then, taking a broken handled spade from a garden shed, Max dug the loose, recently excavated soil; it was easy digging. Within five minutes, he came across a plastic container at a depth of about fifty centimetres; inside was a leather hold-all, full of fifty-pound notes. It took Max some time to count it twice; the total on both counts came out at nine hundred and sixty thousand pounds. Forty thousand short, Max didn't think his dad would mind the shortfall.

Back at Brandscombe, after thanking Mick for losing his lunch break, Max took the hold-all to his dad's study, put it on his desk, and then phoned him. He was in the vegetable garden with Virginia; he said he was on his way back to the house. Christopher walked through his study door.

'What is it, Maximus? I was putting in some bean sticks for your mother.'

His younger son handed his father a leather hold-all that Chris immediately recognised.

'I think this belongs to you, dad.' Max handed the leather holdall to his father. The son explained it was forty thousand short and where he had found it. Max could see Christopher was proud of what his son had achieved at such a young age.

'It could have been dangerous, Maximus. You must remember you are only fifteen; by the way, where is the missing forty thousand.'

'I put it on a horse called Bag of money, running in the 2:30 at Ascot; it came in at 10 to 1.' Chris laughed at his son's answer.

'I have no idea where the missing forty thousand is, dad.'

It was the next day that the inspector called again to see Christopher. He had a plastic bag with thirty thousand pounds inside. The policeman explained that the four detainees had to strip for showering, a regulation before being sent to a more secure detention facility. They found a hidden envelope with ten thousand pounds stuffed in three of the gang's underpants, apart from the Yorkshireman who wouldn't say a word about where his ten thousand pounds was.

Christopher gave the inspector a cheque for two thousand pounds in aid of the Police widows and orphans fund.

9

It is Max's last year at Carrow Abbey, and he had passed his A levels with acceptable grades: Mathematics 7, Science 6, and History 8. These grades will get Max an automatic entry into Sandhurst, subject to formal interviews and non-academic entry requirements. The last term at Carrow Abbey will be sad in many ways, but he was so excited to go to the world's top military academy.

He became a team leader in the Carrow Abbey Rifle Corp having gained top marks on the rifle range for three years running which was made easier due to his experience with his own rifle and his hours of practice on the estate. Max took to shooting quite naturally.

Sark Housemaster, Mr Dobbs, asked Max to become the house prefect, this responsibility he enjoyed, working well with Jeremy Dobbs. The housemaster taught Max a great deal about leadership skills with the use of empathy. The day had come for a sorrowful goodbye at the gym Max had attended for the past three years. He was taught by Pat McCoubrey and his MMA instructor David Chinn, who Max owed so much to for progressing him to black belt standard in Karate and brown belt in BJJ, another form of martial arts. Max had won his last seven hex cage fights on the trot, the last one coming on the night before his final training session at the gym.

Pat and David put on a party for Max's last visit, there was to be no training that night. All the boxing lads and his training mates from MMA were there. Pat put his arm around Max. 'I had high hopes for you, young Maximus; you would have made a decent pro-fighter. I remember like it was yesterday when you came sheepishly into the gym and said you wanted to box. Look at you now Max. Don't forget David and me; we have both grown very fond of you. Good luck in whatever you do, son.'

Max got pissed that night so Pat called a cab to take him back the short distance to Sark House. Mr Dobbs and Rory helped him out of the cab and frogmarched him to the room. 'He's had a good night, sir!' Rory caught the eye of Dobbs, who just nodded with a slight smile and looked away as if he hadn't seen the state of Max.

Back at Brandscombe, things had changed progressively; Archie had taken over as the trainee estate manager. He was totally in his element with innovative ideas for the estate which included pheasant rearing and shoots, paintballing weekends, quad biking and other money-making schemes. He has also got engaged to lovely Charlotte.

Pippa had finished seeing Benjamin and has been involved with many other guys since then including a son of an Earl. That didn't impress Pippa; inevitably, he has long since left the Brandscombe scene. Pippa works diligently on the newspaper and magazines company, breathing modern life into the Hainsworth-Catt publishing empire. It is expected that Pippa will take over the entire running of the press company in the ensuing years. Christopher and Virginia are jogging along at a more relaxed pace and taking life a little easier now, although Christopher still maintains a watchful interest in his companies.

Maximus, at last, received his long-awaited appointment with the Sandhurst Military Academy selection board. Three years in the Carrow Abbey

Rifle Corp and his A-level results should secure him a placement in the academy.

His application to enter Sandhurst as a standard entry officer went in weeks ago. Today he's driving himself to Westbury for his Army Officer Selection Board interviews and assessment process. He thought the questions he was asked as well as the tone they were asked in were edging on a grilling. The board would let Max know if they wanted him to continue the selection process. Max understood that the whole officer training process lasted six to eight months, so he expected further serious interviews. Max left Westbury feeling none too confident. However, he received his reply quicker than he had expected. The confirmation was sent to Max's address at Carrow Abbey school, inviting him to continue the training board's computer tests to be completed and returned. Max was asked to return to Westbury, where he undertook a general knowledge test, military knowledge and multiple-choice questions on current affairs. Then Max had three interviews with group discussions on current and moral matters, finishing off with written essays to write on these latter subjects. Then came the physical test with essential requirements to reach 8.7 on a bleep test, to throw a 4-kilo medicine ball 3.1 metres from a sitting position and to lift 76 kilos in a mid-thigh pull.

Max had practised all these disciplines, and they would not be a problem for him and as anticipated, all went well. He awaited further instructions. Being excused from school wasn't a problem as they expected this from leavers.

After several more interviews, a day on the range and reports from all academy assessors, Max was finally invited to attend a formal consultation with three senior officers, one being the Commandant of the Royal Military Academy Sandhurst. The severe earbashing continued with the usual intimidating questions they expected the potential young officers to answer. The bottom line is Maximus has been selected to undertake an officer training course at Sandhurst. Since he was a kid, this was his ambition. It's now become a reality. He starts in the September term for a forty-two-week training programme split into three fourteen-week terms. Thus, he would be a tad off his nineteenth birthday when starting the famous Sandhurst Military Academy. His last day finally arrived at Carrow School: *"Goodbye, Carrow Abbey, you are a fine school!"* Max mused as he looked back through the gates for the last time.

Max wanted to spend a bit of time with his siblings and worked with his brother, marvelling at his transformation of the estate. Max then went to Pippa's publishing house, spending the whole day watching how she motivated her staff and the speed she worked at. After work, the two young siblings went for a bar meal and continued their catching up chat. Pippa revealed her plans for launching an international magazine called The Single Lady. She had signed off the proofs for her brainchild two days earlier; the first edition was expected to roll off the press in one month.

September arrived and with it came the induction proceedings at Sandhurst. Term one covered basic military skills, fitness and decision making. The first term went quickly; it was made so much easier for him because of his time in the Carrow Abbey Rifle Corp, sponsored by the British Army. Hence, some of the basic stuff, Max had already experienced: Term two was training in more advanced leadership skills. The officer cadets are now expected to choose their ongoing Corp or Regiment. Maximus decided on The Rifles. This regiment is an amalgamation of four of the finest light infantry regiments in the British Army, comprising: The Royal Green Jackets, Devon and Dorset Light Infantry, The Light Infantry Regiment, The Royal Gloucestershire, Berkshire and Wiltshire Light Infantry.

At last, it was the day for Max's passing out parade. He was so proud to be wearing the British Army officer cadet cap and badge with full ceremonial dress. The whole Hainsworth-Catt family were present to see their son and brother at his passing out parade. Virginia was fighting back tears of pride seeing her youngest son Maximus in his officer's uniform. She gasped at her little boy who had morphed into this tall, handsome young man with a bodybuilders frame. Ginny hadn't noticed this in her son until this day. His natural blond wavy hair, the chiselled granite jawline ending with a dimpled chin and the perfect physique of an Adonis. *"Some young lady is going to hit the jackpot with my Max one day!"* Virginia thought with a cheeky smirk and a mother's pride.

The smirk developed into a grin which inadvertently crept over Ginny's face, prompting a question from an amused Christopher. 'What has tickled your fancy, Ginny?'

'Nothing darling, nothing you would understand anyway.' Her smile increased with the added amusement that her husband wasn't aware of her personal ponderings. Finally, the highlight of the event arrived, and with rifle bayonets gleaming on a bright August day, the passing out parade was performed. Maximus received his commission as a second lieutenant and collected his travel warrant. He will join his appointed regiment, the 1st Battalion The Rifles.

Max caught his train at Reading going westbound to Newport, then a taxi to the camp under the first Severn Bridge at Beachley Barracks in Chepstow.

Officially it's in Gloucester but right on the Welsh border. Max was greeted by a corporal who escorted him to the commanding officer's office. 'Come in, lieutenant and welcome to the First Rifles,' Max saluted his new commanding officer. 'I'm Lieutenant Colonel Laurence Abel. Please sit down. Unfortunately, I don't have a permanent position for a second lieutenant, so I want you to assist 1st Lieutenant Paul Gittens in one platoon, B company. As soon as I have a post available, if, of course, you prove yourself in the battalion, then we'll see where you go from there. Any questions?'

'No, sir.'

'Carry on then, lieutenant and welcome to the 1st Rifles.'

'Thank you, sir; I will do my best for the platoon and company.'

Max spent the first few months just fetching and carrying for the 1st lieutenant and also sometimes for B company's Captain Smyth who came across as a total prat, an opinion also held by the other three lieutenants of B company.

It soon became apparent to Max there were many ways one platoon could improve its performance, especially on the firing range, weapon maintenance and speed marching, which at present was a joke. Maximus blamed Captain Smyth as he should be setting the standards for his platoons. Max tried speaking with the captain on several occasions but his aloofness and arrogance prevented Max from having any constructive dialogue with him. He even refused a drink with the young second lieutenant in the officers' mess.

Max was so disappointed and frustrated with everyday soldiering in his temporary platoon. Paul Gittens and B company officer, Captain Smyth, tolerated undisciplined behaviour, always taking the easy option. Max thought one platoon should and could benefit from some significant improvements and needed a bloody good shakeup in their training. The lads of one platoon were a good bunch, but they will get away with what they are allowed to, and they certainly pushed their luck to the extreme with weak NCO's. As the second lieutenant of the platoon, Max's ideas were ridiculed, which is where his frustrations lay. He considered applying for a transfer to another company, but that would not look good on one platoon's men. So Max shelved that idea pretty quickly. Maximus had been at Beachley a year and was getting to the end of his tether when things started to happen.

A corporal found Max in his quarters and asked him to go to the commanding officer's office immediately; Max likened this to being summoned by a headmaster at school.

'Maximus, take a seat. I have some good news at last; I expect you thought I had forgotten you?'

'Yes, sir, I was getting frustrated.'

'Well, I can now offer you your very own platoon. What do you say to that, eh?

'Extremely pleased, sir, but I'm only a second lieutenant; who will be my platoon's first lieutenant, sir?

'Your platoon will be number three and you will be in command as an acting first lieutenant; I am told the regiment is short of lieutenants at present even so I have asked headquarters at Winchester for a replacement, but unfortunately, we have our other battalions on active service, so I'm not holding my breath that my request will be granted. Three platoon has a bad reputation in the battalion as their activity results have proven hitherto. They are the worst by quite a margin in discipline and training. On a positive note, you will have a damn good sergeant in Forbes. I can personally vouch for that NCO. I must speak candidly, lieutenant, you will find three platoon one hell of a challenge and perhaps I'm expecting too much of you! Incidentally, I've been reading your personal file with interest, I see you are pretty handy in the ring and at unarmed combat, so perhaps those disciplines may help. Well, that'll be all, lieutenant. Carry on, and good luck with your new platoon. I think you are going to need it.'

Max instructed his new corporal, Terry Dixon, to bring the platoon's roll-call list to his office. The young acting lieutenant was responsible for twenty-eight men, two sergeants and two corporals. His senior sergeant, Tim Forbes, met Max for the first time and spoke for ten minutes about the men of three platoon. Max made notes while listening to the experienced veteran. The NCO appeared reliable but had negative thoughts about three platoon being under a young Sandhurst officer; particularly with a rifleman named Connolly and his two cohorts.

'Sergeant, I want every man in the platoon on the parade ground in full combat dress and ready to move out in one hour.'

'Yes, sir, but we have done drilling and PT for a few hours; the lads are usually relaxing or resting this late in the day, sir.'

'Just carry out my orders Sergeant Forbes.'

'Yes, sir.'

Maximus was unpacking his gear into his new quarters when his senior NCO knocked on his door. ' Three platoon are all present and correct, sir, and on the parade ground, sir.'

'I'll be right there, sergeant, thank you.'

Now Max knew for a fact that squaddies hated young, fresh-faced officers who have just qualified through Sandhurst. So Max knew he would have to earn their respect. 1st Rifles are to be part of the relieving force and part of the reserve battalion for Afghanistan. Therefore the 1st battalion will leave in four months to start their tour.

Max's platoon was far from ready even for day to day soldiering and certainly not for front-line combat. *"I don't have much time to lick the platoon into shape before Afghanistan; I just hope their reputation is exaggerated."* Max pondered with concern.

There wasn't much Max didn't know about drilling. It had been rammed into him at Carrow Abbey and by the unforgiving drill sergeant at the Sandhurst Academy.

Max ordered Forbes to put the men through their paces. After thirty minutes of drilling with their weapons, Max then ordered a five-mile quick march with a full kit, including a rifle.

'Where's the best route from the camp?' The new platoon leader enquired.

'Route B, sir.'

'Do you know it?' Max asked.

'Yes, sir.'

'Then lead the way and get me a rifle; I'm coming as well.'

'But sir, this is not how it's done; the officer doesn't usually join us on a full kit slog, sir.'

'I know, sergeant, I have just had a year in one platoon. I will be doing things a bit different with three! Tell the men to get used to me doing it with them plus all the other activities. I want to know every single man, his warts and all Mr Forbes, is that clear?'

'Very, sir.'

'Good, we move out in thirty minutes, sergeant!'

'Yes, sir.' As Max expected, there was a lot of dissension in the platoon as they started the march on a gradual incline; Forbes led the line, Max went backmarker. He wanted to observe his new discontented bunch.

The squad had travelled about two miles when the rookie platoon leader heard increased grumbling in the ranks; he had a perfect view of the line marching in front. Max noticed some sideways glances aimed at him from more than a few. The squad's protestations could be heard above the sound of marching at the quick-time pace. This pace was invented by the famous light infantry regiment. It was used to significant effect in the American war of independence and the Napoleonic campaigns. However, keeping up this pace required fitness, which was evidently lacking in the platoon. Max shouted from the back, 'Pick up your pace; I want one hundred and forty strides a minute, don't drop the pace, I'm timing you.'

After three miles the young officer could see he would need to stop his squad as some of the platoon were now fighting for breath and gasping for an intake of oxygen. He gave them a break for five minutes.

'Get them back on their feet sergeant. Put the squad in twos and speed march them back to the barracks, now.'

'Yes sir'

A rifleman with a face that could kill protested. 'This isn't right; we've had a long day drilling and physical training, can't you fucking see we are all knackered, this ain't fucking right, I'm telling you straight.'

'What's your name, soldier?' There was no reply. Max went to the heavily built combatant; Max repeated himself with serious intent. Finally, but reluctantly, the subordinate soldier answered. 'Connolly. Patrick Connolly.' He was a six-foot-three giant of a man with red curly hair and beard; he hailed from Dublin and had a British mother.

'As it's my first day here, Connolly, I'll pretend I didn't hear what you said. Any future insubordination and I will take action against you,' the acting lieutenant spoke in a conciliatory tone. 'Do you understand me?' There was no answer again. Connolly looked around the platoon for approval with a sick grin on his face. Max thought to himself: *"What's the best thing to do? He's trouble. Remember your leadership skills training at Sandhurst."*

There was plenty of piss-taking on the way back, obviously derived from Connolly and directed at the lieutenant. Max knew it was imperative to sort out the Irishman quickly, but perhaps not today, being his first day in charge of three platoon. Max pondered. *"Maybe it would look bad with the commanding and fellow officers if I dished out punishment on my first day in charge."* He didn't know what to do for the best. Max knew it would have to be sorted and quickly. Respect is hard to recover once lost; he saw that with weak teachers who often couldn't control the student bullies at Carrow Abbey.

The platoon got back to base; Max decided to see the platoon again on the parade ground. He will need to stamp his authority quickly, knowing it will not be easy. Matt Harris, the other platoon sergeant wanted to speak with Max

'Sir, can I have a word?' Max nodded approvingly; the sergeant followed his lieutenant into his office for privacy.

'Sir, the men are knackered after a full day's drill; they need a break, sir. Our last officer in number three was very fair on the men, sir.'

'Thank you, sergeant, but I'll be the judge of three platoon's welfare, now get the men back on parade in two ranks.'

'Yes, sir.'

Sergeant Harris returned to Max and saluted. 'Apart from three privates, the platoon is awaiting your instructions, sir.'

'Thank you, Sergeant Harris. Max walked to the paraded men with a purposeful stride. 'Right three platoon, take in what I say, for everybody's sake. I am told that your last officer accepted how you like to be treated; I realise I'm a lot younger than my predecessor and fully aware of your hatred for "Sandhurst Babes." You will, however, all of you, carry out my instructions to the letter. Today is my first day, and I will let these indiscretions go. Tomorrow the bad discipline stops; we then get on with becoming top soldiers befitting the Rifles. Sergeant, dismiss the platoon and have combat fatigues with a complete kit including rifles at 07.30hrs on the parade ground. Sign out twenty-five rounds for each man. Tomorrow I'm changing the weekly routine until I am happy with the standard of our platoon. We will start with a morning five-mile march, again at quick-time; I want the average speed at 140 paces a minute. It will be timed for the whole march; if they fail, we shall do another in the afternoon and another in the evening until we average the 140 paces that I demand,' The NCO could see Max's determination. 'After the march, we will go to the range as I want to see their shooting ability for myself; if I'm not satisfied with the day's shift, then it's more drilling and marching into tomorrow evening. Get this through to the men, sergeant.'

'Yes, sir.' The sergeant understood what Max ordered, but the new platoon leader could see his NCO's reluctance.

'Don't you think it's going a bit too heavy on the lads, sir? It is not what they have been used to; I think we will have serious problems, especially with big

Paddy Connolly, who has the ear of B company's captain, sir.'

'I'm surprised at your attitude, sergeant; I don't care if Connolly has the ear of God. I expect total support from my NCO's. Is that clear, Harris? If you don't like my style put in a transfer to another platoon. I'll endorse the request?' Max was not jesting!

'Yes, sir, sorry, sir.'

'Right, I want no more of what has gone on in the past; that doesn't concern me; our platoon will be judged on its future ability. So where are Connolly and his other two acolytes who didn't show on parade?

'They're in the mess, sir.'

'Okay, fetch the duty corporal of the guard and come with me.'

'Yes, sir.'

Max found the three subordinates drinking in the mess. Max ordered them to stand up. Two did, Connolly didn't; he carried on drinking as if the lieutenant wasn't there.

'Stand up to attention, Connolly, now.' Max shouted. Connolly finished his quarter full glass of beer, stood up and pressed his face into the lieutenant's and belched. *"He certainly was a bruiser of a man."* Max thought.

By this time, the duty corporal and Harris had arrived.

'Take these three men to the guardroom and lock them up until 07.00hrs tomorrow morning. Then, do not release them but escort the three to my office.'

'Yes, sir.'

'You can't do that; I'm going to see Captain Smyth and report this unjustified arrest......sir.'

'Not tonight you won't. Take them away corporal, now.'

'Yes, sir.'

Harris said. 'Sir, please listen to me; I've been with this battalion for four years and ten years in the army; I'm telling you; Connolly is big trouble. I shouldn't say this, but he's already beaten up one of our corporals; we have found it easier to deal with him by turning the odd blind eye. You are so young and inexperienced.... uhh.....I mean just out of Sandhurst and all. Well, sir expect trouble; he's bad news. Those two other lads with him, Tom Palanski and Ceri, really don't want to disobey orders, but they have to do what Connolly says. He makes their lives hell if they don't fetch and carry for him, sir.'

'Thank you, sergeant, for your honesty. How long has this been going on?'

'Several years, sir, he bullies all recruits that join our platoon. The problem is he is unusually friendly with the captain of B company, Captain Smyth. Some say Connolly has something on the captain, and that's why he gets away with so much. We have lost a couple of good NCO's because of his power. I just don't want to see you go down the same way, that's all, sir.'

'I understand, sergeant, carry on and by the way, thanks.'

10

Max read through Connolly's file; it appeared suspiciously like all the registered complaints about him had gone unpunished. All with either accepted mitigation or unreliable witnesses against Connolly and coincidently all signed off by Captain Smyth. It was past midnight when Max had read the performance records of 3 platoon, B company, 1st Rifles. They were, in Max's opinion, appalling compared to the other platoons in B company. Last in target practice, weapon maintenance and training, cross country, assault course, and self-defence. The only success was in boxing and looking at the champion over the last three years which was Private Connolly; that's no surprise, Max thought.

Up and showered by 05:15hrs, and before breakfast, Max went to the guard room and released the three insubordinates. He told them to shower and have breakfast and to be ready in full combat fatigues with a rifle by 07.30hrs on the parade ground. So they skulked off to their billet, with Connolly openly displaying his anger. Max knew there would be trouble coming from Connolly. 'I'm going to get you, youngster, from fucking Sandhurst.' The big Irishman muttered just enough to be heard by the acting lieutenant.

At 07.30 hrs every three platoon soldier was on parade with their complete kit this time. They had been told what to do and what was expected of them in the forthcoming timed march. The squad assumed, as usual, their officer and sergeant would drive to the end of the route and wait at the finish as was the usual practice. The two corporals usually ran the lines of two.

'I'm going with them with a rifle sergeant.' Tim Forbes questioned the acting first lieutenant's decision, but Max waved him away. Max had his stopwatch poised; they were off at the same measured route as the previous night. The platoon got there and back but failed at the average pace of 140 per minute that was demanded.

Max addressed his unit after completing the speed march. Then the officer had his men reassemble on the parade ground.

'Three platoon, your time was a fraction over 132 paces a minute. It's not what I expect nor accept. You will take a thirty-minute break then be back on parade with the same equipment ready to go again.' The grumbling started up once more, and once more, the two sergeants questioned Max's decision; in fairness, they did it for their lieutenant's sake, Max could see that, but he's a Hainsworth-Catt and knew what his SBS grandad would have expected. *"We go again."* Something had to break!

The thirty-man squad moved off in double file with the unmistakable voice of Connolly swearing; the lieutenant ignored it as he wanted this timed march completed. Then, finally, Max bellowed his explicit order.

'Three platoon, we will do it this time at 140 paces a minute; I will lead, so make sure you keep up with me. I will buy the whole platoon free beer for a week if I fail. Did you hear me, Sergeant Forbes?'

'Yes, sir! Clearly, sir.'

Max kept repeating to himself: Don't fail, you mustn't fail. Finally, precisely on two and a half miles, the squad turned back to base; they were marginally below target, but the outward leg was slightly on an uphill gradient, giving them a slight advantage on the return. Max got the platoon buglers to keep the tempo at the pace he demanded. They got to the parade square at an average of 141 per minute. It was a hard slog; some of the guys collapsed on the ground, puffing and gasping to recover their breath. Max called for their attention.

'Okay, three platoon, five minutes pause, and we go again.' There was a deathly hush of total perplexity from the whole squad, including the NCO's. But before anyone could vent their feelings, Max explained with a big grin. 'Relax, you guys, you did it, achieving 141 paces a minute. Tonight I shall buy you all a couple of pints; you deserve it.' Apart from Connolly and his cohorts, a loud cheer went up from the platoon.

'Well done lads, get some grub, and I will see you on the range in seventy-five minutes. After one hour on the firing range with the corporals checking the individual target cards, the results were only average for single shot, rapid-fire and cluster. Not good enough for the new lieutenant. He asked for a rifle and demonstrated all three disciplines scoring 8 out of 10 on the inner ring with rapid-fire, 7 out of 10 for the centre bull cluster and for the single-shot 9 out of 10 and a bullseye. The squad couldn't believe it. Their platoon lieutenant was a great marksman! It really pissed off Connolly, who was getting more bitter by the day and vowed to bring down Max.

Max put down the challenge. 'Any rifleman who beats that set of scores, I'll pay their bar bill for a month. I want three platoon be not only the top marksmen in B company but the best in the battalion, and I know you can do it. So, sergeant, get another twenty rounds per man and let's start again; I will correct any mistakes I see.' The extra practice went on for several days on the firing range as well as speed dismantling their weapon and keeping it dry over a timed assault course. Max made the platoon work an extra hour a day. Not as punishment but to attain the highest possible standards that the acting lieutenant demanded. Max wondered who had been training these guys as some were just like raw recruits.

After two weeks of intensive range training and the continued speed marches, the lieutenant saw massive improvements and was impressed with the platoon's overall progress. The squad had consistently recorded 140 paces per minute on the speed marches and actually began to enjoy it as their fitness improved. The target shooting had attained new levels beyond recognition. The platoon loved competing for the shooting trophies that Max put up for the best performance of the day and a mini-league on the range. Three awards were contested, one for each discipline. Only small incentives, but the lads really tried to win them, which of course, was the idea to improve morale standards and increase banter. Max felt he was winning the platoon's respect slowly but surely from a shaky start. Other platoons in all three companies talked about three platoon of B company and wondered how they had transformed into such an efficient unit. It hadn't gone unnoticed with the top brass at battalion level, including the commanding officer, Colonel Laurence Abel.

The first test was the inter platoon competition for route marching, rifle maintenance and target shooting which were all essential requirements for a rifleman. Three platoon swept the board. The guys and their acting lieutenant were elated; Max took them to the local pub and paid for all their bevvies; there was a lot of back-slapping that night. Then, finally, a slightly drunken speech from Sergeant Tim Forbes, who raised a toast to 3's lieutenant for kicking their arses when it mattered.

A great night! The only exception was the missing Connolly and his cohorts.

The following day and in front of the whole platoon, Connolly was being his usual self, continually taking the piss out of Max.

'Sir, I think we understand one another by now, sir and our dislike for each other......sir. It is customary in the army, indeed encouraged, to offer someone you have differences with into the boxing ring, gentlemanly like....sir. So, sir, I invite you to do just that,....sir. But of course, I would understand if you are too frightened,.....sir!'

'No, Connolly, I will not fight you. I know you would love to give me a good thumping. You just concentrate on your drills. That's all I have to say, carry on, Connolly.'

'We all understand,....sir, it wouldn't be right to see a common soldier of the ranks knock seven bells of shit out of an officer, oh, I mean acting officer,.....sir.' Connolly looked at the platoon, who were all present. He encouraged laughter. For once, he didn't get the response he wanted. However, to a man, they did feel disappointed in their lieutenant for not meeting Connolly's challenge in the ring.

Respect for Max waned after he refused Connolly's offer to fight.

Although discipline was maintained, the platoon sensed Connolly had now got the upper hand over the acting lieutenant. Every night the Irishman bragged how Hainsworth-Catt had backed down to take him on in the ring, making sure everyone he met in the battalion knew the three platoon acting lieutenant was nothing but a coward and not fit to lead three platoon.

Another two weeks passed, and the prestigious annual battalion's boxing championship will start the day after next. The tournament creates keen competition and interest throughout the whole regiment. All ranks can enter, so Max thought he'd give it a go and see if he could remember the techniques and skills that Pat McCoubrey had taught him back at the gym in Windsor.

Tim Forbes reported to Max that he'd heard Connolly bragging to the lads. 'Sir, Connolly is telling everyone that he will damage you severely in the ring. If you remain in the tournament long enough to meet him in one of the rounds. Connolly boasted that you were stupid, sir, for entering the boxing competition. He reckons it's the best news he's heard for ages and bragged it was his chance to legally knock your lights out and do some severe damage! I would think again about entering, sir. He's a bloody animal when it comes to fighting. He has won the boxing tournament three years in a row. Please withdraw, the platoon needs you, and we are off to Afghanistan very soon.' Forbes was almost begging his respected officer to withdraw from the boxing competition and for a good reason!

'I have no intentions of withdrawing Tim.'

'With respect, sir, I think you are barmy; I've seen what he can do to blokes.'

'I can look after myself, sergeant, but I appreciate your concern.' Max replied.

Connolly and Maximus both got through the first and second rounds; it was now the quarter-finals. Max was drawn against last year's runner-up, a chap called Boyd from two-platoon, C company.

Max beat him in the fourth round, a fair well-contested fight. Boyd shook Max's hand and wished him well. He advised the acting lieutenant to watch out for Connolly. 'He's a dirty bastard; he knocked me out in the final last year; he's won the cup three years on the trot, just be careful!'

'Thanks, Mr Boyd, I'll take your advice.'

The draw was made for the boxing's semi-final, and the lads from three platoon were all eager to find out who was fighting who. Max heard on the barracks grapevine that a book had been opened to take bets on who would win the prestigious trophy this year. All the money was again on big Patrick Connolly, of course. The thought of a needle bout between Connolly and their officer got them very excited. The men didn't have to wait long. The boxing head coach made the draw. Acting Lieutenant Maximus Hainsworth-Catt will fight Private Patrick Connolly. The second semi-final will be Corporal James Bainbridge, who will fight private Geoffrey Thomas. The bouts will be four, three-minute rounds next Friday evening at the Wyevale boxing club's gym in Chepstow. Good luck to all finalists.'

Max called the platoon to attention and gave his orders. 'Okay, listen to me, I need to make this clear. I know you are excited about three platoon having two of us in the boxing semi-final. However, we must concentrate on our fitness and preparation for our Afghanistan tour in a few weeks. You have shown me what a great bunch you are. I'm proud to be your lieutenant and will do my best for you. You have consistently beaten your speed march targets and have improved beyond recognition on the firing range. I'm glad none of you have beaten my score; I wouldn't have offered the challenge to pay a months bar bill if I knew then how much you bastards could drink. Today we commence weapon instruction, a medium-fast two-miler and finish off with an hour on the range. Tomorrow we shall get all our kit out that we are taking to Afghanistan. The two heavy machine guns must be stripped down, cleaned, well oiled and sand filters fitted. I think that's about all.'

Max was just about to hand over to the corporal to fall the men out when the silence was broken by Connolly, shouting from the rear rank.

'Acting lieutenant,....sir, I don't think you will be going to Afghanistan......sir, you will probably be in Chepstow general hospital after our fight,.....sir.'

Max was not going to bite but replied. 'You could be right, Connolly, but we will have to see.' The subordinate and his two acolytes laughed; unfortunately, the corporal couldn't control them, and for once, Maximus couldn't be bothered. Was he intimidated? Certainly not! Never give in to bullies; that much Max learnt at Carrow Abbey

The excitement on the day of the boxing bout was intense; money flowed on the bets. Not just from three platoon either. The battalion has always had boxing tournaments but never before was there so much interest. The atmosphere was almost tangible as the men will see one of their own out of the ranks dim the lights of a privileged officer, which meant most, if not all, of the battalion was supporting Connolly. But not three platoon apart from three soldiers, that is. The lads of three had been won over by Maximus and will be in his corner for sure. Most of the battalion's money was on Connolly to win, given his last three years victories.

The fight night had arrived; Max's second was the loyal Sergeant Tim Forbes. The hall was packed; the ring, Max thought, appeared smaller than the one at Pat's gym.

The referee, a civilian from the local gym, took Connolly and Max to the centre and instructed the boxers to keep to the rules and that the bout would be four, three-minute rounds. The ref told them to touch gloves. Max stretched his arm out to touch Connolly's glove as he had done a hundred times at Pat's place but it was ungentlemanly knocked away with considerable force by Connolly. Boos followed from the crowd, especially the group from 3 platoon who were on their feet cheering and shouting support for their lieutenant.

Round one, Connolly came at Max like a huge giant, his arms flailing left and right; Maximus took a step back diagonally, Connolly missed with both attacking fists. Max countered, using his opponent's unbalance to move in to land three or four jabs in succession at lightning speed; the fourth volley caught the big guy on the side of the head that rocked him back; the crowd roared with excitement, but this angered the big Irishman who fumed noticeably. Coming quickly at the young lieutenant again, Max danced away to his right; Connolly wasted two more energy-sapping blows into thin air as Max leaned back, avoiding contact. Max's counterpunch had better timing; it caught the Irishman with a powerful uppercut square on the chin. Three of them in a row, the judges, were scribbling down furiously. Max was well ahead on points when the bell brought the first round to a close. As Maximus turned to go into his corner, Connolly followed him and hit Max square on the back of the neck; the lieutenant went down hard on the canvass. Connolly should have been disqualified, but the severe foul was overlooked. Max was dragged to his corner by Forbes. The ref gave Connolly an official warning, the knowledgeable crowd's support had now swung in an instant over to the young officer! Max, still groggy, came out for the second round.

Connolly, sensing Max was somewhere in the clouds, took advantage and fired a barrage of big punches that hurt and had Maximus reeling back onto the ropes. Forbes looked like he was about to throw the towel in any second; Max protested towards his corner with a defiant no! The officer defended, but not very well, to the end of the second round. Tim gave his fighter smelling salts that cleared his head somewhat but made him cough violently. Max felt better at the start of the third, although still groggy. The lieutenant went after Connolly, perhaps wrong tactics, but he'd had enough of this cheating bully. He used the famous Pat's move, leading with three right jabs that automatically made Connolly move to his left to defend; this opened a sizeable, unprotected area to his opponent's right side, exposing his ribs. Max took full advantage, pummelling Connolly's unguarded right side. Max finished the attack with a left and right to his opponent's face and one square on his nose. The ref came between the fighters to protect Connolly. They parted, Connolly came in to attack again, but this time he'd grown visibly sluggish. Now was the time, Max thought to finish him, which he did with consummate ease. The young lieutenant hit him with an old-fashioned upper cut that left his opponent sprawled out on the canvas with both legs and arms wide apart, looking like a grotesque star. Max was in the final but laying out the thug was more enjoyable! A great roar came from three platoon, all squashed in together at the opponent's end of the ring. Connolly was still out cold five minutes after the knockout. A doctor was kneeling over him, administering oxygen; the Irishman was coming round; with the doctor's help, he staggered to his feet. Connolly was still oblivious to his whereabouts when being assisted out of the ring.

The next day after the fight, the platoon continued its preparations for the Afghanistan tour; the transports were serviced and weapons and personal kits were checked. The three-platoon men had a good day together, and the camaraderie was higher than usual. Just what Max was hoping for before they departed. It's this unity that might save lives in a hostile front line environment. Unfortunately, Connolly was excused due to his head injury and was kept in the sickbay for overnight observation.

Following thirty minutes of firing practice on the range, Tim Forbes walked back alongside Max and quizzed his young lieutenant. 'Sir, the lads have been wondering how and where you got those boxing skills; you fucking hammered Connolly, and he's no slouch in the ring; he's the battalion's three times consecutive champion.'

'From a good friend called Pat McCoubrey. A great trainer and a great man.'

'Be careful, sir, Connolly is bad news, and I don't think you have heard the last from him. Oh, and by the way, you have restored the lad's respect in you good and proper. The platoon really thought you'd bottled it when you refused a ring challenge from Connolly a couple of weeks before the tournament.'

'Thanks, Tim, but stop worrying; I'll be fine.'

Max wrote to the boxing organiser and withdrew from the final; Max would rather see a non-officer win the championship. So Private Geoffrey Thomas of two-platoon was deemed champion by default. Max only entered to give Connolly a good thrashing!

Max sent for Geoffrey Thomas; the private wondered what he'd done; he went to Max's office and saluted.

'A reoccurrence of my wrist injury means I can't fight in the final, and I don't want to compound the damage just before we start our tour of duty,' Max shook the private's hand. 'Please take this £100.00 for a few drinks as my way of saying congratulations, you deserve it.' The young private left with a big beaming smile. Max got his pleasure and reward in seeing Connolly's big mouth shut for a change.

Max ordered more intense sniper practice, fitness and overall teamwork exercises. He could see the men were enjoying it as they became fitter. The firing range action was spectacular at times. Max would confidently put three platoon up against any other unit, not only the first battalion but also the whole regiment!

Ten days had passed since the boxing final. It was now four days before the battalion fly out to Afghanistan as there was a delay with their transports. Everybody was getting excited; all the kit was cleaned and ready for inspection from the company captain before the battalion moved out. Max was due a few days leave but decided to stay with his platoon and complete the preparations. The lads wanted the last night in a Brit pub as is tradition before a tour commences, so they all went down for what might be their last good draught real ale for some time. The bash was good, enhanced by the piano going strong. Max stopped the merriment by standing on a chair and calling the three platoon rowdies to silence.

'I have been here for two years, one year with one platoon and one year with you lot. I've been waiting for the chance to show the world the skills we have worked on together. You were all a bunch of out of control toe-rags when I met you. You are now an inspiring, efficient fighting unit with excellent rifle skills. Gentlemen of the 1st Rifles, you have done your platoon and regiment proud. In forty-eight hours, we fly from Brize Norton to Afghanistan. Tomorrow you have the morning off. So enjoy tonight, and don't worry about any hairy arsed NCO shaking you out of bed. Gentlemen, I am pleased and privileged to command number three. We shall go forth together and show the Taliban not to mess with the 1st Rifles battalion, especially three platoon. So, gentlemen, I raise a toast to you and our regiment. The Rifles!'

A big cheer went up then the singing and drinking took over again. Max needed to phone home to his parents before the battalion left. He had one more beer and said he was going back to the depot. Corporal Terry Dixon asked.

'Sir, I need to phone my parents and fiancée, Laura, she is arranging our wedding, two weeks after our return from Afghanistan. She wants to discuss the colour theme, fuck me, sir, what do I know about that shit? I'll share a taxi with you, sir, if that's all right, sir?

11

Let's walk back to camp Terry; it'll be a doddle compared to our speed marching.'
'Of course, sir, it's a good clear night to walk as well.'

Maximus put two hundred pounds over the bar for the boys; then, the two early leavers left the now rowdy pub. They had walked for about ten minutes along Beachley Road towards Tutshill when Max stopped. He heard an unexpected sound that he couldn't associate with the middle of the countryside. A strange sound for the still of the night with no traffic, although it could, Max supposed, be a wild animal scurrying away. At that particular moment, Max was explaining his ideas to Terry about three platoon duties when they arrive in Afghanistan. Well, the lieutenant thought he was talking to Terry! His corporal had gone.

Max looked behind him and was stunned rigid to see Terry struggling with a dark shadow moving behind his corporal. The lieutenant could make out the glint of the moonlight's reflection, bouncing off a knife blade that was held close to the corporal's neck.

'Stay there.' Screamed the attacker. Max could now make out that the assailant was wearing a dark balaclava.

Max inched closer to Terry but stopped again as the masked man gestured a threatening upward movement closer to Terry's throat.

'Stop and don't move, or I'll fucking slice him!'
Max sensed he wasn't messing.

'Here's my money, here take it all.' Max threw his wallet towards the assailant's feet. But it wasn't money the attacker wanted that night.

Max's concentration on his corporal's situation was broken; from the lieutenant's left side, another masked attacker approached at speed while simultaneously a third man entered the affray, this time from behind Max. He attempted to drag the lieutenant down to the ground with his arm around the young officer's neck, almost choking him. Max moved quickly to his right and spun around to face the third assailant. As this man turned his head to follow Max's defensive manoeuvre, Max lunged with his middle and index fingers spread, finding their targets in both of the attacker's eyes. The counter-assault by Max was so violent that he felt one of his fingers entering deep into the attacker's eye socket, coming to rest against warm tissue. The assailant dropped his knife, screaming and holding his face in great pain. The second attacker threw himself at Max, wielding a knife out in front of him. While this was happening, Terry's assailant, who was still pressing a knife to Terry's neck, was again screaming that he would slit the corporal's throat. The young lieutenant had no choice but to defend himself, being forced to ignore the threat to his corporal as his self-defence skills had already kicked in. Max grabbed the rushing attacker's wrist and pulled him in close, kneeing him viciously in his groin, followed by a head butt planted on the flat of his nose. The semi-conscious man dropped like a stone. Before the one with damaged eyes could recover, Max pounded him with several heavy, well-directed punches to his already swollen face which made the assailant collapse. The now one-eyed assailant held his head, writhing in pain and fell to his knees. Max finished him off with a flurry of well-directed kicks. The young officer now had a moment to see what the first man was doing with Terry. The attacker still had the knife menacingly close to the corporal's throat, and looking over Terry's shoulder, he stared menacingly at Max. The young lieutenant gasped in horror with what happened next. The crazed man in a balaclava slit the hapless corporal's throat with one violent movement. Max couldn't believe what he had just witnessed; it quickly became a surreal blur at that crazy, mad moment.

The vision of Terry dropping to his knees with blood squirting from his neck like a fountain. All captured in the moonlight, like some horror movie. Max had only one course of action; assist Corporal Terry Dixon. Terry was on his knees, still spraying and pumping his red, life-giving fluid into the air. Terry stared wide-eyed at his lieutenant from his kneeling posture as if thinking aloud: Why!

The two thugs struggled to their feet, one helping the other, then they joined their brutal accomplice, the throat butcher. All three disappeared as quickly as they had arrived, through the hedgerow. These vicious men were, at this moment, the least of Max's concern. Terry was dying in front of him. The young officer phoned 999, calling for an ambulance and police. Max explained a man was dying. 'A man has had his throat cut.' Max shouted with urgency. He gave the operator the exact location but didn't stop to answer her many questions, ending the call abruptly! Maximus then phoned his sergeant, who was still in full song at the pub. He told Tim straight, Terry is dying. Max demanded, over the din, that Forbes must get the bar staff to cut a metre of plastic pump-line and bring it to him. Screaming at Forbes to come as quickly as he could, Terry Dixon was running out of time! The young officer ordered the sergeant to borrow or hijack a car and come to the location Max gave him.

'I'll be right there, sir!' The quick-thinking lieutenant removed his underpants and socks to use them as a pad and strapping. He pressed his finger into the open cut and found the windpipe, attempting to stop Terry's blood from being sucked into his lungs. Max was no doctor, but he knew first aid. He could see by his phone torch that his corporal's small jugular vein had been severed, but thankfully not the larger one of the two. The officer could hear air gurgling from Terry's neck, which meant the windpipe was penetrated. Tim Forbes arrived; Max didn't speak to his sergeant but grabbed the plastic drink-line from the sergeant's hand. Max, with Tim, now holding the phone torch, inserted the beer pump-line into Terry's severed windpipe very carefully, ensuring no further blood was sucked in. Max hoped his first attempt at a tracheostomy was successful.

Finally, placing his underpants over the open wound as a pad he then banded this by his socks tied together, holding the makeshift padding in place.

Both Max and Tim tried to comfort their comrade, but he had slipped into unconsciousness. Despite Max's efforts, Terry had still lost a great deal of blood. The sound of the ambulance, police or both was getting nearer; it happened that both the emergency services arrived at the same time. Blue lights were flashing from both vehicles manufacturing a shadowy blue intermittent outline along the hedgerows. Paramedics were out with all the gear they could carry and immediately took over from Max. The medics asked the army officer what had happened and had the victim ingested any drugs. Max explained about the pipe that they could see clearly for themselves sticking out from Terry's throat. To Max's surprise, they left the beer pipe in place, lifted Terry onto a gurney, and into the ambulance. They removed Max's pants and socks to replace them with a clean dressing. Terry was injected and a saline drip was attached to his arm, the ambulance sped away with blue lights flashing and its siren screaming.

The police came across to interview Maximus after cordoning off the road and establishing it as a crime scene. It looked almost daylight with the intense halogen lighting set up. It clearly showed where Dixon was attacked. His blood had drained away to a side ditch, but the dark staining was still evident. The inspector asked Max if he was the one who called for assistance. Max confirmed with a nod. What followed was at least half an hour of questioning; the first motive the police concluded was robbery; why else would a gang of three, attack strangers without robbery as their motive!

Max was suddenly conscious of having no underpants and socks on, although the police gave him a blanket and took both soldiers back to Beachley and returned the borrowed car to the pub landlord. The inspector said he would be in touch, Max explained his battalion leaves for Afghanistan the following day for a six-month tour of duty. The police inspector was not bothered as if he needed to speak with the lieutenant he could via the regiment.

Max got dressed in his quarters and then took a taxi to Chepstow general hospital and awaited news of his corporal's condition. Finally, a doctor from the ICU came into the visitor's room. She spoke in a low but reassuring way.

'Mr Dixon has just come out of emergency surgery. He's a fortunate man. Was it you that was with him when he was attacked?'

'Yes,' Max nodded, how is Terry?'

'He's recovering, but it's still touch and go; he's in the recovery room now and will stay in intensive care for now. The next twenty-four hours are critical for him. Max's thoughts selfishly drifted away from Terry; the young lieutenant was transfixed by the sheer beauty of this young doctor. Maximus tried to see if she was engaged or married, but she had both hands in her scrubs pockets like doctors seem to do. 'I leave for Afghanistan tomorrow. Can I ask a favour? May I have your mobile number to check Terry's progress?' Max blurted out this request.

'Sorry, I don't have a number; I'm about to change it; I dropped my phone down the loo but I'll tell you what, how about you give me yours, and I'll call you when I get my new phone.'

'That's very kind, thank you...........um.'

'Oh my name, yes, of course, I'm Penny Richards.'

Is that Dr Richards by any chance?'

She nodded the sweetest of smiles.

'I'm Max Hainsworth-Catt.'

'That's a posh name. Do you have a title? She mocked.

'Only lieutenant, I'm afraid, but just Max will do.'

'Penny, I feel so awkward asking this, but if I don't, I know I'll kick myself. We leave for Afghanistan tomorrow, so can I keep in contact with you while I'm away?'

'Like a pen friend?' Penny asked.

'Yes, sort of.' Max was fidgety and uncomfortably embarrassed.

'I don't see why not. I'll message you my email address when I get my phone. Now I really must get back to the ward. Oh, good luck and keep safe in Afghanistan. Perhaps you can send me a postcard.' She smiled, turned and disappeared through the swing doors, her hands still in her pockets. What a lovely lady, Max thought; I hope she calls me.

Maximus's spirits really should be lifted by meeting a dream of a girl, but his concern for Terry negated any uplifting mood. He actually felt guilty for sidetracking into the realms of fantasy about a gorgeous doctor. So Max went back to his quarters and packed his non-military stuff, ready for departure tomorrow. Dr Penny Richards was bombarding his mind. Max was still wondering if she had a boyfriend, fiancé or even a husband. *"Damn their pockets."* He thought, a tad frustrated.

Max phoned the hospital at midnight to get an update on the corporal. A staff nurse in ICU explained. 'He's sleeping, pulse better, blood pressure stable and his heart rate has improved. He will be on a ventilator to assist with his breathing for a few days; we have given Mr Dixon a blood transfusion that has gone well. So we are getting more optimistic by the hour. His fiancé is by his bed; she is staying with him overnight. That's all we can say for now. Goodbye.'

Maximus fell into bed and was asleep immediately. It'll soon be morning. After breakfast, there was a battalion roll call, on parade, complete kit, including a rifle. Lorries, personnel carriers and armoured vehicles lined up in the adjacent car park, including their thirty jeeps. All vehicles were painted in desert camouflage. The men had a briefing on respect for the Islamic faith, particularly towards women. It's a very touchy subject in Afghanistan; the Ministry of Defence emphasised the warning. Finally, the transports were lined up all ready to go. Seeing six hundred and fifty troops preparing to leave, the starting of engines and the cacophony of noise was a spectacular military sight and sound. B company that included Max's three platoon was due out at 16.00hrs; all troop departure times were staggered. The first leg of their journey was to RAF Brize Norton in

Oxfordshire. Max had made sure his lot was all packed and ready to leave in an orderly fashion. Max saw Connolly smirking disturbingly; the lieutenant had wished the Irishman was not going to the Taliban country with his platoon. Then, just before he was about to leave, Max had a surprise call from the police inspector.

'We have arrested one of your three attackers. We found weapons, including a knife and the balaclavas they used which all fit the description you gave me. We had to take him to the hospital to see an ophthalmologist consultant; the hospital said he has lost an eye. Did you do the damage to his eyes in the fight?'

'Yes, I tried damned hard to poke the fuckers out for good.' The inspector grunted somewhat disapprovingly and continued.

'We stopped the car by chance for speeding near the scene of the attack. When we pulled them over, two jumped out and made a run for it. The driver was caught; we have him now under armed guard in hospital. The car was stolen and had false plates fitted, as we expected. We have interviewed him at his hospital bed and promised him some help if he cooperated. We eventually wore him down; the breakthrough came in the early hours. He admitted to us a soldier from Beachley had offered them two thousand pounds to mess you up permanently, with an extra thousand to terminate you. What's it like to have a price on your head, lieutenant?'

Max was shocked and asked 'Did you get the name of that soldier?'

'No, he wouldn't say nor who his accomplices were. However, he did surprisingly own up to the attack, probably because we said we had forensic proof from the scene matching fibres from the balaclavas. He wasn't that bright, but we have his confession taped.

We are still hoping to get the soldier's name who was the paymaster. Do you know anybody from your camp that wants you dead?'

'I have a good idea, but you have no proof of linking anybody yet. Thanks, inspector, excellent work. I do appreciate your call.'

'We do our best. You go to Afghanistan today, don't you?'

'Yes, we leave in three hours.'

'Good luck over there.'

'Thanks, and by the way, I've just come off the phone to the hospital,

Terry Dixon is improving by the hour.' Max advised the police inspector.

'Yes, we are kept informed as it could change the charges. Goodbye, lieutenant and good luck.'

'Thank you, inspector.'

It was time to move out; three platoon climbed into two five-ton lorries for the journey to Brize Norton and their awaiting transport planes to sun, sand and bullets. Finally, three platoon arrived in the war-torn country of Afghanistan. Most of the soldiers had boyishly laughed from the excitement of entering this mysterious country. Their naivety was apparent, evidently not aware of the actual dangers that lay ahead for them. The trucks conveyed the relief battalion to their new depot in Kabul. The battalion had a strength of six hundred and fifty men.

The 1st Rifles are in Afghanistan as a planned non-combative role for continued help in training and to assist the Afghan army in case of any Taliban insurgence that was believed to be imminent.

The place is scorching with a dry climate and millions of flies. Nevertheless, the men soon settled into their billet. The experienced three platoon was all present and correct apart from Terry. Max would put his lads up against any fighting unit.

With new equipment they would be better protected now, more than their comrades had been in the past. Their new transport is the Foxhound. Three were delivered to the platoon. These are armoured personal carriers and protect better from improvised explosive devices. The new bombproofing to the vehicles has increased its protection by introducing a V-shaped base. It deflects the main force of an explosion to either side of the armoured carrier.

After five days the men were well into their routine, soldiering with the Afghan national army to develop their skills to protect their own country against the Taliban, Al-Qaeda and the so-called Islamic State whose fighters are now a presence in the region.

The Rifles are a front-line regiment, and when back in the UK, the battalions are on a state of alert and ready to move out in twenty-four hours. Now they are having their second tour of Afghanistan. When three platoon returned from their first patrol in their three Foxhounds, Max had a phone message left from a UK number asking him to phone back when possible. Max immediately thought it must be his mother worrying, as indeed all good mums do. She did say she would phone this week but would leave it until he'd settled in. He didn't recognise the number; perhaps it was Pippa. Max called the number as requested, and a young female voice answered. 'Hello.' The unknown recipient answered. 'Is that you, Pippa?' Max asked, but not confident it was his sister.

'No, this is Penny Richards, the doctor you spoke to in Chepstow General, remember? I hope I haven't disappointed you not being Pippa.'

Max panicked like a schoolboy with a crush and replied. 'Hi Penny, no, no, I'm certainly not disappointed; I'm so pleased to hear from you. I thought you were my mum, no, oh, I didn't mean you sounded like my mum, oh damn, I'm making a mess of this. Let me start again, please. I was expecting a call from my mother; I heard your younger voice answer so I thought it must be Pippa, my sister. But I'm so pleased it was you!

'Well, that clears that up. I have some excellent news, Terry Dixon is out of danger; he's breathing independently, and he should be discharged in about ten days.'

'Penny, that is absolutely fantastic news; his fiancé must be so relieved. Thank you for your call. I hope I can still have your email?

'Mmmm, I'll have to think about that! Okay, I've thought, you seem a nice sort of chap. Write this down. It's *Penny.r@penscope.co.uk.*'

'Thanks, Penny, I'll try not to bore you. Look after Terry for me.'

'I surely will; he's really okay though. He regards you as some superhero, telling me all about the boxing, how you took on and saw off the three attackers on that dreadful night. Wow, and you want to pen-pal me! I'm honoured.' The doctor laughed.

'Thank you, Penny; I'll email you soon; goodbye for now.'

Max didn't think his finish was right; indeed, he felt inadequate, short even. All Max knew was he was so looking forward to their next liaison more than anything.

He cursed himself again for not finding out if she has got a bloke, but it was probably too early in their brief association to ask.

Two months had gone by since the Rifles arrived in Afghanistan; the weather was humid and hot. Three platoon had already completed several patrols, escorts and guard duties. Max received orders from company headquarters that his platoon was to go to an emergency in the Bagram district. Insurgents are reported to have taken over a local police station and have taken hostages. The platoon got to the community outside Kabul; it is a big town of forty thousand inhabitants. Max's unit was in three Foxhounds. They disembarked and moved towards the trouble spot; a captain of the Afghanistan army intercepted them. In a high pitched voice, he tried to explain in English but it was impossible to understand him, so Max called the interpreter attached to his unit to translate the Afghans yelling.

'There is a band of IS backed Taliban fighters holding the southside of the town. They have killed some civilians and have blown up an American mission that was treating sick locals. They have now occupied the main police station with many hostages.'

'Ask the captain how many IS gunmen are there?' Max prompted the interpreter, who translated back.

'He says they have counted between fifteen to twenty; they shot five terrorists in a street battle. The insurgents have automatic weapons, grenades and a few rocket launchers.' The interpreter translated almost instantaneously.

'Thank you.' Max shook the interpreter's hand.

The platoon moved into the lock-down area where the Taliban and IS were holding out. The enemy had captured the fortified police station and it was clear to Max that taking it back was not going to be easy. So the lieutenant split his platoon into three groups of ten, Max took one, and his two trusted sergeants led the others. They knew that the terrorists had decent weapons as they were firing randomly in the platoon's direction. The intel came from the police chief who escaped when his station was attacked by Taliban sympathisers within his own ranks who had enlisted as police officers. They had staged a surprise attack coordinated with the Taliban forces from the Hindu Kush mountains.

The firing from their lines ceased and a white flag was waved but it was not in surrender! A Taliban spokesman popped his head up from the defences. He spoke through a loud hailer and screamed some Arabic sounding garble. The platoon's Afghan translator went to work again. He repeated the demands made by the Taliban guy.

'Unless you release the Taliban second in command, Abdul Muzanni, we will kill the hostages, one every five minutes, starting in one hour. We have thirty-seven locals including women and police officers. You know we are IS Taliban. You know we are serious! Any attempt to storm the building and the hostages will be shot at once. We want a guarantee of safe passage back to our mountains with Muzanni.'

The interpreter used the police megaphone and asked for at least two hours to organise the demands which was surprisingly agreed to. The terrorists would not start executing the hostages for two hours but emphasised that that would be the final timescale.

Max called his two NCO's along with an Afghan army captain and the police chief for a meeting in a nearby shop that had been commandeered and turned into their operations room. Two riflemen stood sentry outside. Max asked the local military man and police chief if either of them had seen this type of crisis before and did they have any ideas for dealing with this situation. The translator interpreted all the conversations. They both said the previous hostage-takings they had witnessed ended in a shootout with the Taliban usually dead, but so were many hostages. It always ended in a blood bath anyway. Both officers said they had no ideas apart from attacking with superior firepower. That way, however, would also seal the fate of all the innocent hostages. They both agreed the insurgents would carry out their threat to kill their captives. IS and Taliban do not make idle threats. 'Do either of you have a picture of this leader they want to be released?' Max asked hopefully.

'Yes,' the army officer replied, opening his laptop and keying in the coded access. First he brought up the Taliban leaders face and profile, like a typical prisoners ID. Then the platoon officer explained a quickly devised plan.

'There must be a local volunteer in your army or police squad that looks like Abdul Muzanni. I understand he wears a pakul all the time, and he sports a beard like most Afghans. So, we want somebody with his height and build who can mimic his voice. We have to act fast and will need the local TV company's makeup artist to give the finishing touches to the disguise, not forgetting the huge birthmark on his lower neck. Show the makeup expert a picture of it to put a false one on our man'. The call for a volunteer was encouraging. Several officers from the police service and the locally based army came forward. Max picked Malik, who was a remarkable likeness in every way. Max knew he chose right after getting Malik to read from a script and act as a terrorist leader might. The lieutenant thanked all the others for volunteering and gave them the equivalent of ten quid each and asked them to stay in a secured cafe until the operation was over. Max thought he couldn't chance a Taliban sympathiser amongst those who had volunteered to play the fake Taliban leader.

Max organised a cordon around the besieged police station and asked both the police captain and the army officer to confiscate all mobile phones inside the ring because he couldn't take the chance of intel getting back to the hostage-takers. Security was paramount.

The chosen Muzanni substitute loved the idea of becoming a hero; he listened to a recording of Muzzani's voice over and over until he could mimic it perfectly.

Max phoned through to Battalion HQ: 'We need to move Muzanni out of his secure cell because many Taliban sympathisers have infiltrated all government services, including prisons. These agents would no doubt phone the Taliban, who in turn would advise the hostage-takers that Muzanni is on his way or not. That information is exactly what we want them to report back to the Taliban.' A senior officer at base reassured Max he would action his request. Ten minutes later a lieutenant called back with confirmation that it had been agreed to move Muzanni out of his prison into another cell covertly. Max required the substitute Malik, to have the same dress that Muzanni was wearing when he left jail. This was another precaution just in case his description was relayed to the hostage-takers. That preparatory work was vital and now complete. Max was confident it would work, but he couldn't afford any slip-ups with thirty-seven lives at stake.

'We must keep our plan privy to as few people as necessary. The ones that are involved must be handpicked and verified. First, we put Malik into cuffs and under armed guard by the Afghan national army. They will carry out the escort duty and bring the substitute terrorist to the designated zone I have chosen as part of my overall plan. All personnel who enter the cordon must remain inside until the plan is executed.' The Afghan army and police officers concurred with Max's plan.

Max called for a meeting with the police captain, the Afghan army officer, his two sergeants, the handpicked eight-man guard, Malik and the interpreter.

'Gentlemen, this is my plan. First, the prisoner, Muzanni, will be switched; Malik, our lookalike, will arrive in a Foxhound vehicle to the spot I've marked off and will be waiting out of sight. Malik will be handcuffed to two of the guards. With the police captain's help, we have taken over the row of houses that run the road's length towards the captured police headquarters. My platoon will be deployed in those houses. They will use single-shot action and have sniper sites fitted to their rifles; we will have two snipers at each first-floor front window out of sight. All the houses are on one side of the road to our right, the terrorist's left. Allowing for the maximum of eighteen terrorists, we will have two riflemen for each gunman if our intel is correct. We have our best three sharpshooters ready to pick off any Taliban that survives the first sniper volley. This is our backup precaution.

Families from the houses have been evacuated by their back doors, out of sight from the hostage-taker's binoculars. The families had been compensated for the use of their homes and moved to a community centre under supervision. Their phones also were confiscated for the duration of the mission in case of Taliban sympathisers. Phase two: We will tell the terrorist spokesman that we have three army trucks waiting and ready to leave with eighteen of the hostages. They will be told Muzanni, under armed guard, will follow in the armoured vehicle. We will ask the terrorists to come out with eighteen hostages and place six in each of the lorries we provide. The other eighteen should be released to us immediately. We will agree to travel about halfway to the mountains. There the exchange will take place. Abdul Muzanni for the remaining nineteen hostages. We will give our word in writing that we will not open fire. Phase-three: They want Abdul Muzanni back as a top priority. We will need to show our handcuffed actor to them as they will undoubtedly wish to verify we have got him. Malik will shout at the terrorists to get the exchange done or there will be punishment. Apparently, Muzanni has a short temper; therefore, we mustn't disappoint, must we? Once we have allayed their suspicions, I think they will want to get on with securing the exchange. The final phase: The nineteen hostages being released will walk slowly to our lines then they will be taken away, medically checked and debriefed. I would imagine the remaining eighteen will come out, each with a captor, closely behind with a gun at each hostage's head. Once they are in a straight line, a flare will be set off on the column's right side; this should distract the captors and instinctively they should turn towards the flare. Each sniper from our platoon will shoot a selected IS target at that precise moment. Each sniper will have a designated target number in order, from front to back. A team of our three best snipers in the platoon will cover any missed targets. The key to this is surprise and timing; my riflemen know they must fire off at precisely the same time at their allocated number in the hostage line. My snipers will keep their individual IS targets in their sights until the distracting flare goes off. So all they do then is shoot precisely synchronised shots. I am trusting in my lads to do just that. Any questions?'

'Isn't this a risk to the hostages, sir' Asked Sergeant Tim Forbes.

'It's going to be a risk whatever we do, Tim, even if we do nothing,' There was silence for half a minute.

'No more questions?...... right, we will carry out phase one, gentlemen. Let's put this plan into action. First, sergeant, place your men into position, and once there they must not be seen! Is that clear?'

'Yes, sir.'

Everything was in place within an hour. The armoured car with Malik, alias Muzanni arrived, and it was time to set up the deal. Six of the eight-man prisoner escort, the interpreter, and Max walked towards the police station with a white flag held aloft. Through the loud hailer, the translator repeated Max's English into Afghan.

'We have what you want; we have Abdul Muzanni in the armoured vehicle. To make the exchange happen, you must release nineteen hostages, leave the police station, and walk to three waiting trucks with the remaining eighteen hostages. You will get into the vehicles and be taken to a village of your choice or the mountains. We will follow with an armed escort; at a designated halfway point, suggested by you, we will then make the exchange. Muzanni for the last eighteen captives. Do you understand?'

'You are trying to trick us; we are not letting half our prisoners go free.'

'Then we have no deal.' Max replied.

Max turned, walking away and got twenty paces before the IS spokesman shouted.

'Wait, let me see Abdul.' The Taliban approached cautiously to within twenty feet of the Foxhound, and Max shouted.

'Stop, that's far enough.' The leader had a group of six guards all looking trigger happy, but they all stopped as demanded!

They got Muzanni out of the back of the armoured vehicle, handcuffed to two guards. The cuffed detainee bellowed at the hostage-taker.

'Get this exchange to happen, now!' The IS spokesman replied instantly.

'Yes, I will immediately, but before I do, please show me your birthmark, sir,

'You are wasting time, we must exchange. You will be so sorry about this; it must be obvious who I am; you should know me, you stupid pig.'

Max thought Malik was overcooking the acting but was impressed with his performance. Malik did sound convincing. He shouted at the hostage-taker again. 'You are wasting time, we must exchange; you will be so sorry about this, do it this minute.' The IS man held his ground in a determined stance.

'I cannot let our hostages go unless I'm sure it's you, sir; I apologise, but I must insist and make sure it is not a trap, so please show me your birthmark!'

Malik fumed; 'Of course, it's me. I have just spent six months in a stinking infidel's prison, and I'm not showing you, a peasant.'

The IS man held firm, stating. 'Then I must return, sir.' Max thought, *"Don't overdo it, Malik; you are losing him."* Malik, however, knew exactly what he was doing. 'Okay, I will show you, I will show you.' The IS man returned.

Malik opened the top of his shirt and pulled it down, exposing the birthmark on his neck.

Malik screamed at the IS leader. 'Get me out of this stinking place, now.'

'Yes, sir, so sorry for doubting you.'

Max walked back with this now very nervous Taliban terrorist. Max repeated the exchange conditions through the interpreter: 'Release the nineteen hostages now by sending them out in a line. Then all your men come out with the remaining hostages. You can then load them up in the three trucks. After that you will leave and travel halfway between this town and your village. We shall follow you in the armoured car with Muzanni, and at that point, we shall carry out the exchange. We shall have an escort of troops to negate yours.'

'Okay, we will do this.' He then returned to the fortified police station.

Max watched as the doors opened at the police station with hostages coming out; he saw a trickle in singles, then twos and threes, through binoculars. Finally, the nineteen were out in the open, walking to the allies' lines; the Afghan medics greeted them and ushered them to awaiting ambulances. Max was delighted, thinking. *"It worked, Malik was bloody brilliant, but it's not finished yet."*

The nineteen were whisked away to the hospital to undergo check-ups.

Now for the vital phase. Max's stomach was churning over with nerves of anticipation; he watched through binoculars. His stomach tightened; the door opened. Out stepped a hostage with a gunman walking close behind, using the hostage as a human shield and moving forward like some weird ritual dance. The Taliban guy was turning his head nervously, left then right then left; it looked bizarre. Max panned round to the row of houses on his right and could not see his concealed snipers; Max hoped all those hours on the range would now pay off. Back at the police station doorway, the line of strange dancers was now a significant number; not long to wait for the action. Max just hoped he had called it right. The procession is complete; hostages and terrorists are all out and in clear view. Max's radio operator was standing by for the lieutenant's signal to activate the loud but harmless flare to his left. The line of hostages and their captors were slowly snaking towards the allies' line, only about seventy-five metres away.

'Now, corporal.' Within two seconds, the loud flare rocket was activated! Instinctively, everybody in the snaking line looked to their right; as they did the line became a surreal sight. The selected targets were hit with one silenced shot each to the head, making the bodies gyrate grotesquely until they lay motionless in the dusty road. For a split second, it was incomprehensible. The hostages were screaming hysterically and couldn't work out what was going on and running in all directions. Sixteen dead IS and Taliban, only one remained wounded and on the ground but still a threat, he lifted his automatic weapon but before he could aim, he must have had at least three bullets in his body that made him do a strange death dance before laying silent on his back, leaking blood from several holes in his blood-soaked skull, those last shots came from the platoon's backup chosen elite snipers. Sadly, a young male hostage took a ricochet bullet which lodged in his brain. He died instantly.

Malik couldn't wait to come out of his hiding place. Everybody all shook hands; the plan came off superbly. The big bonus was Abdul Muzanni is still locked up with only one accidental death! It was a great result. All the IS and Taliban terrorists were killed with one or two shots to their heads. It showed the accuracy and discipline of three platoon's sniper shooting.

Back at their camp in Sharabak, Max called his platoon to order. Max heaped praise on his successful team. Apart from Tim Forbes and one other corporal, it was their first real combat experience.

'We'll have a party to celebrate—bloody good shooting lads.' Max felt so proud of three platoon.

The lieutenant called Malik into his make-shift tent office and gave the talented Afghan fifty pounds for his outstanding performance. Malik welled up; he said it was an honour to serve the famous British Army.

After the Oscar-winning performance with the enemy, Max advised him to take up acting. Malik left the office a pleased and very proud man.

The young lieutenant was called into the CO's office. On the door facing him was a brass nameplate. Lieutenant Colonel Laurence Abel.

'Come in! Ah, it's you, young Maximus. I've heard so much about you back at Beachley, winning the weapon training shield twice in succession, the cross country platoon race, the fastest speed march time, beating the regiment's best average of 142 paces per minute, excellent work. I also heard you gave that bully Connolly a damn good thrashing in the ring as well. You then go on to get to the final of the boxing knockout. The coach told me you didn't have a bruised wrist at all. You wanted only to sort Connolly out; well done! I am saving the best until last. You take on three murderous armed thugs on your own, see them off and went about saving Corporal Dixon's life. I was so pleased he recovered, he's been in 1st Rifles longer than I have. His fiancé must be so relieved as well. Damn it, I hope they call their first boy Maximus. That would be something, don't you know! However, all that back at Beachley pales into insignificance when you consider what you did in Bagram today. The Afghan commanding officer at Bagram told me you devised a plan, then carried it out perfectly. All the terrorists are dead, and just one civilian casualty out of thirty-seven. That's mighty impressive, lieutenant.' I am told that the Afghan government is presenting you with a military medal of sorts.'

'Thank you, sir, but it was only my duty; the credit should go to three platoon and their shooting skills.'

'Well, Maximus, I want you to come to dinner on Friday. There is a private room in the officers' mess at the back. Say 19:00 hrs for drinks; we have air-conditioning, don't you know? The Yanks fitted it before they vacated here.'

'Yes, sir, of course, and thank you, sir.'

When Max got back to his office and tented quarters, he crashed out on his bed. Turning out the light was the last thing he could remember about that eventful, most memorable day.

Max was scheduled for training duties with new Afghan army recruits for the following two days. The men of three platoon were still puffing their chests out with the impromptu rescue mission's success.

12

It was a bitterly cold early Spring morning, one of those crisp, clear days with a cloudless sky but a sharp bite that commanded a heavy warm coat. Penny had an enhanced feel-good feeling that made her even happier this morning. Strangely, she didn't know why.

Dr Penny Richards had that buzz which prompted her to jog to her hospital workplace on such a lovely morning. However, Penny discounted it wasn't just the weather for her uplifting mood. She was strangely excited, Penny was always happy with her life, but this morning the jogging doctor felt a zest that she had not experienced before. Penny had a call last night from corporal Terry Dixon. She played back the conversation in her mind as she jogged. He had brought her up to date with his progress. She recalled the chat, every word:

"My life is more or less back as it was before the attack, and I'm hoping to join up with my battalion in Afghanistan. The battalion has been out there for three months."

"I had asked if Terry had heard from Max lately?"

Terry had answered. *"I haven't for a week, but my good friend, Sergeant Forbes, called me and explained that the very same man who had saved my life, Maximus, had rescued thirty-six civilians from certain death, that he had devised the whole plan himself. It was a clever operation, according to Forbsy. So I am very aware that I owe my life to two lovely people, you and my lieutenant. I will never forget either of you."*

Penny could remember every word of their conversation as she recited it over and over in her mind.

Penny was welling up at what Terry had said, and it certainly wasn't the biting cold that activated Penny's tear ducts. She stopped her run to blow her nose and wipe her eyes. Cheering up immediately, Penny smiled, they were happy tears. So the doctor assumed it was good news from Terry that had put a definite spring in her step.

Penny got to work earlier than she expected, showered and changed into her scrubs for another long shift in A&E. She had a few minutes to spare so she grabbed a coffee and felt the urge to send the hero Max an email. However, she was desperate to speak with him live but had to ask herself rhetorically. *"Why?"*

Across Chepstow, not far from Penny's hospital, a hectic morning was developing inside the local police station. They had apprehended the two other suspects in the Terry Dixon case, the brother of the man already arrested, and the third accomplice. The police had overwhelming evidence against them supplied by forensics; these two detainees will also be charged today, subject to routine police protocol.

The Detective Inspector leading the investigation interviewed the new detainees separately. He put it to the suspects. 'We have forensic evidence linking you and your mate to this vicious, unprovoked attack on the Tutshill road, off the A48. You can think I am bluffing, in which case you will only find out if I am, at your trial. Or you can cooperate, which will mean possibly a year taken off your expected sentence. This interview, as you know, is under caution and recorded, so you may want to ponder or take advice from your solicitor before we continue. Remember, we have charged your brother; we can't do that lightly or without substantial evidence. The same will apply to you.'

The solicitor spoke. 'Can you give us five minutes without recording, please?'

'Yes, of course.' The police inspector agreed.

The inspector re-entered the room and sat down, looking straight into the eyes of the brief.

'My client wants to admit to being at the scene but took no part in the knife attack, and as you can see, he has lost his left eye caused by an army officer in the fight.' However, the solicitor had realised it was better for him, financially, not to challenge his client's case too hard. His client was legally aided, therefore, it will be less work if he pleads guilty, for his ambulance-chasing reduced fee.

'Right, son, give me a complete statement of precisely what happened that night in the lane. Remember, the victim's blood and fibres are on several garments we took from the stolen car. Your statement must correspond accurately with what we know, or you will face an additional charge of obstructing the course of justice, another serious offence. We need the name of the army bloke who put you up to this. We know he's from Beachley barracks; it's only a matter of time before we find out ourselves. Don't let this opportunity slip by in assisting us with our enquiries. We know who used the knife and seriously injured the corporal because of the blood-spattered balaclava we found in the stolen car. So you and your brother should face a lesser charge, but I can't guarantee that. I can only say that the more you assist, the more favourable your case will look to the prosecutors. So tell me the paymaster from Beachley? I want it now!'

After another consultation with the indifferent solicitor, he gave the name they wanted. It tied in with who Lieutenant Hainsworth-Catt had suspected. Mr Patrick Connolly!

At Beachley, the second wave of three hundred troops prepared to join up with the rest of the battalion in three days. Same preparation as the first wave but with more armoured Foxhounds.

All the gossip around the base was more or less the same as all the national and local papers the men had read online. *"British Rifles officer foils escape of most dangerous IS and Taliban leader."* — *"Young British lieutenant saves 36 hostages from certain death"* The local press in Chepstow: *"Local army officer from Beachley barracks, is a hero in Afghanistan."*

The MOD forbade the papers to print the officer's name in case of reprisals from IS terror group cells operating in the UK.

Dr Penny Richards was taking her lunch break when a colleague came across the canteen asking. 'Have you seen this in the local paper? A local army officer from Beachley barracks is a hero. That was the camp where the soldier had his throat cut awhile back, wasn't it?'

Penny looked at the newspaper placed in front of her and replied. 'Yes, I also know that officer, I was told about the story this morning. Penny stared down, almost mesmerised, at her one-carat diamond engagement ring!

Max could still see the anger and aggression oozing from Connolly. There had been unproven thefts and other misdemeanours within three platoon that all pointed to the red Irishman. *"The thug should be hanged."* Max reflected.

The acting lieutenant returned to his quarters, showered, shaved and laid on his bed, quite relaxed in a silk dressing gown that his dear mother gave him. He thought to himself and half smiled, *"I hope the lads don't see me in this; I'll never live it down."* Max's mobile vibrated. It startled the lieutenant as calls at the base are rare. 'Hello, is that Mr Hainsworth-Catt?' The caller asked. 'Yes, who's that?' It's your old pal Rory; how are you, Maximus?

'All good, Rory, hell, it's so good to hear from my best buddy! So what are you up to, still working your arse off in the City?'

'Yes, mate, just gone up the Canary Wharf ladder of skulduggery, insider trading, fraudulent dealing, all that caper, it's stressful but rewarding. All the national papers are going on about an officer in the 1st Rifles; that's your mob, you must know the chap; he's a bloody hero over here.'

'Rory, you must not repeat this, but you are my best and trusted pal. I was in charge of that hostage operation.'

'Bloody hell Max, I'm mates with a national hero. The news says you saved thirty-six hostages from being executed and foiled an escape of a top terrorist at the same time.'

'It wasn't an escape; it was supposed to be an exchange, him for the hostages. One day Rory, I'll tell you the whole shooting match over a beer in the Red Lion; excuse the pun! Anyway, how is your love life going with Stephanie Symonds.'

'Oh, she's a little beauty, Max, I'm dying for you to meet her, wait till I tell her my best mate's the new national hero, shit! I can't; well, that can wait until you go into anonymity again.'

'Rory, we shall have a few beers together as soon as I return in another four months or so. Hey, mate, it's so good to hear from you; thanks for calling.'

'Take care, Max, speak soon. Bye.'

Still lying down relaxed, Max opened his emails. 'Oh yes.' A shot of adrenaline rushed through his body; it was from Penny.

"Penny.r@penscope.co.uk.

Dear Max, I spoke with Terry this morning before my jog to work. He thinks he'll be joining up with you in Afghanistan soon. I told him he hadn't given his healing enough time for a full recovery, but he would have none of it. So please find him light work for a while. He tells me you are playing superhero again; I have seen it for myself, all over the newspapers. I have gone out and bought all the editions. They say you saved thirty-six innocent civilians in Bagram and devised the plan yourself. They didn't mention your name but Terry knew it was you. Well, Mr superhero, can you remember the last time we spoke? I asked you to keep safe. But unfortunately, it doesn't sound like you heeded my recommendation!

Seriously I'm glad you are okay and very well done in Bagram. Now that Terry is mended, do you still want me as your pen friend?'

Keep well and safe if you can.

Regards.
Penny. X"

"What do you make of that Maxi lad? Is the lovely Penny trying to flirt with me? Damn, I still don't know if she's with anyone!"

The next day, Max was ordered to see B company's Captain Smyth. He sure was in a foul mood with Max!

'Sit down, lieutenant; you are getting a bit cocksure of yourself. You think you are the battalion's blue-eyed boy. Well, let me assure you, you don't cut any ice with me. I have received a complaint from a very dependable soldier, Pat Connolly. He has reported that you are picking on him all the time, making his life hell. He has two witnesses to back his statement up. Pat also says you bully him when the rest of the platoon is not around. I'm going to make a full enquiry. Until I have finished it, you are confined to your quarters, it's an order. Is that clear?'

'Yes, sir.'

'What do you have to say for yourself.'

'It's total bullshit, sir.'

'That's what I expected from you, remember, pride comes before a fall, now get out.'

"Bloody hell," Max thought: *"Talk about Mr Bloody Cliche. Five cliches in three minutes of total bullshit. I can't believe what has just happened. I know who Connolly's witnesses are, his acolytes, Ceri Burns and Tom Palanski. There must be something I can do; something is going on between the captain and Connolly; he must be taking it up the bloody arse or something."*

The rest of three platoon couldn't believe what the company captain had done to their lieutenant. What worried Max was Connolly's bullying; the lads will undoubtedly suffer, especially the weaker ones.

Max went to his quarters to think about what to do; he felt frustrated to hell. But unfortunately, Max was under orders from a superior officer, and his frustrations will have to be contained for the time being.

Unbeknown to Max, plans were afoot and happening fast within the platoon. Tim Forbes has taken matters into his own hands; he heard what had happened from Connolly's boasting about it: *"I got that rich shit of a lieutenant into big trouble; good and proper, that'll teach him to fuck with me. Things will be a lot easier again in three."* Tim heard this word for word.

Sergeant Forbes had had enough; he knew the accusations about his respected lieutenant were a complete stitch-up. He and four of the platoon waited for the Irishman to finish one of his heavy drinking bouts. Then, before he knew what hit him, Connolly was bundled into one of the Foxhounds with a pistol at his temple. They strapped him into the seat and went to find his two supporters. With the three now fastened tight, the Foxhound then moved out of the gates. A nod from the sentry who recognised Forbes, waved them on. Tim took the vehicle about five miles out, virtually into the desert. The loyal men got the three captives out of the vehicle and tied them to three separate Mazari palm trees. The small oasis was known locally as the Pani. With much aggression in his voice, Forbes gave his captives an ultimatum.

'Okay, you shits, you either tell us what Connolly has over Captain Smyth, or we will leave you here and inform the Taliban activists to come to collect you. They will then sell you to IS, who will get their film crews and set up their popular TV execution film of infidels. How long they take to get here, who knows? You may even be eaten alive first by the mosquitoes or tree ants. Very uncomfortable either way, wouldn't you say, lads? Then, of course, we will tell the MPs that you three left the Foxhound for some air and didn't return. Please make up your mind quickly before we go; I will now have a slash; I want an answer by the time I've shaken Percy. Think of the headlines for your families to read in papers or worse, see on TV, Ceri Burns and Tommy Palanski, beheaded dead heroes! Do you want that lads? Or do you want a fresh start in the platoon, away from the bullying threats from that wanker Connolly? Your choice, see you after my piss.'

Connolly threatened his two acolytes not to say a word; he screamed, insisting the sergeant was bluffing.

Tim Forbes came back from his finished necessary.

'Well, Percy has had his shake so now we are leaving with or without you. Once in the Fox, we won't hear you, nor will we come back, choices lads.' Tim Forbes, with the other three kidnappers, turned towards the Fox and just as the last man was about to close the rear door, Burns screamed: 'Wait, I'm not committing bloody suicide for fucking Connolly; I've had enough; release me, and I'll make a statement that Captain Smyth is in with it all! He likes young recruits as well!'

Connolly was now going ballistic at Burns. 'I'll fucking kill you for this, you fucking big mouth.'

Tim jumped out of the Fox and told one of the lads to untie Ceri Burns. 'What about you, Palanski? Are you going to die with your friend?'

'No, no, take me back as well, and I'll sign a statement like Ceri.'

First, Burns made his statement:

'Connolly had found out that Captain Smyth was shagging young vulnerable recruits and obtained photographic evidence of his sickening fetish. Connolly blackmailed Smyth that he would not reveal the incriminating photos providing perks he demanded were forthcoming. One night, Connolly was drinking with Tom and me. Connolly was drunk and told us the whole story about Smyth. He said the captain intimidated weak recruits into having his pleasure with them. Connolly bragged that he even had the recruits names who Smyth was turd burgling. He shared some spoils with us, things the captain got him on a regular basis, which of course, implicated us in his blackmailing scam. It was too late; we were in too deep and apart from that, he said he would beat us good and proper if we talked. I didn't fancy a beating from him after seeing him in the boxing ring going mental at opponents. Tom felt the same. In the end, we had to keep doing what he demanded. We think he was also involved with the attempted murder of Corporal Dixon, but we can't swear to that.'

'There's no need to write a statement; we have recorded your verbal information on this phone. Come on, Palanski, you do the same; tell it how it was. He did. It was almost word for word as Burn's statement. Tim took Connolly to the guardhouse, and he said to the duty corporal to place Connolly under arrest but separated from Burns and Palanski. Tim then went straight to the lieutenant's quarters to tell Max what had happened.

'What, Tim, you must be crazy.' Max couldn't believe what his NCO had just told him!
'But it worked, sir. We all knew something wasn't right between Connolly and Captain Smyth. The platoon also knew that Connolly had something on Palanski and Burns. The big thug initially got most of the platoon to play you, but you gradually won the lads over. They began to like and respect you, this of course, pissed off Connolly even more. He made it known to all the platoon that your arrival had scuppered his ongoing perks for easy soldiering. Anyway sir, I have

had the three arrested; they are in the guardhouse jail, as we speak, sir.'

Thank you, Tim, it was very thoughtful and loyal but bloody stupid.'

'To a man, sir, the platoon agreed this was the action to take against Connolly and it worked a treat as well; they all said it was overdue, sir.'

'Thanks again, Tim, now carry on; I'll deal with the captain tomorrow. Good night.'

After breakfast, Max went to the guardhouse. Connolly had gone, Burns and Palanski had chosen to stay detained. Max asked the duty guard.

'Where is Connolly?'

'Captain Smyth gave the order to release Connolly immediately.

Max went to Connolly's billet; he'd gone with all his kit. *"Where the fuck is he? "* Max thought rhetorically.

The lieutenant found Captain Smyth just coming out of the officer's mess. 'Captain Smyth.' Max shouted across the yard at the officer. Smyth spun round and glared at Max.

'I told you to stay confined to your quarters. How dare you disobey an order lieutenant. I want to see you as it happens. Members of your platoon kidnapped Patrick Connolly and threatened to hand him over to the Taliban. What in god's name were they thinking? Did you play any part in this unacceptable occurrence?' Max didn't answer.

'I, of course, released Pat this morning, but I can't figure it out; Burns and Palanski insisted on staying behind bars. That's very strange if you ask me. Anyway, get back to your quarters, lieutenant; I'm going to deal with you later.'

The captain turned away towards his office. Max shouted assertively. 'Your charade is over, captain. I

117

know you have bullied young recruits into having your sordid way with them—and the blackmailing from Connolly. I'm going to see the Lieutenant Colonel right now. Do you want to join me, sir, if you try and stop me, you dirty prick, I'll knock your fucking lights out.'

'Oh my God, please don't, how much do you want lieutenant? Just say anything, listen, I have five grand in cash in my safe; it's yours. Take it all!' The disgraced captain was snivelling on his knees, begging Max to keep his dirty secrets from the CO.

'Fuck off, you filthy bastard and get out of my way, you piece of shit, let go of my arm. You, sir, are a disgrace to our company, battalion and the regiment.'

Max pushed the officer to the ground, with the captain clutching pathetically on Max's leg. Smyth's screaming and pleading caused a crowd of soldiers coming out of the canteen from breakfast to stare and wonder what the hell was going on with these two officers. Smyth was still clinging to the lieutenant's one leg and being dragged along the ground. In desperation, the captain screamed at the watching soldiers to arrest the lieutenant. It was a last-ditch but vain attempt to stop the sordid captain's military career going down the pan in a dishonourable flushing. The B company soldiers ignored their hated captain's orders and watched with amusement at the pathetic sight. Max eventually kicked himself free from the begging officer's grasp and went to the colonel's office. The colonel's secretary asked him to take a seat. 'The Colonel is taking a call from the MOD. it's quite a serious matter from the UK.'

Ten minutes later, her phone buzzed and flashed red, telling her the CO had finished his call from the UK.

She pressed another tab on her multi-functioning phone, she spoke telling her boss that Max was waiting to see him.

'You can go in now, lieutenant.' Max entered his colonel's office with some trepidation; disobeying a senior officer's order is a very serious matter.

'Take a seat, lieutenant. I need to speak to you, but you want to tell me something, so go first, please.'

'Thank you, sir. It's difficult to know where to begin. I'll start at Beachley. There was little or no order in three platoon when you offered it to me. The men of the platoon came and went more or less how they liked. Their marching was substandard, drilling was poor, and on the firing range their shooting was a joke. I also had suspicions that Connolly was behind the attack on me and the attempted murder of Corporal Terry Dixon, who, poor chap, just happened to be in the wrong place at the wrong time,' Max then explained recent events. 'Connolly had control over Captain Smyth, who had groomed new vulnerable recruits for sex; then, Connolly found out about this and blackmailed Smyth. He had photos that compromised the captain. Connolly would only keep quiet about the captain's disgusting behaviour in return for privileges and other favours. Then just yesterday, Captain Smyth confined me to my quarters, apparently on Connolly's say-so to get me out the way. Whilst I was on house arrest, my platoon sergeant and other Rifles took Connolly and his two pals out for a drive; and obtained confessions from Privates Burns and Palanski. I will leave out how they obtained these statements, I will leave that to your imagination, sir. Sergeant Tim Forbes had them arrested and the three spent the night in detention. Bloody captain fantastic Smyth, released Connolly this morning. Still in fear of Connolly for their confessions,

Privates Burns and Palanski chose to remain in the safety of the guardhouse. I saw Smyth just a few minutes ago, and the quivering jelly begged and bribed me not to expose him. Finally, when I first took over three platoon, it was under that bastard Connolly's influence, aided and abetted by Captain Smyth. That's about it, sir. The problem is, I think Connolly has now gone AWOL.'

'Good God, lieutenant, this is outrageous; thinking about it, I've noticed various complaints over the previous months back at Beachley; always Captain Smyth intervened saying he'll deal with it! No bloody wonder. One moment lieutenant.' The colonel picked up his phone, 'Sue, tell the duty MP corporal of the guard to come to my office with two armed escorts at once.' 'Yes, sir.'

The MP's arrived in a moment.

'Corporal, arrest Captain Smyth immediately and detain him until further instructions from me. Here's an arrest warrant for Patrick Connolly, three platoon, B company. 1st Rifles.'

The red cap read the warrant, then acknowledged. 'Yes, sir. Right away, sir.' The three MP's left to arrest the shameful captain and search for Connolly. The colonel continued his conversation with Max.

'Good gracious, what a morning. Right, unless you have any more surprises, I'll tell you some news from home that involves you—about your attackers on the Tutshill road. Three have been arrested and charged with the attempted murder of Terry Dixon. What's more, they have admitted it, confirmed on tape. They have implicated Private Patrick Connolly as the person who offered two grand to carry out the attack, with an additional bonus payment if they killed you. A contract is what the police called it. We need to find Connolly as quick as we can. He needs to be put behind bars and face a court-martial.'

'That is fantastic news; Terry will be so pleased. I bloody well knew Connolly was involved. I even told the police that. What will happen to Connolly now, sir.'

'Of course, he is innocent until the crown court finds him guilty, but that is the civilian route to justice. His military procedure will be through the military justice system and obviously a court-martial held in the UK.

Unless you have any more questions, Maximus, I must go and deal with Captain Smyth, assuming he's hasn't done a bunk like Connolly.'

'No sir, today's events are enough for anyone to take in and digest. Thank you, sir.'

'Don't forget tonight, 19.00hrs in the private function room at the officer's mess. Dinner at 19:45hrs Oh, and black tie, Maximus, carry on.'

Max cringed. *"Shit, what with all that's gone on, I forgot the colonel's dinner tonight; bloody good job I saw him today. So, I have to explain to the lads of 3 platoon I'll have to postpone our little celebration arranged for tonight. They will understand, though."* They did of course.

The colonel put on a lavish dinner for about twenty guests, including the UK's Ambassador to Afghanistan and his wife, an Attaché and his wife, five Afghan government officials and their ladies, two captains from A and C companies and their wives and some senior lieutenants and their spouses. Max, with no female escort, felt awkward initially but it was all very relaxed after a few aperitifs. The dinner got underway, and then came the speeches; God, they went on. The Afghan's took double the time as they had to be translated. Max just about kept awake; the lieutenant stirred, however, when he heard his name mentioned. It was all about the siege at Bagram and the famous plan that got in all the papers. The room fell into applause for Max, with lots of wine glasses being thumped on the table. It was very nice but totally unnecessary and somewhat embarrassing for Max. When the din died down, the colonel was still on his feet.

'Ladies, gentlemen and distinguished guests, I would like you to charge your glasses and toast Lieutenant Maximus Churchill Hainsworth-Catt, the regiment's hero. Today, I have lost a staff member, a certain Captain Smyth, who I hate to say has fallen far below regimental standards; I didn't have to look far for a replacement, however, so it gives me the greatest pleasure to endorse my new captain. I give you Captain Hainsworth-Catt,' another toast completed. The colonel continued. 'I have just received confirmation of his new rank from headquarters. Well done, Maximus, my congratulations.'

Max was stunned at his promotion; it happened so quickly. He thought losing Smyth obviously speeded up the process; confirmation was no doubt the extra pressure from Colonel Abel.

One of the ladies who attended the dinner walked past the back of Max's chair; and with a deft movement, she slipped him a piece of paper and left the room. Intrigued by this apparent covert female's movement, he opened the folded paper to read.... *"Maximus, you don't know me, but I have something important to tell you. Come outside; I'll be waiting for you."*

There wasn't a name on the note, which seemed a bit strange. Max finished what was left in his wine glass and left the room.

Outside, the lady who gave him the note stood there looking weirdly out of place, wearing a most revealing low cut silk chiffon evening gown, this image against a dusty army camp background; the contrast was immense. Max inquired. 'What do you want, madam? Are you okay?'

Max couldn't take his eyes off her full breasts that appeared to be fighting to escape the stunning but very tight dress; it looked as if they were about to win the contest.

'Come here close to me; I need to whisper something to you.'

Still transfixed, Max went to this mysterious young woman, thinking she was a tad tipsy.

She leant towards Max's ear as if to speak but didn't; grabbing his right hand and pressing it firmly against her half-exposed tits. Then, before Max could react, she had planted a full kiss on his lips, trying to dart her tongue into his mouth!

'What the hell are you doing, lady!'

She was not giving up, and probably fuelled with Champagne, she flung both her arms around his neck, losing a high heel in the process. At that very second, a voice growled from the door!

'What the hell is going on out here?'

"Oh fucking shit, it's the colonel!" Max panicked and wondered how he was going to get out of this situation.

The colonel was stepping outside to have a long-awaited nicotine fix from his Havana cigar.

The colonel bellowed a demand to the oversexed woman.

'Get inside and back to your husband, Lauren, now!' She scurried past the battalion commander without a word, looking very sheepish.

Colonel Abel waited until the lady was out of sight, then under his breath, the colonel hissed.

'What were you bloody thinking of Maximus, you have just received your captaincy, and within minutes you are outside ravishing a fellow captain's wife. If this were two hundred years ago, sir, you'd be called out to duel at dawn. So what the hell came over you?'

'Sir, you have to believe me.' Max explained the complete account of what happened, even the juicy bits. But, wisely, Max didn't disclose his almost hypnotic focus on Lauren's knockers.

The colonel, in a more conciliatory voice, replied.

'Sadly, Max, I know what she's like, two bottles of bubbly and the temptress goes wild. I have had problems with her before, she even tried it on with me once; but I shan't go into the lewd details. She obviously took a shine to you, the handsome new captain, ten years her husband's junior. I do believe every word you said, but just watch her; she's a damn dangerous filly.'

'Thanks for understanding sir, also your kind words at the dinner.'

'You deserve it, Max; I'll see you later to discuss your new commission.'

'If you don't mind, sir, I'll turn in now. I'm whacked. They are all still partying by the sound of fun coming from inside. I am knackered; I didn't sleep much last night, the house confinement was on my mind. An incredible day, confined to quarters yesterday, promoted to captain today. Good night sir.'
Things certainly happen quickly in Afghanistan.

13

Dr Penny Richards had booked three days holiday, as did her sister Jenny. The idea was to visit a wedding exhibition in London prior to her planned wedding. She intended to travel to the capitol with her twin sister Jenny and stay two nights to see the sights and take in a show. Graham, her fiancé, objected. The trip was therefore reduced to just a one night stay. Penny was at her flat, a two-bedroom apartment she purchased in her first year as a qualified doctor. It was in the village of Shirenewton, five miles from Chepstow, where she worked. Penny was very proud of her very first but difficult step on the property ladder; something her parents had always dreamed of for themselves. Putting Penny and Jenny through university put paid to their property owning aspirations. They were content, however, in their small council house that the twins grew up in. The young doctor was just finishing her breakfast when her phone rang.

'Hi sis, it's Jen. I'm all packed with my overnight bag. I'll drive us. Are you ready?'

'Yes, apart from packing a small bag. Sorry Jen, Graham doesn't want me staying two nights so it's only one night, I'm afraid. I'm so sorry but you know what Graham is like.'

'That's such a bummer, I was looking forward to being with you for a few days. I don't seem to see much of you since you got engaged to that tosser! I'll be over in about twenty minutes with a smaller bag.'

'Ok, do you want a coffee?'

'No, let's not waste time, let's get to the famous city, especially now our stay is reduced.

'Ok, I'll be ready by the time you get here. bye.'

Penny's fiancé, Graham, who was an absolute control freak, demanded Penny is back by 15:00hrs the following afternoon. His reason, they were driving to his parents in Cardiff. Like they do every weekend. Graham's mother also controls people; it might be a family thing. Penny tried to explain that she and her sister would need two days to view all the available options at the wedding show.

'No, you don't need all that time, just make sure you are back here for us to leave for Cardiff and don't be late. You can do your exhibition in a day. Don't buy anything in London without running it past me first, including the dress. Don't let that stupid sister persuade you to buy things without my knowledge.' There was veiled anger in Graham's voice.

'Ok, Graham, I'll see you tomorrow, and I will try and get back by three.'

'Don't try; get here on time! You know we'll get the wrath of mother if we're late.'

'Safe trip, and don't be late.'

Penny reflected, this wasn't the same Graham who had swept her off her feet a year ago when he had told her how good he would be for her, that he would take care of things for her in every possible way. Quite literally, as it turned out. A strange feeling of being stifled crept over her or was it the most peculiar thoughts and emotions that kept wandering back to another man. The man who she had only spent three minutes with at the hospital. The same man who is over three and a half thousand miles away from her!

Jenny arrived outside Pen's and sounded the horn of her bright red MG.

Penny slammed her door behind her and shouted a greeting to her sister.

'Morning Jen, great you've got the rag-top down on such a lovely day.'

On the way, the mood had edged to sombre between the sisters until Jenny enquired.

'Penny, what's the matter? I know when you have something on your mind, you go within yourself, spit it out, girl, what's up? Have you had a row with the wanker? Oh, sorry, I mean Graham?'

'Jenny, that's not helpful.' But Penny couldn't help a giggle thus making Jen laugh aloud; within seconds they were laughing hysterically.

A lorry driver in the same slow traffic, crawling in the next lane, was ogling the two young sisters legs, accentuated by the very short mini skirts they both wore. He kept pace with the girls. With one hand, Jenny being the young temptress she was, lifted her skirt higher and exposed her skimpy pants; she didn't stop there. 'Watch his face Pen, I'm going to stroke my foofoo.' Using her index and middle fingers, Jen rubbed sensuously slowly up and down on her genitalia. The lorry driver couldn't take his eyes off the naughty Jenny; he momentarily lost control of his lorry, veering off towards the third line of traffic and just missing a white van in the third lane. This created a cacophony of car horns as an accident nearly ensued. This shook the lorry driver back from his dreamland, his eyes now firmly back on the M4 tarmac and gripping his steering wheel tightly. It was fortunate the traffic was moving dead slow, owing to an accident further on. His loss of control made the girls go into another bout of uncontrollable laughter. The embarrassed driver looked away but occasionally threw a glance back just in case he missed something.

'Jen you are incorrigible. That was so dangerous.'

'He's probably tossing off now,' Jenny jested. The sisters broke into yet another giggling fit.

They were soon on their way again, passing the accident between Slough and Windsor, Jen asked quite seriously this time.

'You didn't answer my question, Penny! You don't seem at all happy lately. Please don't make a big mistake. If you are not sure, delay the wedding.' There was a deathly pause, a silence that said much.

'I know something is wrong, Jen, and I am having second thoughts. He's not the same funny guy I first met.'

'What does that tell you then? A couple of months ago you phoned me, and you sounded incredibly upbeat; I thought the best you've been for some time. In that conversation, you explained that you had just dealt with a soldier's throat that had been sliced. That obviously wouldn't have made you upbeat, so what was it? Had you helped yourself to some pick-me-up drug from your hospital pharmacy?' Jenny returned to her unavoidable jesting.

'Jen, that is so weird; I was jogging to work the other day and felt the same feeling you have just described. Oh my God, Jen, the two occasions are connected. The handsome lieutenant. Oh my God.' Jenny was now on a jesting roll.

'It sounds like a film, *"The Handsome Lieutenant"*.

'Tell me more, you dark filly, who is he and did you shag him?' Jenny was at her devilish best.

'Stop it, Jenny, you are disgusting. He has asked me for updates on his corporal, the one with the throat injury. He asked me to be his pen friend, while he's away in Afghanistan. He left only a day after the corporal's attack. He does seem a nice chap, and he's very handsome, I must say.'

'Steady Penny, remind me! We are shopping for your wedding requirements, aren't we?'

They arrived at the underground hotel parking in the capital, took the elevator up to reception, checked in, and went straight out to Earls Court by tube.

They had prepaid online tickets for the exhibition and so they went straight in. Penny was aimlessly wandering around. After an hour, she hadn't spoken to one exhibitor at the wedding exhibition.

'Right, that's it,' demanded Jenny. 'We are going for a drink outside, come on. We can try again tomorrow, but that'll be a total waste of time. So instead, we shall have a bite to eat somewhere, as I want to know more about this lieutenant in Afghanistan. I think he's on your mind more than your wedding preparations.'

Penny didn't argue, almost pleased with the idea of the drink, it might dilute her mixed feelings.

They sat in a trattoria and ordered a spaghetti seafood dish with a bottle of Prosecco. Penny couldn't say much about Max, as there wasn't much to say; moreover, Penny hadn't seen Max since he went to Afghanistan, which was over three months ago. However, she did feel guilty and somewhat disloyal to Graham, having these thoughts for another man.

Penny had met Graham at the hospital; he is a paediatric consultant; and looked down on mere doctors, insisting on being called Mr. Any man would be attracted to Penny; he was no exception. He thought it suited his image to have a gorgeous girl on his arm, albeit an ordinary doctor.

The next day they tried the wedding show again, but nothing stirred Penny who still hadn't made any enquiries at the numerous stands. Jenny thought: *"What a waste of time this is."*

'Come on, Penny, let's get you home. Remember Graham said 3pm, and we mustn't disobey your master.'

Jenny dropped Penny off at her door at 14:40hrs.

Pen walked through the door; Graham had a face that reflected his sullen mood.

'You are cutting it a bit fine aren't you.'

Penny felt like saying: *"Just fuck off, Graham!"*

She didn't of course, just smiled a reply. 'Hello darling, how has your day been? I'm virtually ready to leave; I just need a pee.'

'You're not going in that short skirt, are you? You know how much it will upset mother. You should know what mother thinks of girls in short skirts and low tops; she thinks they are tarts, and for that matter, I agree with her. Can you change please for mother's sake, and hurry, punctuality is my parents byword, as you well know.'

Penny wished she wasn't going and realised how enjoyable it was to have had a day with her sister and laughing like she hadn't done for such a long time. Penny smiled to herself when she thought of the out of control lorry driver on the M4.

.

14

Colonel Abel sent for Maximus. He asked his new captain to continue commanding three platoon for a few more weeks before he could sort out a company for him. Although after some juggling with another jobless captain, the colonel would probably give him B company, thus replacing Smyth.

Three weeks had passed and rumours were circulating the camp that the captured Muzanni had put a price on finding out who planned and carried out the killing of his fighters at Bagram. So naturally, the imprisoned Taliban second in command wanted to know who the treacherous infidel was, the man responsible for killing seventeen martyrs. It wouldn't be long before Muzanni had received Captain Maximus Hainsworth-Catt's name as the British officer responsible. The reward put up for killing the new captain had risen to $75,000.

It was unusual to have a captain lead a platoon, but Max knew number three and regarded them as his own. It was almost an extended family. He met up with Tim Forbes and told him the platoon's orders of the day. 'We are to have three platoon ready to move out with standard rations for three days. We are to escort an Afghan convoy of medical supplies to Kandahar. It's about 500km; we will stop at Ghazni, roughly halfway to allow Afghan transports to collect some additional supplies to take on to Kandahar.'

All the talk in three platoon was about Connolly on the run. The guys were evidently a lot happier now without him skulking around and bullying them.

Connolly was always up to no good. Banter and morale had now increased since the Irishman's demise. The platoon lads had great respect for Max.

The convoy left at 08:30hrs linking up with five trucks full of medical supplies. They had driven about 200km's, nearly an hour from Ghazni.

One Foxhound travelled point; Sergeant Forbes commanded this, code-named Fox-Zulu; at the rear was Fox-Tango, the one Max travelled in, and the third, code-named Fox-Bravo was in the centre of the now increased convoy. The lead vehicle, commanded by Tim Forbes, came through on the satellite phone that was scrambled against unwanted ears. 'Fox-Zulu here, over. Come in Zulu, Tango here, what is it Fox-Zulu, over.'

'Our lookout saw a reflection a couple of times in the lower hills of the mountains to our left; we are specifically watching that area with binoculars. Pass this message on to the captain now. Over and Zulu out.' The radio operator in Tango took the message to Max. After reading the message the captain decided to look out through the observation hatch that doubles as a machine gun position. He scanned the reported area but there was nothing, so he moved away and allowed his lookout to resume his role.

'Keep a sharp eye on your left flank for any movement; if you see anything and I mean anything, tell me at once. In the meantime, corporal, radio call Fox-Bravo, for all riflemen to check their weapons and be ready to stand-to, making sure the men's rifles are loaded with safety catches on. They are to keep them on but at the ready until I stand them down.'

'Yes, sir.'

After another hour of driving, the convoy reached Ghazni. An opportunity for an overdue stretch of the legs. Two lookouts were deployed. A necessary precaution in this hostile district. Both Sergeant Forbes and Max thought they were being watched for quite some time. Max spoke via the interpreter to the Afghan Army CO although he could speak good English. Max asked if there was any insurgent activity around here?

'The Taliban are still smarting over not getting Muzanni freed at Bagram and losing some of their best fighters in the bargain. Our paid informers on the inside tell us the Taliban know who was responsible for their fighters' deaths. The name that has a Fatwah issued, is Lieutenant Hainsworth-Catt. That is you, but you are a captain.'

'Yes, I've just received a promotion.' The interpreter continued.

'Be careful, they seek revenge; you have made them look foolish by duping them. You also have $75,000 on your head; that's a load of money in Afghanistan.

'I'll do my best to be careful, and thanks for the tip-off.' Finally, the translator offered his farewell to Max.

'By the way, I nearly forgot. A lone British soldier was here about a week ago. He said he was on a special covert mission. He took food for about a week, then left.'

'What did he look like.'

'A giant with a red beard!'

'Connolly!' Max cried out on hearing the news.

'Is he one of your men?' The translator inquired.

'He was.'

'I think the loading is completed with the consignment of medicine for your onward journey to Kandahar; good luck and goodbye, sir.' The Afghan officer said his farewell and walked away to the guardhouse to open the gates. With their new urgent cargo loaded, the convoy headed for Kandahar City, another three to four hours drive.

They were still watching the left flank while travelling. The convoy was half an hour from their destination to Kandahar when they entered a mountain pass with steep slopes. The convoy was abruptly halted by a deafening explosion! It shook everyone in the convoy; all vehicles screeched to a stop! The leading foxhound was on its side. Max barked an order to the men to get out of Fox-Tango but stay close to it for protection. Max ran to the middle-armoured carrier, Fox Bravo; he instructed the men in Bravo to do the same as Tango. Max then ran with two chosen men, the convoy's length to the overturned leading vehicle Fox-Zulu. There was a massive crater where the Fox had driven over an IED. (Improvised Explosive Device) By the time they got to it, the men within had crawled out of the wreckage. There were some casualties, but no one was killed, thanks to the new V-shaped designed hull which deflected the bomb's main force.

Max told two of the medics to take the three injured back to Bravo; the others in Zulu, who can, were ordered to stand and form a defensive position. The new captain was worried about rocket launched attacks. Next, Max sent three riflemen forward around a curving outcrop, about fifty metres away, to reconnoitre their way ahead; as it was, they were sitting ducks. Three scouts had almost reached the curve when they received heavy fire by automatic weapons from concealed positions in the foothill slopes of the pass.

The enemy fire was directed at the three exposed riflemen scouting ahead. They were now under heavy fire; Max could see the enemy closing in on his exposed men and realised they were pinned down by rapid machine-gun fire; it was impossible to give the scouts any help from where the convoy was.

'They will be captured and tortured if we don't do something,' Max barked orders. 'Eight riflemen, including Tim Forbes, stay here with me. Corporal go back to the last two Foxes and tell six to come to me. The remaining are to spread out behind the armoured vehicle and fire single-shot in sniper mode at the hillside and mark your targets.' Max shouted to the three scouts to run back as quickly as possible as the Taliban were closing in on them. They responded but the last scout was shot and went down writhing in pain. The other two who were zig-zagging to avoid enemy fire almost made it to the first and overturned Fox-Zulu. They were about ten metres from safety; the second scout took a bullet in the leg and went down instantly. 'Sergeant, get the men to cover me with rapid-fire,' Max ran two paces and dived full length at the injured scout. The captain could see his leg wound was gushing blood. Lying flat Max pulled him, slithering them both towards the cover of the overturned Fox. 'Keep that rapid-firing going men, someone phone through quickly to the rear Fox and tell them to rapid-fire as well. One of you men take Newman from me, put a tourniquet on his leg and do it quickly; he's lost a lot of blood.

I'm going back for Dave Williams; direct your covering fire over there but don't shoot me!' Max pointed to a group of the enemy closing in on the immobile Williams. Captain Hainsworth-Catt ran with his SA80 automatic rifle blazing and bayonet fixed; The officer screamed at Williams to get to him, but Williams couldn't move. Fortunately, Max got to Williams simultaneously with a Taliban fighter. They both momentarily stared at each other; the insurgent dithered in raising his weapon at the captain; that delay probably saved Max's life. However, a lucky misfired shot caught Max in his left arm, just missing the bone. The rookie captain lurched forward, thrusting his bayonet well into the Taliban's neck. A deathly gurgle came from his throat with a mixture of hissing air and spurting blood. He crumpled to his knees, clutching his throat with both hands. Dead.

Max grabbed the injured Williams by his jacket and dragged the screaming soldier to within twenty paces of safety; two more of the insurgents were running at them from behind, angered further by what happened to their comrade. They must have had orders to take the Brit troops alive as Max was sure they could have shot them by now. The captain turned and levelled his automatic weapon at the pursuers; the unfortunate Williams was duly dumped unceremoniously onto the ground. Max fired two bursts of rapid-fire from his hip; cutting down the two pursuing Taliban; they died in the road, their blood now mixing with road dust, forming a brownish paste. Max and his wounded passenger were three metres to safety as six more insurgents took up the chase and got uncomfortably close to their quarry. Sergeant Forbes anticipated the danger to his captain. The sergeant, with six men, ran past Max and Williams. The squad dropped to one knee in synchronised movement and fired, taking the six Taliban out instantly. The much larger enemy group, forty metres back had wisely decided to withdraw from the blanket of well-aimed fire. Max shouted for two medics to take Private Williams to Fox-Tango for medical attention.

Then, still trying to catch his breath, the captain ordered the heavy machine guns onto the observation turrets. The four wheeled drive maintenance truck and a working party pulled the completely damaged Fox-

Zulu out of the road. This now exposed the crater. It was filled with adjacent rocks and sand, fortunately, both in bountiful supply. This engineering task enabled the convoy to progress towards their destination. Max phoned to base and requested helicopter support with air troop-carrying facilities to drop fifty riflemen to the coded coordinates.

'We shall await your arrival but be very quick. Use our rapid response as they will be ready to scramble instantly. Send out a recovery truck and air ambulance with them. We have a knocked-out Foxhound, and with the new tech stuff onboard, we don't want it falling into enemy hands.'

The unmistakable droning, thudding noise got louder and within the hour, three heavy transport choppers landed. Out filed the men of one and two platoons to guard over the sensitive equipment in the incapacitated Foxhound. The returning helicopters took back five wounded, leaving three platoon to carry on with the convoy.

The much-needed supplies were delivered to the grateful garrison at Kandahar. Fortunately, the bullet that hit Max went through the fleshy part of his upper arm just below the shoulder. It was cleaned up, stitched, and his arm put in a sling. They all had a great dinner with their Kandahar hosts, then billeted down for the night, ready to return to base the following morning.

Before retiring to bed, Max sent his report to HQ for the attention of Colonel Abel. It took bloody ages to compile, but accuracy is essential for future intel. His wounded arm was throbbing badly, so he took his own administered anaesthetic in the form of two generous measures of his well-travelled favourite malt, Lochavennie.

Three platoon arrived back in two overcrowded Foxes: Tango and Bravo, the armoured personnel carriers were covered in mud and a thick layer of dust. Max's arm was still in a sling and he was advised to report to sickbay to get the wound re-dressed avoiding possible infection. But first, the captain was to report to his CO, the colonel.

'Maximus, you appear to be having your own private war,' the colonel couldn't help the sarcastic jest. 'can't you keep out of trouble?'

'Funny you should say that sir, a headmaster once asked me the very same question.'

'Did that all really happen the way it was in your report?'

'Yes, sir, exactly.'

'You'll be getting a bravery medal out of this; I'll be bound, of course I will have to debrief Sergeant Forbes to ratify events to satisfy military protocol. Still, after his corroboration, I'll make my dispatches to Winchester HQ. You will feature, sir, with recommendations, sir!' Max humbly replied.

'Just doing my duty, colonel.'

'That sounds like deja vu to me, Max. Didn't you tell me the same thing eight weeks ago, after the siege success? Very well done, Max; you are getting the 1st Rifles a bit of a name back at army headquarters. You took one as well, I see, getting yourself a war wound, eh? Carry on, captain, oh, by the way, you take charge of your very own company next week. You are replacing the ex-Captain Smyth. B company is now yours; congratulations, now carry on. Oh, and off the record, a bit of gossip! Lauren, the man-eater has got caught, this time good and proper by her husband, red-handed; she was in bed with a sergeant and a lance corporal from A company, at the bloody same time! How does that work? She's being flown back to her parents in disgrace. It was only a matter of time, but two men at once? That's what I can't get my head around! Bloody disruptive, the whole sordid mess. Carry on, captain and bloody good show on your convoy. I hope the Taliban don't find out it was you again. I expect the reward for you will rise. You must take care, Max.'

The new captain of B company went to sickbay to get patched up and see how the five injured lads were doing. They were all making a good recovery and out of any danger. Then secretly, Max smuggled them a bottle of scotch under each of their blankets, followed by a cheeky wink and a finger to his lips.

Max mused, wondering how different his life would have been if he'd followed the family's businesses. It would be safer, for sure. Max gave a chuckle at the thought but wouldn't want it any other way.

The captain gave three platoon a day off, and tonight, the beers will be on him in their mess—a little farewell present to his extended platoon family.

It suddenly struck Max: *"Oh shit. I have just remembered that I didn't tell the CO that Connolly had been seen in Ghazni about a week ago."*

Max thought of this significant sighting. He promptly emailed an encrypted communication with this information to the MP's and copied in the colonel.

The following Monday, the new captain called B company onto the parade ground. The company was one hundred and ten men in strength. Of course, his senior platoon will be three. They are now established and battle-hardened veterans with kills under their belts. Max will always be proud of three. Good men. Max introduced himself and promised the men of B company they would be the best in the 1st battalion! The new captain had transformed three platoon, and now he intended to replicate that across the whole of B company. His work will be challenging as the men outside three platoon have had no leadership for some time and apathy had trickled down from Smyth through the NCO's and into the ranks.

15

Penny, somewhat subdued, got into Graham's car and they headed west for his parents home in Cardiff's north district of Lisvane.

After ten minutes of almost silence, Graham finally broke the stand-off.

'I bet you have spent loads of money in London at that wedding exhibition with scatter brain Jenny; I told you not to buy anything without me seeing the items first. It's my wedding as well you know!'

'I didn't buy a thing,' Penny replied in a submissive but almost indifferent manner. 'We just looked round the exhibitors stands but decided to have a meal and a very long chat. I enjoyed Jenny's company very much.' A cheeky smile crossed Penny's face as she devilishly thought: *"I couldn't dare tell him about Jenny stroking her bits in front of a lorry driver."*

Graham happened to glance at Penny and saw the grinning expression on his fiancé's face. 'What is so amusing, I don't think wasting a whole day and night in London is funny.' Another lengthy spell of silence fell upon them.

'You do know we are staying over tonight, don't you?' Graham snapped.

'Yes, Graham, you have told me three times.'

'I'm just popping into Asda to get mother some flowers.' Graham said moodily.

Penny mused, *"I'm not a jealous type, but I don't think Graham has ever bought me flowers, perhaps once, when we first met."*

They pulled into Mill Road, with huge houses on either side; Graham drove through electric gates to his parent's mock Tudor house. Mr and Mrs Price, as usual, were both on the step waiting to greet their son. All four went inside; tea and sandwiches awaited as usual. Mrs Price couldn't wait to start her interrogation.

'Have you named the day yet? Although I thought getting engaged was a little premature and just hope Graham, er, and you, of course, don't regret it. Well, have you?'

'No, not yet.' Pen replied.

'Graham stood up and interjected. 'Actually, mother, we have. It's all booked for two weeks' time; everything is arranged, church, reception venue and the Bands read in both town halls. Just turn up,' Penny couldn't believe what her fiancé had just said. Mrs Price couldn't either, nearly choking on her tea. Before anyone else could speak Graham continued. 'Come on, Penny, let's pop to the Black Griffin for a bar meal to celebrate. I bet you liked my surprise!'

Penny was in shock; She couldn't speak, her brain wouldn't function either. They walked to the Griffin for a bar meal of curry and rice. Graham was still eating when Penny asked. 'How have you organised everything without me knowing or helping? I'm still perplexed.' Penny hadn't touched her food; she couldn't, she felt totally dejected by the earlier shock announcement from Graham.

'I have instructed a wedding planner to do it all. I've paid for everything out of our joint account, but your dad will probably want to reimburse us anyway.'

Penny thought. *"What a bloody cheek, my father can't afford our wedding."*

'I have another surprise for you. I have put a deposit down on a new detached house here in the village. Lisvane is one of Cardiff's nicer suburbs with countryside all around; we'll love it here. I'm getting a transfer to Cardiff University Hospital, and it's only ten minutes drive from Lisvane. If you want to stay in Chepstow hospital, it's easy for you to commute from this village, just down the M4. I will have much better prospects in Cardiff. It's a huge hospital and makes a lot of sense. You can sell your flat in Shirenewton to help with our deposit on the new house as well. The other advantage of living in Lisvane, mother and father can babysit for us, in time, of course.'

Penny felt numb, and negative thoughts would not leave her mind: *"This is insane. What the hell have I got myself into. I should feel happy. This is not right; none of it is."* Penny didn't speak for five minutes. It wasn't petulance, it was utter shock.

'Come on, Penny, I'll show you our plot that I've reserved for us; It's on the Rudry road, five minutes from the Black Griffin.'

'Do your parents know about the house, Graham?'

'Yes, it was them that suggested it, well actually, my mother picked the plot.' Graham hadn't even noticed or perceived the hurt he had caused his fiancé. He was devoid of empathy.

Penny was back at work in Chepstow Hospital; she phoned her parents about the brought forward wedding; they were shocked at the wedding's short notice but pleased for their daughter.

Penny called her twin and told her the news. Jenny, in an alarmed voice, answered. 'I think you are bonkers, but if that's what you want, we must get our skates on. There are only days before your wedding.'

'Sorry, Jen, I only knew myself yesterday at Graham's parent's house. I know it's a damn cheek, but what can I do, Jen?'

'You can tell him to fuck right off, that's what Penny, I hope you don't come to regret this; you know what I think of him!' The sisters agreed to meet up and discuss the wedding plans.

Penny wanted to phone Max; she hadn't emailed or received anything from Max in over three weeks. A friend who bought the local papers told her she had read that three platoon had come under attack transporting urgent medical supplies. There were casualties. Penny was alarmed at the news, and her stomach felt it was in a vice. *"I must see how Max is, I've been a terrible penfriend, but for some unaccountable reason, I am nervous to ring him, but why? I must now find out if he's alright!"* Penny put her thoughts into deeds and made the call she had been mentally avoiding.

'Max, is that you?'

'It certainly is.'

'Sorry to bother you at this time; it's Penny. I've heard through a friend that there was an ambush on an army convoy. Were you involved, and are you alright?' Max replied, still in slight shock that Penny had phoned.

'In short, yes and yes. I am not allowed to discuss it, but all is ok. So much has happened, I have been meaning to ask you something since I first met you at your hospital, but I felt like a nervous schoolboy each time I prepared myself to ask you. First, I wanted to see if you were married or engaged, but you kept your hands in your scrubs all the flipping time. Anyway, after my last skirmish with, let's say, trouble; I vowed to ask you on the next opportunity, so Penny.....'

'Stop, stop, don't ask me a thing, for God's sake, please don't.'

'Pen, whatever is the matter? I haven't asked anything yet; whatever is it, you sound dreadful.' Holding back tears, Penny blurted out. 'I'm getting married in three days, and that's that. Goodbye Max, goodbye.....' Her voice trailed off, and the line went dead.

Penny went for a jog, she had tears falling down her cheeks; she felt confused and kept mulling over in her mind. *"I am marrying a good, honest, hard working medical consultant with excellent prospects, I should be thrilled, yet crazy thoughts keep returning to an army officer somewhere thousands of miles away in Afghanistan. I'm totally mixed up."*

When Penny got back to her apartment, her sister was waiting for her outside in her car. 'Hi sis, I've got a chilled bottle of Spanish Rueda; want to join me for a glass or two.' Jenny could see Penny was back inside herself again.

'Hey, what's the matter, sis? Have you had a tiff with Graham?'

'No, Jen, nothing like that and a very big yes to the white wine; God, I need something, Jenny.'

Penny showered, then curled up in her fluffy dressing gown. Pen took the glass of Rueda from her twin; with the condensation dripping down the side of the cut glass, it looked as good as it tasted. Penny took two whole mouthfuls and relaxed back in her big leather chair, cupping her glass as a comfort thing she didn't want to lose.

Jenny sat opposite her and went straight in. 'Come on, Pen, what's the matter? You look awful.'

'I can't get that soldier out of my mind, and I was so rude to him tonight; I told him I'm getting married in three days, then said goodbye before finishing the call. I put the phone down on Max. I feel so bad; I'm sure he was just about to ask me for a date. Oh, Jen, I'm so

confused and feel damned awful.' Jen thought about
what her twin had said and replied to her sister's
confusion in a decisive manner.

'It's simple, really Penny, do you love Graham?......
Well, do you? Pen, it's a straightforward question.'

'I'm not sure, I suppose I must do really, but he's
so damn controlling. Do you know, he's put a deposit
down on a new house in Cardiff, without even telling
me until he paid the money. Graham is also going to
transfer to Cardiff as well. But what made me really
angry was he's expecting me to sell my lovely flat that
I worked so hard to buy and put the equity from it
towards the house. Bloody cheek.'

'Well, girl, your wedding will be happening soon;
why don't you ask for a postponement?'

'No, I can't, Jen, everything is arranged now.'

'Look, it's a bummer, I know, but it's only a few
grand lost and a few tuts from people you don't even
know; against making a mistake for a lifetime. Pen,
please think about it. All I want is your happiness; you
are a lovely girl and the best sister in the world. You
know I think he's a stuck up prick.' They both looked
at each other and burst out laughing. This chink in the
sombre mood was assisted by chilled wine and had
lightened the mood, if nothing else.

The stag night went ahead in Dublin, the hen night
in Benidorm. In great British tradition, somebody
ordered twelve pink cowgirl hats and T-shirts with
Penny's Hen Party, emblazoned on the front. That went
down great with her friends who evidently had a
memorable time. But who couldn't have fun for one
night in Benidorm, Costa Blanca!

The new B company captain gave instructions to
his three lieutenants to prepare for patrols to Aynac,

southeast of Kabul. He asked three platoon to spearhead the patrol, keeping to the main road from Kabul. One platoon will run parallel, three miles apart on the right of the central force, and two platoon will take the left flank parallel to three platoon.

'We have intel that the village chief in Aynac is being intimidated by some young villagers wanting to join the Taliban. So we need to show some solidarity with a bit of Rifles controlled muscle.'

Ok, gentlemen, be ready to pull out at 08.30hrs tomorrow. We will travel in Fox's'. Three platoons ask the garage for the spare Fox as you busted one of yours.' The other two officers laughed. I will not be going with you because of my arm. However, you will collect your orders from me at 07.30hrs tomorrow; there are a few gifts for the chief as we don't want to lose his support. The balance is very fragile with more and more IS backed Taliban incursions. Carry on, gentlemen, and good luck.' Max got back to his office, where his assistant met him on arrival. 'Sir, I was just coming to find you. A young lady phoned and needs to speak with you. She said it was urgent.

Her name is Jenny Richards.'

'No, not Jenny, it's Penny, but the names do sound the same. Thanks, Paul; where's the number?' The assistant handed a scribbled number to Max.

Max couldn't wait to phone back; he did wonder what Penny wanted him for, seeing that she was getting married in three days.

'Hello, Hi Penny, I'm so glad you called; what the hell was the matter with you the last time we spoke?'

'I'm not Penny; I'm Jenny.'

'Excuse me, but you sound like Penny. Are you winding me up, Penny?'

'No, honestly, I'm Penny's twin sister, really.'

'Oh, sorry Jenny, you sound so much alike.'

'That's where the similarity ends, Pen is beautiful, I'm not, Pen is clever, I'm not, and so it goes on, a mirror twin you see. Anyway, this is not why I want to speak with you. I think my lovely sister is in love with you and she doesn't know it. I spent a lot of time with her recently, when we went to London together and chatted quite a bit. We went to a wedding exhibition in Earls Court, but she just wasn't interested, she didn't even speak with one exhibitor there. I have never seen her so mixed up. It must be you, but she will not admit it to herself or me. I'm telling you, Graham, her fiancé, isn't right for Penny. Graham's a total prick.'

'Pardon me, I don't think I heard that correct.' Max thought he misunderstood what Jenny had just said.

'Oh nothing, just thinking aloud. We have to stop this railroaded wedding Max, do you mind if I call you Max?

'No, not at all, but how in God's name can we stop a wedding, even if I agreed to this mad brain scheme? Penny sounded pretty sure that she planned to marry in three days; she was quite abrupt with me, actually.'

'That's mixed up women for you, I know, I'm one myself. Anyway, I thought if we can get Penny alone with you for just ten minutes and you tell her that you would like to date her; I reckon she would pull out of this mismatched wedding.'

'This is surreal, Jenny; I haven't even asked her for a date. What right have I got to interfere, let alone be part of a wedding sabotage? Another thing, I'm not ready for marriage for some time, if ever, I'm too undecided. The Army is my career; it's no good being the girlfriend of a soldier; being apart from her bloke for so long just isn't fair on any relationship.'

'Will you help, yes or no?'

'Jenny, you are bonkers, obviously caring, and I can clearly see the love you have for your sister but I can't just leave my responsibilities here in Afghanistan; we are fighting a terrorist war. So sorry, no, I can't. Would I want to get to know your sister? I would say, big time. When I met her, I couldn't get my words out, only to bail out of asking to see her. The most I could muster was asking her to be my pen friend.'

'That's a pity you didn't, anyway; who has pen friends these days?' Jenny enquired surprisingly.

'Soldiers abroad and prisoners in jail, that's who. But look Jenny, it's wrong to interfere with your sister's wedding; nobody is making her do it.'

'Ok, Max, I'm sorry, I just thought you were the only way to stop this dreadful mistake. But unfortunately, I think I will have to put on a brave face. Thanks anyway, Max, and I'm sorry to have troubled you?'

Goodbye, Max.'

'Goodbye, Jenny.'

"Well, that's the end of that then. Pity I certainly had the hots for Dr Penny, Richards!" Finally, Max allowed reality to bring him back to his senses.

Mrs Price, Graham's mother, was not particularly looking forward to her son marrying Penny, believing she was unworthy of her perfect son. She eventually had to concede to her son's insistence. Hen-pecked Mr Price, Graham's father, sadly didn't get a say in the matter. It was now just two days before the wedding. Mrs Price, who was always out of her bed in the mornings by 07:30hrs but today she was still lying very still at 08.45hrs. Her husband had just returned from his allotment, where he enjoys peace with his early morning gardening and a respite from his wife's nagging. He opened his front door as he had done a hundred times before and did not forget to take his shoes off. He called out, expecting to see or hear his wife pottering about the house in her normal mode. For once, he didn't get any response and thought she must be out shopping. He went to shower and change, entered their bedroom and gasped! His wife was lying very still. Mr Price tried to wake her. She was still breathing, but it was apparent something was seriously wrong. He dialled the emergency services and asked for an ambulance to come quickly. Mr Price was not confident and did not know how to resuscitate. The ambulance arrived within 10 minutes from the time of the call. Paramedics soon had Mrs Price speeding her way to Cardiff's University Hospital. Mr Price phoned his son Graham, who was actually working at the hospital where his mother was being taken.

Graham went to his mother who was in ICU receiving state of the art attention. His mother had suffered a heart attack. Graham stayed with his father in the adjacent room both waiting for any information about their mother and wife's survival chances. Graham had already phoned Penny. She of course was very concerned, saying she would get over to Cardiff hospital soon as possible. However, Penny had to finish a procedure that she couldn't just leave.

Mr Price shed tears when the doctor gave him the relieving news. 'Your wife is alive, but we will not know if there is brain damage until she comes round.'

The doctor said they both could go in to see Mrs Price, but she could not speak as she had been heavily sedated. Finally, Penny arrived as father and son entered Mrs Price's cubicle. 'You've taken your time, haven't you, Penny? Where have you been until now? Mother is seriously ill and nearly died.' Graham's tone was aggressive and embarrassed Penny in front of her future father-in-law. 'I am so sorry, but I had a patient at the time of your call, you know, as a doctor, I just couldn't leave in the middle of giving treatment. ' Penny's feasible defence was ignored; Graham brushed past her as if she wasn't there.

Mrs Price had regained consciousness the next day; she could now speak. Although weak and still in a critical condition, it didn't stop her from barking out instructions at her son without impediment. 'You will have to postpone the wedding for at least two months; that's how long it'll be before I can go to functions, the doctor told me so.'

'Of course, mother, that will not be a problem; you, of course, must be there.'

'I must,' she snapped. 'so get on with it and tell your father not to forget to put the wheelie bin out tomorrow morning. That's all; I must rest, goodbye Graham.'

Graham phoned Penny and explained the situation about his mother and the necessity to postpone the wedding for two months. So, Penny had no alternative but to agree to the new arrangements dictated by her future mother-in-law.

With Mrs Price fully recovered all the postponed wedding plans were reorganised by the wedding planner.

The marriage between Penny and Graham was about to get underway.

Soon Penny will be Dr Richards at work and Penny Price to her friends.

Penny's stress that morning was like any bride, panic stations! Hair and makeup routine, trying to organise everybody and everything. Jenny came to assist, trying to calm her twin. 'You know, little sis, it's still not too late to change your mind, even now! Do you really want this?'

'Jenny, come on, give it a rest now. In a couple of hours, I will be married, and you will have Graham as a brother-in-law.'

Jenny said under her breath sarcastically, *"I can't fucking wait. Oh joy"*

'I'll be all right, Jen, I promise.'

'Penny, I have a confession to make. Just before your first wedding date, after you had spoken to Max, I tried one last effort to stop you from marrying Graham. I spoke with Max.'

'How so? Did he ring you? Did he mention me?' Penny quizzed Jen, forcefully.

'I phoned him and we spoke about you; I can't remember word for word, it was two months ago. He wasn't too pleased you were getting married.'

'Really, did he actually say that, Jenny?'

Jenny now felt very guilty playing mind games with Penny on her wedding morning but she hadn't changed her opinion of the pompous Graham. It was too late now anyway!

The ceremony began, getting to the vital part, the agreement to marry. Jen prayed under her breath:

"Say no, say no."

Before Penny answered, there was a long pause, total silence in the church, eerily even the babies present stopped crying..........

'I do!'

Penny's sentence, not marriage, had just begun as far as Jen was concerned. *"I do hope she will be happy."* But Jen wasn't too sure Pen would be. She thought of Max and what might have been. As instructed by Graham, the wedding planner organised the reception without any expense spared. He sent the planners invoice of twenty-one thousand pounds on to Brian Richards, Penny's father, without Penny's knowledge. Brian was an ordinary working bloke, not wealthy; however, he withdrew the twenty-one thousand from his pension ISA without hesitation or complaint. Penny was unaware of this. If Jenny had found out about the bill her dad had just paid, she would have gone ballistic at Graham. It was her father's only retirement fund!

Penny chatted to Jenny and a couple of old uni friends, enjoying an impromptu nostalgic reunion. Until that is, Graham shouted across the marquee to his new wife. 'Come on, Penny, that's enough chatter with your friends. You must speak with my family; come on now, this minute.'

'Coming, darling, I'm just finishing off a conversation.'

'No, you've been long enough.' Barked Graham. Penny excused herself and scuttled off to her husband of only two hours.

'Where have you been, Penny? My Uncle Rhys is waiting to meet you. Rhys, this is Penny, my wife. I'm off to the bar to have a drink with my best man!'

Uncle Rhys and Penny shook hands; he kept her occupied with a conversation about his passion for model railways. Poor Penny couldn't get away and rapidly lost the will to live. Mrs Price, ironically saved Penny from Rhys's little trains and interrupted her brother. 'Run along, Rhys; I want to talk to Graham's wife.'

'Well, dear, I do hope you will be a good and proper wife to my son. We are all very proud of him, you know. He's never been any problem to us. He's going to be a paediatric consultant at the Cardiff University Hospital. We are so pleased he has bought a property in Lisvane; he'll be just down the road from us when you move. Graham told me he's selling your flat in Shirenewton to help pay for the one in Cardiff.

That's such a good idea, and it will be less mortgage.' Mrs Price was at her pontificating best.

'I haven't thought about selling it and Graham hasn't consulted me.' Penny retorted.

'It's for the best, dear; Graham always knows what is favourable. You are so lucky my son chose you.' The condescension oozed from Pen's new mother-in-law.

'If you will excuse me, Mrs Price, I need to find Graham.' The groom was still at the free bar arranged by Graham and kindly paid for by Brian Richards.

'Please go steady darling, you've had quite a bit to drink today; come and dance with me. Graham snapped back at his wife of fewer than three hours.

'Don't tell me what to do; Dave and I haven't started yet. Leave us alone, you and I have got years together arguing, now go away woman.'

Penny felt so dejected and very sad. Jenny had been watching her sister. She fetched two white wines from *"Brian's bar."* and told her twin sister to follow her outside to have a drink, just themselves. 'What's the matter Penny?'

'I don't know. It is not how I dreamt my wedding was going to be. Where's the sparkle, the magic and the feeling of love? Graham has been so nasty even on our wedding day.'

'Too late now, Penny, you will have to make the best of it; something about making your bed springs to mind, I'm genuinely sad to say.'

Penny put her wine on the bench table and hugged her sister. 'What have I done, Jenny?'

The bride and groom were staying overnight at the venue, courtesy of her dad, Brian.

It had gone 01:00hrs before the last guests departed.

Finally, Graham left the closing bar, but he grabbed a bottle as the bar shutters came down. The groom didn't speak in the honeymoon suite. He was, yet again, pissed off with Penny over something trivial.

'Graham, for heaven's sake, what is the matter now? What have I done this time? Why are you sulking?' There was despair in Penny's voice. Graham sneered at his wife.

'I was looking for you, and you should be there at my side, not skulking off outside with that fucking stupid twin of yours?'

'Jenny is not stupid Graham, what are you doing?'

'What does it fucking look like you silly little bitch? I'm finishing off the bottle of malt that Dave and I started at the bar. If you don't like it, fuck off to another room.' There was staring aggression on the face of Graham.

'I think I will, goodnight.' Penny went into the suite's adjoining room, collecting a spare duvet from the cupboard. Dr Richards curled up on the sofa and sobbed aloud. A sentiment she couldn't control.

In deep sleep and still dressed in the outfit she had worn to her sister's wedding, Jenny Price was flat out on her bed. Admittedly she had one too many at the wedding. Jen stirred momentarily, disturbed by a sound, she thought. She woke up freezing, so she rolled the duvet around her and laid back down. The noise repeated louder and more frequent. *"What; who......someone's trying to get in; no, it's someone at the door."* She got up and went to the door. Her duvet was now used as her dressing gown trailing behind her. 'Alright, alright, I'm coming; who is it?'

'Jenny, it's me, Pen!'

Jenny opened the door shielding her eyes from the light. It was her twin sister with an unrecognisable face! It was very swollen on one side, bloodstained, and both eyes were closed to slits. 'Oh my God Penny, who did this to you? Come in quick and I'll call an ambulance; I think you need one.'

'No Jen, I've checked myself over; I have no broken bones or need stitches. Can I stay here with you?'

'As long as forever, dear sis! Fuck sake, how did this happen?'

'Graham lost it; he had finished off his final bottle of whisky after we went up to our room. Fortunately, earlier he asked me to leave our bedroom, which I did gladly, I didn't want some drunk abusing me until he fell asleep in a stupor, so I made my bed up in the living room. After half an hour, Graham crashed through the door in an uncontrolled rage. He punched me so many times while I was lying down and still crying; the beating didn't stop. It seemed to go on for ages. The blood that was streaming from me must have shocked him. The psycho repeatedly said, 'What have I done.'

I couldn't stay with him for my safety, so I got a taxi here. Even the cabbie wanted to take me to A&E for a check-up; I explained that I was a doctor. So here I am. I'm so sorry to put on you like this.'

'God sakes Pen, wait until I see that cowardly bastard! I'll swing for him as God is my witness. The jumped-up prick; what did I tell you.'

'Ooooh, Jen, that hurts.'

'Just cleaning the wounds, Pen. I'll make us a hot chocolate, and you can take two paracetamols, then sleep in my bed upstairs until you are well enough to go back to your flat. We'll decide what to do after breakfast. Get up whenever you want; it's already Sunday. I'm so sorry for you Pen, you don't deserve this. Nobody does. I could kill that bastard Graham for doing this to you. Don't go entering any beauty contests for a few weeks, Penny. Have you seen the state of your once beautiful face?'

The following day the sisters had breakfast and needed to decide what to do. Penny could only just about see from one slit, her other eye had closed over completely. She decided it was probably best to get checked over for any concussion or internal bleeding. But first she discussed what she would do for the immediate future.

'Jenny, I'm divorcing Graham; the marriage was not consummated as I didn't have intercourse, I didn't get a bloody chance, he beat the crap out of me. I'm going back to my flat in Shirenewton. He can stick his new Redrow house in Lisvane up his arse.'

'Pen, seriously, you should go to the police, also take out an injunction against him, in case he tries to attack you again. He's fucking mental; anyone who does that to a woman has to be. You can stay here, of course, but it's up to you. I know you like your independence; that's why I couldn't understand you marrying that control freak.'

'Thanks Jenny; I have always been able to rely on you since we were kids. I will make a formal complaint to the police; it makes sense to seek an injunction. You should have seen him, Jen. He was possessed; he really lost it.'

'No matter now Pen, it's all over and if you ask me, I reckon it's for the best. Anyway, you will not require a divorce. You can go for an annulment, providing you have not had sex after you were married, and clearly, you didn't. So officially, you have never been married.

You can go and date Max now, brilliant; I prayed for this, but not this way. Even though I reckon it was worth a beating to make you see sense.' That lightened the sombre mood a tad.

Penny went to Chepstow police station where she knew the officers through their many visits to her nearby hospital. She filed a charge, made the statement and asked for an injunction to be taken out against Graham Price. The police took many photos of Penny's face and bruising. They tracked him down at his parents in Cardiff, where he was staying. He, of course, gave a totally different story about their wedding night. The police cautioned him and took a statement from him. His mother fainted. She had never seen such a scene in all of her middle class, sheltered life. Her husband was also in shock but couldn't believe his perfect Graham could be capable of such violence. 'Both me and my wife didn't much care for Penny Richards; she must have provoked our son.'

He said this to the wrong officers who knew Pen very well; they didn't answer but showed contempt for his comments. After handcuffing Graham Price, they took him, kicking and screaming to Chepstow nick. He spent the night in police custody. The virgin bridegroom was charged with grievous bodily harm and bailed by his solicitor. The police retained his passport.

Four months had now passed since the aborted marriage. Penny had gone back to work, fully recovered, with her outstanding beauty restored to its glowing finest. She thought she would resume her pen pal commitment to the now Captain Hainsworth-Catt. Again the nervous tension returned in her stomach as she tentatively put well-chosen words together.

16

Corporal Terry Dixon was loading up the kit in his transport with another five lads of three platoon as he caught sight of his lifesaving officer, Max. 'Good morning, sir. 'He bellowed from the back of the lorry. As the officer turned to face him, Terry gave an exaggerated salute. After returning the gesture, Max asked the corporal if he was ready to return to wet Wales.

'I sure am, sir; I'm going to walk and run in the rain for bloody miles. I can't wait. Sophie and I are getting married a month after we return. Of course, you are invited sir, will you come, sir?'

'I wouldn't miss it for the world, Terry. Keep out of dark lanes in the meantime, eh Terry!' They both chuckled,

'Yes, sir, I certainly will.'

Max went over to the colonel's office and declared. 'Sir, B company will be ready to move out to the airfield by 14.00hrs tomorrow. Our flight is scheduled for 15.30hrs, sir.

Any requests before we leave, sir?

'Yes Max, sit down. I've some life-changing news for you,' Colonel Laurence Abel went across to his decanter and poured two large ones of malt, handing one to his captain, who stared at the very generous measure wondering for the life of him what the hell this was all about. 'Drink some laddie; you'll need it,' Max was now even more apprehensive. 'You are now Captain Maximus Hainsworth-Catt VC. Son, you are now the holder of the Victoria Cross, the highest, most prestigious award for valour in the military. I am so proud of you and what you have achieved for your battalion and the famous Rifles Regiment.' They both had another large gulp. The colonel pumped Max's hand vigorously up and down. Max couldn't believe it; a VC, his thoughts escaped momentarily to his grandfather Granville Hainsworth-Catt VC. The colonel was talking, but Max couldn't take in what he was saying; it was in a slow-motioned echoed blur. The captain thought and wished Granville was alive to see this; he took another sip and made a secret toast to Granville Hainsworth-Catt VC, SBS. The young captain returned to the real world in an instant. 'Thank you so much, sir; I'm bloody speechless.'

'Well done indeed, Max and no, to answer your question; there's nothing else. Please take this five-hundred pounds and buy your B Company a drink tonight on me; you all deserve it. Carry on Max, damn good show, what.'

It was the last night in Afghanistan, and Max pondered: *"In a way, it will be sad to leave these friendly locals. I just hope they can make a go of their new found democracy. But I fear the Taliban are close to overwhelming that democracy as soon as the last allied troops leave"*

Max will have a few drinks with the lads before leaving them to carry on their serious drinking without an officer's interference. As the colonel had remarked 'they bloody well deserve it.' Max bought the whole company a beer, and good old Sergeant Forbes got on his chair in the crowded mess and called B Company to order. 'Gentlemen of B company, I raise a toast to our brave Captain Maximus Hainsworth-Catt, VC. A big congratulations to him for being awarded this world-famous bravery medal. If anyone disputes the action or says he doesn't deserve it, then I say, sir, you are a liar! I know; I was there and watched his bravery. To our honourable captain, Max-Catt.' Forbes couldn't get out the long hyphenated full name of Max. Funny thing, Max liked his abbreviated name and decided there and then: *"Max-Catt will be the name I will use. So much simpler. So thanks sergeant for inadvertently renaming your captain"* Yes Max could live with the shortened version.

The roar went up to a man. Even Ceri Burns and Tom Palanski were cheering. Before Max left, Ceri apologised to the captain and thanked him for a second chance in three platoon. The incredible night lasted until 03.30hrs leaving a temporary legacy of sore heads, sickness and contentment of a job well done in a hostile environment. Maximus Hainsworth-Catt VC, left with a newly adopted name: Max-Catt VC.

B company arrived at RAF Lyneham in Wiltshire; this was unscheduled as the troops were supposed to land in Brize Norton; some logistical problems had occurred, so they got diverted. Nobody told them why. It didn't matter; in fact, it was geographically better. Lyneham is a lot closer to Beachley barracks and near to the M4. B company climbed into the waiting lorry transports. The armoured vehicles, SUV's and heavy equipment will arrive later tomorrow.

The returning company were soon on the M4. The ETA was about an hour. The convoy looked pretty impressive as it headed west towards the Welsh border and Beachley.

While they were in the air, Max had a few emails suspended owing to no WiFi, but as soon as they were on the M4, Max remembered to turn his mobile data back on; his phone started pinging away like crazy with a backlog of suspended messages.

The captain was in the Land-Rover with his three lieutenants who also had forgotten to turn their phones back on. Max's continual pinging reminded them. There was soon a cacophony of different alerts going off. Max thumbed through his messages on WhatsApp; he had thirty-seven but delayed opening them and went on to his emails; these are reserved for more serious conversation these days. Some from his family, one from Rory. Then Max got excited. *"Oh my God, one from penny.r@penscope.co.uk."* Max's mind raced, he couldn't wait to read it, but he thought—*"Don't get your hopes up, Maxi; she's a married woman by now and probably only writing to a lonely soldier to tell him how happy she was in marital bliss; or to say how sorry she was for being abrupt with me on our last phone chat. But don't guess it read it you chump."* Maximus gave himself a rhetorical nudge.

The young captain did just that, moving his phone away from his junior officers' line of sight; why he did that, he didn't know. It was totally unnecessary as the lieutenants were engrossed in their own accumulated messages.

"Dear Max, I hope you are safe and well. Firstly, I must apologise for the awful way I finished our chat when we last spoke on the phone. I don't know what came over me. I am so sorry; it was entirely out of character.

Anyway, I hope you will forgive me; I intend to continue writing to you and keep you up to pace with local news and gossip.

I won't make this email long as you may prefer not to receive my future correspondence after my rudeness. I would understand. On my part, I hope you allow me to continue with our chats.

How much longer is your tour? Do you know when you might be returning? One of the nurses at

Chepstow hospital is married to a guy in 1st Rifles, and she thinks you return in about a week.

> *Anyway, keep well and don't get hurt.*
> *Kind regards*
> *Penny."*

Max read the email twice and thought hard about its contents.

"What was that all about?" Max mused as he read it another time: *"It was very apologetic and somewhat mysterious—no mention of how she's enjoying married life or even where she is living. But, more importantly, why is she still bothering writing to me. Unless Jenny, her caring sister, told her to, out of pity for me."* Max's thoughts were banging away about the contents of Penny's email. He couldn't work it out. Anyway, he was pleased to be back in the UK and couldn't wait for his two-week leave that starts this coming weekend. He might even get a chance to get up to London and watch his team, Chelsea, play Tottenham at the Bridge. Max converted his best pal Rory to the Blues when they were at Carrow. He is an ardent supporter who loves watching the games and is now a season ticket holder. Max will see if Rory can get some tickets, reminiscing about meeting his pal on Fulham Road an hour before kick-off.

B company arrived back at Beachley with the rain pouring down. There was no surprise about that; however, the feeling of homecoming with the expected inclement weather was so good. To feel the rain with a cold wind biting, added to the freshness on their faces, was what they had missed for eight hot months. Yes, to a man, they were pleased to be back! Max only had a day before his two weeks leave became due. He unpacked his military kit in his quarters, showered and prepared for the main gear to arrive. As captain of B company, Max had to check in all the equipment under his control once it had returned. The next day the kit arrived; it was all present and correct. Max signed the list off. And that was about it military-wise before Max commenced his well-earned rest. The captain would not want to hear another word about soldiering for two weeks.

Max caught the train from Newport to Paddington, London; then on to Crawley. Marshall, the family chauffeur, was waiting to meet Max at the station with great enthusiasm. Travelling back in the family's Rolls seemed light-years from the squalor and filth of Afghanistan. Marshall enquired. 'Do I call you captain now?'

'You had better not; I'm still Max.'

'It's so good to have you safely home, Maximus. Your parents can't wait to see you. We were all so worried when we heard the news coming out of Afghanistan; it was in the papers and the national TV. The media reported how your regiment saved many civilians in a siege. The other big story was your platoon also got ambushed on the way to Kandahar. Were you involved with either of those incidents?'

'I certainly was Mick, up to my bloody neck.'

'I am glad you remembered to call me Mick; thanks for that.'

'Funny that. A great sergeant, Tim Forbes, couldn't get his tongue around Maximus Hainsworth-Catt, and accidentally, while making a speech to B company he referred to me as Max-Catt. This seemed to stick with many of the lads, so I am told. So, if you are Mick, I'm now Max-Catt. Deal?'

'I like the sound of that. It's undoubtedly easier on the tongue.' The two gave each other a cheeky smile.

The Rolls pulled up at the front door of Brandscombe, of course to the good old traditional reception committee, and they were all present. In good micky-taking form, they all saluted in jest as Max got out of the car in a joking acknowledgement of his recent promotion to captain. Max turned and walked the greeting line mimicking an inspection; he straightened his father's tie, told his mum to stand correctly to attention and for Pippa to put her shoulders back. Max bawled when he got to Archie, who lived in his wellies. 'You are a disgrace, sir; you look as if you have just come from farm duty.' The family laughed and the individual hugging commenced with the whole family, including of course, Mrs Cooper and Jarvis. They all went inside to enjoy Mrs Cooper's famous cake and to drink several pots of tea. Max was made to tell his intrepid adventures. The family listened with no interruption from them.

They, as one would expect, fired questions at Max once he had finished speaking. Chris was so proud of his youngest son being awarded the Victoria Cross. 'Two VC's now in three generations of Hainsworth-Catts! Christopher beamed.

Max's parents decided to celebrate their son's twenty-third birthday, combining it with his welcome home celebration. It was arranged for the following week. They expressly asked Max if he could take his leave to coincide with his birthday and to celebrate his VC and safe return as well. They were caring, proud parents but did not need any excuse to put on a good bash. They loved nothing more than people around Brandscombe having fun; that indeed is when the grand old house is at its finest.

Max scanned his old bedroom, it never changes; even his Peter Rabbit sits weirdly on the shelf dividing the books on the military and Bruce Lee. The young captain lay on his bed which happens to be his best thinking posture and thought: *"I had better write back to Penny; otherwise she will think I've taken offence."* So Max went to his writing desk and typed an email to Dr Penny who? He didn't know her married name! So Dr Penny Richards will have to suffice.

"Dear Penny, thank you for your email although I was astonished to receive it. I thought you might still be wrapped up in wedded bliss. I must put you right on one point, however. Our regiment already has returned to Chepstow three days ago.

I was at Beachley for one day sorting out our returning kit but now I'm back at my parents' home in Surrey for two weeks. How did the wedding go? Did Jenny behave herself? I hope the sun shone for Dr Penny Richards on her special day.

I wish that your life is full of joy. Graham Price is a fortunate man and I will finish on that note. I need to unpack my kit, and I want to enjoy the cold rain by taking my quad for a ride in the good old English mud.

Now I'm in the UK for the foreseeable future I don't require news from home, so I suppose this really is goodbye. Thank you, Penny, for thinking of me while in Afghanistan for those eight months. I did appreciate your emails from home. I so looked forward to receiving them from you. Take care of yourself and have the happy life you deserve.

My Warmest thoughts and regards always.

Max."

The young captain wondered if Penny would reply. But then supposed it didn't much matter now as she's married and Max will be a distant pass to her. So the young officer decided Penny was now a chapter finished in his book of life and most probably for good.

Archie asked his brother Max, if he'd like a ride on the quads around the estate. It was strange riding past Rose Cottage; it gave Max an eerie feeling and brought back macabre thoughts. 'It was terrible what happened on that dreadful day in that cottage; the place will never be the same. I'll always have the image of our uncle and aunt's vacant look with neat bullet holes in their faces and lying together like an opened tin of sardines.' Max physically shuddered.

'I pass here most days and I know what you mean. It was terrible how they were murdered. However, I can't grieve for Thomas or Samantha, knowing what they did to our sister Pippa. It was a despicable crime against his own niece.

He got his comeuppance in the end, that's for sure.' Archie mused philosophically.

'He surely did Archie. On a more pleasant note, congratulations on your engagement to Charlie; I'm pleased for you, she's such a genuine lady.'

'Thanks, Max. Now come on, tell me about how you won a VC, it's still hard to believe; an incredible achievement. I'm so proud of you, little brother.'

'Archie situations like that just happen, a spur of the moment decision; I didn't plan it. You can't; it's spontaneous. The whole thing was bloody mad when I think of it. All I did was go on autopilot. I didn't think, I went out and dragged a comrade from my platoon to safety. You would have done it, Archie, I know! Anyway, I am to receive my medal from a member of the royal family no less. So, a trip to *"Buck House"* is on the cards.'

'You say that so modestly, Max, the whole household is elated. My own little brother, a VC. It's hard to believe considering how young you are.'

I'm not that young Archie; I have been in the Rifles three years now.'

Charlotte is coming over for your twenty-third bash, do you have a girl as your escort?' Archie quizzed his brother.

'Yes, of course, a bloody Taliban girl I brought back in my kit bag! No, seriously, I have just got back from the arse-end of the world two days ago. But you mustn't worry about me, bruv, I'm good, really.'

They took the quads over the course that they made as kids. 'I have turned our old quad track into a full cross-country course with water plungers and unusual obstacles. We will market quad hire and adventure, off-roading and all that stuff; it surprised me the amount of corporate enquiries we've had. I might introduce paintballing a bit later in the year as well.' Max thought Archie was improving the Brandscombe Manor business beyond recognition. Max quipped as they turned for home. 'Paint-balling eh, just my cup of tea, although our bullets are for real.' The brothers considered that thought. They finished their ride and returned to the manor in time for dinner.

Max met his sister in the drawing-room; he asked her how the launch of her new magazine had gone. Enthusiastically she explained. 'As you know Max, I launched the new title before you went to Afghanistan. The Single Lady is a smash hit, claiming the second spot in magazine sales and in its first year! We are all delighted, especially as it was my first personal marketing project. The other mags are doing fine, but they need revamping somewhat; this will undoubtedly upset some of the older established readers, but I guess we need to keep changing with new fads and the times. I hope to pay dad his investment back in about another year; although we do need to expand our presses, we can barely cope with the increased circulation.'

'Dad will not mind waiting a bit longer for his investment, he's not struggling for a few quid, but I do understand why you want to pay him back. Dad has always taught us not to borrow or look for handouts.' Max reassured his sister.

'Pity dad's brother didn't have the same standards and principles; if he had, I would still have all my toes!'

Pippa shuddered, just thinking of what Thomas's thugs had put her through. Her younger brother changed the subject immediately.

'I hear you have a new boyfriend; who's the lucky chap?'

'His name is Miles Barclay; he works in Canary Wharf as a merchant banker. He is in Grand Cayman regularly, I asked him to join me for your big birthday bash. Do you mind Max?'

'Not at all Pip, I must say I wasn't expecting a big party though.'

'You know mum and dad, anything for their blue-eyed boy,' Pippa mocked teasingly. 'You have made me and all the family so proud with what you did in Afghanistan. I know you play it down, but you can't fool us; they don't give out VC's like tax demands. We're all so relieved you are home safe now. Please look after yourself; we couldn't bear it if you got.......well you know, just keep safe and let someone else have the chance of being the hero.' Max choked a little and realised then the importance of family love.

'Thanks, Pippa, come here and give me a big sisterly hug.'

17

Dr Penny Richards was sleeping soundly in bed at her flat in Shirenewton. She stirred subconsciously, turning over not really knowing if she had heard something. It didn't get a second thought as she turned over to continue her sleep. Not quite returned to full slumber, Penny raised her head to concentrate on another slight disturbance. Silence! She thought it must be the wind so didn't give it much attention. Penny glanced with unfocused eyes at her bedside alarm clock displaying in big electronic, but blurred red numerals: 03:20hrs. Penny sighed, turned over and pulled her duvet up around her face, settling back into slumber once more. The young doctor was startled again, this time by the unmistakable sound of the handle on her bedroom door turning in front of her now fully focussed vision. Penny pulled her duvet tighter around her body as if it gave her protection. She was scared as she watched the handle turn to its extremity. She froze as the door opened very slowly. Simultaneously, Penny screamed out at the top of her voice. A figure of a well-built man in the half-light edged through the door towards her. 'Get out; I have called the police! What do you want?'

The intruder turned on the light and to Penny's shock and horror, it was the last person she expected or wanted in her room. It was Graham!

Penny's mind was now racing; she tried to shield her eyes from the blinding light. Penny didn't know what was happening or why this dangerous man was here, in her bedroom.

'What the hell do you want?' she screamed at the intruder who she knew well and for that reason Penny was panicking. He still didn't speak a word but inched ever closer. 'You can't be here; you have an injunction against you not to come within a mile of my property or place of work.' Penny felt her words were inadequate and weak against this psychotic man.

'What the hell are you doing here? How dare you break into my home and frighten the life out of me. Get out at once; I never want to see you again, you are just one mad controlling freak, and when your trial is finished you will be put in prison, where you belong. Your hospital suspension was the correct decision because I do not think you are stable and fit for your job. You really do need treatment, now get out and leave me alone. Get out now.' Penny screamed with panic and terror in her voice. She had been on the wrong end of Graham's psychopathic aggression and had the photos of her bruising to proof it. Graham totally ignored Penny's demands by choice or perhaps mental block!

Graham had an evil look on his face that scared Penny. In a threatening, trembling voice he yelled. 'You have ruined my life, you bitch; I am a top paediatric consultant, just about to start a new exciting job in Cardiff.

You never did deserve me; my parents were both correct. They didn't like you from the start. They thought you were a slut with your ridiculous short mini skirts and low cut tops. They warned me that you were not good enough for me, their successful son, but I gave you a chance and you blew it! Anyway bitch, I have come to warn you unless you go to the police and tell them you want to withdraw your original statement as it is untruthful. That you fabricated the whole story about our wedding night, you must tell the police that your injuries were self-inflicted and you caused these to make it look as if I hit you. If you miss anything out I will return and kill you. Are you clear on that? I have nothing to lose, live or die, my life is over, so I will take your life with me. I will get you for screwing up my life; it was all your fault. I wish I had never set eyes on you. Fucking bitch.'

Graham moved closer to Penny; she retreated as far back in her bed as possible, with her body pressing hard against the headboard.

He put his large hands around her neck and snarled, squeezing in ever tightening grip in pulses, demonstrating his control. 'I could snap your scrawny neck like a twig here and now.'

Penny was gasping for air while trying to pull his hands away from around her throat. They didn't budge; he was in total control of whether she lived or died at that very moment!

'I will give you two days to make that statement otherwise, I will be back, don't think I will not finish you off. I will get you! Tell the police you changed your mind about marriage, that you had met somebody else, that you thought by making it look like I'd beaten you up, you could, as you did, get our marriage annulled. I want a copy of your signed statement to that effect and authenticated by the police. Suppose you tell the police about tonight, I will say I have a key and came here to collect my things and left. If you don't make that statement you will always be looking over your shoulder because you will be a victim of a malicious murder one night; you will not know how or when, but be sure I will do it and take pleasure in it. With my forensic experience, I know how not to leave evidence. Remember all that I told you, Dr Richards, forty-eight hours, live or die, easy choice to make. They can't keep me in jail for too long. If you don't do what I have told you I promise you are dead, got that. Dead!'

Graham smacked the defenceless doctor with a back-hander to her face being careful enough not to bruise her this time. He was still cursing as he left the apartment. He kept the key. Penny was in a state of shock; her eyes were red, and her cheek swollen from the slap by Graham. Total uncertainty as to what to do crept in. The hapless doctor didn't know if she should even tell Jenny or anyone? The only person she could discuss things with was her sister. Jen would go berserk, so Penny wondered if she ought to involve her again for her sister's safety. Penny had seen the aggressive side of Graham before, but not as bad as this psychopathic performance. Penny's head was telling her to go to the police and make the statement that Graham demanded. Finally, Penny convinced herself to tell the police it was stressful at her wedding and she didn't know why she had framed Graham. At least doing that would be better than living in fear of a mental psychopath on the loose. Penny thought that action was probably her best option, indeed the safest. Penny knew it was wrong to change her original statement, but she didn't want to live in fear of Graham, especially with him out on bail. Penny eventually made her mind up. She would withdraw the original and make a new statement with the content Graham demanded.

That morning Penny called into work to say she had to attend to something important. The hospital manager had cover for that morning and told his young doctor to come in for the afternoon shift or when she could make it. Penny then drove to Chepstow police station.

Dr Richards wanted to see the same detective constable she saw at the original interview after the complaint about Graham. The same friendly officer who went to Cardiff to arrest him. He was kind and understanding, and she knew him in passing. But unfortunately, she had to accept seeing a younger officer; Penny thought he looked like he'd just left school; perhaps he had. 'Come with me, madam,' The young officer beckoned, 'we shall go to interview room number two. It's the best; unfortunately, the other one has vomit all over the floor from last night. Sorry about that. It's the drunks. Take a seat, so what can we do for you madam?'

Penny sat upright, cleared her throat and in an assertive voice said, 'I want to amend a formal statement.'

'Oh right, I'll have to go and get the correct forms. I won't be a minute.'

By the time the officer returned, Penny had gone!

Penny was sitting in her car trembling; she composed herself and phoned Jenny.

'Hi Pen, you don't call during your work time, what's the matter?'

'Jen, can I see you tonight? It's urgent?'

'Penny, you sound awful. Where are you?'

'I'm in my car outside Chepstow police station.'

'What in heavens name is the matter, have you been hurt in any way? Please wait a sec, Pen, I'll be right back!.....,' Jenny went into her boss's office and returned to her call: 'I've just squared it with my editor; I have booked the rest of the morning off. I'll be right over. Let's meet at the Castle and sit by the river. I'll grab two coffees and see you in about twenty minutes.... .' Penny had no chance of saying no. Jenny had gone.

The twin sisters met by the river, where they arranged. After a quick hug, Jenny was straight into interrogation mode.

'Okay, sister, tell me what is going on; it's that bastard Graham, I'll bet.' Penny, who is normally a practical, clear-thinking person just couldn't contain herself. Penny broke down in uncontrollable loud sobbing. Jenny hugged her sister tight and tried to comfort her. Penny had got the worst of her pent-up emotions out and after blowing her nose and clearing her throat was fully composed.

'Yes, it's Graham! Now when I tell you what has happened, I don't want you going bonkers; I need sound advice, not hysterical revenge, which you are capable of Jen. It's very reassuring having you as a protective sister, but I must make the right choice.'

'Penny, for God's sake girl, tell me what it's all about.'

Penny explained every detail of Graham's intrusion and the death threat; she accounted for pulling out of making a false statement at the police station this morning, just three-quarters of an hour ago.

'He's a bloody psychopath, Penny; we've got to get this sorted. He's bloody dangerous not just to you; he's always given me the creeps. I've never told you this, but it must be evident that Graham and I hate each other with a passion. I'll let you know the reason. About six months ago, I returned a dress I borrowed from you to your apartment. Graham was there. He took the dress from me and offered to make us a coffee, saying he wanted a quick chat. I said yeah, sure and offered to make it. I went to the kitchen and as I poured the hot water into the cups I jumped out of my skin.

Graham was pressing his body right up close behind me pressing his groin against my arse. I couldn't move. He then said and I quote: *"This is nice. I've always fancied having sex with twin sisters."*

I couldn't budge, especially with a boiling kettle in my hand. Finally, I put the kettle down and squeezed round in his grip to face him; he then tried to force a kiss on me.

With a forceful thrust, I kneed him straight in his bollocks. He screamed at me and called me a fucking bitch. I ran out as quick as I could.'

'Jenny, for heaven's sake, why didn't you tell me about this before I married the tosser?'

'I tried several times by dropping hints, but before you met Max, you were so loved up I couldn't shatter your dreams. After what he has just done to you, I just had to tell you, so you make the right decision now. He's bloody mental Pen. Graham should be locked up. I think he will always carry a vendetta against you, so we need to think this through; what is certain Pen you can't take the wrap for his crime. We have to think of another way. Please leave it with me for a couple of hours as I need to think seriously about this! In the meantime, we will go back to your apartment, grab your overnight bag and then you can stay with me until we sort this out. I know we only have forty-eight hours to do so, and yes, I do think he's serious!'

'Jen, there was one other thing I wanted to ask you. I opened an email from Max this morning, saying he's back at Beachley Barracks. That's not unusual, but a nurse at the hospital said the battalion was coming home in a week; sorry, that wasn't the point. He asked in his email if you behaved yourself at my wedding reception, how does he know you and what you are like? I know you have heard about him because I've told you about him wanting a pen friend whilst he was in Afghanistan, but you have never met him, have you?'

Jenny stuttered her reply.

' Not exactly, although I have spoken to him!'

'What, how Jenny?'

'Just before your wedding and after we chatted about him, I thought you seemed different; I mean, you were upbeat, happy and so enthusiastic when you were discussing him. So.....well er, I phoned him in Afghanistan and asked him to try and see you before it was too late. I told him Graham was bad news, that I wasn't happy with you marrying the wanker. He said he couldn't possibly interfere, and it wouldn't be fair on you; apparently you were pretty offish with him the last time you both spoke and even put the phone down on him.'

'All this going on behind my back, hatching plans, discussing me without my knowledge, it would have been nice to have known what you were up to, Jen, surely I had a say. Is there anything else I should know?'

'Penny, I'm so sorry, I did try to get you to postpone your wedding when you told me, but Graham quickly arranged it. It was all for your sake, what I did. I was in such a pickle over what to do to stop you, but you were adamant about the marriage. I panicked as it was only a matter of days before your wedding, so I took a punt on ringing Max. I'm sorry

Pen, I shouldn't have involved Max, it wasn't fair on him or you, I suppose. I am genuinely sorry, sis.'

'I can see you were trying to help me Jen; I'm just so frightened of what's going to happen. I shouldn't have got you into this.'

'Of course, you should; that's what we twin sisters do, ain't it girl?'

'Thanks Jenny.' Penny welled up, allowing Jenny to put her arms around her.

After collecting some personal gear from her flat, Dr Richards went back to her hospital. As soon as

Penny had left, Jenny was already hatching another plan. 'Hi, is that Max?'

'Yes, who's that?'

'It's Jenny Richards. Penny's sister.'

Good afternoon Jenny, the last time we spoke, you were very persuasive in trying to get me to become a wedding wrecker.'

'It's a little more serious now Max; Penny tells me you're back in the UK at the moment. So where are you?'

'At my parents, just outside Croydon. Why?'

'It's a long story, but in short, we need your help.'

Jenny explained the whole story of the wedding, the beating, the annulment and the latest threat to kill Penny if she didn't clear Graham's name by taking the blame. He's making her change her statement to police stating she fabricated the Graham attack.

'He's given her forty-eight hours to sign the new statement clearing him or he will kill Pen. The time is up tomorrow night.'

Max asked surprisingly.

'So Penny isn't married, as it was made void, what a bloody coward this Graham is, hurting and threatening a lady. Has Penny changed her statement to the police?'

'No, but she did get as far as the police station, then got cold feet at the last moment.

'Jenny, tell Pen not to do anything; I'll borrow my brother's car and drive to Chepstow; it will only take a couple of hours drive; what is the address I can meet you at.'

'We both live in Shirenewton, a village just outside Chepstow. Come to 27a Bryn Glas Rd, Shirenewton. You have my number, Max.'

'Yes Jenny, I'll be with you in about three hours, say around 14:30hrs. I'll see you later, bye.'

Max made good time getting to Jenny's place; he pulled up outside number twenty-seven, half an hour earlier than his predicted time.

It was a maisonette, and Max pushed the buzzer of 27a. Jenny answered and Max replied.

'It's Max.'

'Hi Max, come on up; I've buzzed you in.'

Jenny gave Max a continental peck on each cheek, saying. 'It's good to put a face to a voice. I didn't expect you to look like you do.

I can see why my Pen likes you, Mr Hunk.'

'Does she? I didn't get that impression the last time we spoke, although I suppose she did have her wedding on her mind. So where is Pen now?'

'She's at the hospital working, but I've asked her to stay here tonight with me for safety.'

'Yes, about that. I've given it some thought while driving here. We need to catch Graham red-handed. So, therefore, I'm thinking about a trap of some kind. Assuming he will go back to Pen's apartment tomorrow night to see if she has signed his required statement, if he does, I will need to record him somehow, repeating his threat to Pen. I intend to be there, providing Penny allows me. Can we go to look over her flat, do you have a key to it Jen?'

'Yes, we can go now. Do you want a coffee first?'

'No, let's get to Penny's, perhaps have one there. I do need a pee, though. Can I use your toilet?'

Yes, of course, second door on the right.'

They entered Penny's flat, and Max quickly went through her two-bedroom apartment while Jen made coffee. Unfortunately, there was nowhere to hide apart from the wardrobe in the main room. It will mean tomorrow night Penny will have to stay up and watch TV or, better still, read in her living room as the TV might drown out any recording Max intended to make. Max has an HSM listening device that he collected from Beachley. It was intended for covert work to use against Connolly. As it turned out it wasn't required, thanks to Sergeant Forbes's intervention.

After coffee, Max looked for a place to hide. The only realistic hideout was the deep pantry cupboard in the kitchen and he decided that would be his hiding spot after setting up the listening device in the lounge. The HSM mini recorder is the size of a 50p piece, and it will easily fit the sofa's underside just behind one of the front legs and out of sight. It is activated and controlled by a mobile phone.

Max went into the store cupboard to test it, getting Jen to speak in a moderate voice. He replayed it; Jenny's test voice came over loud and clear. If Graham Price turns up, it will record all the conversation.

Jenny phoned her sister and asked what time she would get home. Penny thought within the hour. Jenny and Max decided to wait.

There was the rattling of keys at the front door. Penny came into the living room.

'Good gracious, Max! What on earth are you doing here?'

'I'm here with your sister. I'm here to try and help you. Take your coat off and have a seat; Jen will make us a cup of tea while I explain to you my plan.'

Still bemused, Penny said she would like a shower first, she was a little flustered after seeing Max. Jen made some tea. While waiting for Penny, Max explored the pantry to try it out for size; he removed three shelves and brackets for more space. Thankfully it was about two and a half metre's deep. *"I will need something for me to hide behind."* He thought.

They all sat down in the living room. Max activated his listening device for another live test rehearsal.

Penny said, 'I still can't believe you are here; how much has Jenny told you?'

'Jenny rang me very concerned for your safety; she didn't know what to do.

You were right not to give a false statement to the police; that's a definite. It was brutal what Graham has done to you. I think your sister was right when she called him a psychopath, and if you are okay with the plan, we shall execute it tomorrow night.'

Jenny asked. 'What are you planning to do, Max?'

'Firstly, I think you both should sleep here tonight rather than at the safer place of yours, Jenny. If Pen is not here and Graham turns up tonight, he might get suspicious; who knows what he might try and do. So, what I suggest is tonight you sleep here in the spare bedroom Jenny.

I'll sleep behind the sofa in my sleeping bag; it goes everywhere with me. We will need to pull the couch out from the wall to make room, but it will keep me out of sight if we have an unwanted intruder. Although I don't think he will show tonight, I'll protect you both if he does so don't worry. The object is to nail him, and to do that, we require evidence of Graham threatening to kill you. Tomorrow night, assuming he doesn't turn up here tonight, I'll need you, Penny, to stay up reading a book in here. When he arrives, he'll probably ask you if you have given the police a statement that clears him. I want you to say that you went to the police but panicked and didn't tell them anything, then ask him in a frightened voice, *"Would you really kill me, Graham, if I don't sign the statement?"*

Hopefully, he will say he would and at that point, you agree to go to the police the following day and promise to sign the statement. Ask him what he wants you to tell the police and, hopefully, we'll record what he says. Threatening murder is a severe offence if proven. What do you think, Penny?'

'I don't like it; it's not fair involving you and Jen. Graham hates Jenny so much.'

'Jenny will not be here tomorrow night for her safety and for the plan to work. We really need to do this, Penny, and if we get the recorded proof, on top of charges already against him, he'll go to prison for many years.'

'Yes, I'll do it! I don't like it but understand it's the only way.'

Max replied positively 'Come on, you two, cheer up, let's see if our recording has worked as well as it did with you earlier, Jen.' The bug repeated word for word perfectly.

'Do you have any large boxes or something that can screen me tomorrow night in the pantry?

'I have four tea chests in the garage.' Penny replied.

'That'll do, Pen, and I will need something to give them a purpose and weight. I will stand behind them out of sight. I doubt he'll look in the cupboard, but one never knows. That's it then girls, now who's for a Chinese, I saw one driving through Chepstow.'

Jenny squealed. 'Oh yes, all this excitement has got me famished.'

'I wish I could be as relaxed as you two.' Sighed Penny.

They had a good dinner at the Chinese and returned reasonably early to Penny's, finishing off the evening with a brandy nightcap and retired to their separate beds. Max's was cramped but cosy behind the sofa.

The Rifles captain left early the following day and went to Beachley as he had nothing better to do. He didn't want to be seen at Penny's; the sisters went to work as usual with some understandable trepidation for what lay ahead.

Max popped his head into the CO's office. With a surprised look on his face, the colonel asked. 'Max, you aren't supposed to be here; you are on leave.'

'Good morning, sir, I had to go to see someone in Chepstow, so I thought I'd pop in.'

'Glad you did, Max, I needed to speak to you. The regiment wants to put on a dinner in your honour. However, you know the saying, there's no such thing as a free lunch, well they want you to do the after-dinner speaking; as the guest of honour about the now famous siege and how you won your VC.'

'I don't like those sorts of evenings, sir, with respect, of course. But, if it's good for the 1st battalion, I obviously will. Can I invite three platoon?'

'I'll see what I can do. There's a lot of dignitaries going but leave it with me, Max. I hope that's not blackmailing!'

'Of course not, sir, but the platoon deserves a good night out. Is everything here okay, sir?'

'Yes, we have all our kit back without too much confusion.'

'I'll say goodbye then, sir; I'm picking up a few personal belongings and then getting off.'

'Bye, Max.'

Max went back to Penny's place. The doctor had given Max a key to let himself into her apartment; firstly, he fetched the four tea chests from the garage and put them one on top of the other in the hiding cupboard. The captain put stones inside each one to give them stability; Max then went into his hiding place, all felt good behind the tea chest cover; he activated the recorder on the listening device to see if the signal still worked from behind the chests. It did; Max put the TV on, it recorded perfectly, after which he reset the device. After that, Max felt as ready as he could for Mr Graham Price, a man he hadn't even met but didn't much like. Max thought it prudent to stay in the house in case of the prying eyes of Graham. He could be watching the apartment for a possible trap.

Max watched TV for a couple of hours then decided to call home; Christopher asked his son what he was doing on leave in Chepstow; Max explained he was spending a couple of days with a friend but didn't say what he was up to. The captain made himself lunch, very exotic beans on toast, then went back to the television with a tray. Before today, Max hadn't realised how poor daytime television was; with his patience exhausted from low budget chat and game shows. Finally, Max turned to his written report, obligatory for returning company commanders from overseas tours—adding the finishing touches before sending it off to his CO at Beachley.

It was 5.45hrs when Penny came through her door. Max went to greet her and duly offered to make some tea. Penny responded.

'I think tonight, Max, I'll have a glass of wine, if you don't mind; there's a couple of different ones in the fridge, you select.'

Max poured her and himself one; they sat down on the kitchen bar stools, after chinking glasses Max, toasted. 'Here's to tonight!'

Penny asked. 'Don't you think we should call in the police.?

'Graham sounds too cunning to involve them. He would probably claim entrapment or something. Better we stick to our plan; I've prepared the pantry but remember, Penny, I'll not let anything happen to you, I promise. Just keep to our rehearsed script.'

'Okay, Max, I do trust you.'

'Good. That's settled then.'

'Max, would you like some dinner? I've only got fish fingers and chips or mash. I can't even offer beans with it as I see you've had them for lunch.'

Max thought to himself, *"What a bloody gorgeous lady with a perfect body and such a pretty face, don't mess it up this time as you did when you first met her— bloody pen friend, what must she have thought of me.?"*

Max kept that rhetorical thought firmly in his mind over dinner; both diners attempted light, pleasant conversation. However, the atmosphere was full of tension in anticipation of the forthcoming events later tonight. Penny stuck all the crockery in the dishwasher to hide evidence that two people had eaten here tonight. Penny left one wine glass out. Max retired to his pantry hide, and Penny got stuck into her book, although hard to concentrate, as she was subconsciously listening for any sound, her ears had pricked up more than once over the last few hours. Penny hadn't realised she had finished a whole bottle of wine until having drained the last drop into her glass. She was conscious of repeatedly reading the same lines in her book over and over. She would generally be feeling sleepy at this time of the night but the tension she felt negated the relaxed requirement for slumber.

Max had a couple of old cushions to sit on and propped himself up against the back wall of the pantry hide; he started to doze off when a tap on the door startled the military man into alertness. A soft, whispered voice spoke. 'Max, do you need any water or anything?'

'No thanks, Penny, but from now on, don't move from the sofa or speak. Just read your book and if he comes, try and keep to our rehearsed script if you can. I am here, don't worry.'

Max's bottom was beginning to ache with cramp; A tall bloke stuck in a narrow pantry cupboard is not recommended for too long.

It was 00:50hrs. *"We must give it another hour at least. I'm bursting for a pee but dare not move. Sod's law Graham will bowl up, Max thought wisely."*

There was a definite noise, Max held his breath; the silence in the flat was broken. Max turned on the listening device to the record-setting and watched the seconds of the recording increase past twenty. He knew it was recording every sound in the lounge. A distinctive male voice got louder quickly, and Max could hear all he was saying at this volume level. Then, Graham delivered a scathing barrage of threatening insults.

'You fucking, useless slut. I told you what I would do if you didn't make that statement.' Then it went quiet, as Max could hear Penny crying, but strangely, it was a relief, as he knew she was still physically okay.

'Are you alone here bitch? I don't trust you!'

Max had just moved from around the boxes to inside the door to be quicker for intervention. But, instead, he heard a door open along the hall, Graham had left the lounge; Max darted back behind his tea chest cover and held his breath. Graham went into the guest bedroom then the door to that room slammed. Footsteps were now receding; he's checking out Penny's bedroom; moments later, Pen's bedroom door slammed shut, the footsteps approached, this time getting decidedly louder to where Max was hiding.

The door to the cupboard opened, letting light swarm in. Max's eyes adjusted to the illumination in seconds, holding his breath as he felt the boxes being poked and pushed with an object. It seemed an eternity before he left, leaving the door ajar. Max didn't move a muscle. He was pleased about putting the tea chests in place with weights after Graham's prodding. Graham had left the kitchen and returned to Penny. The young officer could hear them very clearly now. Once more, Max moved to the door, allowing a view into the kitchen through the gap Graham had left.

'Why have you got that knife?' Penny's voice was raised intentionally,

obviously sending a warning message to Max. Graham was armed. He ignored Penny's question, and in a threatening voice, he warned Penny again. 'I told you what I'd do to you if you didn't make that statement to the police to clear me.' Penny kept to the rehearsed script.

'I panicked, I got to the police station, I had a panic attack and couldn't do it. You wouldn't really kill me if I didn't clear you; you were joking, Graham, right?' Her ex-husband had rising aggression in his voice when he replied.

'I haven't brought this knife for fun, you stupid cow; you have one last chance to sign that statement. If you don't by 10:00hrs tomorrow, I'll slit that pretty throat of yours. I will be parked outside the station tomorrow to make sure you do it. If you don't, there will be no more chances. Do you understand?'

'Yes, I will sign tomorrow, I will!'

Graham moved towards Penny, pushing the knife close to her neck.

'God sake Graham, what are you doing.....?'

Take your skirt and blouse off now! I want what was owed to me on our aborted wedding night. Now do it, pushing the knife into Penny's flesh; with his other hand, he tore at Penny's blouse, leaving her exposed from above the waist. He lunged at her pushing her backwards onto the sofa; his strong hands ripped her skirt off, making it easy for what Graham had in mind for the resisting Penny, with one hand he tugged at her very skimpy pants that offered no resistance. Penny was kicking and pushing at her attacker, but it did no good; he was too strong and was getting his way, now he had removed Penny's bra while still holding the knife dangerously close to her throat, but that was as far as he got. With a solid muscular grip around Graham's neck, he was pulled backwards off Penny in one violent movement and onto the floor; instinctively, Graham lunged at Max with an outstretched arm, the sharp blade swished across Max's face, scoring a slash into Max's cheek. David Chinn's tuition came into immediate effect with a stunningly fast reaction; the army captain had secured the wrist of the knife hand and twisted it with mighty strength and impeccable timing that unbalanced Graham. It gave Max a perfect chance to hit him straight between his eyes, followed up instantly with a left, right and another right that pulverised Graham's body. The would-be rapist was laid out and left whimpering on the floor. Max calmly and softly spoke. 'Go and get dressed, Penny. Are you alright?' Max placed the tablecloth around the still trembling and half-naked Dr Richards. She hurried off to her bedroom to dress.

Max couldn't resist another flurry of kicks to the coward's ribs as he whimpered lying on the floor cowering at the feet of Max and begging him not to hurt him further. Two more hard kicks to his rib cage will keep Mr Graham Price in pain for the next few weeks. Probably with broken ribs being the prognosis. He bound Penny's attacker's hands with duct tape and phoned the police. Graham was arrested and taken to Chepstow nick.

Both Penny and Max made statements. According to Dr Penny Richards, Max's bleeding face will need a few sutures. The forensic guys snapped away, the knife, Max's cut face, the messed-up room caused by the beating of Graham and both Max's and Graham's blood on the carpet, gave the police crime scene bods lots to photo and samples to collect in their little plastic phials. You can't argue with a doctor, so Penny drove Max to her hospital and stitched his face for him. All very bizarre, Max thought, *"Husband of six hours gets marriage annulled, returns, tries to rape his ex-wife, and ex-wife stitches up rescuer. You couldn't make it up."*

After being at the hospital, Max went back with Penny to her apartment and crashed out in Penny's spare room on Penny's insistence, after Max offered to sleep in his brother's car. Max was too tired and stiff to argue. It was also nearly daybreak.

Jenny phoned at 08:00hrs to see how the previous night unfolded. Penny explained the whole business. She was delighted that the scumbag Graham was now behind bars and almost certainly would not be allowed bail. Penny had already explained that she wouldn't be at work, the manager understood and advised her to have a few days off owing to the circumstances. Penny was now wide awake from her sister's call; she popped to the local store for breakfast provisions for her sleeping guest.

Penny made Max a substantial full English; they discussed the previous night's events. She expressed her gratitude. 'I don't know how to thank you, Max.

You risked your life against an armed and mental nutcase, thank you so much.'

'Well, actually, Pen, there is something you can do for me. Would you come to my twenty-third birthday party, as my guest? Jenny is also invited. I would love you both to come!'

'Most definitely Max, I was hoping that after the termination of me being your pen pal, it wasn't going to be the end of our acquaintance. Jenny will love it. Give me your address, and I'll book Jen and me a room in a nearby hotel.'

'You will not. You will be staying at my parent's place, we have a spare room, and you, Penny, will be my escort and special guest. I insist.'

'What about Jennifer?'

'Jen will stay with us as well.'

'If you say so, Max, but please ask your parents first.'

'It'll be fine, but yes, I'll ask them. Do you know Penny, the night at the hospital after the attack on Terry? You were standing explaining Terry's situation, and I selfishly wondered if you were married but you had your hands in your scrub pockets all the time, so I couldn't see a ring on your hand. So I was gutted when Jen told me you were getting married.'

'I'm not just saying this, Max, but after I met you, I was all over the place. Jenny had twin telepathy; she pinpointed you for my strange behaviour. That is why she phoned you to try and get you to intervene in my marriage to Graham. I didn't even know about the wedding until a few weeks before. Graham arranged it all.'

'Well, Pen, all's well that ends well, and you are well rid of that horrid Graham.'

18

Penny confirmed that Jenny would love to come to Max's birthday bash and was excited at the thought. Later that morning, Max said his goodbyes to Pen, then headed back to his ancestral home, to the place he loves to be. Max relaxed, fishing in the Brandscombe lake; someone had told him that there are many big pike and carp there since Archie invested in a restocking programme. Max was pleased it had been successful for him. His brother sells a day permit for £50.00 a rod. Max thought. *"Knowing Archie, he'll charge me, his own brother."* Max gave a grin at the thought. He felt pretty darn good that afternoon, the sun was reflecting off the still lake, he didn't have a care in the world. In the back of his mind he knew the real reason for this extra feel-good feeling. Dr Penny Richards is coming to his birthday party as his escort. A satisfying grin spread over Max's face. He straightened his expression when Mick Marshall, the chauffeur, came up behind him at the lake. It was nice to see him and make idle conversation. He asked Max how Afghanistan was and enquired about the VC. The conversation got around as it always does with Mick, about cars. He told Max his preference was the XJ range of the Jaguar or the Bentley Continental. The chauffeur asked Max what was his favourite? Without a shadow of a doubt, the Porsche 911/996

'That's a lovely car Max, very fast as well, I believe. So that is the one you would buy if you could?'

'Not much chance of that, Mick, but yes, I would.' The topic changed again. 'I hope you are joining me at my birthday party, Mick.'

'Yes, of course, if I'm invited.' Mick knew he was. He always went to Brandscombe functions.

'It goes without saying, Mr Marshall.' The subject changed again.

The chauffeur couldn't wait to tell Max the local news. 'Did you know, Max, those thugs that murdered Thomas and Samantha got twenty years each!'

'Serves them right, Mick, dear Pippa has only nine toes because of those bastards. Still, they will not be bothering anyone for a while, that's for sure.'

'Wow, a bite. Mick, get the landing net over here quick! But the net wasn't required. The fish was a pathetic size, so the little Perch was returned immediately.'

"So much for the big fish my brother introduced", Max thought.

At dinner that evening, Max announced he was bringing two lady guests to his birthday party. That got all the family's attention as they were all waiting for the day Max had female company. Max could tell by some of his father's inquisitive questions that he asked that he was getting worried. He knew from personal experience, homosexuality was rife in public schools. Max was not homophobic and had two good chums who batted for the other side, and they were top mates. However, Max could see the pleasure on his parents face. Archie sarcastically remarked.

'About time Maximus, what's her name?'

'Penny,' Max replied with pride in his voice. That bloody gorgeous girl was accompanying him at his bash.

It was the day before his birthday. Max had arranged to meet the twins at The Red Lion, in the nearby village, the family's local. Max borrowed

Archie's car to meet them. The young VC got double kisses from the twin girls and thought, *"that's a first".* So they had one drink in the pub, after which the girls followed Max back to Brandscombe Manor, through the large black wrought iron double electric gates, up the long gravelled drive to the entrance. Max jumped out and went to Jenny's sports car to open the door and said proudly. 'Ladies, welcome to Brandscombe, my ancestral home.'

Jenny said. 'You are bloody kidding me, shit, this isn't your home Max, no way!' The twins were clearly gobsmacked at the size and splendour of Brandscombe.

'It's been in the Hainsworth-Catt family for a long time Jen. I'll take your bags, come in and meet my family.' Max had to fight off Jarvis. He was desperately trying to wrestle the girl's cases from Max's grip in the most dignified way he could muster. It was a scene out of a comedy sketch. The twins thought it hilarious.

Max took the twins into the drawing-room. Virginia, Christopher and Pippa were waiting, intrigued to meet these ladies. Max introduced them both to his family. Next, Mrs Cooper served tea with, of course, her famous *"Cooper Cake."* Then, finally, Archie arrived and was warmly introduced to the twins. He stared at Penny and stood there as if greeted and transformed by Medusa herself. It was embarrassing but funny, it was evident that Archie was transfixed by Penny's beauty. Archie couldn't take his eyes off her; and luckily Charlotte, Archie's fiancé, was not present.

After the tea, Virginia instructed Max to show Penny and Jennifer to the west wing guest suites; rooms six and seven were allocated

'Mrs Cooper has organised your towels, toiletries and dressing gowns; if you require anything else ladies Mrs Cooper will assist you. I hope you have a pleasant

stay at Brandscombe. You are both very welcome.'
Virginia smiled and left.

Max offered to give them a tour of Brandscombe
in the Land-Rover. It's a massive estate that took them
a good part of two hours to complete. He showed them
the pheasant breeding programme which they enjoyed
seeing the many chicks running about. The sisters loved
the lake and the quad off-roading course; both were
duly impressed. Max explained it was all down to the
marketing skills of his brother Archie. After completing
the tour, they went back so the girls could shower and
unpack. As they entered the hallway, Pippa called
across.

'Maximus, can I have a word?'

'Sure, Pips, what can I do for you.'

'You can stop calling me Pips for a start, dear
brother. I was going to help with some birthday
preparations like greeting guests who arrive tomorrow,
however, I have a conference call at the mag in the
morning, so I'll be a little late arriving. Nevertheless, I
will endeavour to get here as quickly as I can. If you
ladies require anything, either of you, here's my mobile
number, please don't hesitate to call me, but I am sure
Maximus will attend to your every needs.'

Both sisters thanked Pippa then followed Max up
the winding stairs to the first floor and on to the guest
or west wing.

They loved their rooms. Max sat on the bed in
Penny's room. Pen kicked her shoes off. 'I've not been
this relaxed for months. What did your sister call you
downstairs. Maximut?'

Max laughed. 'No, my name is Maximus, but
most call me Max, or I like the new abbreviation. I
heard it at our Afghan B company bash, a speech by

my Sergeant Forbes referred to me, by mistake, I think, Max-Catt as he couldn't get the full version out. It shortened my full name perfectly; actually, I prefer it, you know.'

'Oh, I like Maximus; it sounds very Latin, Roman perhaps, yes a Roman Emperor or Senator,' Penny teased, 'I do like it! That is what I shall call you, Maximus. My sacred Maximus. Should I bow when you enter a room, or even if I leave a room in your presence?' Penny was laughing and jesting at the same time, of course. Max couldn't help mentioning:

'It is so good to see you so happy, Penny, after what you have been through at the hands of that evil beast, Graham Price; you appear to be getting back to the caring Penny I first met. Sorry, I digressed from you laughing at my name.' Penny continued about what to call the young captain.

'I have only ever heard you called Max; you even introduced yourself as that at the hospital where we first met. Maximus is a great name anyway, but you didn't mention you lived in a stately home either, Mr Max-Catt!'

'Would you have believed me if I did? What would you have thought of me if I had? Anyway, you know now, however, I hope you do not think less of me because of it.'

'Not at all, how could I? You are my hero; you saved me the other night, ugh, I shudder at the thought of that despicable man crawling over me.'

'Let's not discuss it again, Penny; thank goodness that chapter in your life has been torn from the *"Penny Book";* you are a most beautiful, kind and what I have been given to understand, a talented doctor.'

'Well, thank you, my sacred emperor.'

They both laughed at her theatricals; Max left her, still chuckling at her own jesting.

Max knocked on Jen's door; she opened it slightly as she was in her dressing gown.

'Settled in alright, Jenny? Find everything you need.'

'Yes, Maximus'. She replied with a smirk on her face.

'Not you as well; go on have a good laugh.'

'Thanks, Max, I've had a lovely shower; the room has a beautiful view over the lake. Five-star accommodation for sure.'

'Aperitifs are served in the drawing-room at 19:30hrs. Bye.

A few family members had already arrived for the party including Max's Aunt Pauline, Uncle Alan, his mum's sister and brother-in-law.

Jenny and Penny were introduced to the ever-increasing guests. Max thought it good of the twins asking Virginia if they could help out.

Virginia explained. 'The outside caterers are organising the food so you two just relax; it's nice of you to ask, though.'

Christopher and Virginia seemed to like the twins but who wouldn't. Max slipped away to the recently erected grand marquee where the festivities are to be held. The caterers had supplied plenty of tables and seating. A stage had been assembled for the Pink Flamingos, a talented and sought-after rock band with great versatility in music, allowing the older folk to boogie as well. The band was backed by a local villager who proficiently ran a disco.

Max inspected the rest of this circus size tent, walking the perimeters outside, allowing him to take in some pure Brandscombe air.

His attention was abruptly switched to a flashy, noisy sports car coming along the drive towards the house; it pulled up at the parking area to the side. A man's figure walked across the entrance with a large backpack over his shoulder. As the person got closer, Max recognised him and shouted. 'Rory, Rory bloody Slater. It's great to see you pal.'

'Hey Max, how are you doing, mi amigo?' Rory walked across to the marquee; after a brief man hug Max showed his best mate the party tent then took Rory's bag; the two long term pals walked up to the house that Rory knew from frequent stopovers. Jarvis was hovering on the step, Max commanded. 'I'll deal with this vagabond, Jarvis, thanks.'

Jarvis, still dithering, suggested taking Rory's bag as Jarvis knew Rory very well from many sleepovers at Brandscombe.

'We'll manage, really, but thanks anyway.' Remarked Rory, respectfully.

'It's good to see you, Mr Jarvis; are you well, sir?'

Rory asked most sincerely.

'Indeed I am Master Slater, thank you.'

Rory and Max had another man hug then followed Jarvis into the house.

'Leave your bag by the stairs, Rory, come into the drawing-room. I want to introduce you to my new friends. They are twins.'

Standing in the far corner the girls were being chatted up by Christopher and Archie, who in turn was getting the evil eye from Charlotte, which Max thought was hilariously funny; the friends strolled across the room. Christopher saw them coming first, waving a welcome to Rory. 'Hi Rory, so good you made it, how is the city? I want to have a chat with you about some investments later when you've settled in.'

Rory shook Christopher's hand returning the greeting.

'It's good to be here again, Christopher; anything I can do to help regarding investments, just ask.' Although Max didn't think Rory could teach his father much regarding investments.

'What I hear from Max, you are setting Canary Wharf alight.' Christopher chuckled, patting Rory on the back. Max butted in!

'Rory, let me introduce you to the lovely twins, Penny and Jenny.'

Rory stood there transfixed for a second at their beauty, especially Penny; he composed himself by shaking their hands. At the same time, Archie and Chris moved away to another group of guests.

Jenny was the first to speak to Max's pal, in a playful manner.

'Hi Rory, how do you do? I'm Jennifer, the nicest of us twins.'

'How do you do? I'm honoured to be in the company of such beautiful ladies.'

Penny followed with her introduction but without the teasing. They tended to stay chatting as a four, mainly due to their similar ages. Inadvertently the four paired up, Rory showing an over-keen interest in Jenny. Max thought. *"You've got your work cut out with that one, Rory lad!"*

It was eight o'clock when family and guests started to drift into dinner. First, Rory discreetly ushered Jenny into the dining room. Then, realising it was free seating, Rory took the initiative and pulled a chair back, inviting Jen to sit; he immediately plopped himself next to her. Max teased Rory.

'I thought you were going to sit next to me, us being best pals. I thought we could catch up, Rory?'

'Umm, we shall catch up later, Max; Jennifer is in the middle of explaining her journalism work for a local paper in Newport.'

'Only teasing dear boy, only teasing; anyway, Penny is so much nicer on the eye than you.'

The group laughed at the friendly insult aimed at Rory. Chris did his hosting bit by welcoming everybody to the dinner and hoped they would be comfortable at Brandscombe. Dinner was served with lots of cross-table chatter and laughter. Max thought, looking around; *"It's Brandscombe Manor at its finest."*

After dinner, the girls, Rory and Max, decided to finish the evening down the Red Lion, about three miles away. Max invited Archie, Charlie and Pippa to join them. With seven of them going, a people carrier taxi was called, and within twenty minutes, they were sat in the pub, enjoying the company of good friends and family.

Max noticed Jenny discreetly handing Rory a slip of paper and thought: *"Bloody hell, Rory is more advanced on the dating stakes than me. I have yet to even ask Penny for a date."*

Rory got up, asked for the drinks order and went to the bar. Pippa, Charlie and the twins went off to the loo. Max said to Archie. 'I am always intrigued why women can't pee solo; do they get group discount?'

Max gave Rory a hand with the drinks, and after two trips to the bar, the drinks order was complete. All the guys were back at the table. The girls were coming through from the lounge into the bar from the ladies' loo when a group of four strapping local lads stepped into the girl's path. One made a big mistake; he pulled back Penny, pinched her bum and sniggered to the others. Max was out of his chair and across to join them, moving between the four blokes and the ladies; Max requested respectfully. 'Back off, lads and leave the ladies alone; they are with me; please go back to the table, ladies!' The girls scuttled back to Archie and Rory. The biggest lad, built like a proverbial brick loo, grabbed Max by the lapels, preparing to administer a Glasgow kiss, to most people a head butt. The attack was telegraphed, he leaned back to launch his head forward towards Max. His pals were egging him on. The massive bull-like shaved head was closing in on Max's face. Thank goodness the young captain's reaction was swifter than his attacking opponent. One step to the side, the attacker went forward with full momentum, his head now bowing at Max about waist height. The young army captain grabbed around his neck with both hands and pulled him, he was still bending and slightly off centre to the right. This positioned him facing Max, who raised his knee with great force. The top of Max's knee met the underside of the thug's nose that split it flat; it was a mess and poured with blood.

The thug's nose must be broken in several places; he was totally out of the affray and out cold on the floor.

Two of the gang backed off, but a smaller, cocky one broke a glass and thrust it at Max's face, as David Chinn had said to Max many times. Big mistake, it's reasonably easy to defend, providing you see it coming and have good timing. Max thought of his old master's words. *"Locate the lunging arm, grab the wrist, at the same time pushing back the arm, out of immediate danger; this now opens the body of your attacker's soft underbelly, take your pick."*

Max found the attack with the most immediate effect to immobilise an attacker is the vee-shaped, two fingers thrust into the attacker's eyes. The job was done in under five seconds. The big guy was bleeding profusely. The two badly injured, moaning lads were assisted out of the bar by their two not so brave mates.

The landlord came over with a smile on his face and declared.

'You didn't even have time to say take it outside; I saw and heard everything; they are a group of thugs from the next village. I'm sorry your ladies were bothered. Please have a drink on the house, and if you want a job here Friday and Saturday nights as a bouncer, you've got the job. By God, you were quick; are you a professional?' Max didn't have time to answer; Rory and Archie were over, asking if all was okay!

Max thanked the landlord for the offer of drinks and said. 'I will another time, sir, thank you; sorry about the broken glass and mess of blood.' The landlord laughed. 'It was worth a lot more than a glass to see them go out with their tails between their legs. They have pushed their weight around in my pub for too long. Is that military training I have just witnessed?'

'No, David Chinn and Pat McCoubrey actually, wonderful people.'

It really was over that quick. They sat back down. Max picked up his pint and enjoyed the contents of his first swallow. The table was in silence, and everybody was gawking at Max. Finally, the captain put his glass back on the table, looked around at his staring audience and said. 'What!'

Archie was the first to speak.

'Hell, Maximus, where on earth did you learn to fight like that?'

'Can we please change the subject? They were just a couple of local knobs who had too much cider.'

Rory, however, wouldn't change the subject and told them the story of the Carrow Abbey school bullies.

'Max fought two school bullies in the Big Ring and even got the teachers watching with interest.'

Penny put in her bit and told her story of the Graham incident. But, of course, it was all very embarrassing for Max.

Pippa, Max's sister made a heartfelt toast.

'To Maximus the gladiator in our midst.'

They all went back to Brandscombe pretty happy

Like always, Rory will be bunking in Max's room. His bed had already been made up by Mrs Cooper, who liked Rory and Rory liked Mrs Cooper's cake, a perfect liaison. The girls went west to guest rooms six and seven. They all said goodnight then went off to bed. Rory and Max chatted into the wee hours, catching up on their lives to date. 'Did you ask Jen for a date earlier?' Max quizzed his pal.

'I asked her for her phone number and if I could meet up with her for dinner.'

'Well done, Rory, but what about Stephanie Symonds? Good God, Rory, you were talking marriage only a few months ago?'

'I still see her; indeed, your dad invited her here, to your birthday bash tomorrow, but she wouldn't come as she was going shopping with her mum. But she's not a patch on Jenny anyway.'

'Steady on, Rory, you only met Jen a few hours ago.'

'Do you think they are talking about us, as we are them, Max?'

Jenny was drinking hot chocolate from the self-catering facility, a kettle and a selection of packet coffees, teas etc., were supplied in the room. Whilst sipping the warming nightcap, with her two hands clasped around it, Jen spoke softly to Penny.

'Do you know Pen, you and Max look beautiful together. Has he asked you out for a date yet?'

'No, Jen, but come on, after all that's happened with blokes and me, I'm not looking for romance just yet. He's a great guy from a lovely family. I am eternally grateful to him for saving me from that animal Graham, but I'm not sure I'm ready; I'm still raw from that wedding fiasco.'

'You can't kid me, Pen, when you first met Maximus; I do love that name, you were like a teenager with her first crush. Don't deny it!'

'Of course, I'm aware of a strange, wonderful even blissful feeling, when I'm in his company.'

Jenny gave her sister a quizzical look and replied understandingly.

'I knew that anyhow Pen, it's lovely to see. You deserve all good things in your life Penny Richards.'

'Jenny, I saw you give your number to Rory; he's definitely got the hots for you, girl. I assume you will develop the relationship if given the opportunity.'

'Of course, Penny, he seems a great guy, and I feel very comfortable with him.' She hugged her hot chocolate closer, feeling very content with life.

'Good for you, Jenny. For the last time, thanks so much for making me see sense in not signing the statement for Graham.' Jenny looked up from her liquid chocolate and gave a comforting wink to her twin.

They said goodnight, and Jenny went off to number six next door and bed.

The following day came quicker than usual, owing to lots of chatting through the night. Rory jumped on Max's bed and ruffled his hair.

Max's reflexes, that he naturally possessed and which had been sharpened in recent months, just about stopped him from belting Rory.

'What the.....Rory, what are you doing? I was in such a deep sleep; I nearly gave you a right-hander.'

'Happy twenty-third birthday, Maxi, Here's a little present for you; I hope you like it.'

It was a waterproof, go-anywhere GPS compass.

'Wow, it's better than British army issue, that's for sure, thanks ever so, Rory.'

They went down for breakfast. Then, over a full English, Max suggested they take four quads out around the estate and over the course, made professionally by contractors that Archie commissioned. Max wanted to try it out as he hadn't been on it since the significant alterations.

The girls and Rory were up for the off-roading suggestion.

'We had better go straight after breakfast as more guests will be arriving for the bash; I best be at the house to meet and greet them later in the day.' So it was decided to finish breakfast, change clothes, then go out on the bikes. Max first cleared it with Archie. 'Max, it's your birthday today. You can do whatever you wish. Take the front four quads; they are all fuelled up and ready to go. Have fun and happy birthday, brother.'

After opening up his cards, Max got a big kiss from Virginia and Pippa, then a bear hug from Christopher. The day was starting early, Max met the twins in the hallway, the girls were togged out all in the estate supplied helmets and back protectors. Max gave a brief lesson on how to ride and what not to do. The track was brilliant; they had fantastic fun laughing at each other's caked on mud. Jenny nearly overturned her quad, going over a steep part of the course. After two hours, they were back in the house and showered. It was arranged to meet up for coffee and a warm by the big inglenook fire at 12:00hrs. More guests started to turn up. First was Max's two pals from Carrow, Johnny

Billings the great try scorer and Liam Roberts. Then, Jeremy Dobbs, the Sark Housemaster, arrived.

The two big surprises that Rory must have organised were the two remarkable characters, Max's mentors Pat McCoubrey and David Chinn. Then an even bigger surprise, Sergeant Tim Forbes, Corporal Terry Dixon and even the gaffer, Lieutenant-Colonel Laurence Abel.

Many more of Max's friends and a smattering of far-flung relatives.

It was getting lively, and Max couldn't comprehend that so many people had made an effort to be at his party.

The twins were getting their party dresses on in their rooms while Max and Rory were idly chatting, waiting for the twins to join them. Then Max thought Rory had seen a ghost. His eyes were staring in disbelief!

'What is it Rory, you look as if you have just seen the Brandscombe ghost.'

A girl got out of a flashy sports car on her own. Rory, who was standing right beside Max, cried out!

'Oh fuck, oh fuck, Max; it's Stephanie! What the hell is she doing here? She's supposed to be shopping with her mum, and I have asked Jenny to be my escort at your bash. Shit, shit. What am I going to do?'

Max saw the funny side of Rory's predicament and couldn't hide his smirk.

'I think, first, you need to decide now who do you want to be with tonight. But, unfortunately, you don't have much time to make that decision; Stephanie is coming our way!'

'Max, what can I do?'

'Make your way to our bedroom. I'll intercept her and take her to the drawing-room; I'll sort some tea and cake out for her. It will give you some breathing space, but that's all. What is for sure, you can't accompany them both tonight if you want to live, that is. I reckon you have twenty minutes to decide which one.'

'Thanks, Max, I'm off.'

'Hello, Stephanie, I'm Rory's friend, Max. I didn't know you were coming to my birthday bash. Rory explained you were going shopping with your mother; I think he said. Anyway, come with me. I'll get you some refreshments.'

'I was going shopping but changed my mind as my mother had one of her migraines, so here I am. I got an official invitation from your parents. That guy with you who just ran off looked like Rory?'

'Umm, yes it was; he's got some pressing decisions to consider.'

Penny and Jenny just happened to be strolling out of the house as Stephanie and Max were walking back to the drawing-room. They were heading straight for each other. Max thought: *"Oh, flipping shit."*

As the four passed, Jenny was the first to speak.

'Hi Max, where's Rory?'

'He has some urgent business to consider right at this moment.'

'I asked him to help me choose my dress for tonight. I have brought two, and I want Rory to pick one for me as he's my escort.'

Stephanie's face went crimson in an instant; Max could see an incident developing and ushered the twins over to the marquee to have a glass of bubbly, then he took Miss Stephanie Symonds's arm, guiding her gently towards the house in the opposite direction. 'Who the hell was that woman. What does she mean Rory is her escort? She can't be referring to my Rory; are there two Rorys' here?'

Max avoided a straight answer and left her with Archie, who was asked by his younger brother to look after Steph for five minutes whilst he fetched Rory.

Max found Rory, where he had instructed him to go, their bedroom; Understandably Rory was pacing the floor with worry and was none the wiser about what to do.

'Max, Steph, shouldn't be here. What the hell can I do? Get me out of this mess, mate!'

'First thing you need to do is answer this and only you can! Who do you prefer? It's simple enough Rory. You have raved about Stephanie for a year now; and only known Jen for twenty-four hours. Yet yesterday, you said Jen was a more pleasant person, and you preferred her. So it's make your mind up time, buddy!' Of course, Rory knew this but facing two women who both think they are his date simultaneously isn't great, and it's a new experience Rory dreads facing. The words woman, hell, fury and scorned were tumbling over in Rory's head and he was the one who was getting the fury. Rory knew this.

'I know, I know but Steph had no right to turn up unexpectedly because her mum had a bloody headache and cancelled shopping. If she had agreed to come with me in the first place, this wouldn't have happened. Would it, Max?'

'Just make up your mind, Rory, and be damn quick about it.'

'I have; I much prefer Jen in so many ways, yes, definitely Jenny.'

Stephanie excused herself from Archie, left the house and found Jenny outside the reception with her sister. Stephanie addressed Jenny and asked in a sad, almost pathetic, submissive manner.

'Can I see you privately for a minute?'

'Whatever is the matter, are you alright?'

Stephanie started to sob quietly.

'I must speak with you about Rory. I heard you say he was going with you to the party tonight but how can he do that, he promised to take me! We were going to announce our engagement at Max's party tonight. He asked me to marry him two weeks ago and I said yes. He phoned me this morning and told me not to come as the party was now changed to a boys only bash.

Please don't tell Rory what I've told you; he's got an awful temper. I don't know why I put up with him, I must love him I suppose.'

Stephanie broke into a full flow of wailing with her face pressed into a tissue. Jenny put her arm around the distraught woman and comforted her.

'I'm so sorry, but I only met him yesterday; he hadn't mentioned you at all.' Jenny felt she had been made to look a fool but sympathised.

'You are not the first; he was involved with a married woman just a month ago, an assistant at his trading office in Canary Wharf. We were supposed to move into a flat together. I've been such a fool. Promise you will not mention this to Rory; he'll go mad, and I've seen him get violent.'

'No, of course not. Don't worry; we know what it's like dealing with a violent man from personal experience, don't we Penny?' Pen nodded in agreement. Jenny comforted Stephanie again and felt shocked, misled, and angry at Rory for hurting Stephanie and deceiving her.

Stephanie excused herself to freshen up as her face paint and mascara had reached her chin.

Jenny made it clear to her sister immediately.

'I'm going home tonight, Penny; if you wish to stay, I would quite understand.'

'Calm yourself, Jen, it would be rude to Mr and Mrs Hainsworth-Catt, by going home now. It's not their fault about Rory. You can ignore him if you wish. It's not compulsory to have an escort. I'll explain to Max that I'll be with you for the evening and he will excuse me, I know. It's not as if you've had a date with Rory, so forget him, Jen. It's no big deal.'

'You are probably right, Pen. Okay, I'll stay, but I'm not speaking to Rory bloody Slater.

'Maximus, you must arrange with Mrs Cooper to make up a room for Stephanie Symonds. Virginia was understandably sorry for her. 'She is, after all, Rory's girlfriend. I know it is difficult, from what you told me, there might be some awkward moments between them, but she was initially invited by me on your say so. As you well know, we do not turn invited guests away. Apart from that, she doesn't look as if she's about to leave anytime soon.'

'I understand that, mother, it would be quite funny if it wasn't so serious. Seeing Rory squirm is quite something. I just hope there isn't going to be a problem tonight.'

Rory tried to explain to Jenny, who responded by brushing him away with total contempt. He thought to himself.

"What a mess; why did Stephanie have to bowl up."

Rory was now lumbered with her for the night, with regret ever since he had met Jenny Richards. Rory was a realist and knew he'd blown it with Jen.'

19

The night party was held in the large marquee; already preparations were underway, the band was setting up with all their paraphernalia. The lighting teams were out in force running around testing the power circuit breakers, microphones and sound systems.

Guests not staying at Brandscombe had facilities to change and freshen up; by 19:00hrs most had finished their preparations and moved in steady groups to the marquee to select their seating. The bar was in full swing.

Guests were already mingling; Max considered it his duty to speak to all his guests, making a big fuss of David and Pat from the gym. The fantastic Mr Dobbs was also given a lot of Max's attention. He had conversations too with the lads from Beachley, it was funny to see a battalion commander rubbing shoulders, having drinks and sharing jokes with a sergeant and corporal; this wouldn't have been possible back at the depot.

Max made sure Penny was okay with her sister. Jen, still had a face that could kill, the sisters made an attractive pair and got the attention of many horny males.

Rory sat with Stephanie until she excused herself to go and powder her nose. 'I will not be long Rory, get me another vodka and orange, would you.'

Rory nodded indifferently and went to the bar, passing Jenny and Penny, who were being pestered by two guys desperately trying to chat the twins up. They were harmless enough but the sisters were well out of their league. Unfortunately, it appeared the men had given the free bar a bit of a hammering.

Rory called across the bar, loud enough to make all four in the conversation turn towards him.

'Jen, can I please see you for just two minutes? I will not bother you again, I promise.'

Jenny excused herself and said to Pen.

'If I see him now I can hopefully get a peaceful evening without him keep bothering me. I shall only be a minute.'

'Well what do you want, Rory?' Jenny sternly inquired.

'Please allow me to explain the situation; I want to date you and get to know you. I so enjoyed our short time together!'

'No Rory, sorry, you have a steady girlfriend and by all accounts, your future is with her, not me! So now leave me alone.'

Stephanie had come out of the loo and made her way back into the marquee. She was biting her lip with pent up anger when she saw Rory talking to Jenny so she yelled at him. 'What are you doing? Have you got my drink that I asked for five minutes ago?'

Jenny turned without acknowledging Stephanie and moved quickly back to Penny, who had, by this time, sent the persistent guys on their way.

Stephanie was fuming at Rory, interrogating him about his conversation with Jenny; the arguing couple luckily found a free table to sit at but no sooner had they sat down, Stephanie continued quizzing her boyfriend about what he said to Jenny and she demanded answers. Stephanie then quickly changed tack from aggression to a softer but still mendacious approach: 'We are a couple going steady, I love you and you know you love me. So what are you doing to me Rory?'

'Steph I don't think I do love you; I think you're a bitch, to be frank! Perhaps meeting Jenny made me realise this. Just leave me alone.' Rory blurted out what he had wanted to say for months, and he now felt pretty good.

'How dare you say that to me, you bastard.'

Rory then got a full vodka, orange and ice rocks straight into his face; Stephanie threw the empty glass on the table and stormed off.

A catering staff member who was no more than sixteen and had horrendous acne spots was bringing a crate of ciders into the marquee. Stephanie stepped across the young worker's path, stopping the juvenile and whispered to the crate carrier.

'Would you like to earn two hundred pounds for five minutes of work tonight?'

The night went according to plan for the hosts, Max's parents. They chatted with Pat and David from the gym; both men explained that their son Max could have turned pro at boxing or even cage fighting. The shocked look on Virginia's face was a picture. 'This must have happened when Max was at Carrow Abbey? Did you know our son was visiting a boxing gym Christopher?' Virginia pressed her husband. Chris shrunk back and, in a defensive stance, made his excuse.

'Yes darling, but not until after he left school. However, I was told he used the skill effectively against the school bully.' Pat, seeing a developing situation, changed the subject quickly by asking about the history of Brandscombe, directing his interest and questions at Virginia. Pat couldn't have picked a better topic. One of Virginia's favourite subjects, she went proudly into her well-rehearsed history lesson about her home, she was just pleased to have an audience to unleash her pent-up enthusiasm.

Max did the Hainsworth-Catt protocol rounds of *"meet and greet"* to all the guests and at the same time introduced the twins. They had just about completed the circuit of friends, comrades and family when the band broke into life. Max pointed to a free table. 'Let's grab that table and have a drink. I'm thirsty and I felt like a royal, shaking hands with all these people; it must have been boring for you twins.'

Jenny replied. 'It's better than being with that two-timing jerk, Rory.' But unfortunately, the mood Jenny was in, Max didn't feel it was the moment to defend his friend who he trusted implicitly.

Archie, Charlotte, Pippa and Miles Barclay joined Max, followed by Johnny Billings and Liam Roberts with their ladies. This allowed Max to introduce his two school friends and rugby teammates, Liam, Johnny and their ladies to the twins.

Rory was itching to join Max's table, but he was still sitting alone until a group of older guests joined him, people he had never met. One slightly drunk younger lady was trying to make small talk with Rory. She was unaccompanied and wanted more conversation and given what she was alluding to, panicked Rory. He thought to himself *"Shit, go away woman, I'm in enough trouble with two vexed women."* Rory could see Jenny discreetly observing his every movement.

Jen, whispered to her sister. 'Look at that jerk; he's chatting up yet another woman while Stephanie is away.'

'Leave it Jenny; he's not worth the time or trouble, I've told you before; unfortunately, he's just one of those types of guys and I don't think they can help themselves. Max overheard this and was forced to defend his best friend.

'That's not fair, you don't know the whole story; I'll try to explain. Rory is not a bad person and is a very reliable friend of mine, one I've trusted for many years; please believe me. Jenny, give him a fair chance to expla.... change the subject quick; Stephanie is coming over!' Max stopped the conversation by a whisker.

'Hi Jenny, I would like to thank you for your support and understanding earlier. May I sit with you for a moment.' Stephanie was charming and very plausible. Everybody shifted up to give Stephanie room to sit next to Jenny. There was an awkward moment of silence but the whole table was intrigued with the new guest's presence. Rory frustratingly looked on with some woman telling him her life story and repeatedly stating how she found him attractive. He wondered what the conniving bitch Stephanie was up to with Jenny.

Back on Max's table, Jenny broke the silence by asking Stephanie.

'Is everything alright now between you and Rory?'

No, not really; I'm afraid he will not change; do you have a hanky please? Jenny passed Stephenie a packet of tissues from her handbag.

'Thank you, Jennifer; I'm sorry it makes me weepy just thinking about how he's treated me. Look, Rory is chatting up another woman as we speak,' Stephanie pointed to where Rory was, still under verbal sexual attack. 'I can't believe it.' All the heads on the table turned in the direction to where Stephanie was pointing. Then the transfixed group turned back as the spotty faced waiter came to the tabled group and asked. 'Could you please pass those empty glasses down; we're running out behind the bar.'

Everybody helped by making a human chain with empties being passed to the waiter's basket. Finally, the glass collector thanked the table and left with a basket full of glasses.

Stephanie apologised for her interruption, gave the packet of tissues back to Jenny then left to return to Rory. The lady bothering Rory had left for the loo, probably to be sick.

'Who was that woman you were with?'

'Some drunken lady being a nuisance. What were you talking to Jenny about? Not that I care too much! I'm still soaked and sticky from your vodka and orange attack.'

The two sat in silence which was apparent to the guests on the same table; an elderly lady rolled her eyes at her companions and exclaimed, 'Young love today, eh'.

The band was excellent; they played while guests chose and collected their buffet dinners. The menu ranged from venison to lobster, with ample other meats and fish as well. As always, Virginia had planned the function with consummate precision.

With the dinner crockery being cleared away, the band took a break. Mr Hainsworth-Catt took the microphone and gave a five-minute speech, thanking the guests for coming, how proud he was of his son becoming one of the youngest VC's in modern times and how Max's grandfather would have been so proud of him if he was still alive. Christopher handed the mic to the battalion commander, Lawrence Abel. The senior officer told the Afghanistan story and how the whole regiment is proud of their latest VC hero Maximus Hainsworth-Catt.

Stephanie made one of her dumb remarks and asked Rory: 'What's a VC when it's at home.'

Rory replied. 'Shush, I'll explain later.'

Finally, Archie got up and said how proud he was to be Max's brother, but kept his felicitations short and got the DJ to strike up the famous happy birthday number. With the ceremonies complete, the band started up for their final session.

Stephanie jumped to her feet in panic! 'Oh my God, oh no! My diamond brooch, it's missing; my grandmother left it to me; it's worth at least twenty thousand pounds, but priceless in sentimental value! Oh my God Rory, do something now!'

'Is it the one you keep on your wrap? Because if so, it probably came undone; don't worry, it will be handed in.' Rory was trying hard to calm the distraught Stephanie.

'I'm sure I had it on the bench seat when I was talking to Jenny Richards; I'll go and ask if anyone on their table has found it.'

Stephanie went across and asked the guests at Max's table if anyone had seen her brooch or handed it in. Everybody automatically looked under their respective seats and the table. Nothing was found and they all confirmed they hadn't seen it; someone at the table suggested Stephanie's lost brooch was probably handed over the bar. Stephanie left the table to ask at the bar.

She found the waiter with the face full of zits and asked him if a diamond brooch had been handed in.

He replied. 'Not here, but I did see a lady with a sparkling brooch in her hand; I'm sure she put it in her handbag. I was collecting glasses from that table at the time.' The waiter pointed to Max's table.

'Would you show me who?' The waiter led Stephanie over to the table; everybody's attention turned towards them standing there. Then the waiter pointed to where Jenny was sitting. 'That's the woman who I saw put a brooch in a handbag; I'm pretty sure I saw that when I collected empties. I thought nothing of it really as I thought the brooch must have been hers; I remember thinking how it sparkled.' Jenny was shocked but retaliated instantly at the accusation.

'How dare you accuse me; it's ridiculous what he's implying; it's lies.'

'Look Jenny, that brooch apart from its twenty thousand value was my grandmothers. So just tip out your bag and let us see the contents.'

'This is totally absurd and I shan't empty my bag; it's an insult, how dare you?' Penny spoke up.

'Jen, keep the peace, prove this crazy woman wrong and empty your handbag.' Jenny reluctantly obeyed Penny's persuasion. Everybody in the table group was waiting to see if Jenny was going to empty her bag.

'Okay, if that's what I have to do to prove myself. So be it.' Jenny was trying to hold back her anger but was failing.

The twin of Penny stood up and, with hyperbolising drama, tipped her handbag's contents onto the table. Out fell a purse, perfume, lipstick, mobile phone, a packet of tissues, sunglasses and car keys but there was no brooch.

'Satisfied.' Jenny sarcastically exclaimed with a contempt expression to match. Then, as Jenny exaggerated the violent shaking of the handbag, making her point a diamond brooch dropped out from a pocket within the bag! It bounced twice on the table and slid off onto the floor.

Stephanie turned and screamed at Jenny. 'You thieving bitch! I said to Rory he should never have trusted you.'

Stephanie picked up her brooch and stormed back to Rory to tell him what had just happened, showing him the stolen item. Rory, who couldn't believe it, replied.

'That can't be so, Jenny wouldn't steal, I haven't known her long, but I would never take her to be a thief.'

'Of course she is, it fell out of her fucking bag, the waiter said he saw her put it in her handbag. How much fucking proof do you want Rory? Get Max to make her leave; otherwise I'm calling the police, now do it.'

Rory hurried across to Max's table and asked to see his pal outside. Jenny was obviously in a state of bewilderment and visibly upset and shocked, not knowing what to do apart from repeating her innocence to her sister.

Outside the marquee Rory was very concerned as he spoke to his friend.

'Max, I'm not that enamoured with Stephanie, but she's distraught over losing her family brooch and then seeing it turn up in Jen's handbag.

Do you think Jenny stole it?'

'No, I don't Rory. I think it's a stitch-up. I didn't think the waiter was telling the truth either.'

Rory was puzzled. 'I don't think Jen would steal either, I said as much to Steph. She wants Jen to leave; otherwise she'll call the police!'

'Life is never straightforward, but I'm not sending the twins home. However, I do have an idea, so please go back and keep Stephanie busy, get her a drink and soft soap her a bit to buy me some time. I'll let you know what I'm up to soon enough. Trust me!'

Max went back into the marquee, passing his table of friends and siblings on his way to the bar. He spoke to the waiter with the acne and asked for his help for a couple of minutes.

'I need your help to bring some vintage wine up from our cellar for our special guests. What is your name?'

'Dean.'

Max thought, *"There's a lad with riveting conversation."*

'Follow me to the house Dean.' The young waiter did what he was asked and followed Max into the hall, they went along the passage to access the long winding stairs down to the Brandscombe cellar. This purpose-built wine storage had brick arched ceilings with flying buttresses forming the change of direction, a labyrinth leading off to more tunnels. Each passage has floor to ceiling honeycombed bottle storage that is hundreds of years old. The modern air conditioning unit's quiet hum played away in the background, working to keep the valuable vintage stock at the perfect temperature of between 10 and 15 degrees centigrade. This ensured no fluctuation from changing air temperature outside. Christopher took his wine seriously.

Max could see young Dean was well impressed with subterranean Brandscombe although he didn't say a word to that effect.

Max waited for the right moment; it came! With two very swift movements, first the birthday captain immobilised the unprepared Dean. There was no worry about noise; the cellar was soundproof and secondly Max applied shock tactics on the spotty faced kid.

'Do you want to leave here alive Dean? Do you want to have a regrettable accident that leaves you dead?' Max, with manic eyes, stared close in the face of his incapacitated victim.

'What are you doing? Don't hurt me; what the hell, please, please, what are you doing to me?'

'Be quiet and listen! You will go home to your parents tonight if you do as I ask. If you don't, I have a selection of alternatives. The first is easy because I snap your neck, and for the second, I would use a plastic bag for sublime suffocation, and the third is a blunt but violent bang to your right temple. All these will give you a quick death. I will then drop your limp body down the thirty metre well shaft to the fast-flowing underground stream; never to be seen again. I think it comes out somewhere in Crawley, miles away. But Dean, I will not give you a choice; I'll decide your fate to suit me. I'll pick the one to cause less suspicion about your death. Did you know I'm a professional in hurting people; I just thought you should know that. I was responsible for seventeen deaths in one afternoon in Afghanistan, so one extra little boy will be irrelevant. Hold that thought. Dean you have dishonoured a good friend of mine by telling a lie. You said you saw her take a brooch and put it into her handbag. You know, and I know that's not true. Correct Dean?'

'I did see it, I did!' The sixteen-year-old had already started to piss his pants, the yellow liquid was trickling down his leg and pooled on the flagstone floor.

'That's a shame, and you have pissed yourself, but that means you are taking me seriously. You need to, Dean. How much did Stephanie Symonds offer you? A hundred pounds, two hundred? Very cheap for your life!'

Max took a black plastic bag from his pocket that he'd collected from the caterers on the way out.

He pulled it over Deans head and reduced its capacity by running his hands down Dean's cheeks, expelling the air like a shrink-wrapped product. Max held it tight around his neck until Dean spluttered in a muffled voice:

'I can't breathe, aaaah, please let me go.'

Still choking, still muffled, he screamed at Max.

'You're fucking mad, man! The woman said it was a joke, a bit of a laugh, that was all. She gave me two hundred pounds.' Max whipped the plastic bag off Dean's head. 'The woman said I must say I saw the other lady putting the brooch in her handbag after she distracted the people's attention at the table. I didn't think what I did was that wrong; I thought it was a bit of a lark, and the two hundred quid would go a long way towards the motorbike I want. I am sorry if I've done wrong.'

'Dean, here's another hundred pounds for telling me the truth. I won't tell your boss either, go and tell her you were asked to help me with some bottles.

Now we shall go back to the party.'

'Thank you, and I am sorry. I can't carry on working in these jeans; they are wet through.'

'Come with me Dean; our Mrs Cooper will sort you out with a clean pair. She has all sizes.

Max entered the marquee, followed by Dean in baggy blue trousers; he went straight back to the bar and faced his boss's wrath for going missing.

Max went straight to Rory's table and asked Stephanie to follow him alone outside the marquee. She thought she was going to be told that Jenny was leaving and how sorry he was that she had her brooch stolen at his birthday party. Steph threw an arrogant smirk at Jenny as she passed her. *"You are on your way bitch"*. So the fabricator of lies thought.

'Stephanie, I've just had a long chat with Dean, the young spotty waiter. He has told me everything about the brooch you planted and how you planned to blame Jenny. The waiter confessed that you bribed him with two hundred pounds for him to say he witnessed Jenny taking your brooch and then putting it into her handbag. Don't make it worse for yourself by denying your devious plan. If you don't want me to call the police, you must go home and get back under the stone you crawled out from. Now go or I'll instruct security to have you thrown out. I have arranged a taxi for you, it'll be here in five minutes. You can collect your car tomorrow; it will be quite safe here. Now go!' Stephanie Symonds didn't go back inside but did unleash a venomous tirade of screaming obscenities at Max, who ignored his verbal attacker and rejoined his table. Max was explaining the brooch stitch-up to his group when a screech of wheels interrupted Max's account of the last thirty minutes. The young VC went to the entrance of the marquee, just in time to see the rear of Stephanie's car disappearing down the drive. *"She's mad to drive with what she has had to drink today, but it just shows the crazy woman's character."* Max thought with justifiable reason.

The young captain returned to his table and told everyone about the recent events. Jenny was relieved that her name was exonerated and asked Max.

'I feel awful now; Stephanie probably lied about Rory as well. Shall I fetch him over to join us, Max?' Max replied with a smile.

'No need Jen, he's coming over now, so offer him a seat next to you.' She did. Jenny explained her behaviour to Rory and asked if he still wanted to see her. He, of course, agreed, and things were right back to normal with the twins and their new boyfriends.

After breakfast Christopher and Virginia asked Max if he enjoyed his party. Virginia enquired why Stephanie had left so abruptly and was given a full explanation by her son. Then, after ten minutes of family chat, Christopher asked Max to join him and Virginia outside.

Max could not believe his eyes. Marshall was driving a sparkling black sports car, a 911/996 Porsche came roaring up to the entrance, not fast, but in sports mode making a throaty engine noise. It caught everybody's attention and attracted a small crowd from the remaining guests who had been mingling outside. Max was amazed at the scene, especially seeing Mick Marshall at the wheel with a massive grin on his face.

'Wow, what a fantastic car. Have you just bought it?' Max asked Christopher as he knew his father loved car racing.

'Yes Max, we have just bought it! Do you like it? We hope you do, it's a birthday present from your mother and me, to you, Maximus, it's yours! Happy birthday, son.'

'What? Wow, you two can't be serious!'

'Give it a spin Max!' The happy parents suggested.

Marshall climbed out and handed Max the fob, saying.

'Max, do you know how fast this beauty is?'

'Yes Marshall 0-60 in 3.68 seconds. Thanks, Marshall.'

He just remembered in time not to call Marshall, Mick, in front of his father. Max gave his parents a big hug with many thanks. Then he went to find Penny.

'Pen fancy a spin in my birthday present?'

'Love to Max, that's a real eye-catcher for sure!'

'A bit like your own self Pen.' Max gave Pen a polite kiss on her cheek.

Rory spent the morning walking the grounds with Jenny; they spread a picnic blanket out by the lake's side and relaxed. Jen poured coffee from a flask and opened a pack of sandwiches prepared by Mrs Cooper.

Jenny spoke softly but sincerely to Rory.

'Rory, I am so, so sorry to have doubted you yesterday. Stephanie said some awful things about you. She then lied through her teeth by accusing me of stealing her diamond brooch. I really should have spoken to you and given you a chance to defend yourself. Thank you for understanding, Rory.'

Jenny lent over and pulled Rory towards her, turning her head under his, inching slowly closer until their lips touched. Rory pulled her more meaningfully to his body and pressed himself into a full embrace. After an extended kiss, they slowly parted. Jenny looked into the smiling face of her new love and teased.

'That was very passionate; I hope you meant how it felt, Rory.'

'I certainly did; pass my coffee Jen; it might help me to cool down, if you know what I mean.'

The budding romantic couple heard the throaty roar of Max's new toy approaching the house but decided to stay and finish their picnic. Penny and Max went into the drawing-room; Mrs Cooper brought in some fresh coffee and wished Max a happy birthday as she'd missed his party, someone had to look after the manor and Mrs Cooper was always ready to step into the breach. Max gave his former nanny a loving hug that embarrassed her, prompting her to hurriedly leave the room. Penny took a sip of the freshly brewed coffee, sitting back in a reclining chair, she closed her eyes and remarked in a contented voice.

'Do you know Max, I haven't felt so relaxed and happy for such a long time? I do believe it's down to you. I seem to be thanking you repeatedly. You took control of that awful situation last night with Stephanie, but tell me, how did you get her to leave so quickly last night?

'Let's just say Pen, a little bit of leaning persuasion on that young, lying glass collector.'

'Jenny was so relieved at your intervention last night. She thinks you are such a wonderful man. Penny put her mug of coffee down, went across to Max and planted a big kiss on his cheek and ruffled his hair. It's so comforting to have a knight in shining armour around. I think I now know what a damsel must have felt like.' They both laughed at her silly throwaway remark.

The guests drifted away from Brandscombe Manor throughout the morning. Rory had to get back to the city but promised to phone Jenny the next day; they parted with a new romantic passion.

Max had to return to his unit at Beachley that evening and spent most of his last free hours with Penny. Virginia organised an afternoon cream tea for the remaining stragglers, including Pippa, Archie, Charlotte, the twins, and Maximus.

Virginia caught Max on his way to the loo.

'Max, where did you find Penny? She is an absolute stunner. Is she a model?

No mum, she is a doctor, but you knew that!'

'I was jesting, although she could easily be one; she's beautiful enough.'

Yes, I think so; she's a lovely person with it.'

After tea, Max walked the twins to their car, carrying the suitcases for the girls. Jenny suggested: 'Why don't you drive back with Max, Pen?'

'What about you, Jen? Surely you don't want to drive back alone?'

Max interjected.

'Ladies, let me intervene here. As much as I would love to have the gorgeous Penny Richards sat alongside me with the wind blowing through her hair, who wouldn't? However, I need to spend a little time; now everybody has left, to talk with my parents. Apart from some son and parents time, I do have a serious matter to discuss.'

Penny responded. 'Quite understandable, Max, no bother, you should spend some time with your folks.'

'Before you leave, Pen, may I ask to see you when we get back to Chepstow?'

'Of course, I have been waiting for you to ask me for the last three days!'

Max kissed Penny on the cheek but with no more intent than he gave her twin, Jenny. He waved at Jenny's car as it disappeared down the gravel drive with two arms waving from the sisters on both sides of the MG.

Max asked to see his parents in the drawing-room on their own.

Christopher wondered what surprise their son was going to spring next.

'What is it Maximus? Your mother and I have been on tenterhooks to know why you want to see us?

Your mum thought you might have got Penny pregnant.

'Christopher please!' Virginia scolded her husband with a look to match.

Max assured his parents with a grin on his face.

'It's nothing to worry about and it hasn't happened yet anyway.'

'What is it, Max?'

'I have been in the 1st battalion, The Rifles, for three years now and have enjoyed my military career hitherto, but I need to push myself further with additional challenges. To that end, my dear parents, I wish to volunteer for the UK Special forces (UKSF).'

Virginia gasped with concern.

'Would that be the SAS or SBS by any chance?' Christopher asked, knowing his son's infatuation with the elite regiment.

'Yes, spot-on, dad, I have to see my battalion colonel and ask permission to apply out of courtesy. You met him yesterday, Colonel Laurence Abel.

Initially, I have to pass a battalion-level physical training course. If they deem me fit, the entire training programme follows. Under ten per cent pass and the training takes six months. Endurance over the Brecon Beacons first and if you get through that, it's jungle tests in Belize or Borneo. Then finally, a trial in the English countryside with obstructions stopping the candidate from getting to the objective target.'

Christopher was amazed at Max's knowledge about the criteria requirements of being accepted.

'I knew of your determination since you were a child. I had a long chat with David Chinn and Patrick about your boxing and err, cage fighting. You kept that quiet, and by the way, who signed your permission to allow you to train at their gym?'

'I did dad, sorry.' Christopher continued.

'Anyway, it's a tough life in the SAS; it's changed a hell of a lot since my father's day in the SBS. Don't be disappointed if you don't get in because you know only a small percentage succeed; it's no disgrace to fail son. It must be damned hard.' Christopher shook his head wistfully.

'You will make us go grey early; please don't take unnecessary risks, son.'

'I won't mother, I will always let you know what I'm doing, well, what I'm allowed to that is. So now let me give you a big family hug for my super birthday bash and for getting me the car of my dreams; thank you both for being the best mum and dad ever.'

Max kissed his mother's cheek and gave his dad another big hug.

Pippa, Archie, Charlotte, and the parents, waved at the dust cloud, allowing Max to disappear behind the smokey veil. They all felt a bit silly though, waving at nothing.

The big marquee that was only a few hours earlier bounced with life and blaring music now looked forlorn in the late evening dewy mist descending over Brandscombe Manor. Only the roosting crows and rooks seemed to be the living things left. They were signing off the last fingers of natural light with their eerie evening squawks before roosting.

Brandscombe closed its eyes again as it had done for hundreds of years before!

20

Max drove up to the gate of Beachley barracks and received a customary salute from the sentry, with the officer returning the courtesy. The guard knew him from his success in the battalion boxing tournament; he couldn't help himself as he operated the barrier. 'Smashing car, Captain!'

'Thank you private; it was a birthday present from my parents'

The sentry thought with a smack of envy. *"Lucky bastard, born to wealthy parents and me with a fucking Fiat 500, where's the justice in life".*

As the captain drove past the military vehicle park, he had a random thought. *"I wonder if they ever repaired the blown-up Fox from the Kandahar convoy ambush".* Max settled into his quarters, unpacked and phoned the CO's office. He spoke with the aide-de-camp for an appointment with Colonel Abel tomorrow at 08:00hrs; that was confirmed.

The captain showered, checked his messages that included a few belated birthday wishes; he did no more but crash out onto his bed.

Max had his breakfast early and made his way to the CO's office; he had a strange nervousness about him. Max felt he was betraying his respected boss, Laurence Abel. The colonel had helped Max so much in his military career hitherto. His CO had pushed through Max's captaincy. So yes, betrayal to the lieutenant-colonel is precisely how Max felt.

The colonel's Aide-de-Camp showed Max straight into the CO's office.

'Sit down, Maximus, a lovely do at Brandscombe, what?'

'I'm glad you came sir, quite a good representation of rank from the Rifles.'

'Yes, good show Max; now what can I do for you, looking at the time, I guess it's urgent, captain?'

'Sir this is very difficult for me, and I had it all worked out what to say as well. But that isn't working out now I'm here. You have always been a supporting commanding officer and a bit more besides, so I will cut to the chase. Sir, I want to volunteer for the special forces. Do I have your permission?' The colonel pressed back in his chair and grimaced.

'Maximus I needn't tell you how hard it is to get into the SAS. During my long military career, I have seen many apply for the special forces, only to be sent back to their regiments—some as broken men. I am fond and indeed proud of you, therefore reluctantly and with a heavy heart, I will endorse your request. I do expect you to succeed as a SF candidate, meaning 1st battalion will lose a good officer. I don't know, but there seems to be a captain's curse on B company. It just can't keep its captains!'

'Thank you so much sir; you have helped my career immensely. I will be eternally grateful.'

The battalion, nay the regiment, doesn't forget its Victoria Cross holders either. A date is fixed for you to address the regiment at a formal dinner and presentation in your honour.

It's next month on the 15th. Full ceremonials, and you really should have a lady escort.' Added the colonel.

'Yes sir, thank you sir, I will look forward to it. Can you try and arrange that three platoon get to the dinner, they deserve it.'

'I'll see what I can do but no promises mind. You will have to do an after-dinner speech for half an hour about your Afghanistan experience, so make notes and don't mumble. There will be representation from headquarters, I hear two generals will be in attendance. They'll put me in the bloody back row I'd imagine. So Max, get yourself down to Samuel Brothers and get measured up for your mess dress clobber and bits for a black tie event.

The outfitters are now in Aldershot. Make a fitting appointment and tell them to put the costs onto my battalion account. The army will pay for this. Good luck to you, Maximus. Carry on.'

'Thank you, sir.'

Max sent for his three platoon lieutenants, instructing them for an entire B company parade this afternoon at 15:00hrs in just fatigues dress.

After this order, Max phoned Chepstow hospital to speak with Penny; she was busy on the ward; the receptionist left a message for her to return his call. Max still had to complete his returns report for the colonel that will take him a couple of hours, so he got straight into it. With the information collated, he must now check out the condition of B company's vehicles and heavy weapons after their tour of duty. Max thought *"Another favourite job of mine, boring but essential."* Max's pragmatism didn't help the tedium.

Max went back to his office, replaying the stock-taking dictation from his phone. A corporal knocked on his officer's door and confirmed that B company was all present and correct on the parade ground, awaiting the captain's attendance.

The company was all present and brought to attention. The company sergeant-major ordered them to stand easy. Then, in a necessary loud voice, Max addressed the company.

'B company, I have become very fond of you over time; I have got to know most of you on a one-to-one basis. You excelled in Afghanistan. I am unbelievably proud of how you conducted your job out there. You have kept the famous light infantry at the forefront of the British army. It is with great sadness therefore, I tell you all, I'm leaving to volunteer for the special forces. I will be applying to the SAS 22 regiment for the next Special Forces Briefing Course (SFBC). It is over a long weekend and these assessment courses run twice a year; I hope to get included for the next available one in two months' time. I will up my physical fitness training in readiness, so don't think I've gone bonkers as a fitness fanatic if you see me in the gym every day. I'll miss you a lot but will never forget you. Thank you gentleman, that is all.'

Sergeant Tim Forbes concluded with an impromptu three cheers for the captain, which put a lump in Max's throat.

The captain returned to his quarters, completed his dictated notes, and then sent them to the CO's office, pleased he'd finished them along with the stock-taking equipment list and condition reports from the tour of Afghanistan. Max thought. *"A captain's lot is never done!"*

There was a return call from the lovely Dr Penny Richards. Max's excitement level rose; he could feel the adrenaline starting to pump around his body; this excitement became a regular occurrence when he was ever about to speak to the exceptional young doctor. 'Good afternoon Pen, so good to hear your voice; how are you and your sister after her wrongful accusation at Brandscombe?'

'All good Maximus, all good, so sorry for not returning your call sooner; we had a bit of a flap, all sorted now.'

'Pen would you like to join me tonight for dinner?'

'Yes please Maximus, where and when?'

'I want to take you to the Boat Inn; do you know it?'

'No Max, although I've heard of it, some of the hospital staff had their Christmas party there.'

'It's a lovely pub on the River Wye in Chepstow. I went there with a couple of officers just before leaving for Afghanistan. They do the best steak and Guinness pie I've ever had. The mussels look good as well; I'm drooling here just thinking of it. Anyway, I'll pick you up at 19:30hrs if that's okay.'

'Shall I ask Jen along?' Pen asked.

'No it will not be a date if you do.'

'Oh, so you are asking me out on a real date?' Penny was teasing Maximus and he knew it.

'Yes Pen, I'm asking you for a real date.'

'Just so long as I know, I only ever see you with lots of people around, it seems.'

'Not tonight Josephine.'

Penny thought that was funny and not like Max's humour.

'I had better get home and prepare myself for my first date with Maximus, my gladiatorial hero. Hail Maximus'

'Leave it out Pen; I'll see you at yours at 19:30hrs!'

A very punctual Max Catt pressed the buzzer bang on seven-thirty. Penny answered and said she was on her way down.

She swung herself into the low sports car. It was a short driving distance from Shirenewton to the Boat Inn on the banks of the Wye. After a civilised sort of kiss and polite greeting, Max gave Penny a little history lesson of the pub they were going to. 'It was built at the start of the French Revolution in 1789 and probably used for smuggling contraband throughout the centuries, ideal for such activity, having access from road and river.'

'You know your local history and you're quite knowledgeable for a non-local.' Penny slipped once more into her teasing mode. Max was not biting this time though. Instead he changed the subject by saying how beautiful he thought his date was. Penny blushed and slid out of the car gazing around the pub car park.

Max couldn't hold back anymore; he didn't say a word but went to Penny who was still at the passenger side of the car. He whispered. 'Forgive me.'

Turning her gently, slowly, but with controlled strength that was hard to resist, Max pulled her into his body and brought his strong hands up to her face, turning it delicately upwards to meet his advancing, towering lips. Then bliss manifested to a most passionate level. This pent-up kiss could only be achieved from a man who had waited months to caress his pin-up sweetheart. But at times most recently, Max didn't think this embrace was ever going to happen.

'Wow Max, do that again, please sir.'

It didn't seem real; she willingly went to him; words were unimportant and unnecessary. Instead, they felt natural passion demonstrated by their physical reaction. It was clear they wanted to make love to each other there and then on the bonnet of the 911, a most natural progression from what they had both just experienced together.

The busy pub car park probably stopped the ultimate culmination; Max, embarrassed by the bulge that had developed naturally in his trousers, and to save his embarrassment, removed his jacket and carried it over his arm hiding his evident arousal. They didn't speak again until they were shown to their table and sat down. Penny spoke first.

'Max what happened out there? You overwhelmed me. It was so unreal and ecstatic for me; it was almost animal lust at one time!'

'Pen I'm still shaking; you don't know how long I've waited for that moment with you. I have tried to put it out of my mind so many times but couldn't.' Max replied with equal candour.

'When you told me you were getting married, I was floored. I feel on top of the world right now. Would you join me in a bottle of Champagne fair maiden? A lesser drink doesn't seem appropriate after our car park experience, don't you think?'

'I'd love a glass Maximus, thank you.'

Pen went for the recommended house fish and chips with mushy peas. Max had his favourite steak and Guinness pie, washed down by Moët et Chandon. A crazy combination of food and drink. But not as crazy as their car park experience.

'I have a regimental dinner on the 15th and it is preferred I have a lady escort; would you do me the honour by accompanying me? It's rather a posh event with evening attire. You can't wear the jeans you love so much.' It was Max's time to mock.

'I'll have to check with my rota at the hospital, but I should be able to swap the duty roster with another doctor, so yes please Max.'

They left the pub and before getting into the car, they walked along the footpath of the silver reflecting river, shimmering under the full moonlight. They could not have scripted a more romantic setting. They kissed again, walked, kissed, walked and kissed some more.

Finally, they drove back to Penny's apartment. Then it was at that time! The million-dollar question. 'Would you like to come up for a coffee?' Penny asked in a soft, almost seductive tone. They both knew what it meant.

'I would love to Pen, but I'm night duty officer tonight starting at midnight. He could have kicked himself for agreeing to take the duty for one of his lieutenants.

'Goodnight Pen. Can we do this again this week?'

'You bet Max; I'd love to.'

Another long kiss and Max was back in his car driving back to his camp that was not too far away. He signed on as duty officer at midnight. Whilst in the guardroom drinking a coffee, his thoughts returned to what he was missing right at that moment: Outrageously daring to imagine laying next to the beautiful Penny and snuggling his nose into her perfumed neck.

'Sir can I have a word,' The young captain's fantasy was shattered as he was stunned back to the reality of duty. 'We have a couple of lads drunk at the gate sir; one can hardly stand up, shall I arrest them sir.'

'I'll be right there, corporal.'

The two inebriated squaddies were singing their heads off when Max arrived at the gate.

'Evening sir' the drunk gave an exaggerated salute and nearly fell over doing so. 'Reporting for du....,duteee, shir.' It was Terry Dixon with David Williams, both in three platoon B company.

'It's no good talking to them in their state corporal, call out the duty guard to lock them up for the night. I'll deal with them in the morning.'

Max thought the night was long and tedious; the night duty officer is for junior ranked officers, certainly not captains; however, Max was helping out one of his lieutenants as a special favour. For Corporal Terry Dixon and Williams, tonight was going to be their lucky night as Max was going to be the judge of their punishment.

'Get up you two;' Max shook the corporal, who started to stir, clearly with a massive hangover. Dave Williams was sprawled on the floor with his face in a pool of his own congealed, cold spew. A light kick roused Williams. Both were in a sorry state, but at least they were now coherent.

'Corporal Dixon, Private Williams! I should charge you both. Go immediately to your billet, shower and report to me at 09:00hrs. Williams clean your sick up before you leave. Dismissed.'

At 09.00hrs Max heard the knock on his office door. His assistant was asked to leave the office for ten minutes and to send in the two men on her way out.

'Corporal Dixon I could have your stripes for your drunken behaviour last night. Both of you should be on a charge. Do you understand me?'

'Yes sir, sorry sir.'

'Explain yourselves!'

'It was my early stag night for some of the guys at the camp sir, so sorry sir. No excuses sir.'

'Okay you two, I know you are both good soldiers and sound lads, but you can't come back to camp in the state you were in last night. Terry, you and I know each other well and David, I got my VC saving your arse.

Look, I'm not charging you, but you both know I should. You two are lucky I was on duty last night. Now go and be careful in the future, you daft pair of buggers. Oh by the way, you have a lovely singing voice Terry.' The captain gave them both a wink and dismissed them. They saluted, thanked the captain and left, knowing the trouble they could have been in.

B company had settled into their regular army base routine with no issues. Maximus had applied for the SFBC and was awaiting a reply; it would change his life and outlook forever if he was accepted. Max would lose his rank and the training for qualification is arduous and relentless. But the captain was so looking forward to being in the best special forces group in the world. Max had called his daily briefing with his platoon lieutenants earlier this morning as he had a battalion meeting with the other two captains in the colonel's office mid-morning.

At the platoon leader's meeting, the mood was quite sombre, as they knew their young company captain was leaving soon. Over the past year B company had built an incredible bond of trust and loyalty, not to mention their reputation in the battalion. B company had become the best company in the 1st battalion at all disciplines and the tour to Afghanistan had galvanised the whole unit.

Max asked his lieutenants to increase B company's fitness level and introduce competitions between platoons to include sports, endurance, weapon training and marksmanship. The lieutenants thought this would be an excellent moral boost between each platoon.

Maximus jokingly teased 'I expect my old three platoon to win everything. No bias there then, eh chaps.

I'll put up a shield for the best individual marksman. Every soldier in B company enters with a fiver entry fee and the proceeds go to the local hospital's fund for a new ventilator in their maternity unit. How does that sound gentlemen? I'll match the money raised until we have achieved the target of £7000. If you want to keep the charity competition going after the inaugural year you can decide what charity you want to sponsor. Anyway, with the marksman sniper skills demonstrated in Afghanistan I think it appropriate we call it the Afghan Shield. It will be a perpetual trophy. I think gentlemen, that will be all.' There were no questions and all the officers thought the competitions would be fun and add rivalry. As the lieutenants were leaving the room Max called three platoon's officer back.

'Mike, can you stay behind for a moment.'

'What is it sir.'

'Nothing much Mike, I expect to see three platoon's name first on that trophy; I trained those bastards and they're good. What they did in Afghanistan was incredible sniper shooting. I'd like to speak with them if you don't mind lieutenant.'

'Not at all sir; they are always talking about the famous siege of Bagrami.'

'Mike I'm supposed to be unbiased between platoons, but I have a natural affinity with three.'

'I understand sir.'

'Carry on, Mike and make sure your boys sweep the board in all the disciplines!'

The duty corporal brought in Max's mail. The usual stuff, a mess bill, a letter from home with the Hainsworth-Catt crest on the envelope, giving the senders identification immediately. The third envelope was an official brown one from the Ministry of Defence. It was this one that got Max's interest. He guessed it was a reply to his application for SFBC; Max guessed right, it confirmed that he was on the next course in seven weeks. They asked Max to confirm his acceptance in writing and to give his permission to access his personal army records. They said they would be writing to Max's CO for his endorsement once they had Max's acceptance letter to attend the next SFBC course.

Max wasted no time sending off his acceptance with the necessary permission to review his records. He wrote and posted it in the base mail collection box by the gatehouse within thirty minutes. Next Max called into his boss's office, and out of courtesy, told the colonel of his selection on to the next SFBC course in seven weeks' time and that the MoD will be writing for the CO's permission for Max to leave the rifles

21

Three days passed and Max had fixed up his second date with Penny. He booked a table at the Celtic Manor Resort, a sprawling hotel that hosted the 2012 Ryder Cup, the bi-annual golf tournament between the USA and Europe.

Penny looked ravishing as she came out of her apartment for her second date with the young captain. They drove to the M4, turned west towards Cardiff for only a couple of junctions and were there. The grand winding entrance to Celtic Manor had been extensively refurbished and extended. The romantic setting, an enjoyable meal, with the customary bottle of bubbly had set the scene for the further exciting progression in their relationship.

At the end of their extended meal the young captain spoke in a quiet, soft voice: 'Penny I did ask if you could take tomorrow off work. Did you manage it?'

'Yes all sorted. Are we going somewhere?'

'That's good. Pen would you allow me to book a room here tonight if they have one? There I've said it now. I've been bricking it all day!'

'I would be thrilled to join you Maximus.'

'Stay here Pen, I'll see if I can sort a room out.'

When Max returned Penny was gone! Max assumed she must have gone to the loo and waited at their table. Ten minutes passed and Max was now getting worried. Various thoughts pounded his brain; one in particular was persistent: *"Perhaps she's changed her mind and bottled it because of her experience with Graham. That may have mentally scarred her."* He felt pretty dejected. Max asked the

Matre'd if he had seen her. He said he thought she had left immediately after him. Max was now very concerned; he went to the bar and had a couple of whiskies while keeping an ever-optimistic eye on the exit.

Max mulled over his options: "*I'll give it another fifteen minutes, then go to the room I have paid for; I might as well use it; the room here will be more comfortable than at the barracks and I can't drive my car now anyway.*" But Pen, unfortunately, didn't show up. So it seemed he'd lost the doctor for a second time in their short liaison.

Max was trying to put a positive spin on it by convincing himself it was probably for the best now as his selection training with the SF was about to start. Max tipped the dregs of the single malt down his throat and with massive disappointment took the lift to the third floor. The room was perfect; the Champagne he'd ordered looked decidedly silly and quite pathetic in the ice bucket, He mused *"Champagne is not a drink to drink alone and it certainly cuts a sad image"*. Max laid back on the bed, staring at the ceiling with a medley of thoughts passing through his mind when a noise in the room broke his trance. He bolted upright but kept silent. The ensuite door handle turned. Max stood up in readiness to confront a possible intruder. The door opened revealing an image that would remain in his mind forever! Penny was standing in the doorway with the most provocative negligee ever seen outside of Paris; so subtle, so damn sexy!

'Penny, my God, you look unbelievable; I'm lost for words. Can I kiss you?'

The kiss, this time, developed. Max awkwardly attempted undressing but fumbled. Penny caressed his chest as she opened each button of his shirt slowly, without the same clumsiness as Max. Her slow but deliberate, almost professional, hands moved lower to Max's waist button. While still in a passionate kiss and just with one hand, she twisted the button to release his trousers that dropped to the floor. Max kicked off his sneakers. Penny pushed Max backwards onto the bed and kissed his now naked body from his briefs line and up to his lips and back down to below his navel. Working Max's tight-fitting Calvin Klein boxers downwards enough to expose his enlarged penis. She lingered now caressing the very tip of his fully erect manhood; she worked him to the point of a climax.

At last Pen crossed her arms and slowly lifted her see-through nightie up and over her head, exposing perfectly formed pert breasts. Penny slowly and deliberately pushed Max back onto the bed; with Max's erect penis staring at her, she straddled the well-built, muscled body. She gently lowered herself onto him, allowing him to enter her and taking his full length to its maximum penetration. Penny sighed with a beautiful feeling of love and fulfilment. They made love with so much pent-up passion for each other that they both giggled at their noise, wondering if they had disturbed their neighbouring room guests. Penny kissed the mouth of her new love and whispered to him. 'That was so beautiful Maximus.' She observed his now flaccid body, kissed his back from his firm buttocks to the nape of his neck, lingering there with her tongue darting sensually in small circles that made Max shudder and develop goosebumps.

'Max, my new sweet love, pour us some Champagne; what we have just experienced is worth celebrating, don't you think?'

'As your sex slave Penny, I had better obey.'

They sat in bed together, quaffing the bubbly and their smiles replaced any thoughts or words.

Max suggested they shower together only for the practical reason of scrubbing each other's backs.

Pen laughingly replied. 'Yeah right! I'm not falling for that old chestnut.'

Penny got up and led Max by the hand. She ran the shower and stepped underneath the jets, allowing the stimulating water to cascade over her head and beautiful statuesque body. Penny held out her hand to Max and gently pulled him towards her. She placed his hands over her perfectly formed breasts; they embraced; Max had no control over his returning erection that was accelerated by him sucking at Penny's erect nipples. Max pressed Penny to the tiled wall; he entered her willing, writhing body again. The young lovers sheer passion produced a very steamy, sauna-like, sexual surrounding. They almost collapsed with the heat and fulfilment. Finally sated, Max turned the shower to cold once Penny had hopped out and wrapped herself in a bathrobe. Max stayed under the cold, gushing water looking towards heaven, allowing the unheated water to now cascade over his face and find its way into tributaries down his muscled, heaving and bronzed body. The cold temperature cleared most of the condensation allowing Penny a full clear vision of Max's physique that could be mistaken easily for a bodybuilder. She indeed found his image easy on her eye. His tanned body caused by the Afghanistan sun accentuated his blond hair. She thought. *"This gorgeous 6'2", twenty-three-year-old Greek god with a body to die for is now my boyfriend and lover. What a contrast to that despicable Graham!"* Penny shuddered at that thought. She now felt secure with her man around to protect her.

Max turned, catching her staring gaze. It released Penny from her dreamlike, perhaps ogling trance; she turned away quickly, feeling embarrassed. Max stepped out of the shower and, from behind, kissed the back of her neck. Penny faced her lover. 'Max thank you, tonight has been nothing short of heavenly. I have been so frightened of men since Graham!' No more was said after a loving goodnight caress, both so relaxed, so contented they drifted away into blissful sleep.

The next day after a full English breakfast for Max and scrambled eggs on toast for Pen, they drove to Ross on Wye. After parking the car, they walked hand in hand through the medieval town with its abundance of antique shops. The loved up couple continued browsing the windows when something caught Penny's eye. She noticed a little antique gold St Christopher medallion. She made nothing of it but asked Max if he would go to the car and fetch her wrap as it was getting chilly. As soon as he was out of sight, Penny went into the little shop and purchased the travellers talisman for her young captain and lover.

They walked through the town, making their way down to the river bank before deciding on the Chase Hotel for lunch, selecting a window seat overlooking the wide River Wye and the many swans grazing the rolling lawns of the hotel.

'Pen curiosity is killing me! How did you get into our room last night? I didn't tell you which room it was and I had the two card keys. I looked everywhere for you, even the ladies loo. Finally I went into the bar and had a drink. I was waiting to see if you appeared. Eventually I gave up, but there you were up in the room. How?'

'When you left the table I asked the very accommodating Maitre'd to help me surprise you. He asked reception for our room number, then let me in with a master card key, easy!' He told reception not to mention me when you collected your card keys. The Matre'd was also watching you, ensuring you didn't leave the hotel.'

'I see, you are a little minx. Max grinned with a shake of his head.

They enjoyed their lunch and drove back to Shirenewton. They kissed for the hundredth time that day and went inside Pen's gaff. After coffee with Max sitting next to Pen, he told her that he'd been accepted for an initial assessment weekend with SF, a prelude to complete qualification testing for special forces.

Penny's face dropped; the glow that once was, had gone.

'What exactly does this mean Max?'

'I've applied for consideration to join the SAS.

Before I am accepted there are lots of hoops to jump through. Firstly, you apply for the initial SFBC, the Special Forces Briefing Course. It will last over a long weekend at Stirling Lines in Hereford. It's to see if they like you and that you have a fighting chance to progress. Unfortunately, only nine per cent get through to the finish after about six months of many gruelling tests in Brecon and jungle training in Borneo or Belize and finally a bit more in the UK.

That's it in a nutshell Pen!'

'Oh Max, isn't ordinary life good enough for you? For the first time in my life, I feel something special has happened to me and that is you! It probably started when I first met you at the hospital and dealt with Corporal Terry Dixon. Now you are going to leave me; I know it.'

'Pen come on, it's not like that, anyway; if you must know, I feel the same about you. It hit me for six that day you phoned me to say you were getting married! Yes, it is true, being a soldier means I could be posted anywhere in the world, you know that Pen. That can't change. I'll always want to come home to you, Pen. This love we have, I believe, it's unshakable. I know I'm falling in love with you!'

'Max I feel the same; something truly happened to me last night, a feeling very new to me and I don't want ever to lose it.'

They kissed and slid onto the rug for another bout of sexual lust with each other.

22

It was the 14th, the day before the regimental dinner. The outfitters phoned to say Max's dress suit was ready for collection so Max drove to Aldershot to Samuel Brothers to collect his evening dress for the regimental dinner. It fitted perfectly. The following day Max picked up Penny from her home and headed for the eastbound M4 motorway. They came off the motorway at Newbury and headed south for thirty-five miles to Winchester. After checking into the Winchester Royal Hotel, they decided to have a cheeky scotch in the bar before going to their room to unpack. And, of course, they made time for the now prerequisite sex in yet another different bed. They both showered and Max ironed his new mess dress regimental evening attire. He came out of the dressing area like a new pin.

'Wow! What do you look like? Simply fabulous, that tunic fits you like a glove.' The admiring Penny circled Max eyeing her handsome captain up and down.

Now it was Penny's turn, taking much longer than expected, but when she appeared from the dressing room with her beautiful blond hair worn up, she was indeed a heart-stopping beauty.

Max just stood there transfixed.

'Oh my God! I must take a photo of you right now in this light, this moment must be captured, this special time and feeling. It will always remind me of your stunning natural beauty, wherever I am in the world. I know it will bring me solace.'

'Max stop that; you'll make me blush or laugh. Come on, I've made you slightly late already.'

'No, I must take some shots of you at this moment. Pen, I'm so proud to be be with you.'

She changed the subject, not that she didn't like what he had said. 'Come on, Max, let's go; the taxi will be waiting.'

'Where to guv?' asked the cabbie.

'The Grand Hotel please.'

'There's a lot of you army bods going there tonight; you're my third fare in half an hour. It must be a big army bash, blokes dressed up like you. What is it?'

'It's a regimental dinner for the Rifles.'

'Never heard of them. I was Royal Engineers.'

'That's a fine regiment, The Rifles, however, were only formed in 2007. They amalgamated several light infantry regiments.'

'Here we are. Have a nice evening.'

'Thank you, keep the change. Always good to meet a comrade.' The cabbie saluted and thanked Max.

In they went to the drinks reception. The Grand Hotel lived up to its name, it was huge.

To Max's surprise and delight, he could see some of three platoon standing in a group together. The colonel kept his word; he'd fiddled Max's special platoon in for the dinner. 'Hey guys, it's great to see you here. My word, you all scrub up so well; look at you, a bit different from the days in the blowing sands of Afghanistan. Penny, please allow me to introduce you to the roughest but toughest band of vagabonds you could ever meet.' The guys were not taking in what their captain was saying; they were mesmerised by Penny's beauty.

About ten of the platoon members were present in the group. Max wondered if the others were attending.

A few lads muttered some helloes, but Max knew what they were thinking—the same as he had felt that night in Chepstow Hospital.

'Where's Sergeant Forbes and Corporal Dixon?'

'They are here sir, probably at the bar sir. We are all here apart from Tom Palanski; we all came down by coach. Colonel Abel organised it and even paid for it as well.'

Max noticed one of the platoon talking to a soldier in an Afghan army uniform.

Max went across and recognised who it was. 'Bugger me! Its Malik!' The soldier turned actor who played a big part in the ruse to get the hostages exchanged at the Bagram siege.

'Malik, what on earth are you doing here?'

He turned and gave Max a big hug.

'Your Colonel got me an invite and paid for my flight, hotel and everything; he is a very good man, your colonel Sahib. I'm so pleased to be here. First time in the UK. Who is this lovely creature sir?'

'This is Penny. Penny, this is Malik. He was integral to saving thirty-six locals in the Bagram siege; however he should really be in Hollywood after his performance that day. It's lovely to see you Malik; are the boys from three looking after you?'

'Oh yes sir, very much sir, thank you sir.'

Max then put his arms around Tim Forbes and Terry Dixon, whom Penny had already met. She smiled at the two NCOs.

'Hello Tim, Terry, it's good to see you both again so soon. How is your neck Terrence? Has your breathing stabilised?'

'Yes Penny, thank you for what you did for me. It's great to see you and our good captain together.'

'May I say gentlemen, you both look brilliant in your regimental evening dress.'

Terry replied. 'May I say Penny, you look stunning. Did you arrive in a pumpkin by any chance? Does our captain have a glass slipper for you later?'

Max chuckled at the corporal's mocking!

'Terry, stop flirting; you are getting married in two weeks. By the way, can I bring Cinderella to your wedding ball?'

Terry laughed an approval.

'Of course sir, as long as Penny doesn't wear that dress. Sophie, my fiancé, would go bonkers.'

They all laughed, but it was a valid point. Finally, Tim asked if the young couple would like a drink; they did, and Tim went off to the bar.

The platoon lieutenants of B company came over and made their greetings; they had their ladies with them, so understandably they had restrained comments about Penny. Max couldn't help noticing them secretly ogling her until they got cold scares from their wives, who soon brought the officers back to heel.

Tim arrived with cocktails, assisted by Terry.

'Thanks Tim. It's good to see three platoon make it here.'

'Tom Palanski isn't here sir but he still holds a grudge against Terry and me over our little desert persuasion I think.'

'Oh dear, I thought he had got over that; it's a shame. I thought he was pleased to be back in the fold.'

'Ceri Burns has sir,' Terry Dixon added. 'he has nothing to do with Tom anymore; there was a massive fall out when we got back from Afghanistan sir.'

'There we are; we can't win them all.'

'No sir, that's true.'

'Cheers everybody and thanks for coming.'

Penny and Max moved off to politely mingle. Penny asked Max.

'Why does Tim and Terry call you sir, and you call them by their first names?'

'Military discipline. I wouldn't mind myself, as you probably noticed they called me Max at Brandscombe, however too many top brass from the regiment and even the MoD are here tonight so one has to be formal or one gets an awful bollocking.'

Max and Penny both laughed, with Penny nearly choking on her vodka martini. The colonel had just spotted Max; he excused himself from the group officers he was chatting to and came across to Max and Penny to make an informal greeting.

'Good evening captain and Dr Richards; you both met Margaret, my wife, at your birthday bash; it's good to see you both. Allow me to introduce you to the other battalions commanders?'

The four walked over to the high-ranking officers and Colonel Abel formally introduced Max and Penny to them.

One lieutenant colonel had a bit too much to drink even before the dinner. Max heard him say dreadful lewd remarks to another officer directed specifically at Penny; he continually smirked to the other senior officers. It was disgusting and not what you would expect from high-ranking army officers. Max gave the man a chance to shut up but his remarks became more obvious. Max had enough of the officer's vulgarity. He went over to the offending colonel and whispered into his ear. 'If you make another filthy remark about Penny again, I will knock your vulgar fucking head off without any hesitation!'

Max smiled and moved slowly away as if sharing a joke with the despicable battalion commanding officer. Max went back to Penny, instinctively protective of her. Nevertheless, she sensed something wasn't entirely as it should be. 'Everything all right, Max?'

'Sure Pen, all good.' Max didn't think she believed him as she was looking at the now very flustered officer; his wife was asking him what Max had said. The senior officer was clearly shaken and also extremely angry. He had probably never been spoken to like that before and couldn't handle the confrontation, especially from a lower-ranking officer. His face had turned a puce colour! Max was ready for any eventuality. The offending colonel asked a fellow colonel in their group. 'Who the dash does he think he is?'

'He's the young captain who saved thirty-six innocent lives in Bagram and won the VC on convoy duty. That's who!'

The mood had lightened and with military precision, guests were asked to make their way into the expansive dining hall of the Grand. The tables were marked out on the table planner. Thankfully on Max's table was Colonel Laurence Abel, Sergeant Forbes, Terry Dixon, Mike Stephens, three platoon's lieutenant and his wife, a newspaper reporter and his lady. Dinner was served, and upon completion, the master of ceremonies called everybody to order.

'My lords, ladies, gentlemen and distinguished guests, I would like to welcome to the rostrum on this auspicious occasion the commanding officer of the 1st battalion Rifles, Colonel Laurence Abel.'

The CO went to the stage and welcomed everybody, mentioning Lieutenant-General Tyler-Brookes from headquarters and the other two battalion commanding officers. He said how proud he was of his battalion's achievements on their recent tour in hostile

Afghanistan. 'The men proved superb rifles, conducting themselves in exemplary fashion. So without further ado, I would like you all to welcome our speaker for the evening and the regiment's hero; I give you 1st battalion's Captain Maximus Hainsworth-Catt VC!' There was loud applause around the hall, especially emphatic from the tables seating the raucous three platoon.

The introduction Max had been dreading all evening. Penny, bless her, squeezed Max's hand as a sort of good luck thing and supporting gesture.

'Good evening, I would like to start my talk, not in Afghanistan but at Beachley, our home barracks but first I must mention the hard work three platoon put in before our tour. Their fast marching exceeded 141 paces a minute and they excelled in weapon training and marksmanship. They won the weapons training cup by sheer effort and determination. Please rise three platoon,' Every platoon member stood up apart from Tom Palanski, who wasn't present. They took the applause graciously; it was evident to everyone in the packed dining hall how proud they were of themselves and their comrades of number three. 'Thank you three platoon. We arrived in Afghanistan in uncomfortably hot, humid weather and didn't have proper billets until our dormitories had been sanitised. It wasn't long before we were sent to our first mission. It was in the Kabul district of Bagram,'

Max told the audience of the hostages, the exchange ruse, and the brave Afghan soldier who pretended to be the second in command of the Taliban. Max told how the make-up specialists made him up to look exactly like Muzanni, the Taliban vice-leader. At this point Max asked Malik, the impersonator, to stand up. Malik did. He was so pleased and proud that he started to cry. The audience showed their appreciation with loud applause. Max then spoke about the convoy to Kandahar, explaining how three platoon came under heavy fire but still got the medical supplies through. However, modesty prevented Max from mentioning his solo bravery action that earned him the VC.

'Tom, it's Pat Connolly, can you hear me okay?' Patrick Connolly was calling from a satellite phone from the mountains overlooking Kabul.

'You are crackling and breaking up!' Tom Palanski awaited a better connection.

'I'll have to go outside,' Patrick Connolly the AWOL private went to a better area for a signal. 'Is that better?'

'Much.' Palanski confirmed.

'Is everything in place at your end? Go through it once more; we don't have much time. We can't have any slip-ups; there is too much at stake. I have Taliban fighters waiting to receive the handover of Muzanni from the Afghan authorities when you confirm the deal is done. So tell me where you are with the plan!' Connolly was impatient and concerned.

'All's good here Pat; I've made contact as you instructed with the IS cell here in the UK by using the coded message you passed to me. I met up with them ten days ago and the fucking bastards grilled me rotten! I suppose it will be worth it for the twenty-five thousand dollars each we are getting. The active cell has put an experienced man, Ahmed, to work as a waiter in the Grand Hotel; two others have delivered an adapted wheeled catering bin here that collects kitchen waste. There is added security, owing to it being a military function so they have put a guard on the rear door to check goods in. The IS cell came up with a plan to counter this and have modified a waste container with a false bottom. A unique key at the side is the only mechanism to remove the hidden base. In the void space below are the explosives. These have already been transferred to a drinks trolley. I am, as we speak, dressed as an MP with a bearded disguise; an IS forger altered my army ID. I'm currently in a hotel room at the Grand and will go to the main entrance door with my automatic weapon to cover anybody trying to leave or enter. Ahmed will announce his intentions to the audience imminently. It will happen precisely ten minutes from now at 20.35hrs. We are in place; the trolley is loaded and ready to be wheeled into the dining hall as the port and cheese trolley for the tables.

A signal from Ahmed's iPhone will activate the detonation device. It requires one digit to set the device, a kind of safety catch, the second digit to be pressed detonates the explosives. Ahmed volunteered to die as a fucking martyr. We're ready! One other thing Pat, you are safely hidden by the Taliban while I'm still in the fucking Rifles. I'm not into this martyr shit. You said we would get twenty-five grand each. I hope that is still on.' It was evident in Palanski's voice that he was getting nervous.

'Yes, they want you to get out as quickly as possible; they are happy that Ahmed will be getting his virgins in paradise but aren't bothered about him. They deem you as an asset and want your future cooperation from within the UK military. The newly formed Islamic Revolutionary Front (IRF) want to take more UK military targets so further intel from you is essential which will mean more money for your coffers of course. The terrorists are trying to convert me with their religious crap, hoping I will do their organising for free, but I told them I'm not interested in that, only their fucking money. They know I'm AWOL and wanted in connection with the attempted murder of Terry Dixon so they think they have me by the bollocks. Anyway, listen up Tom, you have to get out quick as soon as Muzanni is released to us; they want you as a mole for other attacks on the army. In particular they want that bastard Hainsworth-Catt dead, if he survives the hotel explosion. They know you can give them so much, through me, like telling them about the regimental dinner being held tonight. So you have to continue being a fucking soldier, got it?'

'Yeah, I've got it and no problems feeding you inside army information providing I get a good payout. Look Pat, I've got to get into place at the entrance. Speak later.'

Ahmed pushed the port and cheese trolley in to the centre of the dining room and placed a bottle of port on several of the nearby tables.

Then at precisely 20.35hrs Ahmed took a mini loudhailer from his trolley, took a phone from his pocket and took a deep breath. Just before this, Tom Palanski, dressed in military police uniform, moved to the entrance vestibule. He took up a position as if he was meant to be there on guard security; he was, but not for the dining party's safety. Ahmed cleared his throat, moved into an aisle for space, and raised the megaphone to his lips but stopped in his tracks. A guest from one of the tables shouted at Ahmed for more wine; the waiter-terrorist ignored his drunken request, but the guy stood up and shouted. ' Oy, you bloody pond life, get us another bottle of Chateauneuf-du-Pape now!'

Ahmed looked at the rude drunk officer, went to his side, and without saying a word, took out a small pistol from his inside pocket and blew the protesting drunk's brains out! The victim's blood squirted the adjacent diners, splashing them with dark red blood from head to waist, causing one adjacent woman to have a seizure. Her dress now resembled a Jackson Pollock abstract painting. Such was the shock and alarm; the dining hall froze in time for ten seconds as if the atrocity hadn't happened.

Then the stark truth hit the room and uncontrollable screaming and panic commenced. First hysterical screams broke out from the slaughtered officer's table. Inevitably panic ensued and spread like ripples in a pond until Ahmed brought everybody back to silence with a shot he fired into the ceiling followed by his shouting into his loudhailer. 'Do not move from any table. There is a sniper rifle trained on the whole room. Anybody who stands will be shot in the head. Like this infidel'

Ahmed went over to the dead officer he had just shot, lifted his lifeless head upright by his hair and released it. The head fell forward and thumped back on the table. The blood was pooling on the white linen, the woven table cloth absorbing the red liquid like blotting paper.

There were whimpers of terror around the hall from ladies who had never experienced such scenes; others were straining to see the dead man. Ahmed went back to his centre-ground and addressed the top table through his megaphone. 'I am Ahmed; I am proud to belong to the Islamic Revolutionary Front. We cooperate with both IS and Taliban. We have the front and rear doors guarded by armed IRF fighters. If anybody uses their phones or tries to escape, we will know. We have spotters for every table and you will be shot in an instant. If you attempt to use your phone you will be responsible for the death of many of the people here. This phone I have here is connected to the detonator that will blow this place into many bits, especially the soft, fat, decadent flesh that's in abundance here. My instruction is simple. You will all walk out of here alive and back to your families if I am obeyed. The most senior rank here, I believe, is Brigadier-General Cox. I want him to contact your Ministry of Defence and tell them to get onto the Afghanistan government in Kabul and release Muzanni. Then I will contact our people in Kabul to collect him. I will receive a call as soon as we have him safe; then we shall leave here without detonating forty kilos of Semtex.

No one will die, apart from one already dead, him over there,' Ahmed pointed at the silent officer with a bullet in his skull. 'The man you are honouring tonight is a different situation. Our leader has issued a fatwah on him. He will be our next target. Captain Hainsworth-Catt. That infidel caused the death of seventeen brave martyrs in Afghanistan by tricking us. We shall seek revenge for them but not tonight. That will be for another time. Our beloved Muzanni's freedom is our only concern tonight.' Ahmed, who was in the kitchen when Max was speaking, hadn't realised Max was in the room.

Penny squeezed Max's hand when the terrorist threatened her man with revenge. The brigadier put his phone on loudspeaker close to the mic so the terrorist could hear the conversation as directed.

Ahmed said he would dictate the message and the brigadier should repeat it to the UK government. The terms for Muzanni's release are to be conveyed over the phone. The conversation was heard loud and clear. Max whispered to Penny.

'I've got to do something; I think that once Muzanni is free, Ahmed will probably blow this place up, along with himself. These groups are fanatical. Pass this note to the reporter next to you with your hands under the table and do it discreetly.'

Penny touched the man's thigh and nudged it. She moved her head, indicating with her eyes downwards. He got the gist and took the serviette from her below the table line. The reporter's wife saw the movement and looked daggers at Penny, thinking she was making a pass at her husband; the pressman opened the folded tissue and read the note with absolute surprise.

"I can't remember your name, but this is seriously important. I'm going to talk to the terrorist, and when I say the word "hostages," I want you to point the flash on your camera directly at the him. Keep your camera hidden until the last second. It could save my life and many others in this room. Don't talk to me or make any gestures across the table. Instead, drink your wine, drain it and lay your glass flat on the table. That will be your signal to me that you understand and you will do what I ask."

Max waited for the flat glass signal which came quicker than expected. The captain thought. *"This has to work"*

He whispered to Pen.

'Stay calm and trust me.'

Before Max could do anything, a message came back to the brigadier. He picked up a microphone and read it out to Ahmed and the dining hostages:

"Out of respect and the close friendship we have with the UK, The Afghanistan government, with great reluctance, will release Muzanni as requested."

The brigadier stopped short of completing the Afghan's complete response. He couldn't let the terrorists know the Afghan government wanted the UK to at least try any other possible option before they let the very dangerous Muzanni go free. So the senior officer held back this part of the message that read:

"Muzanni is very dangerous; we would ask you to resolve this crisis some other way! We hope that releasing the second in command of the Taliban should be the very last option the UK decide upon."

The brigadier finished reading out what he wanted Ahmed to hear.

'The Afghanistan government will contact the UK government when the prisoner is ready for release. They estimated this to be concluded within half an hour.' It was time Max made his move; the captain stood up and shouted across to the terrorist.

'Ahmed, I have a message from Patrick Connolly. He texted me from Afghanistan; it's urgent.' All the diners' attention turned to where Max was and were perplexed with his outburst. The young captain was hoping Ahmed took the bluff. Ahmed responded, but it was evident he was surprised and highly suspicious, but it worked; he turned his pistol towards the young captain and shouted instructions:

'Come to me slowly and put your hands on your head.'

Max tried to calm him by saying. 'I'm part of the plot; my job is to locate Hainsworth-Catt after Muzanni is freed and to make sure he pays for his actions; I have been promised fifty thousand pounds upon proof of his death and another twenty thousand pay-out once Muzanni is released.'

Ahmed was confused.

'Why wasn't I told of this.' Ahmed barked!

'It was on a need to know basis, and with respect, Ahmed, you are way down our pecking order, a disposable commodity.'

Anger replaced confusion in Ahmed.

Max was now facing directly at him and inching closer.

Ahmed asked the question: 'What was the message from Connolly that is so urgent?'

Max answered confidently.

'Patrick said for you to get a message to Tom Palanski. Are you able to do that tonight?'

'Yes, he's guarding the front entrance.' This shocked the men and officers of 1st Rifles. One of their own, a traitor.

They also realised Max-Catt had flushed Palanski out by tricking Ahmed.

'I'll call him and you can speak to him directly so he can confirm who you say you are as well.'

With his pistol still directed at Max it was difficult to call the number. This is exactly what Max was hoping for. The captain shouted in a loud voice to the guests. 'Do you people know why you are HOSTAGES.'

Max emphasised hostages very loudly. The code-word had been activated.

Max-Catt was poised to work his speed to its limits. As the young captain had hoped, Ahmed momentarily looked in the direction of the camera flash; so did everybody else in the dining hall. Simultaneously Max-Catt went in to action, diving at his target's right wrist and grasping it in a vice-like grip. Ahmed hit Max with his other hand to the side of his face, using the flat of his phone as a striking weapon. Although only a phone, the blow felt like Max had been hit with a hammer. Max was able to slam Ahmed's gun hand down on the edge of the drinks trolley three times in quick, violent succession before Ahmed's grip released the gun; Ahmed screamed with pain as the weapon flew across the floor. Then, bravely and thinking quickly, a lady sitting on the nearest table to the action grabbed the gun and aimed it at Ahmed. She fired and missed but came closer to the fight as Max grappled with the frantic terrorist. The lady aimed the weapon at Ahmed, closed her eyes and fired twice with both bullets going through the terrorist's leg. Ahmed screamed out in pain with blood pumping like a red geyser. The lady dropped the gun and fainted on the spot.

Ahmed gave up the fight with Max. He held his leg screaming in pain. Ahmed would die soon through blood loss; the gunshot had punctured his femoral artery. Max used his belt, placing it around Ahmed's leg, pulling it tight and securing it as a tourniquet around his thigh. Men from the three platoon were now with their captain. Max instructed them to get knives, chair legs, anything they could get their hands on to use as weapons, then to follow their young captain. There were no snipers in the dining hall, that's for sure, but Max said Palanski is armed and guarding the front door with another terrorist at the back entrance. Max shouted back towards the brigadier.

'Sir, cancel the release of Muzanni!'

Max split the platoon into two; Tim Forbes led one team to the front door, Max took team two to the guard at the back.

They soon overpowered the unsuspecting young IRF terrorist and tied him up. Some of the lads couldn't resist putting the boot in for what he intended doing to innocent people.

Sergeant Forbes returned with his team.

'Sir, we have searched the whole area. There is no sign of any terrorist.'

'There was one, a traitor; his name is Tom Palanski. I bet he's scarpered as well.' The hotel's ground floor was swarming with anti-terrorism armed units by this time. Police cars and ambulances filled the car park. The platoon went back to the dining hall against a tide of guests flooding out. They couldn't go anywhere as the police had locked down the whole building. The shot terrorist, Ahmed, was taken away in an ambulance with an armed escort; however, with the amount of blood he'd lost, he was not expected to live. Max kept Ahmed's phone as it may lead to Connolly. The bomb squad dealt swiftly with the Semtex hidden in the drinks and food trolley. They were surprised at the quantity the terrorists intended to use. Ahmed was right about one thing, it would have blown the hall to bits with few survivors.

Max spoke with the brigadier who confirmed the release of Muzanni had been aborted! The hotel was locked down for security reasons and to interview all the guests. However, the Afghans were relieved to keep Muzanni in custody; the captured Taliban leader had previously caused many atrocities to Afghan communities, inflicting much pain.

Penny and Max went back to their hotel and their lust for each other had increased through the evening's dramatic events leading to another incredible night of unbridled passion.

Max and Penny drove back to Shirenewton the following day with the conversation very much taken up with the terrorist attack. Penny insisted on Max telling her everything about the plan that eventually overpowered Ahmed. Max reluctantly explained. 'I shouldn't Pen as I have to be debriefed by MI5 at Beachley tomorrow, but as long as you tell nobody, I'll let you know; after all, you were there when it happened. It was all based upon a hunch.

'As you know I am a trained sniper and I also train soldiers in that skill; it is an art to fire a rifle properly. We are also taught observation, how to pick out snipers, a gift in its own right. I scanned the whole dining hall but saw no indication or tell-tale signs of any sniper; therefore, I discounted being shot at. I had no concern about the Semtex either because the terrorist's detonator was his phone and by his own omission, he would need to keep it on and press two digits to activate it. I thought if I could get close enough to Ahmed, and providing I could distract him momentarily, it would give me a chance to get to hold of his trigger finger. My only worry was his gun. The distraction of the flash did it thankfully, as it bought me just enough time to get to him. Connolly and Palanski's involvement was pure guesswork, but Ahmed confirmed my suspicions. Only army personnel would have known about the regimental dinner. Connolly was AWOL in Afghanistan so there was a good chance he had offered his services to the Taliban. With his ongoing connection with Palanski, the only man in three platoon who was not at the dinner. I just put two and two together. Thank goodness it added to four and my hunch turned out to be correct. It made my decision to act easy, knowing that I had no other option. I do believe without a doubt that once they had Muzanni released in Afghanistan they would have blown us up.

Terrorists do not bargain. I'm just glad you're safe Penny.'

'You should be a detective Maximus and with fear of repetition, thank you again for being there for all those innocent people in the hall and me. It seems to be a regular habit and don't think I didn't know you had words with that pervy colonel!' Penny lent across and kissed Max's cheek. Her perfume now reminded him of their beautiful lovemaking; he momentarily lost awareness of where he was, being totally distracted to the point of near disaster. The confused captain drove through a red traffic light, just missing a vehicle crossing his path. Max was stranded in the centre of the busy junction after slamming on his brakes. The man who was nearly T-boned continued blasting his horn at Max for what seemed ages. Cars had to detour around the black Porsche as Max had created an island in the middle of the junction; other angered drivers joined in the cacophony of blasting car horns as they passed the stranded sports car. Finally, the lights changed to green for Max's direction; he was out of there in seconds.

'Max didn't you see the lights were on red?' Penny was shaking her head in bewilderment.

'Sorry Pen, I was in a dream, it was your perfume; I can't tell you what I was daydreaming about! Hey Pen, it would have been ironic if we got injured in the car after what we've just been through. Sorry Pen.' They chuckled together.

'I think I know Max; it has crossed my mind a few times as well.' There was another round of mischievous grins and then they said their goodbyes at her gate. Penny was on duty in just two hours.

'Thanks for another lovely time Max; see you soon my love and brave hero.'

A little wave and Penny had slipped away through her gated entrance.

23

The following day, after returning from the regimental dinner in Winchester, Max was back on duty at Beachley and in the colonel's office. The debriefing took place with strange blokes from the anti-terror department, MI5. They were, by nature, suspicious and asked Max many searching questions about Connolly in particular. They wanted to know how the young VC hero knew Connolly and why Max wished to speak with Ahmed. Max explained that he had strong suspicions that Connolly and Thomas Palanski were involved with the attempted bombing at Winchester and the attempted release of Muzanni. He was convinced that Ahmed would activate the explosion once Muzanni was freed. So Max played his hunch and Ahmed confirmed it. The young captain pointed out that he had no choice when he decided to make his play. It was more or less the same story Max had told Penny; after several hours the grilling finally finished.

The two spooks fully understood what had occurred and thanked Max for preventing a massive disaster at the hotel; they said if Max ever wanted to leave the army they would get him a field job at Thames House, the MI5 London headquarters. They were pleased that Palanski was exposed. They realised he could have done irreparable damage by feeding back military intel to the terrorists; the breach of security he could have caused would be catastrophic. They must now track down the armed Palanski as he may be able to lead them to the IRF cell. The two secret agents left after thanking the colonel and Max for their time and cooperation.

The colonel poured two ample malts and said to Max, 'I think you need one of these after that grilling the spooks just gave you. By the way, I have just received the documents from SF asking for my agreement to release you from the rifles, and reluctantly, I have signed and returned it to the Special Forces Administration. We shall all miss you, Maximus; you are a one-off, a fine officer and a trusted friend.'

The colonel and Max made a sturdy shaking of hands. Max drained the last dregs of the drink, saluted his colonel and left his office.

Max's gym work and increased physical training was going well. Sometimes he'd meet up with Pen; they would jog along the river to Lydney, have a coffee and run back. Max had to continue his exercise regime in preparation for his upcoming fitness tests.

There was another MoD envelope for Max when he returned to his quarters; he fumbled it open in haste; there it was. The confirmation that all the required documentation was in place. Max is to attend the initial assessment weekend at Hereford to see if The Regiment wanted him. The captain had instructions on what to bring and advising him to report to Sterling Lines, Hereford. Enclosed was a special security pass to attend the Special Forces Briefing course; he will leave this Friday morning; the course begins that evening. Max assumed the SFBC would not be too difficult, mainly physical tests. He has already swum one hundred metres fully clothed, well under the expected minimum of three minutes. Several briefings will prepare candidates for tests on basic compass and map reading. In essence, the instructors are looking for something special in their applicants as they do not want to waste the regiment's time and money with unsuitable candidates. These briefings are to ensure the candidate is aware of what to expect when the serious stuff starts.

Max met Penny on a Thursday night and explained more or less what his itinerary would be.

'I should be back on Monday night as the SFBC is held over a long weekend.' They had an early Wetherspoon's quickie dinner of burgers and chips, only because Max needed an early night; this time their date didn't end with a passionate finish.

'Take care, Maximus, good luck in Hereford.'

'Goodbye my darling Pen; I'll see you in a few days.' They squeezed each other in a sincere lover's embrace and parted.

Tim Forbes intercepted Max as he headed for his car.

'Captain, can I see you quickly? I know you are on your way to Hereford.'

'What is it Tim?'

'I thought you would want to know that the police nearly caught Tom Palanski. He was at his sister's in Birmingham, hiding out in her cellar. But unfortunately, he evaded capture by five minutes, our MP sergeant told me last night.'

'That's disappointing news Tim, but they'll get the traitorous bastard. We know Connolly is in cahoots with the Taliban in Afghanistan and no doubt has a connection with the IS backed IRF in the UK. I wouldn't mind betting he will try and get Palanski to an IRF safe house here in the UK. Anyway Tim, thanks for letting me know; I must go. I'll see you on Tuesday morning I expect.'

'Good luck, sir.'

Max was on his way and decided to travel to Ross on Wye on the A449 and turn off to Hereford. Credenhill, to be precise, Stirling Lines, the home of 22 regiment Special Air Service or 22 SAS. It was a reasonably short journey. Max showed his security pass with which he had been issued, then was allowed on to the regiment's hallowed ground. Butterflies started flying about in Max's stomach as he drove through the security barrier.

The young captain was greeted by a confident NCO, there is no rank carried over into this mob from previous regiments so it's back to basics. *"Quite right,"* Max thought.

The briefing lectures started that night and Max thought they went well; Max found himself scribbling away in his notebook constantly. It reminded him of Sandhurst without the snobbery. All of the candidates were billeted together and were a genuine mixed bag of ranks, shapes and sizes.

The usual basic tests went on throughout the weekend punctuated with more briefings. Finally, the course finished with the lead instructor addressing the potential candidates in the lecture room for the last time. He told them their lectures were now complete. He advised that thirteen had left by their own choice; only three were suggested to leave and told it wasn't going to work out for them, the most diplomatic way of saying: SF don't want you!

'We will advise the remainder of you within seven days if we want to see you again and if we do, you will be invited to proceed to the severe stuff when the real fun begins.

Good luck gentlemen and I hope to see you all again.'

Max drove back to Beachley and reported to the colonel who wanted to know how it went in Hereford.

'Well Maximus, was it how you thought it would be? Do you really want to continue to put your body through hell? Notwithstanding your loss of rank?'

'I know it's mad sir, but it's a challenge I want to face. But of course, that is if I have got past the initial appraisal on the SFBC.'

'I'm sure you will Max, from what I know of SAS qualification, it's the next six months that is the killer with only about nine per cent getting through to join 22 SAS. You will always be welcomed back here, but you know that. By the way, when will you know your fate?'

'Next week sir.'

'When do the real tests start.'

'I'm hoping to get on the winter course sir, starting in early January, so I have about three months to wait, that is, if they want me.'

'Okay Max, oh damn bad news about that traitor Palanski. It's a pity the police weren't a bit quicker on the tip-off. The MP boys will string him up by his balls if they catch him first.'

They both chuckled with Max still laughing as he left the colonel's office. Max now had to prepare for the joint manoeuvres with the 2nd battalion next week so went back to the privacy of his quarters to read through the objectives. He collected his post, one was a posh envelope that was neatly handwritten. *"Was it from Pen?"* he wondered. No, it was a wedding invite to Terry Dixon and Sophie's wedding in three weeks time.

Max organised his platoon lieutenants to get the heavy kit, including the Foxhounds to be painted back to army green, ready for manoeuvres in eight days' time. Max sent the RSVP to Sophie's parents as if he left it he'd probably forget. Max phoned Penny and surprisingly she was on a break so got put through immediately.

'Hi Penny love, I'm back; fancy some nosh tonight?'

'Yes please, you can tell me all about the Hereford experience.'

'Yes of course. By the way, are you up for Terry and Sophie's wedding? It's two weeks next Saturday.'

'Yes, I'd love to.'

'Good, I've replied for both of us.'

'A bit presumptuous, Max-Catt! Do you know, I do like your abbreviated name, it has a certain ring to it.'

'I know you, Pen, anything for a free bottle of bubbly.'

'You are courageous when you are five miles away, assuming that is, you are in camp at this time.'

'Yes indeed. I'll pick you up at 19.30hrs then.

Take care my gorgeous doctor and I'm so glad you like my new name.'

Max and Penny had a lovely deep affectionate kiss that reminded him how much he enjoyed being around her. Then he suggested where to eat. 'Let's go to the river pub. I fancy some Guinness and steak pie!'

'Alright just for you, my sweetness and light, that'll be lovely, I'm having fish and chips; I've not had any since the last time we were there and that seems ages ago.'

They arrived at The Boat pub but decided to stroll along the river first as it was a cloudless Autumn evening. The dew was settling onto the grass like scatterings of small diamonds reflecting the dipping sun's last effort to beam light. There was a nip in the air as the sun gradually surrendered to the evening dusk.

Max turned to Penny to face her; he kissed her gently but meaningfully with a momentary pause.

Penny whispered into Max's ear.

'That was nice Max, I have missed you so much even though we've only been parted four days.'

'Pen we have a lot to be thankful for, come on I'm starving. A nice steak and Guinness pie with a pint of real ale. Oh how I missed a good keg beer in Afghanistan.'

They both enjoyed their bar food and Max his couple of pints.

Max told Pen all about Hereford as she wanted to know what he did at Stirling Lines and when he should possibly hear his results.

Max stayed at Pen's for their customary reunion sex. He still has to pinch himself that he's now the official boyfriend of Doctor Penny Richards. Penny was not at work the next day as she worked the weekend shift so Max kissed her whilst she slept and let himself out; he now had a key to this easy-living apartment.

Max got back to camp; the guard on the gate had a message for him to go to the CO's office so Max went straight there as it was urgent.

'Sir you wanted to see me. I've just got back into camp; I haven't had a chance to get into uniform, so my apologies. I would have changed first, but the duty sentry said you wanted to see me urgently.'

'Yes Max, take a seat. Whitehall and MI6 have contacted me, the Taliban are livid with you for thwarting their attack at the regiment's dinner, but worse still, they know it was you that stopped the release of Muzanni, their revered second in command leader, for the second time. British intelligence is convinced that Palanski contacted Connolly while on the run. Palanski must have been watching the whole development in the dining hall and decided to flee when you got the better of Ahmed, who incidentally is under armed guard in hospital; He was in intensive care for a week. The medical staff reckon it was your belt tourniquet that saved his life which is quite ironic knowing they want you dead! Anyway, the Taliban and this new terrorist group, the IRF, are arranging a hit team to take you out. They have contacted a cell in the UK to carry out their Fatwah order against you; you are in serious danger.'

'There's really not much I can do about that sir. But I wonder, does one win a prize or get in the Guinness book of records for having a double fatwah on their head. I suppose I will have to be more vigilant. Thank you for your concern sir; I'm sorry for sounding so flippant; I know this is very serious.'

Max received notification from his father that a letter awaits him. It was from Buckingham Palace. Penny confirmed her availability for the visit to Brandscombe on Saturday. So the couple's visit to his home was confirmed.

24

After their refreshments, Chris presented his son with the royal envelope. As Max opened it he could feel everybody's eyes watching him in anticipation. It was from the Queen's secretary inviting Max to the palace to receive his Victoria Cross in two weeks time.

As directed by Christopher, Max read out the invitation to the waiting gathering. After the reading, Jenny pulled Max to one side and quietly whispered 'Max you have made my sister so happy, all she does is talk about you and I get a detailed account of all your dates. You must know how much in love she is with you don't you?

'I have to say Jenny it's undoubtedly a mutual feeling'. Max's warm smile confirmed his answer. 'So how's my buddy Rory treating you?'

'All good thanks Max, he's a really nice guy, and I have three days holiday next week; Rory has asked me to go to Stratford-upon-Avon with him. I'm so looking forward to it. He has Romeo and Juliet tickets at the Royal Shakespeare Theatre located on the bank of the river Avon.

'That sounds great; you'll enjoy that with Rory.'

The two weeks flew by, Penny was joining Max to collect his decoration at the palace. Things were all in hand at the camp. Manoeuvres were put back for technical and logistical reasons for another two weeks, but that didn't affect B company as they had all their preparations completed a week earlier. They are just waiting on the battalion's go-ahead to move out to their designated war games location.

Pen and Max travelled by train to Paddington; it was a bright sunny day as they stepped out of the train in London, the shafts of light flooding through on the busy platform. It was the day Max is to receive the coveted Victoria Cross. A very proud moment. All the family were in London after the presentation and Max treated the whole family to the famous afternoon tea ritual at the Ritz Hotel. They finished the day off by walking along Piccadilly to Shaftesbury Avenue to see a show. It was coming to the end of a perfect day. Max was hand in hand with the lady he realised he loved beyond a level he thought could ever be possible.

Patrick Connolly screamed at a Taliban plastic surgeon and grabbed his beard with both hands. 'What the fuck are you doing to me you fucking stupid peasant? Where is the local anaesthetic, that fucking hurt, you bastard?'

'Sorry Connolly sahib, so sorry.'

'My name is Jason Fletcher now, not Connolly, don't forget it again, got it?'

'Yes, Fletcher sahib.'

Two hours later, the face-changing operation was complete. Connolly now resembles his new passport of Mr Jason Fletcher with a new beard and longer hair. He had fingerprint recognition for a UK bank account and credit card in the name of Jason Fletcher, the authenticity will soon be put to the test as he was about to travel to London and meet an IS backed IRF group to become a UK-based operational cell leader. Fletcher had other scores to settle in the UK. The killing of Captain Maximus Hainsworth-Catt was first priority on his agenda. In addition, Connolly would collect the increased bounty of $75,000 from the Taliban for revenge of the Bagrami siege killings. Little did the

Taliban know that Connolly/Fletcher would happily kill Max for nothing, Thus, the new Fletcher had thought to himself, a win-win situation.

Jason Fletcher went straight through the security check at Hamid Karzai International Airport in Kabul. He didn't worry too much about this, with his documentation being forged to a high standard so he thought.

He was seated in the departure lounge when the emergency alarm activated causing Fletcher immediate concern as armed guards came running straight for him. He thought there is no way out, he was helpless and no weapon to defend himself with against three guards with automatic machine guns. They were shouting; Fletcher was just about to raise his hands in surrender when the guards ran straight past him less than an arm's length away. They were not interested in Fletcher. There was intel that a Pakistani national was trying to get in on a false passport. Eleven hours later, the transformed man queued in the UK citizens line of passport control at Heathrow. Now his arse was starting to squeak. When he got to the front of the line Fletcher was faced with the automatic E-passport checking booth. He stepped onto the footprints indicating where feet should be placed and looked into the camera; the glass sliding doors didn't open. After a second attempt and placing his passport the other way up it still didn't accept the passport. An officious border agency officer came over, unnerving Connolly, alias Fletcher.

'Give me your passport, sir. Is it an E-passport?

Fletcher replied nervously.

'What is wrong, um............yes, I think it is.'

'Yes, sir, it is a biometric passport; it has a chip that stores all your data, enabling border force officers to detect false or tampered with passports. Step aside and let me try it. The official placed the passport face down on the screen; it started to scan and read the ID. The officer told Fletcher to go and stand back onto the foot placement markers and look into the camera and wait. The flash went and the gates, as if by magic, opened. Fletcher collected his passport then walked through the green channel of Nothing to Declare and into the arrivals hall. Connolly, alias Fletcher, felt good to be back on British soil even though he was a traitor. First he had to check in with an IRF group. He received an encrypted password on his phone which enabled him access to his contact.

The very first thing he was going to do, regardless of what the IS Taliban had instructed, was to visit a western woman along with a decent scotch whisky. So Fletcher headed for Soho where there was plenty of both on offer; he picked up a street girl, negotiated a deal for a whole night stay over; Connolly considered the deal a reasonable price. Next he hired a car to drive them to a run down, sleazy, hot bedding hotel. Fletcher paid cash to the man behind the caged reception then threw another fifty note at him for total anonymity. The desk clerk was obviously the owner and asked.

'Can I get you any drinks.?' The proprietor stuffed the cash into a thick wad of twenty and fifty pound notes then slipped the roll back into his pocket.

'Yeah, a bottle of scotch! Another couple of twenties were thrown on the desk. The roll came out again. In exchange, the seedy owner passed a bottle of scotch through a small square opening in the security mesh.

Fletcher and the prostitute went along a dark corridor with at least ten rooms, five on either side. Halfway along on the left was their room for the night, number 207. The last number on the door, seven, was at a thirty-degree angle. It has probably hung at an acute angle for years, given the state of the olive-green paint. They went into a room that stunk of stale tobacco, cheap perfume and sex. It made a sickly cocktail of unbearable odour.

The torn curtains stretched over a thin rope making it impossible to open them. On a small table, green furry mould cultured on the surface of a half-pint of stale milk. This just about capped off the room's shabby squalor.

The lady didn't hang around; she knew her job well and her bargaining best came to the fore.

'Do you want the special menu tonight? Of course, it'll be another fifty quid but well worth it honey?'

'Just shut your face you whore and get your kit off quick.'

He was very rough, even edging on serious assault. Previous experiences with these sorts of men told her to take it and say nothing. He had finished with her for the time being and rolled off her to reach for the scotch. Connolly didn't bother with a glass, he swigged the liquor from the bottle. Even the prostitute thought sarcastically, *"He's a real class act, this one."*

Fletcher fell asleep with his wallet under his pillow. It wasn't the first whore he'd slept with. At 03:30hrs when Connolly, AKA Fletcher, stirred he unscrewed the now half-empty scotch and took more relaxing comfort from it. The AWOL soldier had missed this sort of life, thinking back to the smelly, cramped conditions of his mountain dwellings as an unwelcome guest of his Taliban paymasters.

Fletcher pulled back the duvet exposing the naked prostitute; he stared at her large tits and thought how out of proportion they looked to her petite body. He noticed many jab marks from heroin on both her arms.

279

Those months in the desert had accentuated Connolly's desire for hard sex. He couldn't or wouldn't wait until a social hour; he shoved her arm and fondled her tits without any hint of romance, just raw lust. Bleary-eyed, she instinctively pulled away until she remembered where and what it was about; she asked out of desperation for some of his scotch.

He snarled back at her with no hint of compassion.

'Fuck off, you poxed ridden bitch, get your head down here and give me the best blow job ever or you will only get half of what I'd agreed.'

She screamed back at him, this time like some streetwise fighting alley-cat.

'You will have to pay more for that, and another thing, you smell of fucking dog shit, what is it?' Connolly went berserk and swung the partly filled bottle sideways, knocking the whore straight out. Blood was coming from a slight gash on her cheek but it wasn't deep. She was still breathing. He turned her face up, slid off her pants, got between her legs, penetrating her again, hard and fast. This time she didn't complain, she couldn't, the prostitute was still unconscious when he had finished. After emptying the scotch, he tied his hired tart to the bed and gagged her with her panties stuffed inside her mouth and held in place by strips of bed sheet. He fell back to sleep on his wallet with the whore lying beside him tied to the bed head. At this point she was still unconscious from the bottle swipe.

The bed's violent shaking awoke Connolly/ Fletcher; it was the tied-up prostitute trying to wriggle free and trying to scream muffled protestations unsuccessfully.

Fletcher dressed, blew the night lady a kiss, rolled up a ten-pound note and wedged it up the crack of her arse, venomously saying.

'That's all you deserve; think yourself lucky I haven't slit your throat.'

He went downstairs to reception and told the shady proprietor 'I'm knocking twenty quid off my bill. That's how much there is left on the prostitute meter. Go help yourself; here's the key, and I'll take twenty quid back. The seedy man didn't argue with the big red Irishman so Fletcher was reimbursed before leaving.

The slimy toad-like proprietor couldn't believe his luck; he went up to the room and found the girl trying to scream but couldn't as her gag was still secure. The dishevelled owner cut her bonds, rolled her over, and exposed her nudity; he undressed and approached her.

'I understand there are twenty pounds left on you.' He giggled more with excitement than humour. He pressed himself entirely onto her, but that was the last he could remember. The empty whiskey bottle was now the weapon of choice for a second time with another knockout within four hours. The prostitute hit him in the centre of his skull. The hotel man went out like a light. The prostitute pushed him from her, sliding out from under his dead weight and checking his pulse; she'd had much experience at this. Many of her weird clients would want affixation to heighten their sensational pleasure to a state of unconsciousness. The grubby hostel owner was alive but would have a sore head when he came round. After relieving him of his fat money roll, the vengeful prostitute dressed, spat on the house proprietor and slammed the door of room 207 behind her. After unlocking the caged reception, she helped herself to another two hundred pounds from his till for added compensation. She thought; *"Apart from a bruised head it was a good night's work money-wise."*

She left the hotel and melted into the crowd searching for her Crack supplier and pimp. But, of course, she would not be declaring her added bonus.

Maximus was pleased with B company's performance in taking the heavily defended position from the opposing regiment at the joint manoeuvres.

Back at his quarters, Max made his constitutional cup of tea, picked up the paper and post, slumped into the well-worn sofa and perused the headlines of the Times momentarily, only to then toss it onto the coffee table. He then picked up his three envelopes. One had the Brandscombe coat of arms, guessing it was one of his mother's regular letters. She detests emailing, believing that e-letters are impersonal and added to the demise of good handwriting, lost forever in these modern times. Max looked at the second letter; this was a brown MoD envelope he had nervously been expecting. He tore it open with fumbling hands and read the contents.

"Dear Mr Hainsworth-Catt, please be advised that following the briefing course you attended at 22 Regiment Hereford, we can confirm that you have been selected to attend our winter course at Brecon, South Wales. It will be a stern endurance and skills test under extreme weather conditions. Owing to the demands on a candidate's body, you will be required to undergo a rigorous medical examination before your trial commences.

You will not be obliged to complete the course and are free to leave and return to your mother regiment anytime. Please find below directions and dates, including enrolment times.

Good luck.
Training officer 22 SAS, Hereford."

Max got butterflies just by reading the content; he had waited so long for this, in fact, since the Carrow Abbey Rifle Corp. The young captain went straight to the colonel's office and gave him the news; he will leave for the Brecon winter programme in three weeks. Max passed the confirmation letter over to Colonel Laurence Abel who, with a loud sigh, expressed his feelings. 'I'm going to miss your battalion input and indeed your friendship Maximus.'

'Likewise sir, I will miss the rifles and the military guidance and opportunities you have given me over my three years here.'

Returning to his office, Max reread the letter to make sure he was potentially joining The Regiment.

He then remembered the third typewritten letter he hadn't opened, addressed unusually without a title prefix, just to *"To Hainsworth-Catt."* Which Max thought was very strange as he dithered to open it for a moment. Now this one did surprise him. It was from Patrick Connolly!!!!!

"You had better take notice of this warning, you pompous know-it-all fucker! I'm back in the UK to finish you off once and for all. You escaped my attempt to kill you in Chepstow, but you will wish I had succeeded then, as I intend to make you suffer badly for ruining my army career and subjecting me to a life on the run. Not able to see my family or walk freely to my local pub. Private Palanski has joined me now and we are in an IRF safe house somewhere in the UK. Keep looking over your shoulder; you shouldn't go out in the dark on your own, that is if you want to extend your miserable life. I will get a fat reward from the Taliban for killing you. They hate you as much as I do. The crazy joy I will get when I terminate your pathetic life will be indescribable. I am getting $75,000 for doing it

but I'd do it for nothing. You'll wish you had never crossed Patrick Connolly. Death awaits you soon, and it won't be pretty. My solemn promise to you.

PC."

.

25

A stunned Maximus sat back on his sofa and wondered: *"How has Connolly had been able to get back into the UK with a description of him posted nationwide including all sea and airports. The letter says he's met up with Palanski, so he must be communicating by phone. Could he be getting Palanski to do his dirty work for him while still in Afghanistan?"*

Maximus agreed to spend the following weekend with Penny. He was, as he expected, collared by her into shopping for new clothes for Terry Dixon's wedding that was on the following weekend. They spent most of Saturday morning at Cribbs Causeway, Bristol, on a shopping marathon. After three hours of shopping Penny was satisfied with her outfit, hat and shoes so they decided to have coffee. Max could sense Penny's brain was working overtime, and sure enough out came the mental computation: 'We are only a few miles from Weston-super-Mare and we do have the weekend to ourselves; let's book into a hotel and enjoy an old fashioned Victorian seaside weekend shall we?'

'Sounds like a great suggestion Pen; let's do it.' They pulled off the M5 at junction 21 and headed for Weston. They booked into the Royal Hotel on the seafront, close to the Grand Pier, which they could see from their room.

After a couple of drinks in the seafront located Wetherspoons, they went on to the Grand Pier that was only across the road. After playing the slot games they entertained themselves like little kids, including a fierce competitive challenge on the simulated F1 car race game. Two ice creams and a bag of chips later, they strolled along the two-mile stretch of golden sandy beach to the estuary of the River Axe and Brean Down. The Down reaches out like a long finger into the tidal Bristol Channel. Finally, they climbed the natural dunes that led across the Weston super Mare links golf course's public footpath. They followed the path across the links to the main road and then back along the seafront promenade to re-join the beach to head northwards for the return walk towards their hotel.

Surprisingly the sea was in, allowing them to kick the surf and play like kids which was a total respite from recent near-tragic events. Max wondered at the two islands out in the Bristol Channel and Penny explained. 'They are called Flat and Steep Holm; you can see them from Cardiff as well. I think they are bird sanctuaries.'

'You are the font of all knowledge Penny.'

Max pointed northwards towards the old Birnbeck pier informing her.

'About fifteen miles up this channel is Beachley, my barracks. Did you know Pen, this channel has the second-highest tide in the world!'

'Is that because the sea goes out a long way for such a long time here?'

'No, the moon controls that; the side of the earth facing the moon creates a bulge, causing the sea levels to squeeze then rise.'

'Hark at you, Professor Hainsworth-Catt.'

They both laughed as Max kicked a foot full of seawater at Penny, who in turn cupped her hands, scooped them full of water and returned the wet compliment.

Max pulled the gorgeous Penny Richards in close to him. There was no resistance from her; they kissed with the ebbing tide rolling over their feet. It was a day they would both remember forever. Max thought to himself, *"I could easily get used to having this beautiful, witty and funny lady around me forever"*. The sun was setting over the channel and dipping into Cardiff; it was a cloudless day. The western sky changed with a crimson glow that bathed the sea, forming an artist's dream of a perfect seascape. Whether it was this aura mixed with the happiness he had never felt before, Max wasn't sure. But what he did know was how his heart yearned to be in her company, how his body felt so natural laying next to hers and how hollow he felt when they were apart. Max knelt in the now shallow retreating tide, he took both of Penny's hands, looked into her angelic face and proposed:

'Penny Richards, please do me the ultimate honour. Will you marry me! I love you so much, and I want to feel like this forever?' There was not the slightest of pauses.

'Yes, my darling Maximus, yes, oh yes.'

Penny pulled Max up to her, and they skipped like kids in the departing surf. They hardly spoke, but it was evident to any passer-by they were deeply in love.

'Max I am so happy; promise me this feeling I have will last forever; my heart is bursting with joy. A feeling not achievable with any other pleasure I have experienced. Max, stop just a moment.'

Penny took a little red box from her small carry bag and opened it; she delicately lifted out a beautifully carved gold antique St Christopher and chain.

'Please always wear this for me in your dangerous world my love.'

Penny opened the chain and placed it around Max's neck, closing the clasp.

'Pen I will wear and cherish it forever. I love you so much.' Max raised his traveller's talisman to his lips and kissed it. They walked barefoot in the surf and holding hands ignoring everything else around them including the diminishing waves and the receding tide.

The loving couple finished their perfect day at an excellent Italian restaurant called Michelangelos, Jim, the maitre'd for that evening was touched by their eventful day and although the eatery was full, he made sure he got them in. Over a chilled bottle of Champagne the couple toasted their promising and exciting future together.

'Do you remember our day out in Ross-on-Wye? We were looking in an antique shop window and I asked you to fetch my wrap from the car; well that was a ruse. While you were away, I bought St Christopher for you. I wanted it to keep you safe, albeit by legend. Today was an appropriate time to give it to you.'

'My darling Pen I am off on a month's mountain trial with UKSF in three weeks. I'll always treasure this.' Max fingered his delicate ornate traveller's talisman. They left the restaurant hand in hand, taking a final brief stroll along the promenade back to the hotel and, of course, the romantic, passionate lovemaking heightened by their extraordinary commitment to each other. The heartfelt proposal on the beach will be an unforgettable day at the famous Victorian seaside town. Max still didn't tell Pen of the threat from Connolly; why should he let that scumbag spoil their magical weekend!

It was all happening at the barracks! The stand-in captain was arriving to replace Max in B company, the boys were organising a stag night for Terry and the colonel had a ding dong with headquarters over budget cuts. Some privates in A company have gone AWOL together and two of Max's B company are on a charge for fighting in a Chepstow pub with the locals. Max thought: *"I've only been away for the weekend and all hell has broken out. It's never dull in 1st Rifles."*

Max went to Terry's stag do in Cardiff; they went to the usual stripper show in the Grangetown district, a sleazy joint aptly named *"Up The Pole."* After several hours of drinking in various establishments, they finished up in the famous Parachute Club, named apparently, as fellas are pretty much assured of a jump there on *"Grab a Granny night."* The boys thought the name of the club was hilariously funny; and soon understood why it was named so. Some old bird tried cuddling up to Max, asking him if he would like to buy her a drink and finish the night at her flat which was enough for Max. He decided to leave the boys and took a cab home, leaving money with Tim Forbes to buy three platoon the last few drinks of the night.

Max picked up Penny at 10:00hrs. Even after toning down her appearance so as not to outshine the bride Penny still looked positively sensational. It had been quite a challenge for Penny not to overshadow the bride. *"God knows what Penny will look like on our wedding day."* Max held that thought with pride. Terry's wedding was at 13.00hrs. Max parked his car as close as he could to the little church in Lydney. St Mary The Virgin, a quaint, spired church with the typical elegance of its period.

Lydney was the birthplace of Sophie, Terry's bride. This attracted a crowd of villagers from the local community who had gathered outside the church awaiting the special event.

"How close dear Terry had come to not being here for this." Max reflected. The young captain was so pleased for this happy day; Terry deserved everything good in his life.

A nudge from Pen brought her fiancé back from his dreamworld.

'What are you daydreaming about this time Maximus, my fiancé ?'

'Oh nothing, Pen, just give me a kiss please.'

'You are so random at times Max-Catt.'

With the congregation settled, the vicar performed the ceremony articulately and ten minutes later, Corporal Terry Dixon and Sophie were married.

'Don't fuck this up or you'll regret it, have you got it?' Patrick Connolly threatened Tom Palanski.

'Yes Pat, no problem.'

'You are only out of the clutches of the MPs and civil police because the IRF cell are hiding you. So we must repay the debt by taking out that fucking Hainsworth-Catt. By completing that pleasurable task, I get seventy-five-thousand big ones, of which you will get twenty plus your freedom.'

'I know Pat. I'll be waiting, engine running one hundred metres from the church.' Connolly explained his plan.

'I am now going to get into position in that big tree overlooking the cemetery and the church's main entrance.'

Connolly moved down the narrow lane with the church to his left, carrying a bagged rifle hanging from his shoulder. He looked in front and behind, about eighty or so metres from the arched entrance. Connolly climbed over the stone boundary wall and in a calm nonchalant stroll made his way to the scattered gravestones and moving out of sight behind a big Yew tree. He took iron pegs with sharpened ends, a hammer and rope from his backpack. Connolly hammered the first two pegs into the blindside of the trunk and pulled himself up by the top peg while standing on the lower one. Next, he hit another metal peg higher. Stepping onto the second spike, repeating the procedure until he had six pegs in position, forming steps to the first major branches. The would-be assassin looked around quickly before hoisting himself onto a sizeable bough. From here, numerous branches enabled him to ascend to the higher part of the majestic tree.

He straddled the high thick bow branch, settled himself and thought: It was the sniper training Max had given him on the firing range, that will, ironically, make the officer's own assassination a doddle. He pushed a cartridge into the barrel, adjusted his telescopic sight to the church entrance, released the safety clip and waited for the congregation to spill out for the photos. Connolly waited patiently. Having time to fine-tune the sights by taking a practice shot at a small bird, probably a sparrow. He adjusted the sights on his rifle, aimed at the perched bird and getting the cross sights in line, breathed in and slowly squeezed the trigger. There was no noise from the muffled rifle, but the little bird disintegrated into feathery bits that disappeared. Connolly thought to himself. *"The sights are well adjusted, my target will be easy, and within half an hour, Hainsworth-Catt will be dead, and I'll be a richer and happier man for it!"*

The wait for Connolly was about to end, the church doors opened!

26

The first to exit the church by tradition was the bridal party, the families followed and then the rest of the congregation. Connolly soon picked out his target, moving his sights along the wedding guests, he soon recognised his nemesis; the captain! *"This is going to be so easy."* The sniper thought. Connolly expanded the magnification on the rifle's sights and adjusting the crosshairs until Max's forehead was intersected. The young officer was standing still, making the assassination even more straightforward than Connolly could hope for. His finger took up the slack on the trigger. Connolly thought. *"In under a second, you are dead! No, instant death is too easy on you; I must make you suffer you pompous bastard."* Connolly lowered his rifle, wiped the sweat from his forehead with the back of his hand and considered his easy options.

Max and Pen were mingling with the guests, they were talking to three platoon lads while waiting to be called by the photographer for the full group photos. Max couldn't stop himself. He took control of Pen's movements as she went to pass him. He swung her into his embrace like some dance routine. The romantic captain kissed her lips. She looked up at him with an expression he had not seen on Penny ever before. It was beautifully serene but with a curious, vacant stare that perplexed and worried Max. Penny's expression transformed to a weird, cold and expressionless gaze. Now her eyes were wild, unfocused, something was wrong. Penny fell slightly forward onto her knees, supported by Max she slipped gently sideways onto the grass where she lay in Max's arms, motionless. Max was able to break her fall and cradled his love. Max couldn't perceive what was happening. He panicked; he raised Penny's head a little, this allowed blood to trickle from the side of her mouth. Max immediately knew this was serious. Pen started to cough and spluttered blood down her chin, splashing her pale blue outfit, and spotting Max's white jacket. The captain was now in a real panic and shouted at Pen:

'What is it Penny? What's wrong with you, my darling?' He crouched over her, easing Penny closer to him. It was then he realised what had happened to his fiancé. A neat 9mm hole was leaking blood; he knew immediately that Penny had been shot in the back of her head and definitely by a sniper!

Between coughing up blood, Penny quietly said to her love: 'I'm dying my darling Max, it's too late for an ambulance or doctor I know. But it's not too late for the vicar! Please...,' Penny coughed up a clot of thickened blood. 'call him from his church; please marry me here before I die. I love you so much my darling. Please always think of me when you have no one to turn to and take strength from. Our unique love and understanding will always pull you through'. Tears from sadness, not pain, were falling down Penny's cheeks.

The vicar responded to the call and ran from his church to kneel beside Penny and Max, who cradled his dying fiancé. The vicar started the rushed marriage ceremony. The gathering crowd were stunned into silence. Incredibly most were still not aware of what had occurred. Penny was hanging on to life as the vicar was finalising the rushed and makeshift ceremony. He didn't marry the hapless couple! His body was flung violently backwards like a gymnast. A neat red hole in the centre of his forehead explained his mysterious backflip before lying face down on the grass motionless next to Max and the dying Penny.

The vicar was dead! Max ignored the demise of the religious man, he had no time; he screamed at the colonel. 'Marry us quickly colonel'

'I've never done this before, but I'll give it my best.'

'Just get on with it, marry Pen and me now; and as quick as you can.' The colonel cut out any unnecessary words and asked Penny if she would take Max to be her lawful wedded husband. Penny coughed up a great deal more blood but managed to say yes. The same rushed question to Max and before the commanding officer could finish the question Max replied, 'Yes, yes, yes'. Colonel Abel then pronounced them Man and Wife. Upon those words the lovely Penny Hainsworth-Catt forced a peaceful smile, squeezed Maxi's hand and looking him in the eyes whispered, Max, I love you so. She closed her eyes for the very last time, slipping peacefully away. Max couldn't release Penny's hand; he didn't want to leave her ever, he buried his face in her bloodstained neck and sobbed like a child.

The wedding guests, who by now realised somebody was shooting at them, ran hysterically for cover back into the church. The choirmaster was kneeling over the dead vicar crying without shame. The colonel was shepherding people back into the church for safety. Max ran towards the direction from where he thought the silent shots had come from, with anger now replacing sorrow for the moment. Max desperately wanted to face Penny's and the vicar's cold-blooded killer.

Connolly speedily but without panic descended the tree the way he went up. He kept the big tree between him and the church, leaping over the stone wall and sprinting a hundred metres to the waiting Tom Palanski; the car's engine was already running and ready to go; they sped off away from the the church. The planned assassination had been well rehearsed, and their escape was assisted by an IRF (Islamic Revolutionary Front) sleeper cell. Connolly's hired getaway car was returned and he went to the IRF house as arranged. Palanski decided to stay at a safe house of a friend rather than with the terrorist cell. He didn't trust them. He planned to keep off the streets for a while.

Asim, the IRF cell commander, was livid with Fletcher AKA Connolly and demanded why Fletcher had not killed the intended target, the hated Maximus Hainsworth-Catt when he had the chance.

'His bitch got in the way at the last minute and there was a load of soldiers who were guests coming after me. I had to get out of there but you have my word, he will be dead within the week.' Asim was still angry and warned Connolly not to make any more mistakes. Asim had made a threat to the wrong man!

Max got to the tree and soon noticed the iron pegs in the trunk and the fresh footprints around the base. He knew straight away this was where the weapon was fired from that killed Penny and the vicar. Each shot's angle was about mid-tree height. The assassin, not surprisingly, had gone. It was therefore no point in Max continuing the search for Connolly. *"But why didn't he kill me, why my darling Pen, he couldn't have missed from the tree's distance. Was he playing with me by destroying Penny, just making me suffer longer? I wished it was me and not my darling wife that died today"!* Anger and hatred towards his wife's assassin had stimulated a new motivation of revenge within Max! At the foot of the tree from where the lethal two shots were fired Max vowed to avenge his wife's killer!

Max ran back to the scene of carnage and stayed kneeling over Penny's body that he had covered with his coat. Fortunately, the ambulances arrived soon after Max had got back to Pen.

Max was in shock as he left the distressed crowd crying and screaming in various groups. The police, by this time had cordoned off the scene and had already started interviewing guests. The bride was sobbing in the arms of her new husband, Terry, who didn't know what to do but console his distraught wife.

Maximus explained to the police what had happened and made a complete statement. The young captain explained his suspicions and Connolly's motives. But of course, they didn't know his pseudo name was Fletcher. Max gave the police a copy of the threatening letter he received and told them that Connolly is wanted by the security forces for orchestrating the attempted murder of Terry Dixon and his involvement in the Grand Hotel attempted bombing.

Max travelled to the hospital in the ambulance holding Penny's hand all the way. At the hospital Max asked to stay with her; he couldn't leave his lovely wife. The mortuary staff allowed Max to say his goodbyes. Max was in a real bad way and he unashamedly broke down, crying his heart out. Max couldn't concentrate on anything nor wanted to. The young captain had never felt so sad in his life; he was inconsolable and felt his existence now meant nothing.

It was 22:00hrs and the mortuary staff finally led Max to reception. Max had lost his beautiful wife of just a minute. The hospital had lost a top A&E doctor, and the whole mood within the hospital was sombre. They called Max a taxi; he left, still in a state of numbness with his world blown apart. He told the cab to take him to Penny's apartment in Shirenewton. He went through her wardrobe, holding her clothes to his face and inhaling her particular unique scent. Max prayed for the first time since he was a child, asking God to care for his darling wife and for her to wait for him. He knew he would never fall in love again. He repeatedly kissed the St Christopher that Penny gave to him. It will never leave his side. Max cried himself to sleep, hugging Pen's dress close to him.

Colonel Laurence Abel phoned Max the following day and offered his deepest condolences. Max thanked him and apologised. 'Sir I am so sorry for barking at you yesterday, I was losing Penny fast and you were the only person who could marry us. I am so distraught but so grateful to you for performing that rushed marriage, it meant so much to us both. The police had better catch that bastard Connolly before I do. Connolly will rue the day he crossed my path.'

Max told his commanding officer about the threatening letter from Connolly.

'Bloody hell Max, why did he not kill you yesterday when evidently he had you in his sights.'

'He should have sir, because he will regret he didn't when I find him.'

'Don't throw your promising career away by doing something stupid Max; leave it to the police. We have not had this conversation. However, I do understand why you want your revenge. Just think about the consequences, please.'

'Thank you sir.' The boss was right, Max realised he will need proof it was Connolly.

'Take a few days off Max, no need to rush back; I have your replacement, so we are not understaffed. Just call me the day before you return.'

'Yes sir, and thank you so much.'

27

Max planned to go straight to Brandscombe for solace; however he knew he had to meet Connolly's threat head on. It was now his number one priority. He thought Connolly must have an alias with supporting identification documentation. He couldn't have got through the UK border control otherwise. It was probably organised and paid for by IRF.

Max's dilemma is how to track down Connolly before he gets to Max. There was only one connection the captain could think of to find out Connolly's new identity.

Ahmed, the terrorist who tried to blow up the Grand Hotel was currently in a Winchester hospital, still under armed guard. Max had to speak with him covertly, without any witnesses around.

Max worked out the basis of a plan. He will need to visit the medical officer at Beachley to get some ketamine which can render a person unconscious for twenty to thirty minutes with one dose. Max calculated that period would be the minimum he needed to make his plan work so Max went to sickbay. The captain knew the MO well enough. They played together for the battalion rugby team and had many beers together afterwards both in Beachley and Afghanistan. He knew Max but still quizzed him about the ketamine request as it was a potent drug.

'Ryan please trust me on this; it's so important; I promise I'll tell you why I want it after I have used it.'

'I shouldn't, Max, but I do trust you; I know you are a decent guy. But I can't supply it to you legally.

Ketamine should be entered into the poison book. Any potent drug does. So please be careful with it. I'm only going to give you one dose.'

'Thanks Ryan, that's all I need .'

Dr Ryan Hurst gave Maximus a quizzical look, raising his eyebrows to their highest point on his forehead.

They went to the pharmacy together and Ryan took a small brown bottle from the top shelf and tipped two ten-gramme tablets into a small tablet box and handed it to Max. Ryan didn't enter the tablets into the poison book so it wasn't written up as a transaction.

'Thanks for trusting me Ryan. I appreciate your help.'

'What help? I do not know what you are talking about.' The two friends looked at each other with a cheeky grin. Max left with what he came for.

Back at Penny's flat Max found disposable scrubs in her wardrobe. He went through Penny's medical bag and took out a stethoscope and a lanyard with her hospital identity card hanging from it. Max kissed her name and swore revenge. That particular moment shook him, realising he would never enjoy those special moments they shared, ever again. Max thought no one could understand the sheer happiness they experienced together. Shaking himself back into reality he used Penny's laptop and printer to print out the name of Doctor Timothy Nalder. Tim was going to be a relief locum. Pen had taught Max enough medical jargon to talk his way out of trouble if need be. Finally he must find out if Ahmed was still in the hospital in Winchester. Max phoned the hospital on the pretence of being a family member of Ahmed's.

'My nephew has been at your hospital, his name is Ahmed. Can you confirm he hasn't been discharged and also can you tell me your visiting hours please.'

'One moment sir,' The receptionist checked on her computer. 'Hello. Yes, Ahmed Zaheer is still in here, but you need special clearance to visit him I'm afraid. He is deemed a flight risk; therefore, he is under armed guard. You will have to get clearance from the police. I am told you will need identification in the form of a passport. They will carry out a clearance check on you while you wait at the Winchester main police station. That's all I can help you with at this moment. Goodbye sir.'

Max had miscalculated the visiting restrictions on Ahmed, with the almost visa-like security pass required from the police to visit the terrorist. The captain realised he will have to rethink his hospital visit; he certainly will not get clearance from the police. They know Max was the soldier who stopped Ahmed at the regimental dinner in Winchester. Max will now put his plan B into operation, but must move swiftly as Ahmed will, no doubt, be transferred any day to a secure prison. So Max will activate his move for tomorrow night.

'Jen I haven't until now discussed events with anyone in detail apart from the debriefing with MI5. However I wanted you to be the first to know the details of the death of your sister and my lovely wife.' Max was holding back tears as he explained to Jenny over the phone.

'Max I am proud to be your sister-in-law. But God knows I'm going to miss her so much.'

'Jenny what would you say if I decided to try and avenge our Penny by attempting to get the bastard who shot her?'

'I'd say do it every time, give me a gun and I would kill him myself.'

'That's what I thought you would say, if I was able to deal with Connolly would you act as an alibi for me?

'Yes Max, without hesitation.'

'Thank you Jen, it may involve me stealing a car, impersonating a doctor and ultimately murder!

Are you still able to cover for me?'

'Sure Max, I am a law-abiding citizen, but the bastard who killed my twin sister should pay with his life, not just put in a cushy prison with all the mod cons. We should never have abolished hanging! I'd string the piece of shit up by his balls if I had my way.'

'This is very serious Jen and I want you to sleep on what I have asked of you; let me know you if you feel the same tomorrow.'

'My answer will not change, but yes, we'll speak tomorrow.'

'Goodnight Jenny.'

The young captain stayed at Pen's as he wanted to feel her things around him for as long as possible. Apart from that, he needed the solitude to grieve alone. Max was fully aware that time was running out to kidnap his hospital patient who is the only lead to finding Connolly.

'Hello Jen. Well, what's the answer?

'As I said last night, whatever it takes to get Connolly. I'm in all the way. That means anything goes!'

'Good to hear that and thanks Jen, I knew I could rely on you. Do not mention what I am doing to anyone, even close family.'

Jenny Richards promised silence about the covert work ahead.

Max went shopping for a wheelchair and some other tools he'd need.

It was 16:00hrs, torrential rain was hammering down in Winchester; just what Max needed, he thought sarcastically.

The young officer made his way on foot to the multi-storey car park he had selected. Max had purchased clear, thick framed glasses, a false beard with tinges of grey and a pork pie hat to complete his disguise. He felt conspicuous but the disguise was essential. He waited for the next suitable vehicle to arrive. Waiting behind a concrete pillar, he fumbled with keys as if looking for his car fob.

A businessman arrived in his car and got out carrying a black briefcase and umbrella. He was probably a sales representative making his last call of the day; he didn't know Max had chosen his car to borrow. As soon as the businessman was out of sight, Max went around the blind side of the car. It had automatic locks but that was no problem, although the would-be thief will need to work as fast as possible and certainly before the owner's car fob's signal is out of range of the car. Max took the recently purchased tools for the crime out of his bag: a putty knife, a plastic wedge, pliers, and a thin improvised welding rod. He used disposable gloves. It was easy to slide the putty knife down through the top of the car door. Max covered the thin scraper with cling film so as not to scratch the car's paintwork. With a slight gap opening, Max pushed the plastic wedge in and with a couple of hits from the palm of his hand he opened a gap wide enough to slide the rod down onto the window rocker button inside. Slight pressure lowered the window and Max was in. All within twenty seconds. He couldn't delay, so stuck his foot on the brake and pressed the start button; thankfully the car fired up. Max gave it five minutes for the owner to leave the car park. The captain drove the borrowed vehicle to where his car was parked in a quiet road with no cameras. Max transferred the wheelchair to his new stolen transport and carried out a mental checklist: scrubs, ID badge, gloves, stethoscope and the two tablets.

Max placed false number plates on the new stolen vehicle with Velcro tape then drove to Winchester General Hospital. He put on the scrubs and a surgical cap in the car park, hung his stethoscope and ID badge around his neck and confidently walked into reception. The young officer parked up the wheelchair with a casual, almost nonchalant swagger. Max lent over the counter and explained to the receptionist while flipping his ID towards her.

'I'm Dr Timmy Nalder, locum; I've been sent to check on patient Ahmed Zaheer; he's had a complication with a leg injury. His consultant has asked for a second opinion on his leg infection!'

The receptionist checked her computer screen, returned her gaze to Max and told him 'Mr Zaheer is in West Ward 3; take the lift on your left to the third floor, turn right, fifth door on the right. You should find it okay doctor.'

'Thank you for such detailed directions.' Replied Max.

Max collected the parked wheelchair and couldn't help glancing at himself as he walked past the full-length mirror next to the lifts. He thought he looked the part of a doctor.

The lift stopped on the second floor and a doctor entered; he nodded a little quizzically and asked.

'Are you new at the General?'

'Yes I'm a locum, I have been asked to cover for holidays. The lift stopped on the third floor and the doors opened. 'This is me,' said the bogus doctor. 'See you around.'

Max left the elevator with the wheelchair and headed for the ward. The ward sister confirmed the room Max wanted. She pointed down the corridor where he could see the armed guard at the far end leaning against the wall. Max thanked the stern looking nurse and headed towards the guard who didn't take any notice of someone in a white coat with a medical hat on and pushing a wheelchair. Max stopped and spoke with the armed copper and said 'I need to check on Ahmed Zaheer. Is he in there?'

'Do you have your signed pass sir? I can't let you in without that clearance?'

Of course. I was dressing his leg this morning but left my pass just inside of the door on the medicine shelf. I showed it to your colleague but forgot to pick it up. Can I get it?'

'No, not allowed, but I'll get it for you.'

The unsuspecting officer went in to the room, he had only made his first step when Max placed his muscular arm around his neck while clamping it in place with his left hand. With his strong arm behind the neck of the now incapacitated policeman Max squeezed his carotid artery pressure point restricting the brain's blood flow and temporarily rendering the guard unconscious. Quickly he taped the guard's hands and legs together then stuck a gauze cloth bandage in his mouth with sticky tape across it to keep it in place. Max had to move fast. The shocked Ahmed Zaheer couldn't believe what had just happened. He didn't raise the alarm but shouted at Max.

'Have you come to get me out of here?'

'Er yes.' Max explained Connolly had organised it and that he was down in the car park waiting for them.

'I can't walk far.' Ahmed complained.

'Don't worry, take these two tablets; they will relieve the pain and mildly sedate you. However, they will make you drowsy for about ten minutes so don't speak once we have left the room.'

Max put the tablets into a glass of water, Zaheer drank it down in one; The bogus doctor pulled the wheelchair into the room and told Ahmed to sit in it. Next Max attended to the reviving copper whose muffled objection sounded comical. The captain sat him up and dragged him into a large store cupboard, shutting, but not locking the door.

The ketamine was already starting to work; the terrorist was getting delirious, mumbling and dribbling simultaneously. God knows what he was trying to say. Max looked at his watch; he gave him another three minutes, as Max wanted him, non-compos mentis before they left the room. The young officer made one last check on the guard; This set the captive into another tirade of violent head shaking and more muffled screams. The impersonating doctor closed the door on him once more. Ahmed was completely unconscious now; his head had rolled onto his right shoulder. Max stuck the pork-pie hat on Ahmed and opened the door, pushing his pretend patient along the corridor to the elevator and retracing his incoming journey. Max avoided eye contact at reception and didn't stop. No one appeared alarmed or interested in them and Max made it uninterrupted back to the stolen car. He made a quick check for watching eyes then lifted the dead weight of Zaheer into the boot. He then pushed the wheelchair into the bushes and drove back to his own car. Max took the false number plates off the stolen vehicle and disposed of them in a commercial refuse bin nearby, leaving the car parked up in a location where it could easily be found. Max was in surgical dress for the whole escape plan, including gloves so there should be no trace of his presence. With Zaheer still out cold, Max thought it wise to secure him so he bound his legs with duct tape and put some over his mouth as well. He was still handcuffed from his hospital detention. The young Rifles officer drove his own car alongside the borrowed one and transferred Ahmed, with some difficulty as Ahmed was a dead weight, on to the back seat of his Porsche. Max had earlier decided that the best place to interrogate him would be Brandscombe. He still had the key to his lodge so that was to be Max's next destination.

Max had a pay as you go phone that was still in the box. He installed the sim, and after charging the phone in his car, he was surprised it worked. A message came through to say he had £4.50 worth of credit. Max phoned the hospital and spoke to the receptionist, probably the same person he had spoken to earlier in the day. He now mimicked an accent he had picked up in Afghanistan as best he could. 'This is the Islamic Revolutionary Front; we have taken back our hero Ahmed Zaheer. You infidels are not as smart as you think. We shall rule the world one day. You have a pig inside the cupboard of the room where Zaheer was. You'd better get him out! Allah-hu-Akbar.' Max put the phone in a drain after removing and destroying the sim thinking that that call should keep the security forces off his back for a while at least.

28

Max drove into Brandscome Manor, the saddest homecoming he had ever made. Revenge for his dead wife spurred him on. He parked his car by the garage totally out of sight of the house. Jarvis answered the door. The family were not expecting him and he surprised them with his visit. Max received much sympathy from his parents. It was still hard to bear, reliving that dreadful day. Max welled up with more outpourings of grief reminding him of what he'd lost. Finally, Max excused himself. Understandably so his parents thought. Their youngest son went to his bedroom, waited twenty minutes and then made his way out to the fire escape at the rear of the big house. He left the fire door off the latch for his covert return. His car still held the now wide-awake terrorist.

Max drove slowly to his lodge, switched on the lights and closed the curtains. His lodge was a substantial timber and stone cabin; it had a useful cellar accessed by a trap door with steep stairs. The sub-ground level was a large, ventilated room. Max had played there on many wet days as a child never imagining what was about to unfold tonight. He received a muffled greeting from Ahmed as he hoisted him out of the cramped back seats of the sports car. Max cut free the would-be-bomber's legs from his tape straps to assist the rear seat extraction. The prisoner was pushed through the lodge door towards the stairs that led down to the cellar. The accommodation was spacious, on the ground floor was a living room, kitchen, bathroom, study and a bedroom; the first floor comprised two bedrooms and a bathroom. However, the cellar was chosen as the most suitable place for what Max had in mind as it was soundproof! Zaheer muffled a scream that Max assumed was a protest about his injured leg. Max gave him a shove to encourage his reluctance to descend into the underground room. It was out of earshot of the house so there would be no witnesses to what was about to happen.

Max tied Ahmed Zaheer to a chair; his hands were still restricted by the police cuffs, but taping him to the chair was an additional precaution. The best Ahmed could do was stand up and topple over. Max had put on his disguise, greying beard, thick spectacles and a bobble hat replacing the surgical cap he wore at the hospital. Max removed the tape from his captive's mouth.

'What do you fucking want from me; you said you know Connolly; where is he? Who are you?'

Max replied with anger in his voice.

'Shut your foul mouth and listen good. You are going to tell me where Connolly is. This is why! If you don't you will lose a digit off your hands every minute until you have ten stumps down to the first joints; it will be damned hard to pick your fucking nose after I've finished with you. I would imagine you will probably be brave at first, of course, to see if I will actually cut your fingers off. I think you may even get to three amputations before you tell me.' Ahmed's voice was parched.

'Who are you? I will have you killed, you don't know how powerful we are! Where is this place? Are you a British agent?'

Max didn't answer any of his questions but delivered his last ultimatum.

'You must tell me the exact location of Connolly within a thirty-second countdown, 30-29-28............5-4-3-2-1.'

Max didn't speak but walked around Ahmed's back, picked up a small pair of bolt croppers and took the terrorist's smallest finger off at the first joint, as easy as removing a rotten twig from a bush. Max couldn't even feel resistance with the precision action of the tool. With indescribable agony Zaheer screamed at the top of his voice, he stood with his secured chair attached and then lurched backwards nearly toppling his chair over. Max steadied it. The blood was like a dripping tap onto the heavy gauge plastic sheet placed there for that sole purpose. 'Next one Ahmed!' 30-29-28.......5-4-3-2-1.' The index finger from Zaheer's right hand dropped onto the sheet accompanied by increased blood loss. The dripping noise from the two partly amputated fingers made a weird, almost macabre, musical tapping rhythm onto the sheet. It was drowned out by further screaming from the terrorist. Ahmed Zaheer sobbed, swearing in Arabic at his torturer. Max took a photo with his phone of his captive's dripping hand and showed Ahmed what he couldn't see behind his back. *"It's surprising how messy finger removing can look."* thought Max, thinking of Penny which negated any compassion he might have creeping into his head. Max didn't speak this time but started counting again. '30-29-28........5-4-3-2-1.

Snip! Part of a thumb joined the two pinkies already on the plastic sheet. The thumb offered much more resistance, with a thicker bone and more robust sinews, but a neat piece of guillotining all the same. The screams and wailing were ear-piercing but as these abated the pleading started.

'If I tell you will you let me go?' Max thought, *"Here comes the bargaining."*

'Of course, you'll be as free as a bird. You will be taken to a deserted place and left to get yourself sorted out. 30-29........'

'Wait, I'll tell you. You are a madman, who are you?' Max showed no emotion but asked. 'Where? How do I know you will let me go?'

'You don't, but you don't have choices; I do.'

'Why should I believe you.'

'Because I'm the one with the bolt croppers.'

'Okay, okay, he's in a safe house in Luton.'

'Address. I want that fucking address.' Still silence from Zaheer.

'30-29........5-4-3.'

'152 Elmsville Road, Luton. Please don't tell them I told you, please, I beg you.' The now sobbing Ahmed was clearly scared of his terrorist cell.

'I will bandage your hand for you and I have set up a rabbit water feeder with a litre of water in it. You will have to piss your pants as I will not be back until I'm sure Connolly's at the property you said. No one can hear you so save your breath.' I need a description of Connolly's new face as he must have changed his appearance to fool the UK border agency. What does Connolly look like now and what does he call himself. If you get this wrong you will lose more fingers, if not all of them when I return until I get the right information.'

'I can describe him; he has a passport in the name of Jason Fletcher. I only know his name, Tom Palanski told me on the night of the planned Grand Hotel attempted bombing. He was still in Afghanistan at that time so I have never met him. Can I have painkillers for my hand?.' Max ignored Ahmed's plea and demanded he continue with the information he had on Connolly.

'I did hear that they interrogated Connolly for some time before offering him a deal. Our people in Afghanistan believe he is mentally unstable but as he could offer them big targets here in the UK and promised to find and assassinate Captain Hainsworth-Catt they took a chance on him. That's all I know, I promise.

Max thought: *"That's Connolly, alright."*

Max went back to the house via the fire escape, took off his disguise and explained to the family that he had to leave for the barracks. Instead he drove to Luton and located the house. He kept surveillance on 152 Elmsville Road with binoculars, watching for any movement in or out of the property. It was a substantial three-storey place that was no doubt alarmed, with security lights and probably heat sensors. Max got a KFC bucket of chicken nuggets as he hadn't eaten in two days. He was watching and eating but nothing stirred for an hour or so. Then a pizza delivery moped pulled up outside 152 so Max got to him before he could ring the bell. 'I'll take the pizza's; how much?'

Max offered the pizza man a fifty-pound note for the takeaway nosh. The delivery man said the pizza's had already been paid for by card over the phone. 'I know that, this is for your tip.' The surprised young delivery biker thanked the captain and passed over three pizzas. The young captain thought he should be able to recognise Connolly even with his new disguise. His size and body shape would give him away. He rang the doorbell and heard footsteps on the other side of the door. A Middle Eastern man opened the door and went to take the Pizzas; Max pulled them away from the reaching hands. 'There is forty-five quid to pay mate.' Max relied on Connolly's temper to react to the disturbance at the front door. If indeed he was there but instead it was an older man who came to the door opener's assistance.

'What's the problem?' The older man asked.

'This guy said I have to give him forty-five quid for the Pizzas; I thought you paid for them and I heard you give your card details over the phone.' The door opener insisted.

Max shouted louder so anyone else in the house would hear him.

'Unless I get the forty-five quid you ain't getting the pizzas so pay up.' Max's trick worked as two more men came to the door. The temper from the big guy proved it—the unmistakable Irish accent of Patrick Connolly.

'What is your fucking problem? Do you want your teeth pushed down your throat?'

Max thought that's definitely Connolly and answered in the most timid way possible. 'There's a mistake. I'll ring the shop.' So Max pretended to ring the pizza shop.

'Hi is that Joe? Did the order for Elmsville Road pay by card as I had a message with the order to collect payment?' Max looked up to see the four men squeezed together at the open door glaring at him.

'The boss is just checking.'

Connolly couldn't hold back and pushed towards Max, trying to grab him but Max stepped back. Connolly missed his target and just about kept his balance only because he was supported by one of the other men.

'Okay Joe, my mistake,' Max finished his pretend call. 'Here we are guys, your three lovely pizzas.' The older man held Connolly back and took the food delivery before slamming the door in Max's face.

Max chuckled all the way back to his car, thinking mission accomplished. Connolly had his face changed, obviously with plastic surgery, but Max knew Connolly's traits. That was Connolly, no mistake.

Max drove back to Brandscombe Manor. Ahmed was relieved to see him and begged Max to let him have a pee. That was the least Max could do so he released his legs and guided Ahmed outside for a piss; and didn't he pee!!!! After replacing his leg tapes, Max disposed of the blood-stained plastic sheet and threw the two half finger digits and a half thumb down the loo, flushing them to wherever. Max then bundled Ahmed back into his car and drove to Winchester. He walked into the police station with Ahmed and spoke to the custody sergeant. 'This guy hitchhiked a lift with me and is wearing handcuffs which looks pretty suspicious to me and I think he needs to go to the hospital. I'm on double yellow lines. I'll park up and come back to explain what he told me. You had better put him in a cell in the meantime. Give me two minutes officer.' Max hurried out of the station with the sergeant shouting 'Wait a minute.' But Max was gone with no intention of returning. He couldn't say he had returned the prisoner in good condition.

The young captain returned to Penny's apartment to think. After a restless night, Max woke early to the electronic sound of his phone's alarm. It was 04:30hrs; he had packed a rucksack the night before with the required bits and pieces he may need. Max returned to Luton and arrived at 06:45hrs, parking across the road from number 152. He'd arrived early enough, he hoped, to watch any of the occupants of the safe house leave.

Drinking coffee from his flask at 08.00hrs and periodically glancing at his watch was the most exciting things that were happening. Still nothing stirred at 152. Another forty-five minutes passed and Max was just finishing the dregs of his fourth coffee when the door of 152 opened. Three guys, including Connolly, left the house, walking in the opposite direction from Max so he had to wait for the fourth one to leave 152. Max was now dying for a pee and couldn't wait any longer, so he opened the car door and peed in the gutter. The relief was such that it would have been worth a police caution. Unfortunately, he hadn't finished peeing when the door of 152 opened again but Max couldn't just stop. He was in full flow! The last occupant was the older guy who saved Max a thump from Connolly last night. Max only just got back into his car before the cell member reached the other side of the road. As the older man passed by the Porsche he turned towards Max, who prevented himself from being recognised by burying his face into the newspaper he had bought earlier at a service station. The headline read TERRORIST RECAPTURED. The captain was intrigued so read on. *"An unidentified person handed the escaped terrorist Ahmed Zaheer into a Winchester police station last night. The terrorist had some of his fingers amputated crudely. The man in custody would not say why or how he was returned. Police believe it was a rival faction; this is yet to be confirmed. The police would like to interview the man who escorted Zaheer into the police station to help them with their enquiries. This is an artist's impression of the man they need to trace. Please contact Winchester police headquarters if you know or have seen this man."* Max considered the sketched drawing of a man with thick glasses, a greying beard and a pork-pie hat to be a good likeness of his disguise. Max thought: *"I got away with that one by the look of it."*

The captain waited another half hour and decided it was time to move. He walked briskly to the door where he had delivered pizzas. He rang the bell three times finishing with one extended ring. No answer. With his little box of tricks Max quickly opened the door. He had learned how to deactivate basic alarms and put this experience into practice at 152. With the security system deactivated, Max moved through the ground floor; the place stank of stale curry. In the kitchen last night's pizza boxes were stacked on the draining board. Max shouted upstairs but expected and got no reply. Firstly checking out the whole ground floor, Max moved up to the first floor that had three bedrooms, two separate doubles and one with two single beds; this would account for the gang of four.

Max cleared this floor with military precision and then moved slowly up to the second floor. Max couldn't believe his eyes when he opened the door to what he thought was just another bedroom. *"Fuck me; it's a bloody bomb factory"* Max gasped to himself. There were detonators by the dozen, hundreds of kilos of explosives, automatic weapons; a complete arsenal that could mount a small war. The partition walls had been removed forming an open space. The right thing would be to report this to the police anti-terrorism unit and the bomb disposal squad but Max, selfishly perhaps, wanted to face Connolly first. What to do? *"He decided he must get Connolly on his own. The best option is to wait and watch for the opportunity of him leaving the house alone."* Max pondered this new twist in his pursuit of Connolly.

Max took photos of the third-floor arsenal and rigged a concealed listening device in the main living room where he guessed most of the chat occurred. He searched through the bedroom drawers, eventually finding what he was looking for, Connolly's passport. It confirmed what Ahmed had said. Connolly is now going under the alias Jason Fletcher. Max kept the passport and then reactivated the alarms before leaving the house.

He had a good view of 152 from where he was parked. Several hours later the occupants of 152 returned; first the older and younger came back together and ten minutes later Connolly arrived. And finally the fourth and final resident was back inside 152.

Max could hear the conversations clearly, recognising the older man's voice; he appeared to be the leader. Max gathered from the conversation that his name was Asim. Not knowing he was the same man who organised Connolly to assassinate Max at the wedding. The recording of a discussion from 152 took a more serious tone that concentrated Max's attention. The leader advised the others about a planned bomb attack on the Luton shopping mall. They discussed bringing forward the target date because the UK security status had been upgraded to critical owing to the Winchester failed bomb threat to get Muzanni freed.

The boss mentioned that Ahmed had been kidnapped but had been mysteriously returned. They couldn't determine why or who took him from the hospital and returned him to the Winchester police station. The terrorists at 152 were definitely getting edgy.

Connolly, alias Fletcher, stated: *"My priority is to kill Hainsworth-Catt then collect the seventy-five thousand dollars reward from the Taliban via you Asim. I've lost track of him since that wedding. I should have shot the bastard then instead of his fucking bitch when I had the chance."*

Max's fists clenched on his steering wheel with the venom he felt for Connolly followed by another bout of grief. Little did Connolly know that Max was no more than a hundred and fifty metres from where he was speaking. One of the terrorists then asked Connolly where his friend Palanski was. Connolly replied. *"He is with a friend staying low; he didn't trust this safe house because both the military and civil cops are after him but I'm meeting him in a pub up the road later. He's helping me to get that fucking captain."*

As it was only the middle of the afternoon Max had a long wait as he planned to intercept Connolly at the pub rendezvous with Palanski. It was definitely Max's best opportunity. The residents of 152 moved into another room making it impossible for Max to make out what they were saying. He waited for what seemed an age before more activity came through from the listening bug. It was an incoming phone call that Asim answered. He spoke to someone for about three minutes; it appeared the caller was his senior as he was giving instructions. When Asim finished the call he shouted up the stairs to the others. Asim relayed his received instructions. 'We do the Bluegate shopping centre on Thursday. Our leader has also issued a hit on Ahmed Zaheer in case he does a deal with the authorities and tells them about us. They don't trust him'

That is only the day after tomorrow! Meaning Max will have to move on Connolly very soon or he will have no alternative but to report him to the anti-terror squad and report the imminent planned attack on the Bluegate shopping centre in Luton.

This evening will be Max's last chance or abort his revenge mission. It had just gone 18.40hrs when two of the residents left the house, walking in Max's direction; he looked the other way as they passed by. He hoped that Connolly would hurry up and go to meet his friend Palanski. At 19.30hrs Max was beginning to think he had missed Connolly or perhaps he had changed his mind about meeting the other traitor but Max's patience was rewarded five minutes later. Out stepped Connolly who turned away from Max. The captain got out of his car and followed Connolly, keeping a hundred and fifty metres behind him on the other side of the road. Connolly turned left, another left, crossed the road, turned right, and at the end of the road, about three hundred metres on the left was the Hare and Hound public house. It must be the rendezvous for meeting Palanski. It was.

29

ax waited for ten minutes before he followed Connolly into the pub; it was pretty busy for an early Tuesday evening. Max went to the bar as any other customer would and made small talk with a chap, a bar-fly, who had probably been going to this pub for years and pounced on anyone who would listen to him. Max ordered a pint of guest beer and continued chatting to the local man. This helped Max scan over the bar-fly's shoulder around the large room. Sat at a window seat were the traitors, Connolly and Palanski. Manoeuvring to the other side of the bar-fly, Max was given an unrestrictive view of the pair hidden by his new best friend, Charlie the bar-fly. The army officer thought he'd wait for Connolly to have a piss and then follow him in and deal with him. The captain's thoughts ceased instantly. Max cringed as Palanski came to the bar only a few feet away from him. Palanski ordered another round of drinks; he didn't give Charlie and Max a second glance.

Once Palanski had returned to his seat, Max ordered another beer for himself and bought Charlie one too. Max thought he'd go and check the loos out before his intended move on Connolly. *"Plenty of room to do what needed doing. All good."* Max thought and went back to his buddy to carry on drinking whilst watching Connolly's every move. Palanski went to the loo first and returned a few minutes later, but no move by big Patrick though as one might expect. They sat there together quaffing their ale. Palanski then came to the bar for another round. This time bloody Charlie, who unknowingly was Max's cover, started a conversation with Palanski. Charlie took a sip of his free beer and went into bar-fly mode:

'Are you part of the new customers convention here in the Hare and Hounds tonight?' Charlie pointed to Max. 'This guy has not been here before either. Do you know each other? Max and Palanski both couldn't help but look at each other and for an awful moment Max thought Palanski had recognised him as he asked Max his name!

'Your face does look familiar. Do you live around here?'

'No, I'm on the major construction works up the road and living on-site in a Portakabin. I'm from Brighton.'

Why Max had said Brighton, he had no idea.

Palanski quickly lost interest in the pair at the bar so picked up the two pints and went back to the window seat to rejoin Connolly. Max thought. *"I could have done without that scare "* Charlie wasn't to know; he was just being friendly.

Max paid lip service to Charlie, but he did talk so much crap, as most bar-flies do, and Max needed to keep an eye on the window seat. Max thought: *"I have peed, Palanski has, and even the half-wit Charlie has been to the loo. Come on Connolly, I want this sorted. Please go for a piss. They are talking seriously about something though. Probably about my future demise!"*

At last Connolly got up and came to the bar,

Max started a conversation to hold Charlie's attention long enough to prevent him from starting chatting with Connolly. However, Max couldn't risk Connolly recognising the man in the same disguise as the pizza delivery guy!

Max said with deflection in mind: 'Charlie how long have you been coming to this pub?'

His eyes lit up. He loved nothing better than talking on his chosen subject— about his local. Max got the other side of Charlie to have his back to Connolly.

Max could hear Connolly order two pints as Charlie replied with his drawn-out account about his long association and love for the Hare and Hounds.

Max nodded at Charlie in approval but didn't take in a single word he was spewing out. The young captain was intent on what Connolly was doing. The dangerous Irishman had put the pints down at his table but stayed standing. *"Good, he'll come back for a piss."* Max guessed. He didn't; he downed the pint in one leaving Palanski a whole pint to drink! Connolly slammed the empty glass on the table and belched so loud that Max could hear it from the bar.

Max couldn't believe it. Where is he going? Perhaps home; maybe his meeting is finished with Palanski. Max had to think and move fast if his whole plan wasn't to go down the pan. He excused himself from Charlie and went through to the lounge, exiting into the car park on the other side of the pub. Max looked around the front corner just in time to see Connolly's shape disappearing from view.

He was heading back down the same road they both used to arrive. Max assumed the Irishman was returning to 152. Still keeping Connolly a hundred metres in front, Max phoned Colonel Laurence Abel on his personal phone. 'Colonel just listen and don't speak. Do you have a pen? Write this down quickly. Hare and Hounds pub, it's near Elmsville Road in Luton. Send two or three armed MP's from the nearest barracks; if there aren't any military nearby then get the local armed police response cops; but without their sirens on. Tom Palanski is in the pub, but only until he finishes his pint. I must go now. I'll phone and explain later, sir. Do it as soon as possible sir. You have the clout and he mustn't get away again.'

'I'm on it Max.'

Max kept up with Connolly's pace, keeping fifty metres behind him; along the first road and turning into the next, getting ever closer to Elmsville Road and safety.

Halfway along the road Connolly disappeared into some high Cypress trees that formed a house boundary. The dirty bastard was pissing in someone's front garden.

Three police cars entered the Hare and Hounds car park silently; they were not taking any chances; they were all armed response officers and had rehearsed these tactics many times.

One team went into the lounge entrance, the other into the bar where Palanski was still seated but with only two fingers of beer left in his glass; the police had just made it before Palanski left the pub. The squad leader shouted for everybody in the pub to put their hands on their heads. Charlie called 'What me as well.'

'Everybody. Now.' He moved around the room, and although Palanski turned his head away in the vain hope of not being recognised, it only made him look more suspicious. He was immediately spotted and cuffed. The police knew exactly who he was from his photo that was distributed to every police station in the UK as the most wanted terrorist. He offered himself up, knowing that to evade arrest he would be tasered at the very least. He wasn't going to give them any trouble, that would have been suicide. The police led Palanski away with an armed escort to a secure location for debriefing by MI5. The police sirens blasted from the car taking him away. It compensated for their silent arrival.

Max thought the delay in the pub had probably turned out for the best as it was now dark; the conifers made the perfect cover. Max-Catt stealthily followed Connolly into the front garden hidden by the coniferous trees. He saw just two metres away the big Irishman pissing away, seemingly without a care in the world and facing away from the captain. With his shortened cosh, Max belted Connolly's upper neck, impacting on the brain stem. This stalk-like portion of the brain controls consciousness. A strong enough blow can also kill as the brain stem also controls the body's breathing. Max wasn't too worried about that outcome. As it happened Connolly was out cold but still breathing. So Max taped Connolly's hands, mouth and ankles together and left him in the undergrowth of the trees, then looked for an easily recognisable landmark to return. After checking all was clear he hopped out of the foliage to run back for his car. Passing 152 Elmsville en-route Max looked at the door and thought. *"I know one joker who will not be staying there tonight!"*

Max drove back and collected Connolly who had regained consciousness and was writhing about on the ground amongst the trees.

Max dragged him to the pavement and after checking all was clear, opened the passenger door and lifted the very heavy Connolly into the car. Max strapped him in then drove from Luton to Brandscombe. Max assisted Connolly to the lodge. He cleared the furniture away from the main room to assemble a temporary fighting cage, three metres diameter and two metres high. Max had purchased this cage to help him with extra training in the school holidays. Max opened the door and pushed Connolly in. Max followed him in and locked the door behind them. Max cut Connolly's ties. Feet, mouth and finally his hands.

Max took his thick glasses and greying beard off and removed his bobble hat. Connolly's face was an absolute picture, then he screamed.

'Fucking Hainsworth-Catt, you bastard, I'm going to kill you with my bare hands,' the big guy raged. 'You have made a big mistake cutting me free; you are dead.' Max replied in a slow, meaningful voice.

'Just the two of us now Connolly or should I call you Fletcher, no rules, the key to getting out is in my pocket, all you have to do you total scumbag is get it.'

'That will be easy and my pleasure; I should have shot you at Lydney Church and not bothered with your whore. My mistake'

Max could feel his veins throbbing as the blood pumped through them and pure adrenaline took over.

Connolly came at Max like a man possessed; both arms were flailing but missed their target. Max countered with a high kick to the side of his head. It opened the gash he'd given him earlier with the cosh. Before the Irishman could recover Max hit him with a left and two right jabs to his face; Max's knuckles were bleeding from catching a blow to Connolly's teeth. The Irishman spat his loose teeth out on the floor, projected by a mouthful of blood. Connolly was now raging and caught Max with a kick to the thigh that hurt beyond his normal pain threshold. The combatants exchanged a few half-hearted blows; Max worked him to the cage wall and pummelled his body with quickfire jabs. As the army deserter leaned forward Max saw his opportunity and grabbed both of Connolly's ears. These made perfect gripping handles that Max used to significant effect by pulling Connolly's head towards him landing a forceful head-butt that smashed into Connolly's nose breaking it in two places.

Blood was now pouring from Connolly's face and mouth; the big man was tiring but was still viciously dangerous driven on by his manic obsessional desire to kill the captain. A left hook from Max sent him spinning to the cage side, crashing into it face first. Connolly bounced off the cage wall allowing Max to meet his rebounding momentum with a full extended fist that he planted on the Irishman's already broken face; Connolly did a twirl and collapsed to his knees in front of Max. The vengeful captain couldn't resist a final blow to the side of his head and yelled at him. 'This is for my beautiful Penny.' Bosh. Blood spraying from the assasin's head covered the front of Max's shirt. Connolly crashed sideways, his head only stopping its violent movement when it thudded against the bars of the cage. As a result, he bounced off and finished up motionless on the floor not moving a muscle. Max said. ' Get up you murdering bastard.

He didn't reply. Connolly couldn't; he was dead. Long after his death his body's weird nervous spasms giving persistent movement to one of his legs as if it didn't want to succumb to the finality of death.

Max would have had naturally sincere regrets for killing someone in a sporting arena, but a strange, peaceful calm washed over him. He felt eerily satisfied but questioned his standard of humanity. After several minutes of reflection Max went to his car and fetched the military body bag he had taken from the camp. He placed Connolly into the bag and before zipping it up, he looked at his wife's killer and thought. *"He doesn't look like either the old Connolly or the new Jason Fletcher, he's unrecognisable"*. Connolly's face was a total broken mess. Shamefully Max wondered how he could have disfigured a fellow human so badly. These thoughts immediately vanished when his mind flashed back to Penny's death. Max zipped up the bag and took Connolly's body to his car. Max squeezed the body across the cramped back seats and covered it with a blanket. Max showered back in his lodge and changed his blood-spattered clothes. His blood-stained shirt and chinos were put in to a sealed bag and thrown on the Porches's passenger seat. Max left Brandscombe feeling strangely relieved that the revenge for his beautiful wife had been achieved. Yes, Max felt pretty good.

30

Max stopped in a country lane to pour petrol on his bag of bloodied clothes and watched the fire die to grey embers. Now Max must dump Connolly's body and he decided that the Luton area would be his best option given that is where Connolly was last seen. Even before the cage fight, Max realised he would be a major suspect for Connolly's demise, having had a strong motive to kill his wife's murderer. For that reason, he had to put distance between Connolly's body and Brandscombe tonight. Max headed back to Luton ensuring he kept within the speed limit. Max was still on an A road near the M25 when he noticed an unmistakable and unnerving blue flashing light in his rear mirror. *"Oh fuck, fuck, fuck! This can't be! The police are flashing me to pull over; this is going to be a murder charge"*. Max slowed down; the police pulled alongside and asked Max to follow them. He started to think, albeit stupidly: *"I could wait until they stopped and then speed away. They would never catch me, I could dump my car and say my car has been stolen; I am in the shit, that's for sure."*

Max did as directed and followed the traffic cops to a deserted lay-by. He stopped his engine but not his mind. It was being bombarded with crazy ideas: *"Should he put back on his disguise quickly, attack the unsuspecting police officers, secure them and leave them in their police car. Put false plates on the Porsche and make a run for it?"* This plan with some even more stupid ideas flashed through his head in an instant. Max didn't have to decide. It was too late for that! A burly traffic copper was tapping on the

Porsche's side window. The police officer then turned his attention to the car and walked around looking closely at the front as if inspecting it for any law-breaking additions. *"What if someone had seen me bundle Connolly into the car in Luton, perhaps taking my registration number. The police may have circulated it nationwide! "* Max's mind was torturing him again. At that moment the army captain accepted he was finished. He was now much calmer and buoyed in the knowledge that Penny had been avenged. Max was at the point where he considered stepping out of the car and offering the coppers his outstretched hands for cuffing. He now was thinking of mitigating his crime. He could say it was a private cage fight for money and he panicked when Connolly hit his head and died. He could show them the blood and teeth in the cage! Max couldn't stop his brain from spewing out crazy thoughts again! Then Max's brain stopped its nonsense and concentrated on the immediate reality. The burley lawman came back to the driver's window. This time he stayed.

Max opened his window as requested, the officer peered in and said the usual police lines: 'Is this your car sir?' 'Yes officer, I wasn't speeding, was I?' Max replied.

'No, no, I just love Porsches and I said to Bob, that's my buddy, I thought by its shape it could be the new 911/996. So it is isn't it?'

'Spot on officer, well done.' Max felt suddenly awkward by being too nice to the copper, almost grovelling.

'Would you mind if I sit behind the wheel sir?'

"Oh fuck no, fuck, fuck!" Max's racing thoughts had taken over again.

'No, not at all, officer, be my guest; Shall I start her back up for you?'

'Oh yes.' The car enthusiast was like a schoolboy in a sweet shop.

Max fired up the engine and played the throttle in sports mode for him before vacating his seat. Max then invited the copper to slide in behind the wheel.

'Listen to that throaty noise.' He squealed with delight as he pressed the responsive accelerator.

'The policeman called his pal from the squad car to come and take a picture of him. The scenario was becoming bizarre. The first copper, still sat at the wheel, couldn't know there was a dead body almost touching his back. It got worse, the second copper, who took the photos suggested to his pal. 'Ask him if he'll let you drive it.'

Max couldn't take much more of this suspense, he took another dry mouth swallow caused by panic, not knowing how to answer when the police car radio crackled into life. The second cop ran back to his car. Seconds later he shouted at his pal who was still sitting in Max's car. 'Come on Shaun, we've got a bad accident on the M25.' The cop slid quickly from the Porsche, shook Max's hand and thanked him and ran back to his car. They left Max gasping for air! He had got away with the whole incredulous thing. *"How the fuck did I get away with what just happened; it was just mad?"*

Max continued his incredible journey with his hands still trembling on the wheel.

Max reached Luton without further incident. He parked in an unlit suburb but didn't know Luton apart from Elmsville Road and didn't know where he was in the town. It helped that it was dark and tree-lined. Max waited for a dog walker to pass; it was a typical cold, wet night. *"I had to meet a bloke out walking with his dog that happened to sniff and piss on every tree he passed."*

As the dog walker disappeared Max thought twice about dumping Connolly at that spot. After nearly bumping into the persistently pissing dog and its owner Max decided to drive on and look for a more secluded spot. After ten minutes Max pulled onto a secluded piece of waste ground. He slid the body bag out of his car with great relief that it was, at last, out of his vehicle. Max opened the bag, knelt over the body and with his knife carved the letters I S on to Connolly's forehead, the knife penetrated deep, forming both letters, blood smudged them, but the initials could be read easily. He thought it was sensible that he changed the dumping site; the dog walker would have easily identified his black Porsche.

Max slid Connolly out of the military body bag and dragged him into some bushes stuffing the Jason Fletcher passport into the corpse's pocket. The captain packed the empty body bag into a plastic container and drove away south westward. Once well into the country, Max pulled into a deserted lay-by, took the body bag out of his car, poured petrol over it and threw a disposable lighter at it. He watched the body bag burn to ashes. When the last embers died away he drove non-stop to Shirenewton and Penny's apartment. He poured a big Lochavennie malt, laid back in the easy chair while holding Penny's St Christopher gift and he spoke softly to Pen.

"I got the bastard my darling; we are now free of that scumbag of a man that ruined our future together. I'll always remember you my only love." A little tear trickled down Max's face as he thought of his lost love.

Max finished his drink and started to drift off, thinking of the events of the last couple of days. Suddenly Max bolted upright in the chair, knocking his cut-glass tumbler onto the floor.

'Shit! The Luton Shopping Mall bombing.' He fumbled for his phone to activate the listening App to listen to the latest recording. He heard a lot of uneventful chatter, but the terrorists did discuss the shopping centre attack saying where, how and when the attack would happen, more than enough information to incriminate the residents of 152 Elmsville Road. Max phoned the anti-terrorism squad on the number he was given after the attempted bombing in Winchester and explained to an inspector. 'On Thursday there is a planned bomb attack on Luton's Bluegate Shopping Mall. I know who the bombers are and where they live.' The Inspector blew out his cheeks and sarcastically replied.

'I suppose these bombers have told you all this information sir. Do you know how many hoaxes we get and I hope you realise the penalty for such a hoax sir? Now do you wish to continue this conversation?' The officer's indifference dumbfounded Max and he retaliated. 'No, you are right; I do not want to continue our conversation! Put me through immediately to the most senior officer on duty who will take me seriously. Do it now!'

'I don't think that's a good idea sir; you will be told the same, and it will be worse for you by wasting police time.' Max got angry and demanded.

'Just put me through to a senior officer; I will not speak with you further!'

'On your head be it sir.' A gruff but enquiring voice came on the phone.

'I am Detective Chief Inspector Wallace, Anti-Terrorism Unit London. This had better be genuine.

332

How can I help you.' Max explained all. How Max wanted to locate his late wife's murderer through Palanski, who himself was wanted by the police for his involvement with the Winchester Bomb attack. Max went on to explain that his enquiries led him to a property in Luton that he broke into and placed a listening bug in and discovered a bomb factory.' Max was abruptly interrupted by DCI Wallace. 'What's that about a bomb factory?'

'I discovered it on the second floor, enough weapons to start a small war. I am a professional army officer and know about weaponry but chief Inspector, please believe me, I am deadly serious!'

The DCI took Max's name and immediately recognised it from the failed bomb attack in Winchester. 'Mr Hainsworth-Catt, I will ring you back, stay with the phone you called on!' Max agreed.

Literally in under a minute Max had the callback. 'Where are you Mr Hainsworth-Catt?' Max gave Penny's Shirenewton address. I'll send a local police car to pick you up; it will take you to Luton Police Headquarters where I will meet you; we need to move quick!'

Max was soon heading east along the M4 towards London in the back of a high-speed unmarked cop car with blue lights and sirens full-on. Max thought: *"This is crazy; I kill a guy, dump his body in Luton, drive to Wales, drive back to Luton in a police car all in the same day; remarkable!"*

The squad car pulled into the rendezvous police station in Luton. The DCI was already there to debrief Max.Then to the police chief's astonishment, he realised the seriousness of what was unfolding. Wallace had sent for specialised anti-terrorism squads in readiness. With four armed response teams and bomb disposal units parked in the Luton police station car park as back-up, the convoy moved out led by Wallace's lead car accompanied by Max as a passenger. The police chief halted the squad about half a mile from Elmsville Road.

They approached the target house on foot with stealth and military precision. Max-Catt and Wallace were now in the unmarked operations wagon parked in Elmsville Road. Max turned on his phone and opened the listening App tuned into the bug; the voices came over loud and clear. Max recognised two voices; one was the older chap who talked aggressively to the other one. The senior was Asim, the cell leader. They discussed the whereabouts of both Jason Fletcher aka Connolly and Tom Palanski.

Evidently they were getting very fidgety.

DCI Wallace knew he couldn't delay the operation for long and gave the signal to his men to go in. The team leaders confirmed everything was in place and they were ready to move. The synchronised time was ten seconds then it was Go Go Go. The three teams started attacking the front and back of the property with synchronised timing and skill. Max thought it was brilliant to be there to witness their professionalism. Stun grenades broke the silence as the teams did their well-rehearsed drills. Unbelievably it was very quickly all over. For their own safety all the neighbours had been secretly evacuated earlier. In less than three minutes the raid was over and was a complete bloodless success.

'Could I go and retrieve my listening bug.' Max asked the police chief.

The commander slapped Max on the back and said. ' Of course, I'll come with you. I know all about you and what you have done!'

Max's heart was in his mouth, he was thinking. *"They've found the body and traced it to me; somebody saw me, perhaps the dog walker who got my number plate".* The DCI allayed Max's fears in an instant.

'Yes you were the army officer who prevented the bomb attack in Winchester at a regimental dinner. A VC holder and now this. Would you like to join the anti-terrorism squad in London? It's a good life if you can put up with all the shit we get from some of the Human Rights Brigade! I'd get you in straight away. Do you know I have never met a VC holder before. Let me shake your hand and can I have a selfie with you.' Laughed the senior policeman.

'Thank you for the offer sir, but I'm hoping to join UKSF soon.' The DCI blew out his cheeks.

'I've been told that's bloody hard going, but good luck to you captain. Come on, let's get your listening bug.' The DCI led Max into number 152.

Max phoned Jenny and asked to see her and explain the events of the last twenty-four hours. They arranged to meet the following evening at a pub that was one of Pen's favourites in Chepstow. Max got a lift back with the Welsh copper who took him to Luton and he was dropped off at Penny's flat.

Max met Jenny as arranged and, ensuring no one was in earshot, told her over dinner. 'Your sister's murder had been avenged, accidentally, as it happened. It should be in the news anytime. Also, and with a bit of luck, we got his accomplice, Tom Palanski, who was arrested in a Luton pub.'

Max explained the bomb factory and the raid on the terrorist's safe house and how a swift raid prevented a major bomb attack on a shopping mall.

'You've been busy saving the world again Max! Incidentally how are you coping?'

'Not very well Jen; I'm trying to concentrate on my forthcoming SF training next week. I have things to tidy up at Beachley first; then I'll head down to Brandscombe to see my family before I go. Would you like to travel with me? I could give Rory a shout to see if he can make it as well.'

'I would love that Max. I'll ring Rory also. He'll want to see you before you leave I know.'

'That's settled then Jen. I'll pick you up on Friday evening, I'll be leaving Brandscombe to come back late Sunday afternoon as I need to pack my things and complete my farewells at the base and of course we have Penny's funeral on Monday. So I'll stay at the camp Monday night and get ready to leave. I'm to report to the Brecon training officer on Tuesday. I've got a lot to pack in before that. At least Connolly isn't going to be getting in my way or murder anyone else, that's for certain. I almost forgot, I'll have to clean up the cage and pack it away in the lodge. Remember Jen, not a word about Connolly. It's only between you, our darling Penny and me. God I miss her Jenny.'

Jenny got up from the table and gave Max a big hug. 'I'll always be here as a friend Max, you can always confide in me. I would like us to keep in touch and not just because of my relationship with dear Rory.'

'How are things with you two Jen?'

'Let's say they are developing quite satisfactorily.' Jenny gave a warm, beaming smile across the table to Max that told him more than her words could ever do.

'Jen do you remember that we have an appointment with the undertakers tomorrow. They have booked Penny's funeral for Monday; it's the only day they could fit in before I leave for Brecon, which is the following day. Shall I pick you up?

'Yes that will be good, thanks Max, what time?

'We have to meet Mr Holder, the undertaker, at 09.30hrs; I'll be at yours at 08.45hrs.'

'Okay I'll be ready.'

Max and Jenny arrived at the undertaker's reception at 09:10hrs. The place was decked with a fantastic display of beautiful fresh flowers. Max and Jenny decided on a quite delicate but straightforward casket. It was something Max wasn't expecting to be doing just a week ago. With all the arrangements complete, Mr Holder confirmed with the crematorium and the vicar for the funeral to be on Monday at 10:00hrs.

31

The following day Max returned to Beachley Barracks and reported to Colonel Laurence Abel who greeted Max with an unexpected, almost fatherly, hug. 'You have taken weapon training and fitness to new levels; I insist that my officers follow your high standards. I like the idea of the shield you are putting up as an annual charity shooting contest and your financial contribution too; Sergeant Forbes told me about it all and is genuinely enthusiastic about it.'

'The battalion has a good, no-nonsense colonel in you sir. It's been an honour and a pleasure to serve under you in the battalion. You helped me so much when I first came here as a green second lieutenant just out of Sandhurst. Your support and advice has been invaluable to me. I'll never forget that sir.'

'Thank you Max. Now prepare yourself for the arduous tests you are about to face. Good luck Max and do the 1st Rifles proud; I know you will give it your best shot and please keep in touch.'

Max returned to his quarters. On his way, he watched B company being addressed by his replacement, Captain Munro. It seemed strange seeing somebody else directing his men. Max's thoughts went back to Afghanistan to the discipline and bravery they had shown, especially three platoon. Max approached the new captain and discreetly asked if he could address B company as he was leaving on Tuesday.

'Of course captain, I have some big shoes to fill by what the colonel has told me.'

'You have a good company of men Mr Munro; you will do good and they'll serve you well. Thank you Mr Munro.'

With Sergeant Forbes alongside Max he called B company to attention and then stood them at ease. 'Gentlemen of B company, it has been an absolute privilege to have led you. Together we took on the Taliban and defended the innocent in Afghanistan. You did your duty with courage, discipline and pride. I leave next Tuesday for special forces training and assessment. Respect Captain Monro as you have me. Don't let Sergeant Forbes get you down'. This brought immediate laughter from the company ranks. 'So goodbye B company and remember, always give it your best.' Sergeant Tim Forbes called for three cheers. Max formally saluted his loyal B company, shook Munro's hand and thanked him before going to his quarters feeling quite choked.

Max was in the middle of emptying drawers and just for a split second wondered if he was doing the correct thing; quickly dismissing that negativity. His cases and trunk were filling up and he hadn't realised how much junk he had accumulated over his three years at Beachley. He cleared out one of his desk drawers and came across a letter with his darling's distinct perfume. He read it with trepidation. It was so sweet; her words were almost poetic but meaningful. He kissed the paper and held it to his face to have a momentary reminder of their happy days together before packing it with his other gear. Max was very pleased for finishing Connolly but that will not bring his wife back to him.

Max had just finished packing his last suitcase when a corporal knocked on the door.

'Three platoon are on the parade ground as you instructed sir, all present and correct sir.'

Max addressed the men of his old platoon. 'Men, my chosen men of number three. I will give you something you may come to hate me for. I'm going to bestow upon you a unique name for your platoon. it's entirely unofficial, but you can say your previous captain named it. You must make three become a legend; you and your successors must make sure the name is taken forward as a military inheritance. You must always pass this down to new platoon members of three and tell them what is expected. It will mean you must endeavour to always be the best platoon. It'll mean more continued challenging work, practice and pain to stay as the leading platoon in the battalion. You have earned this position through those attributes that must never slip or be forgotten. The name I'm going to give number three is the *"Invincibles"*, it's not official, but you guys know it to be true.

Max returned to finish his packing when his phone rang; the CO's office summoned Max to go there straight away.

'Come in Max; this is Inspector Kimber.'

Max shook hands with a police detective inspector. They both sat down at the colonel's desk.

'I have a few questions I need to ask you Mr Hainsworth-Catt regarding two terrorist suspects, Mr Patrick Connolly alias Jason Fletcher and Thomas Palanski. Firstly are they both known to you?'

'Yes of course they are, they were under my command in three platoon here at Beachley. Connolly was the person who hired three thugs to kill me. Palanski was his accomplice and the latter was actively involved with the attempted bomb attack at the regimental dinner in Winchester.

He fled the scene and linked up with Connolly to claim the seventy-five thousand dollars reward for killing me and collecting the bounty put up by the Taliban.'

'Why did they want you dead?' The detective asked quizzically.

'Because I thwarted the release of one of their important leaders in Afghanistan. This is already well documented in my interview after the Winchester attack.'

'Yes indeed, we do have that information but I noticed upon inspection your name has been listed in this depot's absent register for the last three days. Where were you?

The colonel interrupted the Inspector.

'Now wait a minute inspector, what are you implying. Captain Hainsworth-Catt has just lost his wife, murdered at the wedding of a fellow comrade. I actually suggested he took a few days off to grieve!'

'I'm not suggesting anything at this stage colonel; we are trying to piece together a string of events that don't add up. Firstly, a terrorist suspect named Ahmed was charged with attempted murder and related terrorist activities for the attempted bombing in the Winchester hotel. He was recovering from two bullet wounds to his leg. He was placed under armed guard and while he was recovering in hospital he was snatched from his hospital bed. We thought his own terrorist cell members got him out. That's why Ahmed Zaheer was handcuffed to prevent such a breakout. The armed guard was incapacitated but left unharmed. Someone phoned to say he was bound and in the store cupboard. Who ever heard of a caring terrorist? We thought if they were friends of Ahmed they wouldn't have left the guard alive. Ahmed, in the meantime, was returned to a police station minus two fingers and a thumb. He could but would not say who took him, why he was tortured or what they wanted. We then get a tip-off where to arrest Palanski. We know that it was you who asked your CO here to arrest Palanski. Another tip-off was from you about a bomb factory and a planned attack on a Luton shopping centre. You sir, gave us all those tip-offs, and of course, we are most grateful. It probably saved hundreds of injuries and deaths at the Luton shopping centre, but we need to know how you got this valuable information and, to that end, your whereabouts over the last three days as I asked you earlier. Moreover, adding to the case's complexity, a male body was found on waste ground in Luton. This body fitted the description of a Mr Jason Fletcher with a passport in his name found on him. Forensics, however, advised us he is Patrick Connolly. His army medical and dental records confirmed this; he is also linked to your wife's death. DNA matched Connolly's on the tree he used to fire his deadly shots.

He was beaten to death in the last twenty-four hours by a gang of several persons given the injuries he sustained. We believe his killers were the so-called IS. We are assuming he may have double-crossed them. Connolly had received high-quality plastic surgery; our forensic people think the face work was carried out in a foreign country. Border Control supported this, confirming a Jason Fletcher came through Heathrow ten days ago. Can you assist us any further or fill in the many of the frustrating blanks we have?'

Max thought the inspector was a bit condescending but only doing his job and indeed a lot of action had taken place over the last week. Max had expected to be questioned sooner or later, but giving the police the tip-offs was too important not to take the risk of getting caught.

'Inspector I would like to think I'm a law-abiding citizen who takes discipline seriously. My information involved a person whose name I'm not going to divulge for his safety; he gave me information about Palanski. He came to me after the attempted bomb attack in Winchester. He said he had been informed by someone who was friends with Palanski and that Palanski had blabbed to him one drunken night that they, being him and Connolly, were going to get even with me for stopping their lucrative activities in this camp. Their insubordinate action involved another captain. The colonel here knows all about it. Connolly had instructed three men near these barracks to ambush and murder me; this went horribly wrong for them and poor Terry Dixon got his throat cut. The three perpetrators are now locked up after confessing that Connolly was the instigator of the attack. We were in Afghanistan when the news came through to the colonel here confirming Connolly's orchestration in the attempted murder and his mucky dealings with the dodgy Captain Smyth. This meant the net was closing in on Connolly and confessions from his frightened acolytes in Afghanistan, put him in the guardhouse.

Worried about his own dirty dealings, the frightened Captain Smyth released Connolly, who knew he was finished, so he went on the run and obviously joined the Taliban to escape. He worked with them to get me. You have been told why they put a Fatwah on me I expect. Anyway my informant was disgusted with Palanski when he actually carried out his brag to bomb innocent people in Winchester so he came to me. He told me that Connolly had arrived from Afghanistan into the UK and had gone to a safe house at 152 Elmsville Road in Luton so I went to look for Connolly; I watched the house and counted four occupants but I didn't recognise Connolly as one of the four because, as you said, he had a face job. Well, I searched the place and planted a listening device in the living room. Then on the second floor I discovered a bomb factory with lots of automatic weapons and explosives. So I left and waited to listen in. By the way, I explained all this to the armed response commander DCI Wallace. I was with him at the raid in Luton. I got information that Connolly was meeting with Palanski in the Hare and Hounds pub.

I rang my colonel here, who arranged an armed response team to pick Palanski up...,' The colonel interjected.

'That is all true inspector, thanks to Max not only did he stop perhaps a hundred fatalities in Luton but caught a highly wanted terrorist and deserter.'

'Yes colonel I have been fully briefed on the captain's brave exploits. Please continue captain.'

'I also heard they didn't trust Connolly because he failed a mission; he took it on himself not to shoot the designated target, me! The cell deemed Connolly as a loose cannon and a liability; they thought he might jeopardise the whole Luton target so they said they would call in their field operators to deal with him which I assume meant to bump Connolly off. My listening bug was getting crackly at that moment so I can't say how their conversation finished. I then left to go to see my sister-in-law, Jenny Richards, in Chepstow and to get some sleep. I am sure Miss Richards will be happy to corroborate this.' After intense interviewing the detective left.

'That wasn't so bad Maximus.' The colonel deliberated.

'No sir, he's only doing his job.'

'Are you all packed? The stand-in captain can't wait to move into your quarters.'

'Yes sir, just about, but remember my last night in the depot is Monday night so don't go giving my bed away until Tuesday.'

'I will certainly not Maximus; we shall have a last farewell drink before you go.'

'That we shall sir!'

Max called Jen and they used her SUV to pick up his trunk and suitcases from the base. They certainly wouldn't all fit in to Max's Porsche. Max drove as he thought Jenny looked tired. On the way he told Jenny about his interview with the police and how he thought it went well. Max said to Jenny that he didn't think they would be bothering her for a statement. Max and Jenny arrived at Brandscombe at 15:00hrs.

'Maximus, did you come to Brandscombe a few nights ago? Jarvis swore he saw the lights on at the lodge while he was putting in some mole traps on the side lawns.' Chris couldn't wait to ask Max.

Not wanting ever to deceive his father, Max replied.

'Yes, dad, I needed my rugby kit as we had a tournament at the depot against a local team—a charity match. I popped in late and didn't want to disturb you.'

'Well, that clears that mystery up, son.'

As Jen knew about the cage fight Max whispered in her ear. 'I must clean the cage, take it down and stow it away.' 'Show me Maximus, I want to see it.' Said Jenny.

Max told the family he was going for a walk with Jen as she wanted to surprise Rory so they were going to Max's lodge until Rory arrived. The cage was now quiet and innocent, a total contrast from the other night when two gladiators fought primitively in a locked cage. Jenny gasped.

'My God look at the blood and bits of flesh, it's splattered everywhere, look there's even teeth on the floor.'

'It wasn't pretty Jen, but it was unashamedly satisfying.'

'Max I want to clean this up; I want to be a part of the revenge pact for my sister. I must do this. I'll boil some water. Have you any cleaning liquid.?'

'Yeah in the kitchen out the back. There is a kettle as well.'

Jenny scrubbed every part of the cage from the top to the floor; she rubbed it all down and polished all the bars until they shone. Jen would not let Max clean a thing. They both unbolted the floor frames to put them back into the storage area, probably never to be used again.

'I feel much better for that, now I'm a complete accomplice in revenge for our Penny. 'So give me a big hug brother-in-law; you are a good man Maximus. I hope you always regard me as an exceptional friend and a sister!'

Max squeezed Jenny with sincere feeling, quietly saying. 'That applies both ways dear Jenny. I'll always be at your side if you ever need help in any way.'

They hugged again; the embrace was sheer affection for each other. Then they strolled together back to the house where they awaited Max's best friend and the love of Jenny's life, Rory.

Virginia put on her usual excellent dinner. Over this there were questions from family and friends on the recent exciting exploits of Max. Everyone carefully avoided the wedding carnage and the death of Penny, the late Mrs Hainsworth-Catt. Due respect was evident and very much toned down from the usual merriment they have all come to expect from a Brandscombe dinner.

The visitors had a hearty Mrs Cooper's breakfast then they all said their goodbyes and left the family home.

Max couldn't help giving Jenny a sideways look as they passed the lodge. She met his glance. They were no doubt thinking the same!

Max went to the funeral with Jenny. Rory travelled up from London and met them at the crematorium. In fairness to Mr Holder, he organised the service exceptionally well. Max was grateful to see his parents, Archie, Charlie, and Pippa at the service that was befitting Max's late, lovely wife. Max said his last goodbyes as he kissed the gold St. Christopher she had given him on the sandy beach at Weston-super-Mare. Max vowed it would never be far from him, ever!

The young SAS candidate took the opportunity to say his farewells to his parents and siblings again. It was a sombre occasion, cremating his wife of only a few minutes is far from a natural occurrence. He thought sadly as his darling went through the curtains of finality. *"You were so beautiful and loving. I will always love you, my sweet, lovely Pen. Wait for me."*

The guests drifted away from the wake; Max needed time to take in his loss. He said his farewells to family and friends. They understood it was solitude Max required at this time. He drove back to Beachley and, for the last time, crashed out on his bed there. Apart from the promised drink with the boss he had no more goodbyes to make.

It was 08.00hrs when Max's alarm went off, it wasn't necessary as Max was up, shaved and his packed bags were waiting by the door. He dropped his used bedding off at the camp laundry. After clearing his quarters for the eager stand-in captain, Max went to the CO's office. They drank a glass of the colonel's best malt; he hugged Max and wished him the very best and insisted that Max keep in touch. That was it. The fat lady had sung. Max-Catt was on his way to Brecon with a high degree of sorrowful pain!

32

'Captain, just a minute.' Sergeant Tim Forbes ran out of the NCO's mess across the parade ground towards the car park. Max stopped and looked back. Tim handed Max a gift-wrapped box.

'This is from B company as a small thanks for changing our lives, particularly three platoon.' Max replied with sincerity in his voice.

'I will miss the lads, their banter, professionalism and courage that was demonstrated in Afghanistan. It's been a pleasure throughout my time with them. Support your new captain and help him settle in as you did me and make sure the Invincibles are always the leading platoon.' With that Max and his loyal sergeant had a brief hug and then Max turned away.

He was driving from the base with the unopened gift on the passenger seat of his 911/996 Porsche. The tension in his stomach was as high as he had ever encountered in his military life hitherto, including the tour of Afghanistan on the front line. The tour helped get his promotion to captain but that rank isn't worth diddly squat in the SAS as all new trainees and recruits are defaulted back to private, unlike any other British Army regiment.

Max's thoughts were jumping around between what to expect in Brecon and his recent macabre past, flooding back to Connolly, the cage fight, the bomb factory in Luton, the persuasion of Ahmed to give him essential information and the sad, premature death of his beautiful wife Penny. A strange chapter of his life that he is now leaving behind.

Max's destination was not that far; he headed west for Brecon, some fifty miles into Wales. He was to join up with his fellow candidates attempting to be accepted into the elite SAS regiment, a most gruelling challenge of endurance and personal fortitude. Out of an average of a hundred and twenty-five candidates who start the tests only ten will pass out and receive the coveted beige beret and winged dagger. The fear of failing was the cause of the knots in Max's stomach. The journey was enjoyable and the weather was a typical winter's sunny blue sky, although cold he had the roof down on his cabriolet 911. Max turned off the M4 at Cardiff West and turned north along the A470 to Merthyr Tydfil, passing the old slag tips of Dowlais Top, a reminder of the area's mining and industrial pedigree. Max turned north west for Brecon through the most picturesque landscape. The wind was biting at his muffled face, but it was exhilarating rather than uncomfortable. To his left the pine bordered reservoir dam was a picture of total tranquillity and a perfect example of the beauty of the British countryside. An image that Max often thought of when he was on the front line dug in in some fly infested shit hole in the Middle East. Max could see the snow-capped famous Pen y Fan mountain in all its splendour to his right; he wondered if he would be thinking of it with the same affection and beauty at 03.00hrs with a full bergen on his back and fighting for every foothold. He turned off at the next junction on to the A4215 towards Sennybridge and the military training centre.

Upon arrival at the high-security checkpoint Max was instructed where to report. The checkpoint is obviously aware that one hundred and fifty plus SAS candidates, just like Max, were arriving today.

After being kitted out and introduced to his fellow hopefuls they met the assigned NCO instruction sergeant, Andrew Jenkins. Max received his first set of instructions for the following day. All communications with the outside world were now terminated. The torture is about to start for Maximus Hainsworth-Catt, not captain; as from now his commission is not worth a jot.

Selection phase 1-: Endurance started at 24:30hrs; Max and his group set out in the dark with their weighted bergens on a timed hike over the Brecon Beacons and Black Mountains of South Wales. They had to navigate between checkpoints where the directing staff checked the candidates in and out again without encouragement or criticism.

It was damned hard work and strong, fit men cried with pain. Max was chilled to the bone and wet through and was wondering what the fuck he was doing here in this God forsaken place which was a far cry from the fierce heat and humidity of Afghanistan. Even the sheep had the sense to shelter in the lowest crags of this bleak hell as the heavy snow made visibility reduce to about twenty-five metres. Max's bergen straps were biting into his shoulders, wryly he thought he would swap this freezing torture for a dangerous front-line position in Afghanistan surrounded by Taliban fighters, anytime. Max could not allow his body's coldness to numb his decision making. However, the insane cold was taking its toll on Max's concentration, a nagging self-preservation voice banged away in his head telling him to pack this excruciating pain in now! He had nothing to prove to himself; he'd done his bit under fire in a war environment, being shot at, wounded twice, and decorated with a VC!

Max got weaker as the hikes of endurance got longer; the subconscious voice who thought Max should quit increased its negative advice pounding at his logical senses. His comfort side hammered at his thoughts again. *"You have wealthy parents! You can work in the city! Partner Archie on the estate! Why this? Why this hell? Give up and go home!"* The demons of easy street were persistent. *"The rewards for giving in was a warm duvet, bacon and eggs every morning if you want and much more income!"* These demons would not leave Max alone.

Then Granville, his late grandfather, came into Max's mind, interrupting the comfort demons.

"Lad, you are my grandson of whom I am so proud of, don't listen to your tormentors. Become SAS and once you are in this elite group, nobody on earth can take that proud feeling away from you. Now beat the great Pen-Y-Fan!"

The bergens were made incrementally heavier at the regular checkpoints which didn't help; Max felt he just wanted to collapse in front of a marshall and let the medics fly him back to the warmth and comfort of the base. He didn't think in his wildest dreams that the trials would be as inhospitable as what he was enduring. His Sandhurst training was always under constant instruction from NCOs bellowing at him what to do. Here in this north pole of the UK, you make your own decisions, trying to navigate with a shaking field compass, hardly able to hold it still long enough to read it with every part of your body shaking at once. Max couldn't describe how cold, tired and defeated he felt at that moment. If one dared to piss it would freeze within seconds of release before hitting the ground.

How Max got through those first two weeks he didn't know. The resilience and the Hainsworth-Catt determination, especially the spiritual connection he felt with Granville, pulled him through. The surviving candidates who didn't quit or were asked to leave are now to face the long drag challenge. This forty-mile hike with a bergen pack weighing 55 pounds must be completed in twenty-four hours or it's an immediate failure and elimination. What the applicants have just experienced on the mountains was a stroll in the park compared to the Big Drag. This next trial was nicknamed the Fan Dance. The candidates were told that at least twenty-five per cent would fail this gruelling test of man. Some wokey people in civilian jobs say it's too hard on a human's mental and physical capability. Max finished it in twenty-three hours ten minutes, not the quickest time but not the slowest either and then a long soak in the communal bath with lashings of hot water. Max stayed submerged until the water got uncomfortably cold. His blistered feet caused him to hobble badly. His condition was not helped by his rubbed-raw shoulders that were bleeding from the pack straps that had cut into his flesh. To get from the cold bath to his bed was a challenge in itself. Max collapsed onto it, wrapping himself in the high tog duvet. Bliss!

Max got his results through by 10.00hrs the following day. The brown envelopes were on Sergeant Jenkin's desk. It was just like waiting for his GCSE results Max thought; the other hopeful candidates gathered around in anticipation. Maximus passed, but there was no congratulatory slap on the back, only an order to report to a nominated venue with sixty-eight other successful survivors. They were not aware of what they were about to face next. Phase two was about to begin.

There was no time to enjoy the exhilaration of getting through the gruelling Welsh mountain torture. Instead the survivors of the tests were billeted together for a few days awaiting their next phase. Their orders came within two days which gave Max's shoulders a chance to heal a little.

The diminished band of candidates now numbering just sixty-nine were transported to RAF Brize Norton in Oxford, a familiar place for Max. The new destination was Belize for their jungle survival test. By this stage, guys had started to pal up, typical in such scenarios, usually to get information or compare notes and give each other support going into the next phase.

The group finally arrived at this humid, hot Central American country with its eastern side meeting the Caribbean and, in the west, the candidate's destination, dense jungle. The kit for the next tests was delayed in Belize City so the men had a few days leave. They were put into four-man teams. It made sense to stay in their groups of four allowing each team to get to know each other better. Myers, one of Max's group, had hired a car and offered to drive his other three group members into Belize City. They all thought this was a good idea for bonding before they set off into thick jungle.

The four introduced themselves formally before setting off to the city. Phil Myers had asked the training sergeant if he could be in the same four as his mate, Nathan Brookes, who he had palled up with back at

Brecon. The group of four were Max 1st Rifles, Jamie Cuthbert 2 Para, Nathan Brookes Royal Marines, and Phil Myers RAF regiment. Jamie and Max hit it off immediately, but they didn't take to Phillip Myers who was a big muscular guy who threw his weight around as well as his mouth. He'd heckled with nasty piss-taking insults to many lads who struggled in Wales. Max had heard some rumours about Myers and Brookes but didn't know exactly what. The three team members waited outside the base gates for Phillip Myers to pick them up in the hired car. There was always a local chap outside the camp, a taxi man named Delroy but he answered to the name of Delboy, the name given to him by the British garrison at the camp. Delboy asked the three if they wanted some nice ladies, very clean and cheap. Then he tried selling them some fake gold jewellery. He was persistent that was for sure.

Myers arrived with his car and drove towards Belize City. They arrived in the city centre, parked up and headed for the first lively bar. 'That one will do us.' Myers exclaimed. He was already across the road and entering the Ship pub. The bar was crowded and too cramped for the number of drinkers using it, with more customers pouring in. Myers was first to push his way to the bar, 'Four beers.' he shouted, not bothering to ask what the lads wanted, but nobody complained. They took the beers outside as there was no room inside to scratch your arse.

'We'll have a couple here and move on to the next bar.' said Myers, again dictating to the group. He did seem to be taking charge of the team. *"Perhaps good leadership skills."* Max considered. 'I'll get these.' Nathan Brookes, the Royal Marine, was up and collected the four empty glasses. He battled his way back into the madhouse for refills. Myers went with him, which, as it happened turned out to be a disaster.

Breaking the busy and loud background chatter in the bar from locals enjoying their weekend, came an ear-piercing scream from women and the unmistakable sound of breaking glass. It was a brawl. And it involved Myers and Brookes. It was challenging to get into the bar as the crowd was spilling out as fast as possible.

'Come on, we've got to get out of here, now.' Screamed Myers. He ran at pace around the corner of the block with Nathan Brookes chasing close behind. Not knowing what the hell was going on, Max and Jamie followed them; it seemed the thing to do as they were supposed to be a team. So they went down back streets and across a main road until Max shouted. 'Stop, what the fuck are we running from?' It took a good couple of minutes before his breath returned to enable Nathan Brookes to say 'I didn't see anything; it was all so quick' Myers quickly butted in with the full version of the events.

'Some geezer pushed me in the back and said something like fuck off you Brits. I turned and hit him three times and kneed him in the bollocks then pushed his head down onto the bar. He collapsed on the floor. Tell them Nathan.' Brookes, an obvious quiet type, confirmed.

'I heard you shouting at the guy behind you and I saw you smash his head into the bar and then watched him jerk backwards and slide to the floor. I stopped another guy trying to get at you and then people were screaming everywhere. It was mayhem so we legged it as it looked like it was about to kick off with others joining in.'

'We can't go back there; we must wait until dark then collect the car to get back to camp; a good job we were not in uniforms or we could be in big trouble.' Myers directing the other three again with aggression in his voice.

The newly formed team waited for it to get dark and returned to the hired car. They headed back to the camp. Just as they turned onto the main highway that led to the base they could see a traffic jam with a line of stationary vehicles ahead of them. Temporary arc lamps had been set up. On either side of the road were the unmistakable flashing blue lights of police vehicles. Myers slammed the brakes on and spun the car, scraping the rear wing.

He turned the lights off and started to drive back the way they had come. 'What the fuck' Max screamed. It was still the rainy season in Belize and a storm had made visibility very poor which enabled Myers to turn around unnoticed. Myers took them on for about another two miles before they turned off the main road. They were on a farm track of sorts, stopping abruptly after about half a mile or so. 'We need an explanation and now.' Max demanded and grabbed Myers' arm. Myers swung round to face Max; he was losing his self-control and with raw anger in his voice replied, 'It was nothing but a punch up in a bar, it happens all the time in Liverpool where I'm from.'

'Why not go through the roadblock then which was probably for some drugs operation anyway.' Argued Max. Myers was getting very angry. Then, in a loud voice, barked 'I don't want a bar fight to end my chances of getting into the SAS so I'm taking precautions. You lot can fuck off out of the car and walk if you don't want to come with me. Who hired this fucking car anyway?' It was evident to all of them with the rain hammering down and in the middle of nowhere they were not going to leave the car. Jamie suggested they head along the track and check the map and their GPS position. The road branched into three tracks joining the one they were on, they took one of the tracks hoping the road was not flooded or closed off. If they hadn't had the hire car they could have improvised as this is what they were being trained to do. It seemed unreal and part of a dream, but this was happening, running from authorities in a country they had just arrived in! Max wanted to get Nat Brookes on his own and ask him why he was so nervous around Myers as he had seen back in Belize City but being stuck together in a car made that impossible.

Max was tempted to report the incident to their training sergeant, but that is not part of the regiment's ethos. Not to drop your comrades in the shit. But something wasn't quite right and Max didn't trust Myers one bit.

It wasn't until they got to within five miles of their camp that another problem faced them. They saw another police roadblock ahead with similar lighting as the previous one. Again, Myers screeched to a halt, turned the car round and drove it into the driveway of a private house.

Myers inexplicably stabbed the front tyre of the hired car but said nothing and walked to the door on his own. A woman opened the door. All the population of Belize spoke English so Myers had no problem conversing with her even with his scouse accent. He pointed to the flat tyre and explained they were at the British army training camp about five miles away. She knew the base well enough and was not surprised as she had met many a soldier in Belize over the years. Myers returned to the vehicle and explained what he had arranged. 'I told the old girl that we had a puncture and were on leave from the camp and that we must report back so I asked her if I could leave the car in her drive until the morning as we need to bring a new tyre and she agreed.' Myers said it would be better to go cross country and skirt past the roadblock. Again Max was not pleased with this decision but couldn't see how it affected him so he went along with it although he considered it an overreacting plan. The rain had eased but it was still very muddy and their casuals were not designed for hiking at night through light jungle terrain such as this. Finally, they came across a farmhouse and open cultivated land and could see their camp half a mile away.

The sentry asked for the four's ID's and then told them to report to the guardhouse probably because of their muddy state. The duty corporal phoned through to the candidates' section and spoke to their assigned instruction sergeant. After a brief exchange, the corporal bid the four good night and they were on their way to the barracks. 'I'm going to the mess for a beer, are you guys joining me?' Myers growled.

Jamie and Max walked towards the communal billet ignoring Myers; Jamie threw Max a quizzical glance. Myers insisted Nat Brookes went with him.

"All very strange and he's definitely controlling Nat." Max was convinced. 'Something isn't right and I intend to find out before we head in to the jungle.'

Myers finished his third pint without a word to Nathan, who was still only an inch down from the top of his first one, letting out a massive, prolonged belch into the face of the subdued Royal Marine.

'You know you cheated in Brecon on two occasions, and I saw it all Brookes; I told you I wouldn't dob on you providing you kept your mouth shut about what happened in the bar. That big-mouthed bloke had it coming to him anyway. He will be all right; he'll suffer more from the kick in the bollocks I gave him than the bar-slamming that I finished him off with.'

'This is wrong Myers, you should tell them what happened; you know it's wrong. I just don't know what to do.' Myers pushed his face into Nathan Brookes's and whispered, 'Forget what you saw or your career is over, do you understand?' Nat left without a further word and with lots to ponder.

33

The kit arrived two days later so they had two extra days preparing the equipment; they scrounged some buckshee stuff that they could lay their hands on. No one had seen Myers for two days. Finally, the delay was over and all quartets were issued field instructions. Off they set in a shuttle bus to the helicopters that will take the candidates to a cleared landing strip miles into the thick inhospitable jungle. On their way inflight Max asked Myers. 'Where have you been for the last two days? It doesn't take that long to repair a tyre and return a hire car.'

'Get fucked and mind your own business.' Myers glared at Max.

That ended any further conversation between the two of them on the flight. The chopper hovered above the helicopter landing site and from now on it will be the last time they will speak to anyone outside their group of four unless captured or emergency dictates it.

The air was appreciatively cooler in the jungle but very humid. There was a definite elephant in the room as both Jamie and Max weren't happy with Phillip Myers's attitude and previous conduct. The tension was apparent and Nat Brookes didn't help with his subdued mood.

The team of four had an arduous task ahead of them. They had maps and a compass and needed to avoid active troops searching for them to simulate being behind real enemy lines. They had to evade capture with only basic rations and collect water from rat-infested streams and rivers and with dangerous jungle dwellers sharing the water. Their water purification tablets were their only protection from a number of diseases that could render humans ill or dead from contaminated water.

The first objective was to rendezvous with another quartet of candidates so each group was given target coordinates; this was not too difficult as they were all accomplished map readers. They hacked their way towards their first target position, spreading out with all four taking turns at point (Front Man) No speaking or noise as the searching patrols will be hunting for the teams everywhere. Besides that many other sources of danger were lurking, snakes, poisonous frogs, scorpions, spiders and much more. It was essential to make a cover at night; mosquito netting was needed to keep malaria carrying flying insects and rabid vampire bats away. The following morning the four continued towards their target with Jamie on point, his job was to signal back to the others if there was any movement or sound from the front. Jamie's fist pumped upwards in steady but deliberate movement; this is the signal to stop in their tracks and kneel awaiting further signs from Jamie. He turned and put his finger to his lips commanding silence and for them to be on full alert. He slowly laid flat on his stomach; the rest copied his every movement. It was the first sight of a searching patrol they had seen so far.

The patrol was no more than eight feet to the team's left but they were not aware of Max's team's presence. A patrol of six was hacking their way past the group. The patrol was thrashing with machetes and were now within touching distance of the four. If they reached out in the group's direction it would surely mean capture. It was a tense situation. Their hacking and beating at the undergrowth disturbed a hive of bees angered by the human attack on their home. Nathan Brookes was the one that copped it. He got stung on his face, neck and hand several times; how he didn't cry out was down to the self-control of the ex-marine. The bees moved the search patrol away from the four much quicker than they arrived with several of them screaming expletives. The team waited for ten minutes before Jamie gave the all-clear. He moved into the crouch position and stretched upwards as if watching something, but he was only scanning the adjacent jungle with his ears pricked for any sound. There were plenty, but not human anymore.

The team's rendezvous was about six hours away and, thank goodness, the near brush with the search patrol didn't delay them. They rested for a while and attended to Nat's stings, which he tried to brush away as nothing, but they concerned Max and Jamie. The stings had swollen up badly and looked nasty. Unfortunately, those stings are more severe and infectious than the Northern European bee. Max acted as a medic and gave Nat some antihistamine tablets and hoped he'd be ok. So, on they moved slowly cutting their way through the thick jungle but not speaking, the point man stopping every so often to listen. The quartet was thirty minutes from their rendezvous when their point man, which was now Myers, halted them. He turned towards the team and signalled for them to get down, but it was too late; his movement was restricted by two combat clad search troops with more of them behind them. With a rifle in his back Myers couldn't do a thing; the team had lost one of only two chances allocated to them to complete phase two. It was a significant setback for the team and it was still at the beginning of their mission.

Fortune raised its hand for Max's group for the second time within a few hours! It soon became apparent that it wasn't the enemy searchers who had captured Myers, it was the other team of four they had to rendezvous with, a massive relief for both teams. The order from the base was to locate each other and obtain the next instruction. After the teams realised they had stumbled across their specified targets by accident the eight men from the two teams were shaking hands and back slapping. It was a silent celebration however. They exchanged the sealed envelopes with further instructions. They had a brew together, wished each other the best of luck and after a bit more back-slapping they said their farewells. Max's team decided to study their next assignment before the natural light faded. Agreeing to camp for the night in what looked to be a safe area, they cleared the ground and threw their mosquito nets over tree branches and set out their bed bags in this makeshift tent. Dry rations were for dinner as a fire would alert the many searching patrols who were desperate to find them. They had used the last of their clean drinking water and from now on will rely on filthy sterilised river water. The team went to bed happy in the knowledge that they still had their two chances intact.

Breakfast was the same as dinner, dry rations. The four took murky water from the river and filled their canteens, adding the purification tablets to make it safe but they couldn't reduce the pungent smell or taste. They unanimously agreed that it tasted and looked like shit. Nat's bee stings looked pretty bad and the swelling was worsening; he was in severe pain but was trying not to show it. It was now evident to the other three that Nat's pain was increasing but infection now a bigger worry.

The next objective was to steal the radio from a jungle field station operated by a platoon of the Reserve regiment with a lieutenant in charge of about twenty-five men.

The new instructions directed the team to take the radio across the Macal river three miles downstream. Once across, the group of four are to call the base and confirm their position. They would then be issued with their final instruction. But first they had the difficult task of getting into the camp, stealing the radio, and getting out again without being caught.

The compound was well guarded but the small garrison was not aware of Max's team's planned mission so they had the element of surprise on their side. The compound was a week's march away and their pace was slow through the thick jungle; cutting it away with their machetes was their only way through in some parts.

34

The quartet had made slower progress than they had hoped. It took them eight days instead of the estimate of seven. In that time they encountered three more search patrols. One was no threat and a hundred metres away, the second was not too much of a concern but the third was very close. They actually appeared to be tracking the quartet of candidates until the pursuers headed off on a ten degree change of course to Max's team.

Finally on the eighth day they reached a well-covered ridge that overlooked the entire camp. This was their target and from this elevated position they could clearly see the camp's layout; a sentry on the main gate, a few men walking about in khaki shorts and singlets and two men working on a small RIB obviously for use on the Macal river nearby.

'What's the plan to get in there?' enquired Jamie. Max replied 'We could send one of us in half-dressed and dishevelled pretending to be a lost tourist that required medical help for dehydration or something.' Myers interjected.

'Yeah he could let the rest of us in after lights out!' Jamie also thought it a good idea and this plan would get over the problem of breaching the perimeter fence. Max quickly had a re-think about his own suggestion musing that the reserves might take the bogus tourist back to Belize city for hospital check-ups or even to the SAS base and that would scupper their test programme. Maximus explained his misgivings to the others and all but Myers agreed to think again. It was still bugging Max who wanted answers to the strange actions of Myers before they left for the jungle test, in particular him going missing for two days. Max was also concerned about Nat's obvious pain as the bee stings were still very swollen indicating an infection developing.

For now, both concerns had to be put aside as there was only a specific time window to steal the garrison's field radio, get across the Macal and report to base. Myers gave Max an aggressive stare and said, 'If you're so fucking smart, give us a better plan.' He was definitely getting to Max, but Max had to think of their operation first and took comfort in promising himself he would get to the bottom of Myers's behaviour and his apparent hold over Nathan Brookes!

Max suggested they mull over their task and asked the team to develop ideas and options, but they couldn't take too long about it. Their kit was limited to two weapons to protect themselves in the jungle, a rope, a collapsible grappling iron, flares, machetes and a deflated small dinghy with no paddles. That was about all the kit they had apart from personal stuff and the essential dry rations. Jamie thought they should reconnoitre the perimeters of the enclosure that was built from timber poles four metres high and forming a square. The entrance was a pair of gates made of the same construction. There were two guards at the gate chatting to each other. The team could see that electricity was supplied by a large generator housed in a shed at the rear. It would need to be put out of action once they had secured the radio, which was unanimously agreed between all four of the team.

The time had come to agree on a plan to get into the camp. Max's second plan was put forward: it had to be a night op and as it was still raining they would have better cover with poorer visibility. The power hut was about three metres from the rear fence so the intruders would get cover from the shed. They all accepted this. It was not a high-security field base nor was it a war scenario so this would help their mission. The garrison were briefed to expect some action but they didn't know what or when. As there was no appointed leader in Max's group for unilateral thinking and decision making, the plan Max put forward had to be agreed by three-quarters of the team which it got unanimously.

'We go in with two men at midnight, we skirt around the camp and get to the rear side where the power hut is. Then using the well-practised leg up and onto the shoulders routine we will place the padded grappling iron on to the top of the fence to avoid noise. If it's all clear we'll drop the rope and climb down and cross to the hut, checking for any guard's position. The mess should be empty at that late time, with most of the garrison asleep. Max's team knew where the communications room was because of the aerials and satellite dish on the roof which Max doubted was being used or guarded. They should get the radio within two minutes and then get back to the rope, one of the team will climb the rope and hoist the radio up and lower it down to the other side then return the rope over the wall for the other man to exit.'

'Sounds simple right? Can anybody improve on the plan?' Asked Max. There were no improvements forthcoming.

'It sounds too easy but it makes sense to me.' Jamie nodded his approval.

'What do we do about the generator?' A good point made by Myers.

'If we are detected we cut the cables to escape in darkness; if we are not seen then we leave well alone and make our way to the river crossing; that way it gives us a head start.' It was decided that the injured Nat shouldn't go. They tossed a coin between the three others with protestations from Nat. Jamie and Max would carry out the operation, helped with Max's piece of coin trickery which no one noticed.

'Be ready to leave for the river as soon as you see us returning from the camp.' Max said to Nat and Myers.

They stayed in the tent to get some rest and at 23.00hrs they packed up their kit, broke camp and walked the half mile to the compound. 'Are you ready Jamie.' Max enquired. Jamie Cuthbert replied with a nod, and with blackened faces the two left the other two, moving slowly forward along the ridge above the compound; from there they crawled the last hundred metres to the camp, stealthily skirting the enclosure to the rear. The base appeared to be in silence and darkness. They moved into position by the hut; Max gave Jamie a leg up and as planned he attached the grappling iron, with cloth taped on it to reduce the noise, on to the fence. Max pulled himself up, straddling the top. Next Jamie climbed the rope; the two were now on the top of the fence looking into the camp. There was no sign of guards so they lowered themselves in to the compound. Both stood flat against the perimeter fence. First Max moved slowly and silently three metres to the hut, Jamie followed. They had already identified the communication room through binoculars, so they knew its location in the dark. The two intruders crept towards the hut. The long shadow created by the main barrack block made their movement visually undetectable. The target hut was in darkness, Jamie shone his pencil torch through the window scanning the room. He spotted the radio they were after. Then they both froze at the unmistakable sound of boots striding closer towards them. In the darkness they moved silently back around the corner of the building and pressed themselves against the wall; there was no time to do anything else. The guard stopped, lowered his rifle, and both thought they had been discovered. They couldn't believe what happened next. He lit a fag, exhaled towards the sky and walked past Max and Jamie who were no more than two feet away. Max and Jamie both looked at each other in total bewilderment after the guard had moved on. The SAS candidates tried the communications room door, surprisingly it was open. Max went in first and scanned the room with his pencil torch.

'Who's that?' a voice from behind them pierced the silence; Max's torch illuminated a guy sitting up in his bed.

'We are from headquarters and are billeting in the camp here tonight; I need to call base to confirm we have arrived; your lieutenant told us to use the field radio here.'

'I know nothing about this.' 'I'd better just check with the guardhouse.' He was still half asleep.

Jamie moved behind him and with a powerful arm lock around his neck, making sure the guy could hardly breathe and certainly could not speak. Max showed him his lethal-looking knife and gestured with his finger to his lips not to talk. The poor chap couldn't work out if it was a bad dream or for real. They taped his mouth and tied him to his bed and, with a nonplussed expression on his face, he just watched the two raiders help themselves to the radio. They checked the batteries were charged for remote use. Jamie collected the spare battery and the two left the way they came in.

"So far so good." Max thought. The pair moved slowly back to their rope; Max pulled himself up and straddled the top of the wall as before. Jamie hitched up the radio, enabling Max to pull it up and swing it over the timber perimeter and lower it down the other side. Once safely on the ground, Max released one end of the rope to throw it down to Jamie, who was soon up over the fence. Myers and Nat were there with all the kit and ready to move off to the river.

'How did it go' Asked Myers.

'No complications as such, now let's get across the river before we are discovered.' Max replied.

The Macal river was in flood and it certainly didn't look inviting although Max thought it would be a beautiful place to explore in different circumstances with the rainforest edging its bank on one side and a rocky terrain on the other. The quartet left the jungle side, aware of the dangers that a fast-flowing river can bring. Myers inflated the small boat which was almost a toy and quickly made two paddles from palm leaves and bamboo. Myers and Max paddled the little boat which was kept tied to a tree as it needed to be sent back for the other two, guiding it slowing out in to the river. It was two fit, strong men against the current; unfortunately, the river was winning the battle of human versus nature. After a strenuous effort they neared the opposite bank. The dinghy was way downstream to their target landing area and had run out of rope. Myers could see the problem, in an instant and without comment, he made a brave leap to the bank. Only just making the overhanging tree branch with one outstretched hand, he pulled himself along the bough like a chimpanzee but without the grace of that dexterous mammal. It was all Max could do to keep the inflatable near the bank, fighting the current now singlehanded. Myers knew what to do. Cutting a long sapling tree quickly, he offered Max to grab it from the boat. He then pulled the inflatable to the bank. They tethered the dinghy, securing the rope to a mature tree about a metre above the water-line. The rope straddled the banks of the Macal, straight across from where Nat and Jamie were on the jungle side. Myers stayed on the far bank while Max pulled himself back across, using the rope and not the paddles. The river used the best of its powerful strength to challenge Max's upper body. Finally with a gentle and purposeful rhythm of step and brace, likened to a tug-of-war competitor, Max eased the boat back to Jamie and Nat.

The next job was to get the radio across. Max asked Jamie to take it across the river using the same method as he had, securing the radio in the inflatable Jamie crossed the river as Max had.

It served two purposes: getting the radio across the river and giving Max a chance to get Nat alone!

Max wasted no time in grilling Nathan Brookes.

'How are your bites feeling Nat? They look terrible?'

'Those antihistamine tablets have helped to reduce the swelling thanks Max.'

'Nat I want straight answers, what happened at the Ship pub in Belize City?'

Nat paused before looking quickly up and then turned away after a nervous glance at Max.

'Just a punch-up that got out of hand, as Myers told you.'

'Nat something else happened in there. It was obvious to both Jamie and me because when we caught up with you and Myers after we ran from the pub Myers threatened you, we heard that much. Come on man, tell me what's going on between you and Myers; he has been controlling you since our drink in the city.'

Nat turned away with a definite mood change; he was clearly physically shaken.

'I've been an absolute fucking twat; it started in Brecon on our phase one test. I couldn't go on with the long drag; it was the fifty-five-pound bergen that done me. I stupidly removed the weights and replaced them with branches to bulk out my pack; I should have just thrown in the towel there and then, but no one was interested in checking my bergen contents and that made my cheating easier to carry out. I swear I would never have completed that forty miles, the bergen straps had rubbed my shoulders raw and they were bleeding from the chaffing. I couldn't have coped with the indignity I would have felt with my fellow Marines had I returned to 3 Commando at Stonehouse Barracks in Plymouth as a failure.' Nat was near to tears as he admitted his failings to Max. Nat admitted it was a load off his mind especially since the pub incident and the blackmailing.

'You bloody fool Nat, what the hell were you thinking of? It's not a disgrace to fail; so many do man!'

'That's not all Max, I swapped bergens when we got back and Myers saw me; I knew then he had caught me cheating in the long drag and Myers had me by the bollocks then. I didn't know what to do and I've felt like shit ever since.'

'Both Jamie and I knew something was on your mind; we knew it wasn't just the bee stings.' Max was sure Nat was about to tell him what really happened in the pub but at that moment he noticed Myers pulling himself back across to collect one of them and was just about in earshot of their conversation. Max needed to keep Nat and Myers separated so said he to Myers. 'Nat and I will cross next to give you a rest Phillip.'

Max and Nat got in the dingy along with the tents and half the kit. As they were crossing the river it struck Max; this might be his last chance to quiz Nathan alone as Myers was always hovering around him.

'Come on Nat, tell me, what has Myers done to blackmail you into keeping your mouth shut?'

Nathan took in a lung full of air and blurted out.

'Myers stabbed a guy in the pub, he knifed the bloke with military precision, his knife moved in the blink of the eye, I don't think anyone saw it other than me. I only saw the blooded knife as he slipped it back into his pocket. Myers is sure the bloke will be ok but I'm not sure. I've been worried sick. Myers said if I did anything to jeopardise his chances of joining the SAS he would implicate me in the fight and tell the training staff I cheated.'

Nat was clearly troubled. Max told Nat not to repeat anything he'd just admitted which would give Max time to think about what to do with Nat's situation. They dropped Nat and the kit off then Max returned to collect the remainder of the equipment and Myers for the last shuttle across the river.

The new day was breaking and the early morning misty tranquillity of the river was shattered in an instant. Gunfire! Ten camouflaged soldiers came charging towards Myers firing their rifles into the air so Max pulled himself to the bank as fast as possible. Unfortunately, it was too late to do much as half the garrison was bearing down on Myers. Max shouted for Myers to leave the kit and release the rope from the tree; he wouldn't have had time to untie it, so Myers gave one blow with his machete and the rope was severed. 'Jump for the boat now'. Max screamed. Myers did and nearly knocked Max into the water. The guys on the other side could see the trouble their comrades were in and started to pull frantically towards them. As they were doing so, Myers attached the end of the rope to the boat's bow. The inflatable was twenty feet out when the first couple of soldiers had reached the bank, it was that close. Max recognised one of them; he was the guy Jamie had tied up back at their camp.

If they were the real enemy the inflatable would have been shot out of the water by now, although the SAS candidates would have made other contingency plans, if they were real enemy. Instead, Max and Myers had rocks and anything the stranded territorials could pick up thrown at them. Jamie and Nat pulled their comrades quickly to safety. Although the team of four were now safely on the other side of the river and jeering at their pursuers they had lost a lot of their equipment that had to be left on the other bank. However, they did have the radio which was their objective. The team knew the garrison would be immediately in pursuit having discovered their radio had been stolen. In addition, they had a Land-Rover to assist in their pursuit.

The map showed the nearest bridge was about ten miles downriver, so the team estimated they had about three-quarters of an hour head start on their hunters. The garrison territorials hadn't a clue who the SAS candidates were or why their field radio had been taken.

.

The noise and activity from the opposite bank caught the quartet's attention; a Land-Rover had arrived with a trailer and four guys were unloading a

RIB with an outboard motor. 'Shit.' Jamie was the first to see the latest problem. The team increased their speed as their pursuers would be across the river in no time at all. Max advised strongly. 'We need to get moving fast and head for jungle cover; we not only have the enemy patrols from our headquarters but half the garrison from the outpost hot on our heels.' They also had a time limit of just another hour to report into base camp for their final instructions. They needed to evade capture from the garrison who were just about to lower their motored RIB into the river.

The four candidates ran as fast as possible into the jungle, melting into its dense cover of ground plants and trees. They had no idea where they were going as they hadn't had time to take bearings. It was unanimously agreed to hide rather than keep on the move; Jamie was bang on when he said. 'We need to make sure we do not disturb the growth or break branches; we must not tread down our path route' It was challenging but the jungle was so dense the team could cover their tracks.

They found a decent area for observing their pursuers, they separated about twenty metres apart, all within sight of each other and covering themselves with broad leaves and grasses. They settled down to silence and waited. It wasn't long before the team heard the thrashing about and chatter from the garrison; they sounded determined to retrieve their radio. The pursuers were fifty metres away, but thankfully the noise soon reduced to silence. The SAS candidates gave it another fifteen minutes before signalling collectively with a thumbs up and moved out together. The team set up the radio with Jamie working the dials on the secure band and was surprised how quickly he got through; Max listened on the twin headset. Jamie asked for the training officer Sergeant Andy Jenkins.

'Hello boys, you just made your time limit, well done.' Max thought: *"Fuck me a compliment, the first one I've heard from anyone since the tests started."* Max interrupted the call. 'Sarge we need to rush you as we are surrounded by hunters who want our blood; please give us our next assignment and coordinates before we are captured.' Without another word, the coordinates came through. Latitude 17.4995 Longitude 88.1976: Philip Godson Highway, Banco de Centro Americano.

Your clue to work out the combination number is: *"At last, it's your birthday"* The answer to the clue will give you the four-digit number you will need for the combination lock that will open the deposit box in the bank. You have three attempts to crack it. Of course the bank has been set up to receive you, but you will not be able to open the deposit box without the correct code. The deposit box is 591. You crack the code and you are in. Good luck.'

Jenkins asked Jamie to repeat the information and he obliged. The radio-phone clicked off, confirming they had the correct information. Max asked the other three to think about the clue; was it about birthdays? Was it a combination of their birthdays or the anniversary of the regiment? Max was mulling it over in his brain but nothing was obvious to him. That night, as they slept under the netting, Max went over and over the clue. *"At last, it's your birthday."* He mused. *"There are four of us, joint birthdays perhaps! But it's only four digits."* Then a moment of inspiration, *"It's your last birthday. Could it be the last digit on the four of our birthdays?"*

Max asked for the last digit in all the candidates birthdays; the four numbers he wrote down were 6 7 8 8. Max played around, writing them down in different sequences. He first got 6878; these numbers were put in order of age. But what was the order. It could be in reversed order or length of military service.

Max's money was age order giving the combination of 6878. They shall see, if they indeed get to the bank. Only three stabs at it, that was the problem!

35

The four set out towards the received coordinates; it took them back along the banks of the Macal river, over the first bridge in an easterly direction. Their electronic map showed the main road was about five miles away which is where they headed for. Fortunately, they hadn't encountered hunter patrols. After over three weeks in the jungle on basic rations they all felt pretty confident in making their final task and getting back to base; but three weeks behind enemy lines had taken its toll.

Max still had the worrying problem about the stabbing and how he would deal with it. But what is for sure, Max can't let it lie. It would be wrong.

The team soon got to the target road that led directly to Belize City; they soon realised it must also be the main road to their camp as military traffic was constantly using it in both directions. However, it was evident to Max that it was too risky to use the open road; any of the passing trucks could easily be part of a patrol out looking for the teams. According to the maps, one choice was to take the road that swings east or cut back through the jungle. The team decided the latter as it was the safest option on Max's suggestion as they had come too far to get caught now. This option was unanimously agreed upon so back into the jungle they went.

The quartet had no idea how many hunter patrols were active in this area of the jungle or where they were so they confirmed their bearings and after re-programming their new route, the team cautiously moved off. It was fortunate that this final stage had no time limit so they could travel as conditions dictated. The group estimated it should take them two to three days to complete the trek providing they incurred no further delays. The bonus was, they still had two lives still remaining in the *"not getting captured stakes."* The lack of intel was frustrating, not knowing if patrols had increased or were concentrated in their area. Nevertheless, they carried on as before, sharing point duty and maintaining silence as they progressed. The light was fading fast as it does in the deep jungle; setting up camp on the raised ground made good sense. They were using the same procedure with the mosquito nets covering them all and their sleeping bags unrolled and laid out. Having a fire was still impossible, that is if they didn't want to get taken by the search patrols. So no fire or hot food that night which was no different from the last twenty-five and only whispering when they needed to communicate. They camouflaged the netting and retired inside for another long boring night without lighting.

Max was sure Myers had twigged that Nat had told him something about the pub incident as Nat's downbeat mood was not only caused by his now worsening bee stings. Nat appeared to be a genuine lad and Max could empathise with him. The dreaded anticipated humiliation when returning to his parent regiment, The Royal Marines.

Max took the first watch and wore a makeshift head net, looking more like a beekeeper than a sentry. It may look out of place, but essential in this inhospitable jungle, particularly with vampire bats out at night. Jamie filtered and purified the stinking drinking water and handed the mugs to the team for their bedtime drink. Myers took two mugs from him and gave one to Nat who was dabbing his stings. Jamie took Max's out to him, it tasted like liquid shit, but they needed fluids. The men settled and went off to sleep; Max completed his sentry shift for three hours. Finishing his stint, he peeped under the netting. The three guys were away with the fairies; Max shook Myers, who took over sentry duty. Max squeezed into his bag, turned over and slept.

His rest didn't last long, he was awakened by Jamie, pushing his shoulder and shouting. 'Nat's having convulsions, you are our medic, what's wrong with him?'

Nathan Brookes was writhing and gasping for breath; he was sweating buckets and choking for air. He said he couldn't feel his arms and they were the last comprehensible words Nat uttered. By now Nat was shaking and convulsing. He was also crapping himself; the smell was horrendous and then he fell into unconsciousness.

'I don't like this at all; I'm calling HQ. It could be the bee stings or the infection.' Max suggested

Myers stuck his head into the tent asking what was going on? He also warned to keep the noise down as he thought he heard a nearby patrol. Jamie explained that Max was going to ring base for help.

'You can't do that, it will abort all that we have done and waste our efforts.'

'You selfish fucker, can't you see he's in a seriously bad way.'

Max contacted HQ and reported the situation to the base radio operator confirming what quartet they were and gave him their coordinates; Max quickly asked for Sergeant Jenkins to come to the phone. 'This had better be good; I was in the bloody shower.' The NCO snapped.

Max explained the state Nathan Brookes was in and requested an air ambulance immediately.

The helicopter lowered a stretcher and harness into the cleared area within forty minutes. A medic was lowered by a winch harness. He took one look at Nat and could see he was in a critical condition. He administered oxygen and put Nat on a saline drip. Next Nat was rolled onto a stretcher and the medic signalled for the helicopter to hoist the stretcher up. The medic was lifted next; the chopper banked eastwards and was away.

'We have to break camp and quick; the enemy hunters would have seen and tracked the helicopter so they will be on us in no time.' Max warned. The team of three broke camp quickly and moved out in a necessary rush. The trio heard the hunting patrols moving in from at least two sides. Max thought: *"Are these bastards just after us? What about the other twenty or so quartets? It seemed every man and his dog is out chasing us."*

They carried on through the night, stopping to listen, but all was quiet. Morning brought more heavy rain together with instant flash flooding which ensured their passage was wading through nearly a metre of surface water compounded by swollen streams that had breached their banks. Leeches became their new problem, sticking themselves to any piece of exposed flesh. These sucking parasites can pass on Syphilis and erysipelas, a serious infection of the skin and some bites can cause extended bleeding.

Jamie and Max were concerned for Nathan and not just for his illness; it was the end of his attempt at joining the regiment. At least on this attempt anyway. Myers strangely appeared more confident since the premature departure of Nathan. His arrogance increased noticeably. This prompted Max to wonder if Myers had anything to do with Nat's demise.

The trio pushed on soaked through; it was mid-morning before they stopped to rest and removed the sucking leeches from their legs. Shorts were cooler to wear but gave them no protection. It wasn't until now that they thought they were safe enough to stop. Jamie pulled out the field radio and kicked it with some venom; it rolled over twice from the force. Max looked up at the angered Jamie and was surprised at his temper.

'There is no battery life, it's fucked.'

'Where is the spare one we took from the camp.' Jamie explained that it was in the kit that was left on the riverbank when the garrison arrived at the river crossing. Providing they have no emergencies, they should manage without it. 'Do we carry on or should we go back to base and support Nat?' Max put the question to the two other team members

Myers said 'We couldn't do much and we would probably be in the way, besides we are so close to finishing the final phase of our tests'. Jamie agreed with Myers for once even though he felt terrible about Nat. So on they went for another thirty miles of heavy going in torrential rain. The trio finally left the jungle at the far eastern end close to the main road. There was only one more attack from this green wilderness, a bite from a spider; it was on Jamie's thigh, but it didn't look too severe and certainly didn't warrant the ex-Para flattening the poor creature with one thump of his clenched fist.

The team jointly decided to take a chance on hitchhiking on the road; they selected a single vehicle for a lift and waived down a military lorry; the driver was on his own but stopped as he could see the thumbing men were in military camouflage. 'Where are you lot going?' The driver shouted down from his cab.

'Bloody anywhere away from that fucking jungle.' Grumbled Jamie rubbing his bite simultaneously.

'I'm going to the city to collect supplies for the camp.'

'We only have to pick up a document in Belize for Sergeant Jenkins and return to base. How long will you be before returning to the camp?'

'About two hours I expect.'

'If we get our business done in time and get back to this highway could we scrounge a lift back to camp?'

'Yeah, but it'll cost you guys a crate of Belikins. Max knew this to be the favourite beer for locals and the squaddies.

'You are on.' Myers butted in answering for the three appearing full of himself once more. The trio of soldiers climbed in; Max dragged himself up in the cab with Myers and Jamie getting into the back. Max-Catt checked his coordinates and told the driver they needed to be about thirty miles down the highway and well inside the city.

'Steve, the next junction appears to be the closest one to where we need to go; we really appreciated the lift. If we get finished first, please look out for us at this junction and we will make it three crates of the local beer.' Steve agreed.

They bid the driver goodbye, walked off the slip road and hailed a taxi. Their kit just fitted in the taxi's boot with some on the guys laps in the back.

'Banco de Centro Americano please.' Without answering the taxi pulled away and five minutes later the trio were outside the bank. They looked strange; three filthy and wet through soldiers with complete kit walked into the bank in mud-caked khaki shorts. They approached the entrance but their passage was abruptly barred; two guards with submachine guns stepped into their path. The senior one of the two guards asked the soldiers what their business was in the bank. After Max explained this the guard lightened up but told the three they would be arrested if the police saw them with guns albeit carrying only blanks. The three were told two of them must wait with one of the guards outside and the other one would be allowed to enter with the senior guard. Max had the guessed password number, so he went in without a weapon. An official from the bank met them and explained he was expecting four soldiers some time today. 'You are from the British army camp I assume?' Max nodded and he beckoned Max to follow him to the bank vault and safety deposit boxes. 'I assume you have the number of the box and the combination code you will need?'

'Yes.' Max confirmed box 591 and the bank official led Max to that box. Max spun the combination 6878. It was correct first-time; the box opened. Max was so chuffed that he'd worked out the riddle given to them by Sergeant Jenkins. Unlike in the movies, where there was always diamonds, gold and cash inside bank deposits boxes, this box just had an envelope with their quartet team number written on it. Max opened it; all it said was *"You have completed your mission return to base at once and report to Sergeant Andrew Jenkins and give him this confirmation envelope. Get it stamped by the bank, proving you have collected it."* Mission accomplished. Another Taxi took the trio to the highway; the furtive driver tried it on with the price until Myers threatened to punch his lights out. Problem solved. They waited for their promised lift unless they saw another army truck come past first. No military vehicle did and an hour later, Steve, the chirpy lorry driver pulled off the road; they all jumped into the back and mostly slept on the journey to the base.

The lorry pulled up at the barrier to the camp. The three in the back all lurched forward.

'We are here; come on out everybody.' The team of three unloaded their kit from the lorry; Max went to the cab and voiced. 'Thanks Steve; we'll catch you in the mess for those beers we owe you.' Another thumbs up from Steve and Max joined a small queue to wait his turn to be checked in. The jungle team was ordered to the guardhouse as routine security and the duty corporal asked his questions then sent them to report to Sergeant Jenkins, the training instructor for the jungle phase.

The three entered the NCO's office and Sergeant Jenkins asked them to sit. In a harsh, ominous voice he said 'Before I get to why I have summoned you here, I must ask if any of you know anything about a stolen SA 80. As you will know it's the army's automatic rifle general assault weapon. The day before you left for your jungle training it went missing from this camp. We have interviewed all of the three hundred and fifty army personnel garrisoned in this depot, most of the returning SAS candidates from the jungle, the ones captured and failed, plus some teams that just gave up. They have also been interviewed. Your team is one of the last groups to be checked. I don't have to remind you how serious this theft is. The civilians who work in the camp are high on the MP's suspect list as many locals have links to the various drug and human trafficking gangs in Belize mainly coming over from Mexico and Guatemala. Our redcaps are making ongoing investigations. An SA80 would be first on any local gang's shopping list and would fetch a top price.'

'How was the rifle stolen? Surely all weapons are signed in and out of the secured armoury?' Enquired Jamie.

'It was taken from the back of one of our trucks just inside the main gate. A six-man patrol, which was just about to leave the camp, had left the truck momentarily to collect their main kit from the quartermaster. The driver was still in his cab waiting. On returning it was discovered one of the SA80s was missing. The armoury register shows it as being signed out approximately twenty minutes before the theft was discovered. We all know the driver should have been more attentive and kept guard as is standard practice when weapons are involved. The driver will get disciplined for that anyway. If you know or hear anything about its whereabouts you must report it immediately to the MP captain or me at once. Is that clear?' A collective yes came from the nodding three.

'I now have to inform you of the current health of your teammate who was airlifted from the jungle. Nathan Brookes is in a critical condition. When he arrived here he was placed immediately into intensive care and put on a ventilator. He is at this moment fighting for his life.' It was evident from the tone of the NCO's voice that he was very concerned for Nat. 'What? I can't believe what I'm hearing, how is that possible just from bee stings?' Max replied in an incredulous tone.

Jamie asked Sergeant Jenkins, 'What's he got wrong with him?'

'He's having tests but it doesn't look at all good.' Just then, there was knock on the door and a medic stepped in and whispered into the NCO's ear.

Sergeant Jenkins had the three's attention.

'Gentlemen the doctor who is treating Nathan wants to see you all now; I've sent word for him to use this office so please wait here.' The doctor came into the room clad in what doctors always wear, pale blue scrubs with the trademark stethoscope around the neck, a surgical mask hanging below the chin, allowing him to speak. He looked very concerned. 'Your comrade is gravely ill and I don't expect him to survive the next twenty-four hours I am sad to say. I asked to see you as I have just received Nathan's blood and urine test results from the pathology laboratory. What is baffling is that the pathology reports confirm that Nathan Brookes ingested a deadly toxin into his body. It's the most lethal poison on the planet, Tetrodotoxin. It has a nerve paralysing effect that causes vital organs to fail followed by loss of breath. Humans can die sometimes as quickly as seventeen seconds after ingesting it. To humans Tetrodotoxin is deadly. It is up to 1,200 times more poisonous than cyanide and there is no known antidote. It only needs 2 or 3 milligrams to cause death. It's why I'm sure Nathan is sadly going to die. I've not asked to see you just to tell you about your friend's demise. How he received this deadly poison is a serious concern to me and no doubt the investigative authorities, including our military police who will undoubtedly want answers. The only natural source of Tetrodotoxin is from a Tetraodontidae, commonly known as a Pufferfish, or a Brachycephalus, a saddle backed toad. The latter is a highly coloured frog from the Cloud Forest Mountains in southeast Brazil.

As neither one of those inhabit the Belize region Private Brookes must have been poisoned deliberately or have been unfortunate to eat some flown in Fugu or pufferfish, a Japanese sought-after delicacy that entails expert preparation from a Fugu chef. To train such a chef takes two years in which he will learn the skills of removing, very delicately most of the fish's anatomy, only the flesh is free from the deadly toxin. The liver is believed to be the most toxic. Therefore, the lethality of the fish is taken very seriously by every Fugu chef,' The doctor was getting carried away with his poison knowledge. 'Where was I, ah yes, I don't believe he's eaten Fugu, being in the jungle and certainly not in a top Japanese restaurant; therefore, he must have been administered the poison either accidentally or probably intentionally. I must add I can't see how this toxin was given to Mr Brookes accidentally. I am not a detective, but I will be calling in our MPs and putting in a report to the Belize police who will, I am sure, want to investigate this matter further.'

Another knock on the door; an army nurse entered and whispered something to the doctor. They went outside the room. Moments later, the doctor was back to address the three-man team.

He gave the trio of soldiers and the sergeant the worst but expected news and in a sombre voice addressed the men.

'It has sadly just got a lot worse! Private Nathan Brookes has died. Tetrodotoxin overwhelmed his body five minutes ago.'

Sergeant Jenkins interjected.

'This is now very serious, and given what the doctor has just said, I am sure all three of you will be questioned. Until further notice all of you are confined to barracks. Go to your billet and shower and change in to clean fatigues.

Then go to the mess where I can locate you. You all understand this is entirely out of my hands now; carry on.'

36

An hour had passed since the jungle team of three had returned and they now met up in the mess. Myers had been very withdrawn since the doctor spoke and was now looking subdued. Max perceived this change and wanted to talk to Jamie independently but didn't get the chance; Phillip Myers was on them like a rash.

The MP Captain Lewis Titcombe entered the mess and asked Jamie to follow him to his office and asked Max and Myers to wait in the mess until called.

'Tell me what happened out there in the jungle Mr Cuthbert. Was there any fighting amongst you? Did anybody buy fish before you left? Was there any bad feeling between individuals? I want all details no matter how unimportant you might deem it.'

Jamie recalled what happened nervously!

'We acted like a team who hardly knew each other; we only met a couple of days before we went into the jungle. You must understand that the four of us were selected as a four-man team by Sergeant Andy Jenkins. Nothing happened in the jungle, but we did have an altercation in a bar in Belize City a couple of days before we started our jungle test.

It happened in the Ship bar in the city centre. Two of our lads got into a punch-up with some locals, you know, usual thing, civvies don't like the army chaps around taking their women, need I say more captain. Maximus Hainsworth-Catt and I were outside and didn't see what happened. Only Phillip Myers and the late Nathan Brookes were inside when the fight broke out.'

The enquiring MP nodded. 'This throws a totally different light on the matter. A local man known to the police was stabbed in that bar and later died in hospital, I think on the same day your group were there.

The Belize national police come to the camp as a matter of practice if it involves UK military law infringements. If you look on the general noticeboard you will see their request for witnesses or information asking for person or persons who might have visited the Ship bar on the Saturday before your jungle trip. The very day you guys did. Tell me exactly what happened there again.'

Jamie explained again the whole account including Myers avoiding police roadblocks.

The captain folded his book and asked, 'Why was this not reported when you returned to HQ?'

Jamie replied. 'In hindsight, of course, we should have, but it was just two days before we started our jungle assignment and that was all that was on our minds and what happened in the city was just another Saturday night in a bar with guys letting off steam. So why wouldn't we believe Myers' version of what happened? Indeed, it was corroborated by poor Nat Brookes.'

The captain said to Jamie. 'Is there anything else that happened out of the ordinary in the jungle?'

'Only the convulsions Nat had on our last night, the helicopter airlifted him back to here and that's all really.'

'That will be all for now but do not leave the barracks unless I say so. Understood?'

'Yes sir.' Replied Jamie. Jamie headed for the door. 'Please send in Maximus Hainsworth-Catt for me.'

'Yes sir.' Jamie was sweating from the questioning and had a dry mouth brought on by nervousness. He wondered if this whole incident might scupper their SAS qualification and after all the time and previous effort it took to get this far he shuddered at the thought.

'Max, the MP captain wants to see you next; come on, I'll show you to his office.'

'I need to speak to you as well! And now. What did you tell him, what did he ask you, what's going on?' asked Max anxiously. 'I told the MP captain exactly what happened; what else could I tell him? We thought something was strange and that it appeared Myers had something on Nat. You had better get in there and tell him how it was.'

'You don't know the half of it Jamie.'

Jamie gave Max a quizzical glance and thought to himself, *"What did you mean by that Max!"*

'Sit down Mr Hainsworth-Catt and tell me everything that happened at the umm, the...,' The military police captain went back on some pages of his notebook and continued 'Ship bar on Saturday before you left for the jungle. Also, any incidents that occurred later in the jungle leaving nothing out.'

Max told him everything he knew, explaining to Lewis Titcombe that both Jamie and he were surprised with the strange behaviour of both Myers and the late Nathan Brookes after they ran out of the pub.

'In what way strange?' the MP interjected.

'When Jamie and I caught them up Myers was speaking to Nat in a threatening voice and did so again later in the mess. Myers made Nat drink with him. I know it sounds daft, but it appeared that Myers had some sort of influence over Nat. The first time I had the opportunity to get Nat alone was at the river crossing; I had to coax it out of Nat as he was reluctant to talk about the Ship incident and why his mood had changed so much after that. I was stunned when Nat blurted out his admission of guilt and his failings at Brecon and the cheating by removing the weights from his bergen while on an endurance run. Myers had seen Nat's cheating and was using it to blackmail him. Nat had also witnessed Myers's fight in the bar which we all knew about because Myers told us himself. What we didn't know was that Myers had stabbed the guy. Myers threatened Nat that if he told anyone what happened he would tell of his cheating in Brecon and that would finish his chance of getting into the SAS and the shame he would face on his return to 3 Commando. Nat was beside himself with guilt and anguish over his stupidity for cheating and withholding evidence about the stabbing. On our return we were informed by Sergeant Jenkins that a person was stabbed and had died in the Ship and the Belize Police were asking for witnesses. Of course, I have not had time yet to come forward and say all this until now.'

After listening intently, Lewis Titcombe demanded. 'If there's anything else you remember, you must let me know, anything, do you understand?'

'Of course.'

'Send in Myers will you.'

Titcombe warned Max not to leave Belize City.

"That interview will be interesting." Max mused.

'Myers come with me and I'll show you to the interview office.'

'What have you said to him.' Myers asked Max.

'The truth Myers, the truth.' They didn't speak again. Max left him at the door of the interview room. Myers knocked and went in with his usual confident swagger.

After they both settled in their seats the captain opened his book, 'Tell me all you know about what happened from the day you arrived in Belize until now and don't leave anything out, is that understood.'

Phillip Myers explained. 'The eighty-plus guys who succeeded in the Brecon Mountain trials arrived in Belize for the jungle phase. We were billeted here at this camp and put into teams of four. Our kit was delayed in arriving, so we had a couple of days leave.' Phillip Myers explained his embellished side of the story. Keeping to the general points that happened but leaving out the stabbing and blackmail which didn't surprise the military police captain.

Myers returned to the mess but not to Jamie and Max. Instead Myers stayed drinking at the bar pondering his next move. Max and Jamie went for a walk to try and work out their situation as things had moved so quickly and they required answers to some questions. Max started by retracing events beginning at the Ship.

'What is your take on the events at the pub Jamie?'

'It's all extraordinary, but like you I don't trust Myers one bit.'

'I haven't had the opportunity to tell you this because Myers has been present most of the time and then we had the questioning by the MP Captain,'

'For God's sake tell me Max!'

'Myers stabbed the bloke he fought at the Ship.'

'Fuck me, he'll get done for murder,' Jamie was clearly shaken. 'How do you know this Max?'

'Remember when we were at the river crossing after we took the radio across, well that was the first chance I had to get Nat alone. I pressed him into telling me what was going on with him because his mood had definitely changed markedly after the pub incident. I was as shocked as you are now when he told me about the knife attack and there's more. Nat hit the wall on the forty mile drag in Brecon. He removed his weights and packed out his bergen with branches; and then he swapped packs around at the finish, Myers saw what Nat did so he blackmailed him. Nat felt awful but couldn't face failure and the shame. He didn't want the indignity of facing his comrades in the Royal Marines.' Jamie was stunned but sympathised.

'He shouldn't feel a failure for not being able to do the long drag, more than half of the candidates couldn't hack it and didn't get here to the jungle test.'

'That's exactly what I told him at the crossing'. Said Max.

'What are we going to do Jamie? We could both be in the shit over this.'

'I don't think so' said Jamie 'At the time of events in the pub we were outside; we only followed by chasing after Myers and Nat and at that point we didn't know what had happened. We had no control in the back of the car at the roadblocks either. I suppose we should have reported the incident when we had the two days at camp waiting for our kit to arrive but we have been taught comradeship above everything so we couldn't report Myers for what we only thought was a pub brawl at the time.'

'Unfortunately, it wasn't just a pub brawl though Max, was it?'

'I have already explained all this to the MP, so we shall see what develops; I don't think we will have to wait long. I reckon Myers is going to get nicked for the murder.'

'What do you think about the poisoning of Nat Brookes? Do you believe Myers had something to do with that as well?'

'It looks like it Jamie, but how?' Max asked, almost rhetorically.

'Let's see if the captain has updates on the stabbing.' Suggested Jamie.

They waited ten minutes before the captain saw them and before Max and Jamie could sit down or even speak with the MP, he exclaimed. 'We have arrested Myers on suspicion of murder and he's now in custody in the guardhouse; we expect to charge him within the next twenty-four hours.'

'From the evidence we received from you both we can hold Myers for twenty-four hours; we will need more proof though to charge him and make it stick. The only witness, it appears, is Nathan Phillips and he's dead. So it's only your word against Myers. I'm afraid that what Nathan Brookes divulged to you will not stand up in a court trial. The Belize police investigator told me they had interviewed all the remaining customers in the ship and they all said they didn't see the incident. The Belize law enforcement guy explained that getting witnesses is difficult because of the drug cartels as they use Belize as a stepping stone to the lucrative USA markets. He went on to say that most shootings, stabbings and other murders are carried out by the drug gangs against other gangs for turf rights. Ordinary folk see nothing and say nothing. It's their safest protection. So the officer doesn't hold out much hope of getting a conviction; it's just the way it is here.

'I think Myers is guilty; his strange behaviour, the avoidance of police roadblocks, surely add up to guilt but proving it will be difficult, I do understand that. By the way captain, what is happening with the poisoning investigation?'

'So far the pathologist has passed his findings to the district coroner's office, as the tests were not conclusive. The coroner has ordered a post mortem on Nathan Brookes. By the way your confinement to barracks is lifted for you both, but do not leave Belize without checking with me first.'

Jamie and Max left the MP, relieved their confinement was rescinded.

'Do you know what I think Jamie? Let us try a different approach; we both want to nail Myers, if only for poor Nat Brooke's sake. The authorities apparently will not get far with the stabbing; we will have no chance if the local police can't. The poisoning with Tetrodotoxin that killed Nat was no accident; it couldn't have been, so we should look at the facts and see what we can establish. Firstly, we know from the experts that the cause of Nat's death was through paralysis, organ failure and his heart stopping brought on by Tetrodotoxin. Secondly this poison can only be produced from the pufferfish or that frog the doctor told us about, so we know what the weapon was. Next is motive, you and I didn't want Nat dead, why the hell would we? We only met him when the four-man teams were selected; who would wish Nat dead?'

'Of course, Nat might have said to Myers he wasn't sure he could lie about the stabbing and Myers perhaps didn't want to risk him reporting what he had seen, Myers stabbing the guy in the Ship pub!' Jamie at last could see a motive for Myers wanting to kill Nathan. 'What can we do Max? It comes down to proving it and we can't.'

'The doctor categorically told us that Tetrodotoxin could not be found on plants or any species apart from the pufferfish and that Brazilian frog, the name I can't remember; the doctor was sure none of that poison could be found in the Belize jungle. We know he hadn't eaten that Fugu pufferfish delicacy so the only possible way Nat received the deadly toxin was from the person who gave it to him in some form or other. The speed at which the poison acts suggests ingestion must have been taken on our last night in the jungle when Nat fell ill. Myers must have poisoned Nat, but how and where did he get the deadly poison from.'

'He was with us all the time apart from the days before we went into the Jungle while we were waiting for our kit to arrive.'

'That's it Jamie, of course. Myers went missing on his own for two days; that's when he must have sourced the poison but from where and who?'

They had a few days leave before their briefing and return to the UK which will allow Max some time to locate possible local stockists of this highly lethal toxin. Max searched online for pharmaceutical companies in Belize and came up with several possibilities who were around Belize City and on the Mexican border. Max intended to visit these places as a start. But first he needed Myers's photo from the captain.

37

'Back so soon Mr Hainsworth-Catt, so what can I do for you?'

Peering over his glasses, the military police captain gestured for Max to take a seat.

'I intend to go to Belize City to look up suppliers of Tetrodotoxin and I might strike lucky in finding the stockist who sold the poison to Myers.'

'It's not your concern, keep out of police matters, you are a soldier so stick to soldiering.' Captain Lewis Titcombe fidgeted with annoyance. Max could see the MP officer was getting worked up but the SAS candidate persisted in his request. 'I would very much like your help by obtaining a photo of Myers; you must have taken some when he was arrested. All I want is a mug shot of him for Nathan's sake. We must at least give it a try!' Maximus had a determined tone to his voice.

The captain blew out his cheeks in exasperation and told the persistent soldier to wait while Titcombe left the room. Returning within a few minutes the MP captain slide an envelope across his desk towards Max. Inside was a prison photo with a front and profile of Phillip Myers.

'You can have this but don't get involved apart from enquiries and promise you will call me with any news or developments. It's on those conditions I'll let you have theses photos.' Max accepted the MP's terms, took the photos, thanked him with a firm handshake, and left.

Max carried on checking the largest pharmaceutical companies in Belize City online; two were close together at Ambergris Caye situated in the San Pedro district. He thought this was as good a place as any to start his investigative work. The SAS candidate hired a car to visit the city; thanks to the Sat-Nav, he got there within an hour. Max parked and walked to the famous swing-bridge and bought his water taxi fare from the caged ticket office and went through security. He waited for the next open boat to take him to Ambergris Caye, San Pedro. Seventy minutes later he was on the island making his way up Main Street, according to the guide map he bought at the swing-bridge. The street layout was Main Street, Front Street, Middle Street, Back Street and Back a Back Street. The latter looked as if it was a tag-on and indeed it was. An additional street was added behind Back Street. Max knew this because his first call was to Collins & Sanchez Pharmaceutical Supplies, on that very tag-on street.

Max hired a golf cart that appeared to be the only local mode of transport in Ambergris. Driving up Front Street away from the ocean the narrow, cobbled streets were full of parked golf carts, some with open pick-up style backs for carrying goods and people; the golf buggies were parked strangely but efficiently at forty-five degrees in the same direction and on every road.

It was 10.40hrs by the time Max had weaved his hired golf buggy to Back a Back Street and pulled up outside Collins and Sanchez; the display board read licensed to sell drugs and poisons. The soldier, turned detective, went inside and asked if an English military-type had called in a few weeks ago and purchased some Tetrodotoxin. The startled look on the assistant's face was quite apparent. She exclaimed. 'Do you know how dangerous Tetrodotoxin is?'

'Indeed I do. May I speak with your boss or the head pharmacist please?' She laughed out loud and said.

'I'm the only qualified pharmacist here, there's another girl who helps, but she is out doing deliveries.'

'Well, my apology, so my same question to you again.' She fetched a large leather-bound book and confirmed.

'I have checked through the dates going back a month and there has been no dispensing of TTX in our poison register; it's a rare request and very expensive.'

'I assume TTX is the scientific abbreviation for Tetrodotoxin?' Max enquired.

She replied with an affirmative nod.

'Would you tell me what this lethal poison is used for?'

'Sure, it's a modern painkiller, and it's starting to replace the opiates that can easily become addictive. In addition, TTX appears to last longer in pain suffering patients for a lesser dosage. It's in the early stages of trial testing that is still awaiting scientific and the World Health Organisation's approval. It also appears to benefit nerve-associated pain and acts as a blocking element.' Max was impressed with this young lady's knowledge.

'Wow, you know what you are talking about; by the way is there another pharmacist nearby licensed to sell TTX over the counter?' The young chemist answered immediately.

'Yes, Carmichael's on Middle Street, about halfway up on the right. As you have probably gathered all the streets are one way.'

'Where are Collins or Sanchez?' The young pharmacist laughed. 'That's how I knew you were not from around here. Are you with the British army?'

'Yes, am I that obvious?' Max was not surprised as everybody must know everyone else on a small island like San Pedro. 'Anyway,' she explained 'both Messrs Collins and Sanchez retired five years ago; I'm Donna Collins, the niece of Trevor Collins. He opened this place in 1987.' She said with pride in her voice.

Max thanked the lady for her help and kindness. He left the pharmacy that time had forgotten and headed for Middle Street and Carmichael's. Although Max didn't hold out too much hope he had to eliminate all possible sources of this evil poison that caused the death of Nathan Brookes.

Back in the hired golf cart Max thought to himself: *"It's funny what goes through one's mind when driving; this paradise, worlds apart from the fly-infested, sand-swept frontline of Afghanistan or the minus ten degrees freezing on Pen Y Fan mountain in Brecon"*. He had a mental chuckle to himself at these thoughts.

Max soon learned the local art of not hitting golf buggies that pull out in front of you, at the same time as negotiating pedestrians who seemed to be coming out of the tightly packed shops like rats scurrying about their business. Five minutes later Max parked two hundred metres away from his next port of call as there was nowhere nearer to park; he left the buggy outside a liquor store and walked to Carmichael's. The intrepid soldier was accosted in the most friendly manner from shop keepers competing with the street vendors selling everything from queen conch shells to the famous panadas, a doughy envelope filled with meat, fish and cabbage covered with homemade habanero, a local spicy sauce. Unfortunately, Max had no time for one; the cooking filled the air with an aroma of spices that made him drool.

Carmichaels was a larger establishment; it had several assistants buzzing around the shop serving customers. Max asked to speak with the head honcho and waited twenty minutes to see Mariano Gomez, the head pharmacist. Max explained the same to him as he had to the prettier, more helpful, Donna Collins. After hearing what Max required, Gomez passed Max on to one of his female colleagues who thought his request unusual and lectured Max on the deadly TTX. She checked her poison book which showed a negative result, but suggested Max try NTM Pharmaceuticals in Neils Pen Road, Belize City. The pharmacist said it was near the Collett canal and explained that they were major suppliers and wholesalers in pharmaceutical products. Max thanked her and left.

On the way back to his golf buggy, Max couldn't resist a panada, it was too tempting to pass up for a second time. Max returned the golf cart to the seafront buggy hire and walked along the sugar white beach edging the clear, turquoise Caribbean Sea. It was accentuated by the barrier reef that spans the length of Ambergris Caye. The giant white waves were rolling over this natural reef, a surfers paradise. Max had the same thought as he had earlier, thinking back to the last drag on the bone-chilling mountain of Pen Y Fan in the Brecon Beacons, it seemed like worlds apart. Max asked himself. *"How can one's body feel so different and only a few weeks apart, insane to think of the freezing exhaustion when the body doesn't stop shivering all night to this, this paradise with the warmth of the sun on one's back".* The perfect sea breeze was just about retaining the break out of sweat from his forehead. It was truly paradise!

The sound of an ambulance siren jolted Max back to the rigours and reality of life and the work in hand. He made his way back to the water taxi terminal, where luckily one was about to leave. Max showed his return ticket to the man on the pontoon and hopped aboard the open top speed boat that returned him to Belize City. He picked up his hire car where he had left it and set the satnav for Neils Pen Road, a strange name, Max thought. He found it easy enough and mused at the many tiny coloured houses, almost shanty like, along this main road; in contrast they stood cheek by jowl with prosperous real estate that strangely blended in perfectly.

The satnav directed Max to right outside the door of NTM Pharmaceuticals and he went in the main entrance to the reception. He introduced himself to the receptionist explaining he required information about the sale of TTX poison. The receptionist asked Max to take a seat and somebody would come to see him.

'Mr Hainsworth-Catt I am Conrad Dyer, sales manager, how can I help you?' Max shook his hand and replied.

'I am trying to find out if you sell or can source Tetrodotoxin and if so, have you sold any TTX in the last few weeks?'

'Are you police?' Dyer asked suspiciously!

'No I'm here for a friend who asked a Phillip Myers to source some TTX for him, he wanted to know who sold Myers the poison as he now requires some more and he thinks it might have been NTM as you seem to be the largest suppliers of drugs and toxins in Belize.'

'One moment sir, I shall fetch our poison register.'

Max nodded and sat back down, watching the elevator move slowly up to level three and stop. The manager returned looking furtive and definitely uneasy. 'I'm sorry sir, I can't help you; it's data protected you understand.' Abruptly he ushered Max to the door, too quickly for Max's liking. The SAS trainee left the building bemused but convinced the poison book was kept on level three! He must try and get to that register.

Max decided to look around the spacious building and made his way to the back of NTM towards the despatch area. A guy was leaning against a wall smoking and looking as if he hadn't a care in the world. Max asked him about his job, pay and conditions; it hit a nerve as he wondered who the fuck Max was! Max assured him 'I'm a backpacker just looking for some casual work.' Max offered the agitated man a cigarette which relaxed him a tad.

'I must be truthful,' Max thought of a better approach. 'I work for a Mexican medicine and drugs conglomerate who is looking to buy out NTM and any assistance that you can give me may work well in your favour. Do you get my drift?

The man shrugged his shoulders and became more interested. Max elaborated. 'I need the actual size of the building as the Mexicans will only take a specific sized buy-out. I get a healthy finder's fee if it comes off, and I promise you will not be forgotten for your information. Also, I need the entire layout of the building on all three levels. Can you get me that information?'

The smoker asked Max to wait while he went inside the building. He returned with another guy. Max was a little worried, thinking he may have been bubbled. 'I can tell you about every nook and cranny in this building; I'm maintenance here,' before Max had time to answer he continued. 'It'll cost you three hundred Belizean dollars.' Max had wondered when a deal was going to be offered.

'I'll give you one hundred British pounds now and five hundred if the deal goes through and I will also put a good word in about you two if the Mexicans buy this business.' They shook hands on the deal. All Belizeans love British pounds.

Max warned, 'You must not mention this to anyone; the Mexicans will back out if the owners find out about a takeover'. The maintenance man drew a rough plan for all three floors and handed it to Max to study. Max could see the plan was detailed and showed all the rooms. He paid the map sketcher a hundred in cash and left the two overalled workers with smiles on their faces.

Max went back to his car, took out his bag and walked to the nearby Collett canal and sat on a park bench overlooking the flowing water to gather his thoughts. He considered breaking into NTM, perhaps a long-shot, but worth a try. Max was about to return to his vehicle when his phone vibrated into life. 'Yes.' it was Jamie Cuthbert ringing from camp. 'Hi is that you Max?'

'Yes Jamie, is anything the matter?'

'No not at all, but listen to this; we have a massive breakthrough on Nat's death. You remember before we left for the jungle training nobody had seen Myers for two days, well it turns out the taxi driver, Delroy, who is always outside the camp gate, told me Myers approached him and asked him outright if he knew any people in Belize City who can *"get things"*. The cabbie told him he did but, and this is the best bit, Myers asked him if he knew anyone who might be interested in buying an automatic weapon. The taxi bloke asked Myers what sort of weapon was it that he wanted to sell. Myers told him it was a front-line British infantry assault rifle SA80 and his friend had a spare one to sell. The driver asked how much. Myers told him four hundred pounds; he made the point that a Heckler and Koch SA80 automatic assault rifle is the best part of nine hundred quid,'

'What happened then?' Max was hanging on Jamie's every word. 'the cabbie said he did have a contact buyer for such a weapon and asked Myers if the gun for sale was the same gun Myers had put in his boot. Myers admitted it was. The cabbie agreed to take him to his contact but warned Myers not to say a word and let him do the deal. The cabbie phoned the contact and took Myers to meet the interested party to do the deal. The cabbie drove Myers to Orange Walk Town, about an hours drive north of Belize City on the San Antonio Road.

The cabbie pulled up at the meeting place, a seedy bar, and was greeted by two nasty looking bodyguard types who showed them into a back room where their boss was. The cabbie said he introduced Myers to a man named Aguila. Myers didn't do what he was advised by Delroy, in that he jumped straight in, asking Aguila if he could source poisons like arsenic or cyanide. Myers said he would want poison plus cash in exchange for the SA80. The cabbie told Myers that Aguila could get anything. The gang boss said to Myers he would make a call and while he was doing this, Myers was asked to fetch the SA80 from the car. He returned with the bagged weapon. Aguila told them that he could source some poison far deadlier, a thousand times more toxic than cyanide and almost instant death. He said he could get the poison the next day if the weapon was up to expectations. Myers unwrapped the rifle and it was inspected methodically by Aguila, who took it out the back and fired off several rounds in auto mode. He liked it and said to Myers that he had a deal. Aguila would have the poison by the following day before 13.00hrs. The cabbie said that Myers was invited to stay the night with Aguila as he had some other business to discuss with him. Myers accepted the stop-over, then the cabbie said he returned to the base after agreeing to pick Myers up at 13.30hrs the next day.'

'Bloody hell Jamie, that clears up a lot of questions, enough to nail Myers as well methinks.'

'Where are you, Max?'

'I'm in Belize City. So, tell me Jamie why did the taxi guy offer you all this information? I'm intrigued!'

'Because the deal was more of an exchange rather than a cash sale, an SA80 for a phial of poison, no money changed hands. The gang boss took his dangerous new toy, gave Myers the phial, and told him he wasn't getting any cash. Aguila then strongly recommended that Myers should leave quickly for his safety and warned him that Orange Walk Town was not the place to hang around for too long. The cabbie endorsed Aguila's advice, saying he wouldn't take his cab to that district after dark. When the driver and Myers got back to the base Myers refused to pay the introduction fee and told Delroy he could swing for the money. It led to a quarrel and Myers left the taxi driver in a rage which Myers made matters worse by thumping the cabbie. The taxi driver wanted revenge and intended reporting Myers to the MP's at the base but after cooling down he realised it would incriminate him as an accessory after the fact so he decided against telling the MP's. He didn't want to jeopardise his taxi concession at the camp or worse, get arrested.

'The cabbie wanted retribution so while we were away in the jungle the taxi driver made enquiries using his connections at the base and he soon discovered that Myers had gone on a jungle exercise and wouldn't be back for weeks. The cabbie was told who the other team members were. When we returned to base, he tried contacting you, Max, but he couldn't find you, then he looked me up; the cabbie also knew that Nathan had died. Finally, he got a note passed to me by a cleaner friend of his who works in the mess. The message asked me to meet him at his taxi stand this morning. He couldn't wait to tell me his story about being ripped off by Myers. I gave him four hundred Belizean dollars for his information and asked him not to mention it to anyone else to which he agreed. I concluded by asking if he would testify against Myers. Delroy's reply was emphatic. No! It's safer to see and say nothing in these parts.'

'We know that Jamie, from the witnesses who kept schtum in the Ship pub, it must be a nightmare for the prosecutors here.' Max blew out his cheeks in disbelief.

'That's excellent, you have done damn good work. I'll go halves with you with the money you gave Delroy.'

Jamie remembered. 'I forgot to mention that Myers was released without charge this morning due to lack of evidence.'

'Let's hope Myers doesn't influence Delroy.'

'I shouldn't think that's likely as Myers will stay clear of him as he owes him money,' suggested Jamie.

'What do we do next Max? We leave for the UK in two days.'

'Yes, I know Jamie, I'm fully aware of that. We need proof against Myers and I'm positive it's in the poison register at NTM Pharmaceuticals. It's 14:00hrs now, can you meet me here by 16:30hrs this afternoon? Bring the collapsible grappling iron and rope from our jungle kit, gloves and a pencil torch? I'll buy the other bits that we'll need. I'll explain the plan when you get here. Get the cabbie to bring you then you can return with me in my hire car. Don't mention meeting me. Tell the cabbie you are shopping in the city for souvenirs before leaving for the UK. Meet me at the bridge, 144 Belize, on the Collett canal. I'll watch out for you around 16.30hrs. You had better get your skates on right now.'

'Sure Max, I'm on the case; see you later.'

38

The balance has now changed dramatically in their favour Max believed. They now have a solid link between the rare pufferfish poison and Myers and a witness confirming that he stole the SA80 although the witness will not repeat this evidence to the authorities. Likewise, Myers' meeting with Aguila's exchange of the TTX for the rifle but again no conclusive evidence.

Max realised he must substantiate the unproven facts he already has and is convinced the factual proof is in the poison register book at NTM Pharmaceuticals. Max intended to get that proof with Jamie's help and the handwritten plans of the whole building, courtesy of the smoker. Max thought back to when Conrad Dyer left him in the reception of NTM to check the poison register; he took the lift to the third floor and returned from same floor. He didn't go to another level. The information they need is on floor three, Max was sure of this. Dyer gave Max a very significant clue when his total personality changed upon his return to the reception, perceived immediately by Max, who felt sure Dyer was hiding something.

Max went off to complete his shopping list for the planned job.

It must be done tonight as it's their last free night before thier return to Brize Norton. Max had already found out what time NTM closed and although there were security alarms on the windows and doors, Max didn't see any surveillance cameras internally or outside.

Max had a plan; he purchased a lab coat, a clipboard and a headband fixed torch. After completing his shopping list, he grabbed a takeaway coffee and sandwich. He waited for Jamie by the canal, eventually surrendering to the persistent ducks that nagged him for the remnants of his bread. Then, intrigued with the waterfowl fighting over the last crumbs of his sandwich, he looked up to see the unmistakable outline of Jamie Cuthbert getting out of the taxi; Max also recognised Delroy, the taxi driver. The cab pulled away and Jamie, with a backpack in his hand, looked around for Max. With arms frantically waving, Max shouted across the canal. 'Jamie over here,' Mr Cuthbert crossed the bridge to Max, they embraced as true friends. Both had come through a lot together in the last month or so and it seemed natural for them to cement their comradeship.

'Thanks for coming Jamie; we have to nail that murdering bastard Myers.'

'I feel the same way Max; we can't let Myers get away with this, what's your plan, I'm intrigued?'

'Let's go to my car and I'll explain it all to you; did you bring the kit?' Jamie nodded a reply. Max explained the plan to get the proof they need to convict Myers as they couldn't rely on the dodgy cab driver to give evidence against Myers and certainly not against Aguila. Max explained his idea of getting to the poison register to link Aguila to the purchase which will in turn connect Myers. Max knew that NTM closes at 18.00hrs and that there are no security cameras that could be seen, but the doors and windows are alarmed and activated at 18.00hrs when the last senior staff member locks up for the night. Then two or sometimes three cleaners arrive at 18.30hrs and finish around 19.45hrs. While they are in the building the cleaning supervisor deactivates all the alarms. Max intended to get the register between those times. 'Do you follow so far Jamie?' asked Max.

'Yes, but I have some questions.'

Max acknowledged Jamie's comment but continued. 'The building's layout is as follows, on the ground floor there is the reception, waiting lounge, toilet block, lift, stairway, and at the rear, a large mailroom with a loading bay. The second floor is mostly administration, a couple of middle management offices, a toilet block and the dry goods stores. The third and top floor is virtually all laboratories with a wing that accommodates two senior managers offices, a liquid store, a toilet block and a board room. Outside there's a large car and lorry park to the side and rear.'

Max and Jamie poured over the hand-sketched but detailed plan of the building for the three floors.

'Your questions Jamie?'

'Wow, where did you get this plan of the building?'

Max explained. 'After being asked to leave NTM briskly by the dodgy Mr Dyer, I surveyed the building for a possible covert entry; I went to the back to the despatch area. A guy was there having a fag break. His pal was the maintenance worker who drew up these plans of the whole building. Naturally they fell for the Mexican takeover deal and of course the part payment of cash I gave them, helped. Now Jamie are there any more questions?'

'Yes, how are we going to get in?'

'We are not, I am, I need you on the outside. So here is the entry plan!

You and I will go to NTM Pharmaceuticals an hour before they close. There are gangs of young kids begging and generally making a nuisance of themselves all along the canal, we shall use their disruptive behaviour to help in our plan. We'll pay two of them to go into the reception area just after you have entered. While you engage with the receptionist asking for directions or who their buyer is, anything to distract her attention, the kids will go past you and start splashing the water in the ornamental fountain making a distraction. I will show the kids the fountain through the side window prior to you going in.

'What will you be doing when me and the kids are in reception?' Jamie enquired.

'While the receptionist is dealing with the kids I will come into reception wearing my white lab coat with a clipboard in hand and walk briskly to the lifts. If the receptionist doesn't go to the kids to turf them out you must tell her she must as they are damaging the fountain or something along those lines. That should move her but I'm sure that'll not be necessary. According to the bribed maintenance man, there is a dry store cupboard that is never locked. I will hide in there until 18.00hrs when hopefully all the staff should have left or are leaving by then. I will have half an hour before the cleaners arrive, if they come early and I haven't found what I'm looking for by then I will say I'm a lab technician working late. Are you happy with that Jamie?'

'Sounds like a good plan to me Max. So what do you want me to do?'

'Have the car parked in the loading bay at the rear ready to move off quickly or just in case I accidentally trigger an alarm. I will be in contact by phone, also don't forget to pay the two street kids their earnings as promised, but only after the job or you will not see them for dust. I will leave the window open in the store cupboard but the alarm may still go off so get ready to move out fast.'

'I'll be ready Max!'

'Let's go and sort out our partners in crime.' They drove to the NTM offices and found two street urchins who eagerly signed up to do the task. It was made clear to them that they would not get the cash reward until the job was finished then Jamie would pay them. That completed, Max then took the boys to the window and showed them the fountain they were to make a disturbance in. Next, Max gave the boys instructions. 'You two are to stay around here and wait for us, this man' Max pointed to Jamie 'will go into the building and you boys count to twenty then follow him in, you know where the fountain is so splash the water and make as much noise as you can, got it?'

Both the boys nodded and one of the the cheeky street kids asked. 'Are you robbing the place mister? If so we want a cut!' Spoken in near perfect English, it made the two special forces candidates chuckle at these streetwise urchins. Jamie made it clear it was not a robbery.

Max put on his lab coat, backpack with grappling iron, torch and gloves and was ready to move in. The two kids were there waiting to follow Jamie. Max stayed back as Jamie met the boys outside the entrance with a briefcase in his hand, looking every bit the part of a businessman. He gave the kids last-minute instructions and walked confidently into the reception of NTM.

The boys were counting down the time agreed to follow Jamie in. Max moved near the entrance and waited for his moment. It came almost instantly; the kids were in place splashing about with youthful enthusiasm. Max watched the receptionist dash from behind her counter and run to the fountain shouting at the kids. Jamie followed, blocking her view should she look back; there was no fear of that; she was on a mission to protect her fountain. As Max entered the reception, he heard the receptionist screaming at the boys to get out or she'd call the police. Max hurried to the stairs and climbed to the second floor. So far so good Max thought. He looked at his makeshift map and headed to the dry goods store. Just as the maintenance man had said, it wasn't locked. The storeroom was fitted with standard metal storage frames. Max climbed to the top of the shelves and made room by moving boxes down to the lower shelves, leaving a line of cartons to make a screen. He covered himself for good measure with overalls and work clothing. Max closed his eyes and waited for 18:00hrs when all the staff should leave, he hoped. After ten minutes of Max's arrival the storeroom door opened and closed again. Max held his breath as he heard footsteps walking below him. Max's mind was racing. Had the kids or the maintenance man reported him? Perhaps it's somebody just getting stock from the room. Max heard the window open behind him, the same one he hoped to use as an emergency exit. Then it was blatantly obvious why the person had come in. The pungent smell of cigarette smoke wafted up, hence the opened window, which didn't seem to be diluting the smoke. After a few minutes the window closed, and the sound of footsteps passed; the door opened and closed again. Although not tempted to look for another couple of minutes, Max was alone in the room once more apart from the lingering smell of smoke.

The wait seemed so long until the next loud noise; although muffled, it was not far away. People were chatting and walking so Max assumed it was home time; a glance at his watch confirmed this. He waited until he heard no more sounds then extricated himself from his jumble of boxes, packages and overalls. Max pulled off the alarm sensor from its position adjacent to his planned escape window. He did the same to the sensor on the storeroom's door; it was now 18.00hrs, meaning he had thirty minutes to get to the poison register that should be on the next floor up. Max stealthily moved up the next flight of stairs to the third level; he turned left and froze on the spot. Facing him was a suited bloke who looked as startled as Max. The military training, Pat's gym and Sandhurst kicked in, Max's right leg moved quickly behind the right leg of the stranger. Max's upper body weight was thrown forward with full force ploughing into the startled man's midriff toppling him backwards to the floor. Max was soon upon him; the poor bloke looked frightened to death. Max gestured with his finger to his lips indicating that he didn't want him to speak. To his surprise the restrained man nodded. Max whispered that he would not hurt him and would let him stand up. Max also showed his knife and indicated he would use it if the man uttered one word; the frightened man frantically nodded his understanding. Max helped him up. The poor chap looked like he'd crapped himself, but the special forces trainee knew he had to keep up his verbal aggression. Max told him to quickly show him where the poison register was kept. The frightened worker said, obviously trying to please Max, that he knew where it was. The SAS candidate followed the man.

'Don't think I will not use this knife'.

'I will do what you want, just don't hurt me, I have five kids.' He led Max to the end of the corridor, luckily, he had keys and opened the door to an office. It was now 18:17hrs, Max knew he had to get out before the cleaners arrived.

'Where is the book? Get it quick!' Max upped his verbal aggression although he meant no harm to this innocent man.

'Okay, okay, It's in one of these cabinets; I have the keys.'

The employee's hand was shaking too much to open it so Max snatched the keys from him. 'I'll do it.' Max flung the door open; he saw it, a leather-bound book that had to be the poison register and fortunately it was.

Max flicked through the pages at pace and got to the date when Myers obtained the poison, and with horror, he saw the corresponding entry page had been deliberately torn out. 'Fuck it.' Max cursed out loud, composing himself and thought that just maybe Conrad Dyer may have thrown the page into the waste bin as it was probably only this afternoon when it happened. Max suddenly had renewed hope and went to the two bins, quickly rummaging through them; he got further pissed off, having put his finger into a half-empty yoghurt pot so with sticky fingers he continued. Nothing in either bin.

'Bollocks, he's taken the page.' Then with a last straw grasping chance he asked the quivering man.

'Where's Conrad Dyer's office?'

'It's just over there' he said pointing to a room about five metres away.

'Do you have a key?'

'No.' He replied in a worried voice; Max believed him.

With one massive kick from Max, Dyers's door flew open.

The noise of the alarm was intense. It was ear-splitting!

'It's not my fault, it's not my fault' screamed the suited man.

'Just shut it', Max shouted over the screaming alarm. He ran to Dyer's basket and tipped out the contents. The secrecy was over so it didn't matter about being quiet or discreet anymore; he did, however, need to move sharpish 'It's bloody well here.' Max screamed with delight.

Bold as you like, twenty grams of Tetrodotoxin signed for by a Mr Aquila. *"Got him!"* Max thought.

'I have what I need on this page torn out from your poison book; I'm hoping to put away a murderer who used this deadly stuff to kill a good man. Now we will walk out of here and you my friend, you will help by telling any interested parties that there was a scare in the lab but it's now under control, got that?'

The man appeared more relaxed now and agreed with a nod. They went down in the lift to reception where they saw the three cleaners with machinery and mops looking perplexed but not moving. Max's temporary hostage had already turned the alarms off at Max's instruction. 'Everything is all right; we had a problem upstairs in the lab, but it's all clear now. We had to force open the door of Mr Dyer's office; you can carry on now but don't forget to reset the alarm when you leave.' That bit surprised Max, an accomplished performance from the frightened man.

Once outside Max turned to his now freed hostage. 'Thanks for your cooperation.'

'No need to thank me, I hate that bastard Dyer; he's nothing but a crook. I will not be able to explain his office break-in and I will have to say you forced me to open other doors, but I will not describe you accurately even to the police. I believe you. Will you shake my hand?'

They shook hands and Max left.

The SAS candidate saw Jamie and they jogged together around the corner to their car.

Before either of them had a chance to speak there was a tap on the side window. Jamie expecting trouble grabbed the wheel wrench conveniently situated in the passenger's footwell. He was out of the car in a flash. 'Hold it Jamie; it's my map writer and his buddy that got me into the building.'

'Sorry guys, you can't be too sure these days' Jamie backed off and got into the car.

'No problemo mi amigo.' said the map writer.

Max gave him his promised balance of five hundred pounds.

'Let's see where we are; we know Myers stole the SA80, we know he exchanged that for twenty grammes of TTX with Aguila in Orange Town Walk, we know Aguila bought the poison from NTM in Belize and we know Myers gave Nathan Brookes the poison. All the dates correlate as well. We nearly have him Jamie; all we need is the cabbie to sign a statement that he took Myers to meet Aguila and we've got him bang to rights. All the dates and events stack up; even the timeline points to Myers poisoning poor Nathan.' Max said to Jamie before they drove away.

'We need to see the cabbie as soon as possible. We leave tomorrow night for the UK; by the way, what is the cabbie's name again?'

'The taxi man is called Delroy, but you never know if he uses a pseudonym while working, especially with his dodgy connections.'

'He might sign a statement for a bit of cash, having missed out with Myers giving him nothing.'

'We'll see Jamie, but first let's see Delroy and then our MP Captain Lewis.

39

'Can you go to Delroy and ask if we can see him for a chat.' Max thought Jamie might be the one to persuade the cabbie. So Jamie went to where Delroy parks his cab just outside the camp gates; unfortunately he wasn't there.

The camp sentry called over to Jamie. 'Delboy, the taxi geezer has just left with a couple of our guys. He should be back soon.' Jamie thanked the guard with a wave and found a low wall to sit on to await Delroy's taxi.

While he was doing that Max reported to the captain of the military police.

'I have plenty to tell you captain.'

'Take a seat Maximus and tell me everything.'

Max explained Jamie's conversation with the cabbie, Delroy, and his revelation about Myers' meeting with Aguila, the SA80 exchange for the 20 grams of TTX and retrieving the entry page in the poison register at NTM. Lewis Titcombe looked at Max incredulously and scowled.

'That's aggravated burglary with menaces and possible assault! So this bloke you attacked, is he okay?'

'Yes he hates Dyer anyway and after I explained everything he was on our side. He walked out of the building without coercion from me and he explained a plausible reason to the cleaners why the alarms went off on the third floor. First, of course, we need Delroy to confirm his introduction and the deal set up between Aguila and Myers for the trade exchange of the SA80 for 20 grams of TTX. Jamie is locating him right now and I hope to speak with him about making a witness statement this evening as we are leaving for the UK tomorrow night. I want to nail that bastard Myers before I leave for Nat's sake.'

The MP captain sighed again and spoke quietly with concern in his voice.

'This is military police business Max, but I can see that if we get involved now it will probably frighten off Delroy completely. He is the only person who can give us the final piece of proven evidence we need to bring charges against Myers. I say to you unofficially that this conversation didn't occur so do what you must but I can only give you another two hours before I have to intervene and take over. Don't let me down Maximus!'

'I'll try not to sir and thank you for your trust.'

It seemed strange for Max calling the captain sir as he was also a captain back in his parent regiment but not now under the SAS system of stripped rank and where all are equal.

Jamie phoned as Max was leaving the captain's office.

'Jamie here. Delroy is in his cab waiting for you, can you come right now? He has a pick up in twenty-five minutes.'

'I'll be right there Jamie, don't let him leave.'

Max slid into the back seat of Delroy's cab and was introduced to him by Jamie who appeared to be like old chums with the cabbie.

Max went straight in as he knew his time was limited.

'Delroy I have been told by Jamie here that you have explained to him your association with Myers. You told him Myers admitted to you that he had taken the SA80 from the truck and asked you if you had connections to get things. Is that correct Delroy?'

'Yes that's right, you sure you ain't a copper?' Delroy looked into his central mirror at the face of Max!

'No I'm the same as the man sat next to you, we're just a couple of soldiers trying to get justice for a comrade. 'He turned around to face Max and said in a nervous voice.

'I'm no way going to be a witness so let's get that straight for a start. I can't, you don't know what it's like for squealers around these parts. I shouldn't have told Jamie here all I did; it was only because I was so fucking pissed off with Myers not paying me for introducing him and taking him to meet Aguila.'

'You were there with Myers when he did the exchange, the SA80 for the poison in Orange Walk Town because you told Jamie that.'

'Yes, I was there alright but I didn't get paid for my trouble; if I make a statement, would I get into trouble about the rifle that I transported for Myers?'

'I am not the authorities Delroy so I can't speak for them, but as I see it you were just a bonafide taxi driver just taking a fare. I admit there may be something to answer for because you knew the stolen SA80 was from the base, but I would think the fact you would be helping to put the murdering scumbag Myers away for good, they are bound to take that into consideration.'

Jamie interjected. 'Would you sign a witness statement in the military police captain's office now?'

'I've been thinking about that, it's bound to get back to Aguila if I split on the deal he had with Myers I'd be dead with a bullet in the back of my head within the hour, day or night, so sorry guys I just can't, I'm too scared, you don't know Aguila, he's one nasty dude.' Jamie pleaded with him but it was to no avail; Delroy had bottled it.

'I have to go now guys, I really am so sorry as I hate that bastard Myers as well.'

The two SAS candidates slid out of the taxi allowing Delroy to speed off to his fare.

'He won't help us Max, a total waste of space that dodgy little twat.' Said Jaime. They walked back through the camp gates, the sentry knew who they were and waved them in. The two candidates went straight to see the military police captain who was in the officer's mess. Max asked the duty steward to fetch him.

'Yes gentlemen, what do you have for me.' The captain was just about to have his dinner and a cheeky gin and tonic.

'We have just met with Delroy and' Jamie was stopped in his tracks by the captain.

'Stop, let's go to my office; I'll take my G&T with me, come on.'

'Right Mr Cuthbert, finish what you were saying.'

'Simply sir, Delroy will not make a statement. I pleaded with him, and Max has tried as well, but we could see he was too frightened of Aguila!'

The MP replied 'I'm not surprised; I've heard many nasty stories about him; he runs a massive operation in drugs and human trafficking in Belize for his Mexican associates. The police can't touch him as he has contacts high up in the police and government on his payroll.'

Max interrupted 'If you two would allow me to speak I'll explain how we have cracked it,' Lewis Titcombe and Jamie both stared at Max.

'I have all the conversations recorded on my phone, listen!' Max placed his phone on the desk and turned on the recording. The device played back every word starting with Jamie and Max's recorded sounds of getting into Delroy's cab, the introduction and the whole conversation with Delroy. Then the goodbyes with Delroy speeding off.

The captain was excited and now in a jubilant mood.

'That's brilliant Max, bloody brilliant, we've got Myers now, bang to rights, that's for sure.' Jamie joined in.

'You sly bugger Max.' Slapping him on the back.

'We did this for poor Nat Brookes.' Max replied sombrely.

'I must now write out a charge sheet; I'll need you two for this so we will have to start from the beginning.'

40

'Who is it.' Myers spoke into his mobile.

'It's me Delroy, you owe me money dude, and I want it. Now listen up I have had a meeting with the two guys you were in the jungle with, Catworth or something and Jamie Cuthbert. They know all about you and the poison but I hold the key, because if I make a statement to the MP captain, you are fucked, understand? Now I have just spoken to Aguila, who said he would get you out of the shit you are in, but you will have to act fast. There is a big cash bonus for both of us if you can deliver.'

'What does he want?'

'Twenty-five SA80's and delivered tonight!'

'Fuck off, that's impossible; how the fuck can I get them out of the armoury?' Myers said.

'Myers you are fucked anyway; this Catt bloke discovered where Aguila sourced the poison so they are bound to get you pretty soon even without my statement. They could do a deal with Aquila to talk, who knows.'

This revelation made Myers's heart pound and his temper rise to bursting, trying to think what to do.

He realised his time in the armed forces was finished now and he needed to avoid the inevitable.

'Okay listen, you piece of shit, I'll do it but you must get your taxi into the base to collect them!'

'Sure I go in regularly to collect top brass and take them to the British High Commission in Belmopan. Squaddies in the depot know me as Delboy for some strange reason and now I even answer to that name. It's easy for me to pick out any newcomers like you when they arrive. So what's the plan.'

'You bring your taxi in and park it next to the side entrance of the armoury in thirty minutes exactly; you do know where it is?'

'Yes I know the camp like the back of my hand. I've helped drunken soldiers into their barracks enough times; as you lot say, I'm one of the family.'

'Good, then be there and don't make the mistake by pissing off or I'll snap your scrawny fucking neck.'

'I'll be there; make sure you are and with the guns, or you will be dead meat. Aguila has no sympathy even for his brother who he killed two years ago over a double-cross.'

'Be there in thirty minutes.' Myers had the last word.

Phillip Myers changed into his combat dress and beret and walked confidently into the armoury; the duty guard looked up from his desk and addressed Myers.

'Hi what can I do for you, soldier.'

'I require these for tomorrow's manoeuvres; here's the signed chit.'

Myers placed the blank piece of paper on the desk and walked around to the guard's side. Before the armourer could protest Myers grabbed the hair of the seated soldier, pulling his head back and with his free right hand severed the armourer's windpipe with one lethal swish of his large knife. The gurgling noise was sickening, blood and air mixed, pumped out over an arm's length away from the shocked man. The victim had a look of horror set on his face. He laid there hunched up with his face looking up at the ceiling now dead! Within a minute a pool of blood had covered a metre square of flooring but continued to flow, searching for the lowest point to pool. It reflected a macabre, dark crimson, shining glow from the fluorescent strip lighting above the gruesome scene.

Myers went to the desk draw and pulled out a bunch of keys. The entrance door already had the key in the lock, Myers locked this door, securing the front. The double murderer had difficulty unlocking the reinforced cage of the armoury and cussed. Finally after several minutes of panic-fuelled fiddling with the keys he found the right one on the bunch. Myers had accessed the first door; the next key gave him an easier entry and he was quickly through the second door. Myers was now amongst the guns, hundreds of them, hand grenades, machine guns and many lethal SA80s, all hanging in numbered order. The smell of refined machine oil was quite overpowering. He moved fast and took the SA80's from their holders on the walls.

He moved the rifles to the side door in a heap, ready to load up Delboy's boot. Then the front door handle turned and rattled in front of his eyes, somebody banged heavily on the door and shouted for entry. Myers moved to the door and thought quick.

'Sorry we can't unlock the door, we are stocktaking because of the stolen SA80. We should only be another twenty minutes.'

'No bother mate, I'm returning the gun oil we had, that's all; it can wait until tomorrow.'

'Okay that's fine.' Myers waited for a few seconds of silence and returned to removing the rifles. The oil-bearing soldier will never know how lucky he was that night by not being persistent!

A tap on the side door this time and the unmistakable voice of Delroy was there with his taxi. The cabbie tapped the side door again and called 'Are you ready to load up?'

'Yeah' Myers opened the side door with yet another different key. The door opened and Delroy stepped in. The first thing he noticed was the stream of blood coming from behind the desk, following the trail with his gaze that led to the crumpled body of a soldier.

'What the fuck have you done Myers?'

'You didn't expect him to help us load your fucking taxi did you? Now shut the fuck up and start loading these into your boot and be quiet about it. Delroy filled up his boot and scratched his head.

'There is more than twenty-five rifles here'.

'Shut it and load them on the back seats.' They loaded the last SA80's into the car and threw a cover over the back seat. Myers switched the lights off, locked the side door, and climbed into the passenger seat of the taxi next to Delroy. They moved slowly towards the gatehouse; the guard looked out, saw Delboy and waved him through and out onto the road heading for Orange Walk Town to meet Aguila.

'So Maximus what have we got. We have Nathan Brookes killed with TTX, a stolen SA80, the fatal stabbing of a civilian that we know was at the hands of Myers and a rendezvous with one of the most dangerous criminals in central America. Now the recording confirms Myers is associated with Aguila. I will charge Myers with theft from a military establishment, the murder of a Belizean citizen and a British soldier.

I need a copy of that tape and witness statements from you and Jamie. With all that I will arrest and charge Phillip Myers; he'll probably be where he usually is; in the mess getting rat arsed, I'll get the charge sheet typed out and arrest him within the hour.' The MP captain concluded.

The captain looked for Myers to arrest him with two other MPs, but he was not in the mess. The captain put out a call over the PA for Myers to immediately report to the camp guardhouse. After thirty minutes of searching and calling him they realised he was off base. The corporal of two platoon, the same unit that the armourer was in, went to the armoury to relieve his colleague and secure the weapon store for the night. He was very surprised, indeed shocked, to see the lights out and the armoury all locked up. The NCO thought this was strange; the private doesn't have the authority to lock up for the night or leave the armoury unattended and retain the keys. He pressed his torch up to the window and looked around the store; nothing looked out of place until his eyes scanned round to the weapon storeroom; the security door to the weapons cage was wide open; another breach of army regulations. The corporal tried the door but it was locked. He went to the side door and that too was also secure. Something was seriously wrong; the NCO hurried to the guardhouse and asked for the duty officer. 'Sir something is wrong at the armoury. I went to lock up and relieve Toby Jackson and secure the armoury for the night and I couldn't get in, both doors are locked, the lights are out and nobody's there.The worrying thing is the weapons store is a high-security door but it's wide open.'

'That is serious corporal, come with me; we will check this out; I'll just collect the spare keys.'

They stepped inside the armoury door and as soon as they passed the desk they saw the horrific scene of the dead private. Toby Jackson was lying in a pool of his own blood, eyes wide open, staring at the ceiling. His throat sliced wide open, a deep and dark cavity line across his throat, congealed blood trying to seal the severed windpipe.

The captain of the military police was called with his two subordinates to the scene. He took over matters and ordered the armoury to be taped off, declaring it a crime scene and therefore out of bounds. The duty officer confirmed forty SA80s were missing from their racks, adding to this grave matter.

The captain phoned Max who immediately came to the armoury as requested. 'Fucking hell sir, what's happened here.' Max asked in a shocked voice.

'A soldier has had his throat cut and forty weapons were stolen.'

'This is the work of Myers for sure; is he still missing?'

The MP captain nodded. 'I'm afraid so. I have got three patrols out searching for him with warrants for his arrest.'

'He's in Orange Walk Town by now, I'll wager. Have you pulled Delroy in for questioning?'

'Not yet but he's first on my list of enquiries.'

41

It was the same procedure as their last visit to San Antonio Road, Orange Walk Town. Two heavily armed bodyguards escorted Myers and Delroy to the back room; Aguila greeted them with his arms raised and said. 'Did you get my guns, Mr Myers?

'Yes, but not the twenty-five you asked for, far better we got you forty of the little beauties. Now, how about the money you promised.'

Aguila scratched at his beard and said, 'According to Delroy, you killed a Brit soldier; that changes everything. I pay you nothing. But I can keep you alive.'

Myers went bonkers and ran at Aguila but was stopped in his tracks by a solid wall of bodyguards.

'Careful, Mr Myers, do that again, and I'll send your head back in a bag to your camp.'

Delroy said to Myers, 'He's not joking; he will feed your torso to his pigs.'

'You are well informed and correct, Delroy.' Aguila sniggered.

'These are your options, Myers; you can walk out of here with nothing and go on the run, or I can get you a different identity and passport to go back to the UK if you want. Take it as a present from me for the guns. Or better still, you can join me and help me run my business here; I can protect you from getting arrested in return for your undivided loyalty. But, remember, you will be wanted by the whole British army, especially those deadly SAS people that are seriously vengeful when one of their own is murdered. Delroy has told me all about your caper; you are in deep shit.

What's your decision?'

'What choice do I have but to join you.' Myers agreed reluctantly.

'Correct choice Mr Myers, take him to his digs and make sure he stays there until things quiet down. I'll see you later, Myers, to discuss your new employment with me. Delroy, get the SA80s from your car and put them in the SUV in the yard. Esteban go and help him.'

The rifles were unloaded. Delroy went back to Aguila.

'Now, where's my payment for all those rifles?'

'Aaah yes, well done, you must keep up this excellent work for me! Come follow me, Delroy; I need to show you something before you leave.'

Delroy duly followed the drugs boss into his rear yard. They started walking towards the pig pens about a hundred metres from the house.

Delroy asked nervously.

'Where are we going, Aguila?'

'Just over here.'

'Why?'

'Too many questions Delroy, that's your trouble, you know.' Delroy was now really shitting himself.

'I don't want much money, Aguila!'

'Good.' That was the last word Delroy heard from the gang boss. Aguila moved so quick with a short cosh to the side of Delroy's head. He collapsed in a heap. Aguila didn't bat an eyelid but grabbed Delroy by his polo shirt collar and dragged him the last three metres to the pen wall.

With apparent ease, Aguila lifted the slight Delroy up onto the flat copings of the metre-high stone pen wall and rolled the unconscious cabbie into the muddy enclosure.

First, a sow came to see who their new guest for dinner was, followed by a huge boar who pushed his lady out of the way with no manners.

The noise stirred the rest of the herd, about ten in number came trotting over to the exciting disturbance. The boar was first to attack the human dinner, his great jaws ripping through the left arm of Delroy. The obvious pain woke the taxi man to his nightmare horror. He hit out at the large boar to no effect; it only served in exciting the herd further and they joined in the melee.

By now, at least three of the largest pigs were tearing at Delroy's limbs; he was still desperately fighting for his life. trying to fight his losing battle.

It had become an eating frenzy with Delroy now dead, probably of shock and heart failure; the pigs were now crunching the bones of the cabbie. Only blood, mud and scattered red fleshy bones remained, but even the disintegrated skeleton will eventually disappear by the time these omnivores finish their human snack! Aguila smiled, turned from the pen and went in for his own dinner. 'Sanchez, take Delroy's taxi and burn it.

That was Aguila's last order of the night before sitting down with his family for food.

The MP captain, Lewis Titcombe, was fuming at the atrocity of the slain armourer happening right under his nose. However, the MP officer evidently exercised restraint when speaking to Maximus Hainsworth-Catt.

'You have gone beyond the call of duty Max; I'll get that fucking bastard Myers. I know you are leaving for home tomorrow with your group; I wish you well and good luck with the final phase of your SAS test.'

'Thank you, sir.' Max could still sense the anger in Titcombe's voice.

'Max, I respect you. However, I know from earlier inquiries I made when you were a joint suspect for Brooke's death, I discovered you are still a captain outside SAS remit. That means you are still an officer to me, therefore call me Lewis, if you please.'

Max replied, smiling. 'Thank you, Lewis, it does seem strange after all our meetings and chats, now calling you Lewis, but it does seem more natural.'

They shook hands on that. Max said encouragingly. 'I hope you get that bastard Myers. Please let me know when you get him.' Here's my UK mobile number.

'I'll promise to do both. Bye, Max.'

'So long, Lewis and good luck!'

The next day, Jamie and Maximus were standing on the tarmac of Belize airport, awaiting their transport plane home with the other jungle candidates. There should have been two more with them; however,

one was dead and already back in the UK, flown home with military honours and the other somewhere on the run in Belize. Nevertheless, Max was not sad to be leaving this place. They landed in Brize Norton, the Oxfordshire airbase they had left seven weeks earlier to commence the killer phase jungle training and survival in Belize.

The trainee candidates walked out onto the Oxfordshire tarmac into the driving rain and easterly wind to climb into the waiting RAF lorries that took them to the air station's lecture hall adjacent to the airfield.

There were about eighty-two in number and they sat like schoolkids in a large classroom awaiting their teacher to arrive.

In strode three officers of the SAS training team. 'Gentleman, please settle down, we have put you through hell, and it's a privilege to be addressing fine examples of the British army. From nearly two hundred applicants at the start of the tests and who set out to join the best regiment in the world, here you are, a reduced group of just eighty-three sat here. The average fallout after phase two is always around ninety per cent, and the list in front of me indicates we are not bucking that trend this time.

Understand, it is just those who have the strength and fortitude to take what we throw at you; it's aptitude, thinking outside the box, self-discipline, initiative, keeping your vital equipment clean and serviceable at all times and looking after your team. All these attributes are given points, and that's how we get down to the elite soldiers we require.

You have all completed a week's briefing course, a gruelling mountain aptitude test or, as we lovingly call it, the Fan Dance, ending the four weeks in Brecon. You have just returned from your seven weeks in the Belize jungle undertaking your TTP (Tactics Techniques and Procedures) and SOP (Standard Operating Procedures) assessments.

You should all be incredibly proud of yourselves for getting this far. Let me tell all of you ninety-eight per cent of men in your age group would not and could not complete the courses you have undertaken. Unfortunately, this brutal selection continues, and only eleven of you will now continue to the third phase: Survive, Evade, Resist, Extract and Interrogation.

The vast majority of you will now be leaving us. The remaining few are to stay seated.

I will now call out the successful candidates. If you don't hear your name called, collect your packs and travel warrants and report back to your parent regiments. I say goodbye and tell you that you have one last attempt to join The Regiment, but you will have to wait for the summer test now. So, unfortunately, you will be required to start from the beginning again. Good luck, gentlemen and goodbye.' Max's stomach was churning with fear of rejection. It means so much; the wait was intolerable.

Both Max and Jamie's names were called out. The relief for Max was immeasurable. They had passed and are now candidates for the third and final phases.

The SS (Squadron Sergeant) spoke to the remaining few in a commanding voice with not a hint of praise for what this small group had achieved.

'Right then, gentlemen, if you thought your previous testing was brutal, let me tell you that your third phase will seem insane. You will start with a brief period of E&E (escape and evasion) techniques taught by experienced Blades (badged SAS men). After this, you will be on your own, dropped off into the British countryside, where you must avoid capture by the Hunter Force made up of special forces (SF) who will use their proven skills to find and capture you. They will take you in for questioning. You will be given waypoints to get to. If you remain at large for three days, you must turn yourselves in for interrogation. Again, use the skills learnt from your lectures. You will be made to wear a vintage heavy WW2 greatcoat to impede your movement. Your maps will be handwritten, not printed. You will be given basic field rations. Your billet will be in this camp until the morning when you start your E&E lectures. Hainsworth-Catt and Cuthbert come with me.'

They followed the SS NCO to an office where a civilian police detective and two MP officers were sitting. They asked Max and Jamie about Nathan Brookes' poisoning and the missing automatic rifles. Max explained everything he could and referred them to MP Captain Lewis Titcombe at the British army base in Belize for further details and onward investigations. The UK police apparently have already had conversations with Lewis Titcombe, but they wanted Max and Jamie's account for their ongoing enquiry. However, they did say that Myers will be found guilty In Absentia (in his absence).

'We are satisfied owing to evidence from the phone taping and your written statements that arrived from Belize. Myers will be found guilty thanks to you two. Your effort to discover evidence and your actions assured your selection to the final phase of your SAS testing. I'm not saying you wouldn't have passed anyway, but the initiative to work alone was a big plus in the eyes of your instructors. Well done to you both. Unfortunately, forty SA80's are in dangerous hands in Belize.'

42

After a week of lectures and special survival training, the eleven survivors were taken to open countryside somewhere in rural England, issued with antique, mothball smelling heavy WW2 greatcoats, maps, instructions and meagre rations. The small band were separated and instructed to go and not get caught for three days, after that, captured or not, they must make their way to TQ (Tactical Questioning). Of course, it had to be pouring with rain. Max covered himself with his smelly coat and studied his handwritten map to direct him to his first waypoint objective. All the time, striving to evade capture from experienced 22 Regiment hunter patrols trying to find them. Compass in hand, he could see his way to travel at least three miles NE. Max had twenty-four hours to make it to his first waypoint. Max could see from his map a wooded area that looked like it went on for some distance ahead of him.

Max made a personal target to keep moving through the night between the dark and the wood; he has a better chance of evasion that way.

The movement was slow, made so by the thick undergrowth of early spring. No apparent paths were going his way, so it was a case of twisting and turning around trees and saplings. Not like Belize, here it's devoid of dangerous insects, vampire bats, snakes and scorpions. Max had travelled 2.4 miles according to his mobile, and so far so good. It was getting dark, and he debated whether to leave the woods now to gain time with better speed on the road or stay in the woods with more cover, but much slower. He weighed up his options and decided who dares wins.

Max left his shelter behind and headed further north than before. He didn't want to put himself under time pressure for the last stint of his journey, so he picked up the pace, almost into quick-time marching. Max thought. *"This will make up a bit for the slow woodland pace"*.

Max was using a B road with hardly any traffic. It seemed a doddle compared to 'Pen y Fan' in Brecon with a 55lb loaded bergen.

Max heard the distinctive noise of traffic approaching from behind him; he didn't have time to run anywhere for cover; if it was the Hunter force coming, he would be in full view in about ten seconds. Max dived headfirst into the roadside drainage ditch, which hid him from the road. The ditch had approximately thirty-five centimetres of water that submerged much of his stretched-out body. Max held his pack above the water in the grassy bank to keep it out of sight. An army convoy with the yellow markings and flag indicating a hunter patrol out looking to capture any of the eleven surviving candidates they could. They would probably enjoy the interrogation they would bestow upon their captives. The convoy passed very close to Max; the road was minor and not very wide. Max felt the vibration as the trucks thundered past. He felt sure the driver in the lead truck had seen something jump into the stream. They started to slow down and perhaps troops would get out to search for him.

Max knew that if the driver looked out of his cab, he was bound to see him lying in the ditch. Only the darkness was his friend at this point.

The two lorries and one Land-Rover drove by. Max thought he'd made it, sighing with relief. He arched his back to rise from the water but dropped back under the water. His relief was premature as the small convoy stopped, and the troops in the back got out about sixty metres past him. Max thought they were coming for him. Instead, they all hopped over a fence and came back after a couple of minutes, climbed back into their transport and off they drove. Even soldiers need to piss. Max thought he could now leave the stream confident the patrol had moved on. Max got out of the ditch. The soaked, much heavier greatcoat impeded him, but he had to continue along the road, unable to afford to delay. Max could see the necessity to veer NNE from his map in about half a mile. It was fortunate for him; he looked ahead and saw what looked like a roadblock. Another hunter unit Max was sure. He got off the road and skirted around them, going across a field of cows, who paid little interest to a furtive figure moving amongst them. When Max was clear, he returned to the road well behind the military checkpoint.

Maximus turned right at the next road junction and thought it quicker for the time being to stay on the road, but his waypoint location will eventually take him across more fields and through another wooded area. Max imagined that the Hunter patrols would increase as he got closer to his target. He was not wrong. Another five miles were completed with roughly ten to go. It was dark; he was wet and cold but still nothing like the bone-chilling nights in Brecon. That place was a frozen hell; he shuddered at the thought. Another hunter convoy with three lorries filled with troops and a Land-Rover drove by. No problem this time as he hid behind a hedgerow, and being dark, they drove past without noticing, even with searchlights in operation. Max was now where a change of direction was required, going through open fields towards large woods having skirted the areas to be less conspicuous and keeping tight to the hedgerows intertwined with bramble. It seemed sheep were the only creatures interested in him. Max entered the woodland at 21.00hrs. It was too dark to negotiate a passage through the shrubs and trees, so Max decided to rest up until morning as he couldn't use the torch in fear of being seen by the increasing number of patrols. Max climbed a tree and secured himself on two sturdy boughs with rope and used his greatcoat as a cover and a degree of warmth, albeit still wet through from the dive in the ditch earlier. He dozed and eventually fell into an uncomfortable sleep.

Max was startled into consciousness by human voices; a cramp had developed in one of his legs owing to an unnatural position slightly twisted around a bough. Torch lights beamed everywhere but upwards. Max was alerted to the realisation of where he was and why he was sleeping up a bloody tree. If they only knew he was directly above them—moving their light beams from side to side, Max thought it only a matter of time. Please don't look up and see my pack tied to a smaller branch Max prayed. The patrol was right below him, and Max could make out their conversation; they were that close. They were complaining about night patrols. *"Please don't look up."* Max held his breath and closed his eyes, concentrating on not moving. Max was begging them to move on and not stay here; for God's sake, move away. They did, and eventually, Max got back to some semblance of sleep. Catnapping was more accurate.

Max woke to his vibrating watch alarm telling him it was 06:30hrs and time to move off. He could smell smoke and could see it coming from a campfire which alerted him and concentrated his wakening senses. He trained his Leica binoculars from where the smoke was rising. He could see five obvious hunters having a brew with one missing, probably on guard or having a crap.

Once more, Max was forced to circumnavigate their camp as it was the direct compass line he needed to take for his waypoint.

Max was about a mile out from his destination when he stopped dead. There were at least thirty hunters in a line combing the edge of the wood and moving his way methodically.

There was no way he could get past this cordon of searchers; if he moved either way, he would be spotted without a doubt. They were about a hundred and fifty metres away and steadily moving in. Max's only chance was to keep a big bramble bush between them and himself. Max hurriedly gathered grass branches and leaves without leaving tell-tale holes in the foliage. He dug frantically with his knife at the base and centre of the bush, already bleeding from the hostile bramble. He made a shallow pit; thankfully, the surface was loose with deep mulch, allowing him to complete his hide quickly. Max needed to; the sweeping line was nearly on him. Max squeezed into the bush's centre and covered himself with loose mulch, leaves, and branches, slipping his arm in last. It will have to do as he couldn't afford another movement or noise.

Max laid as still as possible and hoped his foliage camouflage did its job.

The hunters were either side of the bush and sweeping past. One stopped at the bush, no more than half a metre from the hiding hole. Max held his breath as he felt warm liquid pouring down on his back, neck and face. He closed his mouth for obvious reasons. The stench of ammonia confirmed his horror; Max was being pissed on and had to accept it.

A voice bellowed out from a distance. ' Come on, men; we have only caught five of the bastards. We can flush more out, keep your eyes peeled; we've got to stop them reaching the waypoint target. Think of our reputation.'

The line moved off, thrashing at the overgrowth but thankfully getting quieter. Max waited until it went completely silent, apart from two wood pigeons cooing at each other nearby.

The young candidate sat up and spat out muck from his mouth and thanked goodness the greatcoat stopped some of the piss, looking back as he left he was satisfied with his mulch hideout made in record time.

With under a mile to go, he moved off, although wet through and smelling of piss; Max felt pretty good as he exited the wood.

He could see the destination village where the waypoint was. Now he needed a plan to get into the target building, undoubtedly having many more hunters in and around it. Finally, Max got within view of the target waypoint finish; he could see two hunters hiding in the grounds through his binoculars. They will try to stop him at the last hurdle; how to get in? Max thought hard! He went back to the pub he had passed. Max received some strange looks, as one would being dressed in an old WW2 coat, unkempt and strongly smelling of piss.

Max asked a group of lads drinking if could he join them as he wanted to put a proposition to one of them. Max got some extraordinary stares from all of them. Nobody spoke. Max explained his mission and showed them his military ID.

Max explained he wanted one of them to put his greatcoat and beret on, then go to a house. However, there is a snag; Max explained, 'They have two guard hunters waiting in the garden. So I need a volunteer to walk towards the house and wait until you see the hunters approaching, which they will, so then you run as fast as possible away from the house. They will, of course, catch you, and you can say who you really are, then you will be back in this bar with a hundred quid in your pocket. Not bad pay for five minutes work, eh lads! So while the two hunters are distracted, I'll nip in on the blindside and complete my mission.'

'I'll do it; sounds a bit of a laugh and a hundred smackers as well.' Said one of the lads who turned out to be a uni student on half term. He introduced himself as Tom.

'Come on, then Tom, get this coat on and follow me.'

Tom did what was asked, sniffing at the arm of the greatcoat and screwing up his face from the smell of urine he was now wearing. It was pretty entertaining to see the hunters who jumped out at Max's decoy soldier, Tom. As instructed, he ran away; the hunters chased him down the street and out of sight. Max sprinted the fifty metres from cover to the building that the MoD commissioned for this sole purpose. Max let himself in and declared his presence to an SAS officer who sat at a desk in the middle of a large room, specifically for the registration of successful SF candidates.

'Come with me, Mr Hainsworth-Catt, where is your greatcoat?

Max told him the story, which made him laugh out loud. He sent somebody to retrieve it from Tom.

'Okay, this is your certification to show you have completed your test within the time limit with no points deducted. Well done, Hainsworth-Catt; we have caught all but three of your fellow contenders, and with only thirty-five minutes remaining before penalty points are added for the last two candidates, their score is sure to be reduced, if indeed they are not caught by our hunters first.

You can shower upstairs and get some food.

Tomorrow you will be given your next waypoint.

Max felt much better after the shower and a change of clothes supplied by the house and then went to the pub, paid Tom a hundred quid, sat with the lads, and quaffed a couple of beers. Max thought it was the best he'd felt for some time. Perhaps it was the chase in the wild that increased the pleasure of this real ale brew!

The next test was almost completed, with similar scrapes encountered, until the last evading test. Max got captured by a hunter patrol ten minutes from his final waypoint. But with only ten minutes of penalty points deducted, he believed he would be home and dry. However, the most challenging and final test was about to be faced. Capture and Interrogation!

It was every bit as gruesome as the instructors had warned it would be at the briefing lectures. They were not exaggerating, that was for sure. They tried all ways to break Max and the remaining surviving candidates down.

The interrogators used mental cruelty, waterboarding, disorientation, all unlawful methods but the worst, in Max's opinion, was sleep deprivation for forty-eight hours. It was mentally unnerving with sounds and floodlighting going on and off repeatedly. Not knowing whether it was day or night. Bribery was the last attempt to break the candidates, who had it drummed into them by their experienced instructors to give the interrogators the big four: Name, Rank, Serial number and date of birth. The interrogation testing stage was now completed and Max hoped his marbles were still intact. He now awaited his result with a few others who had made it past the final field stage and prayed. *"I hope to God, after all that had happened, the sheer effort and torture. I make it into the Regiment"*

The few remaining candidates were taken to an Army teaching depot to await their fate. Then, finally, it was time, all the pain, stress, freezing and torture came down to one word: Yes or No. the results were read out; Almost in a matter of fact way.

Max heard his name; he couldn't hold back. 'I'm in; I'm in.' His outburst got Max a hard stare from the NCO instructor until Max shrunk back into his seat. Max will receive the beige beret with the famous winged dagger insignia; however, these are usually a formality after completing the gruelling phases. They will now prepare for the domestic stage, including employment training, ACSIC (Army combat survival instructor course) and the SF parachute course at RAF Brize Norton in Oxfordshire.

Max attended his surveillance and reconnaissance course for two weeks and an army combat survival course for another two weeks. Max then took part in the parachute training to advanced HALO level for another four weeks. After this, he completed Counter-Terrorism training, another fortnight and signals instructions for a further week. At last, Max finished his patrol training and squadron induction courses for the final two weeks.

Max and Jamie were sat on a bench outside a Hereford pub, soaking up the sun on a cloudless day. It wasn't just solar energy the friends were soaking up; they had just drained their third real ale. After a mild belch, Max remarked. 'If I'm not fucked in the head or not returned to my mother regiment I will be joining an operational Sabre squadron at 22 SAS at Hereford for sniper and demolition training to include further HALO jumping (high altitude low opening) and HAHO (High Altitude High Opening) special training in high altitude jumps. Max could hardly believe it was happening. Jamie laughed but concurred and went for re-fills. Indeed, it was a day to celebrate after their gruelling experience getting to this incredible conclusion.

After three months, Max got his reward; He received his draft into a squadron at Hereford. It has been a long, gruelling and bizarre six months to get to this point. So many problems were left behind in Belize, and Max wondered what damage Myers and the drug gangster Aguila might do with forty SA80's; perish the thought Max mused.

It was good to have Jamie with him on the employment training course, along with eight other lads who started with them in those freezing weeks in the Welsh mountains. But, God, that seems a lifetime ago now.

Max will relish the chance to soldier alongside his new comrades. However, he dearly wished he still had his darling Penny to phone with his news about his exciting new career in the special forces. How he misses that beautiful person.

Max travelled up with the other successful volunteers to the 22 SAS in Hereford, all with excitable nerves on edge. The new SF recruits were met by the staff sergeant, Andy Jenkins. 'Welcome back lads to Stirling Lines Hereford, home to 22 SAS regiment. I'll give you your troop tomorrow; it will be one of the four A, B, D or G. You are now troopers; you already know you have lost any previous rank you may have held, so don't expect saluting. Training starts tomorrow. Today you settle into your billet, and I'm standing you all a beer at The Bell in Tillington. You all deserve it. I've got transport to leave this garrison at 19.00hrs. Bring some cash as we'll have more than one, won't we, lads.'

Max felt so proud to be part of this world-famous and elite regiment. As they were leaving, the sergeant called out 'Hang on a moment, Max; I think you should know something. Jamie didn't pass the last phase but failed only by a small margin; however, he was selected because the Captain MP in Belize told our Operations Officer about the business in Belize and the sterling work you and Jamie did by nailing Myers. The murderous bastard who is still at large, our boys out there will get him eventually, but only thanks to your investigating prowess. For that, Jamie will be joining the best regiment in the world.'

'I think he will make a great Blade Sarge. I'd pick him for my team every time.'

'Thanks for letting me know, I'll see you at 19.00hrs with the other lads.'

That night in the pub, they all bought each other beers. The gruelling torture they had put their bodies through was all forgotten. Max knew he was in a unique band of brothers.

The start of their final training of bomb disposal and first aid, working in small groups to clear buildings of hostile enemies and of course, the parachute training at Brize Norton where they will take in advanced HALO jumps.

The eight new SF recruits were allocated their squadron placements. Max thinks Andy Jenkins, the staff sergeant had a hand in what squadron they were joining as Jamie Cuthbert and Max went into G squadron together. Both were delighted they would complete their last part of training together. Finally, after two more months of strenuous testing and training, the last few got presented with their Winged Dagger cap badge, beige beret and of course, the prized dagger. Maximus Hainsworth-Catt, now known to his G squadron comrades and now his friends simply as Max-Catt.

ABOUT THE AUTHOR

Bill Diamond left school with no, or very little, education and served a full apprenticeship as a bricklayer. After educating himself, he learned most facets of the building industry and property development. Bill started a management company that was established in 1979 and is still enjoying success today.

He has ridden competition horses at Badminton and Gatcombe Park, having bred many of his own horses.

Recently, he had the privilege of flying a Spitfire over the cliffs of Dover to Canterbury Cathedral and it remains one his most memorable experiences.

As an avid reader of spy/thriller novels, he has often criticised books that had too much 'padding out', even though the storyline was strong and indeed entertaining. With Max-Catt and his *"rogue"* tendencies, the author has tried to create a not so respectful hero, who his 'lady of the manor' mother would not tolerate if she knew.

Bill hopes you enjoy his shared opinion of this fast-moving thriller with so many twists and turns.

Although this is his first book in the Max-Catt series, two more have already been completed.

Printed in Great Britain
by Amazon